CatStronauts

ROBOT RESCUE

CatStronauts
ROBOT RESCUE

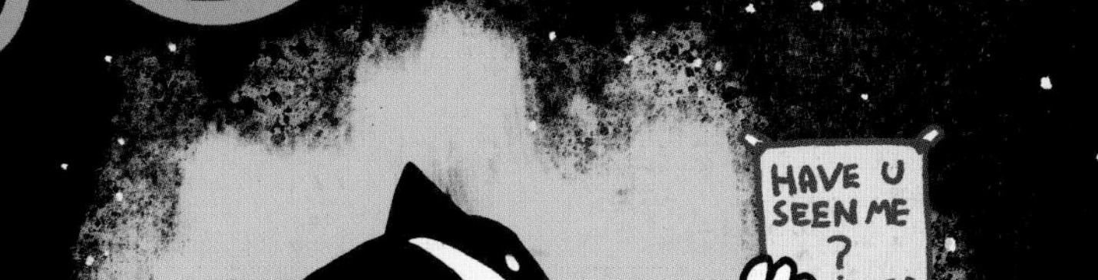
HAVE U SEEN ME ?

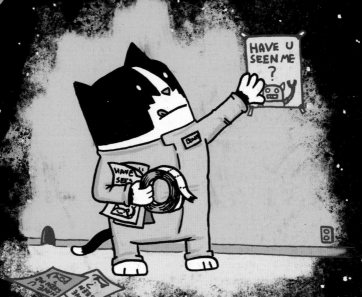

BY DREW BROCKINGTON

LB
Little, Brown and Company
New York Boston

Copyright © 2018 by Drew Brockington
Catstrofont software copyright © 2016 by Drew Brockington
CatStro_Thin software copyright © 2017 by Drew Brockington

Cover art copyright © 2018 by Drew Brockington. Cover design by Angela Taldone.
Cover copyright © 2018 by Hachette Book Group, Inc.

Little, Brown and Company
Hachette Book Group
1290 Avenue of the Americas, New York, NY 10104
Visit us at LBYR.com

First Edition: April 2018

Little, Brown and Company is a division of Hachette Book Group, Inc. The Little, Brown name and logo are trademarks of Hachette Book Group, Inc.

The publisher is not responsible for websites (or their content) that are not owned by the publisher.

ISBNs: 978-0-316-30759-8 (hardcover), 978-0-316-30756-7 (pbk.), 978-0-316-41219-3 (ebook), 978-0-316-41217-9 (ebook), 978-0-316-30755-0 (ebook)

Printed in China

1010

10 9 8 7 6 5 4 3 2 1

For my mom

CHAPTER 1

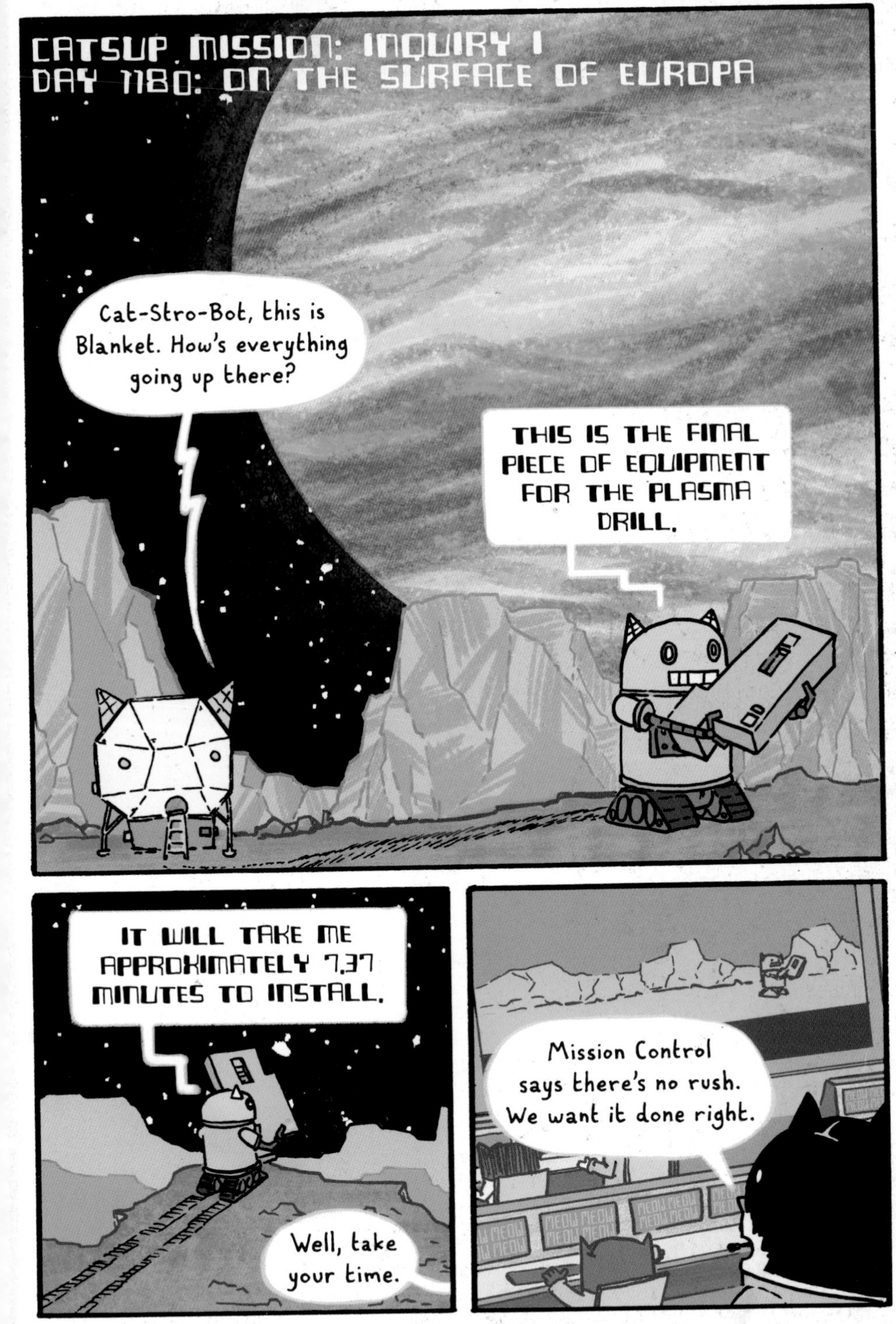
CATSUP MISSION: INQUIRY I
DAY 1180: ON THE SURFACE OF EUROPA
Cat-Stro-Bot, this is Blanket. How's everything going up there?
THIS IS THE FINAL PIECE OF EQUIPMENT FOR THE PLASMA DRILL.
IT WILL TAKE ME APPROXIMATELY 7.37 MINUTES TO INSTALL.
Well, take your time.
Mission Control says there's no rush. We want it done right.

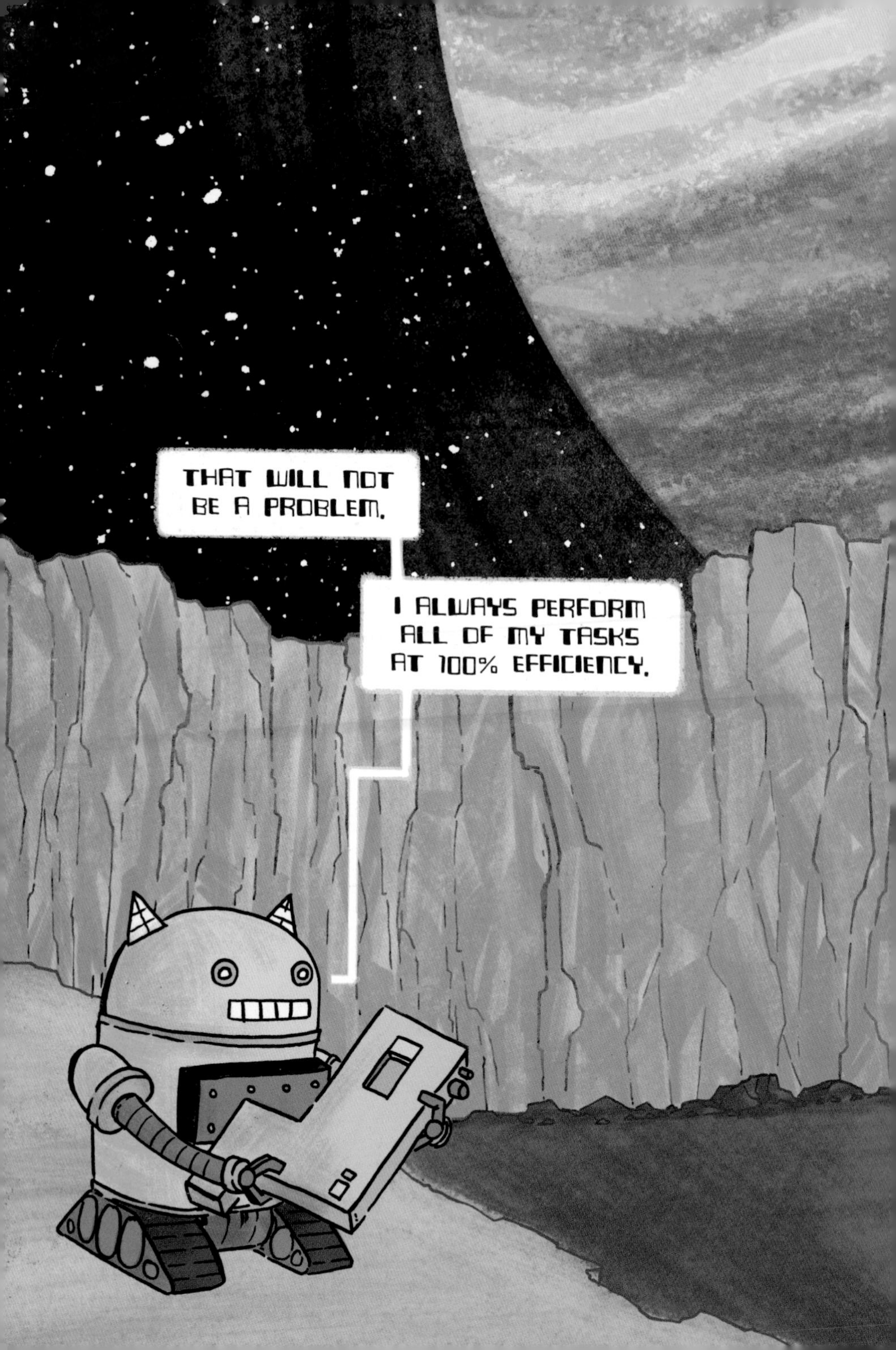
THAT WILL NOT BE A PROBLEM.
I ALWAYS PERFORM ALL OF MY TASKS AT 100% EFFICIENCY.

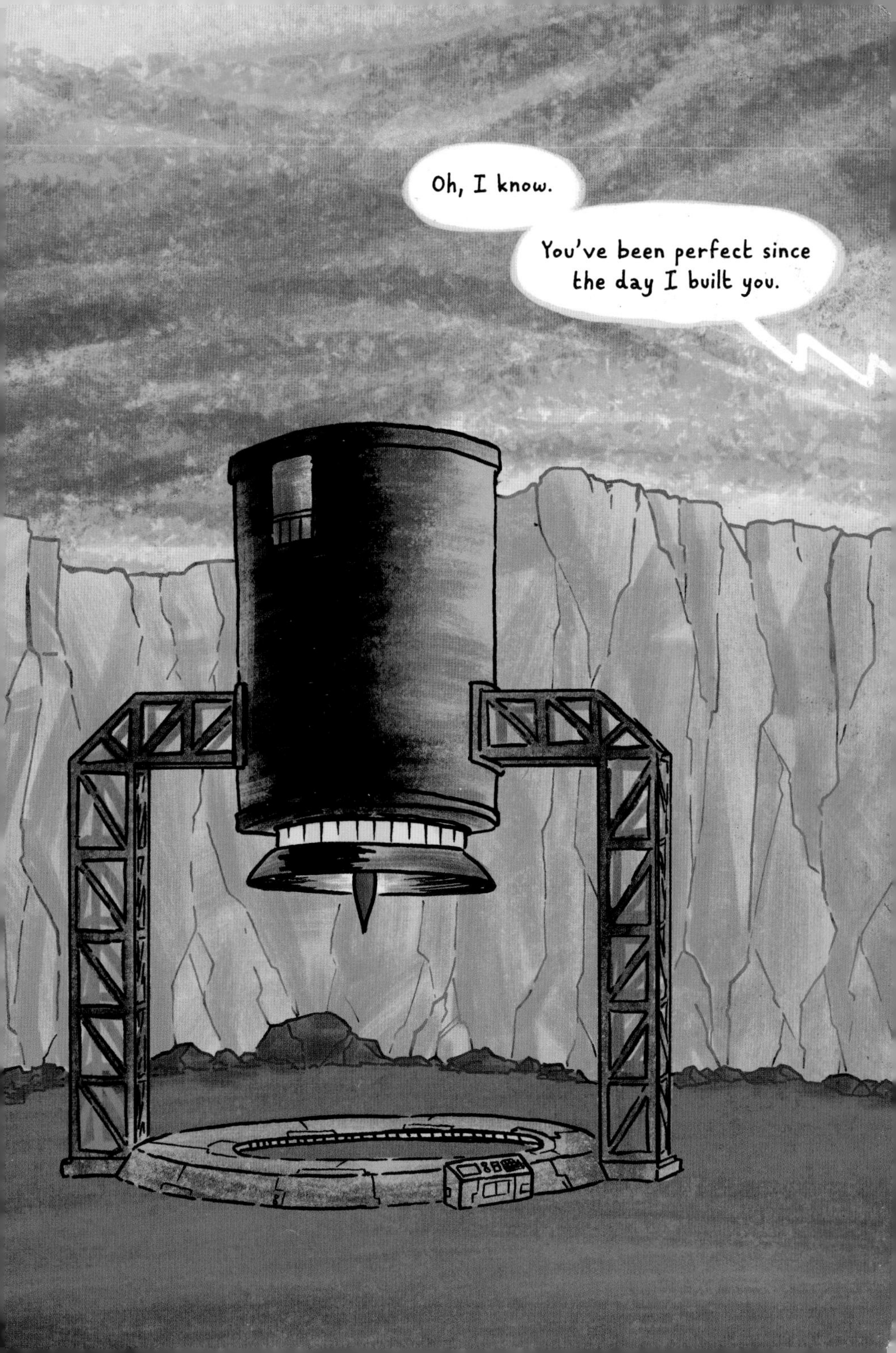
Oh, I know.
You've been perfect since the day I built you.

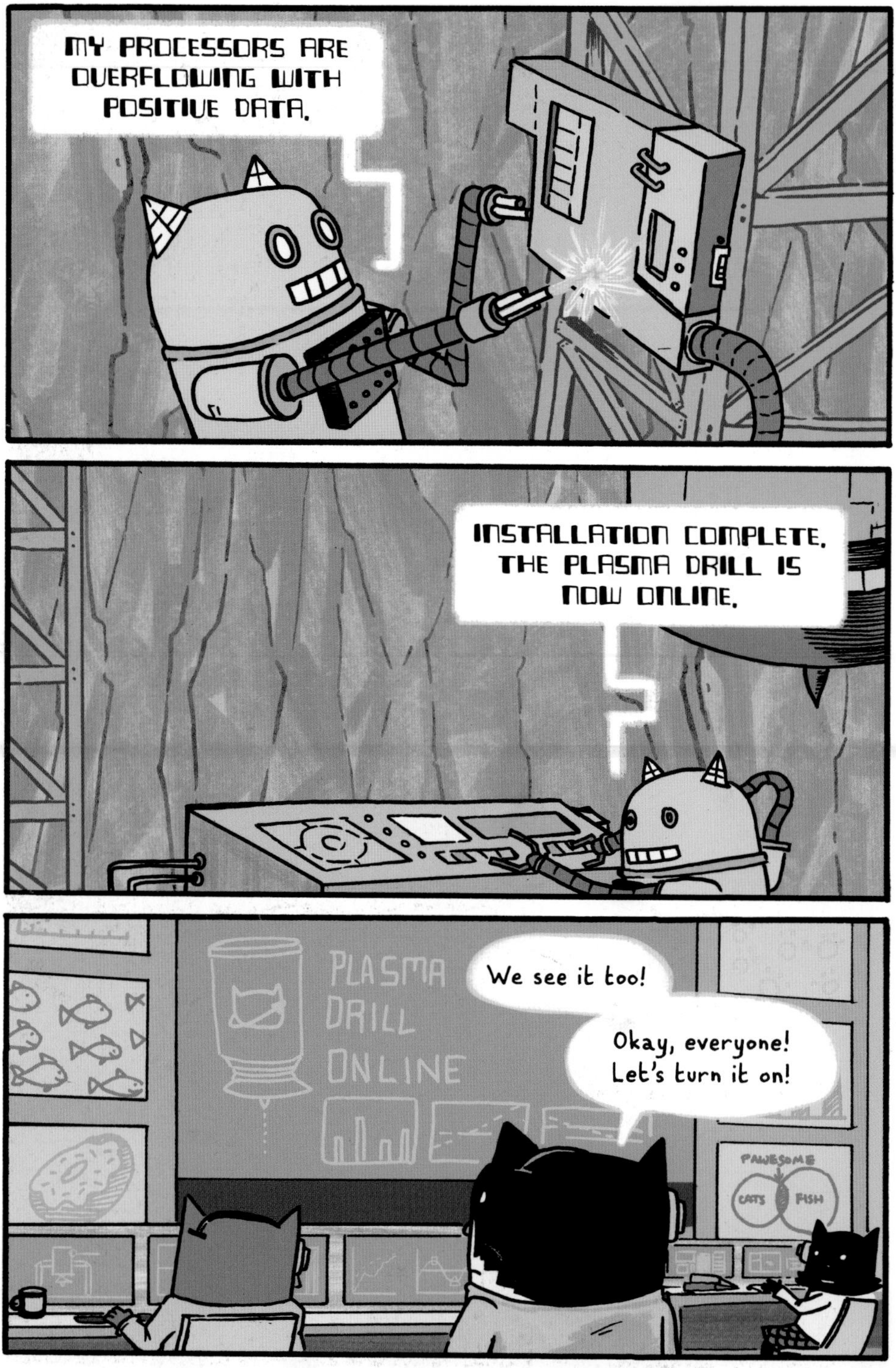
MY PROCESSORS ARE OVERFLOWING WITH POSITIVE DATA.
INSTALLATION COMPLETE. THE PLASMA DRILL IS NOW ONLINE.
PLASMA DRILL ONLINE
We see it too!
Okay, everyone! Let's turn it on!
PAWESOME
CATS
FISH

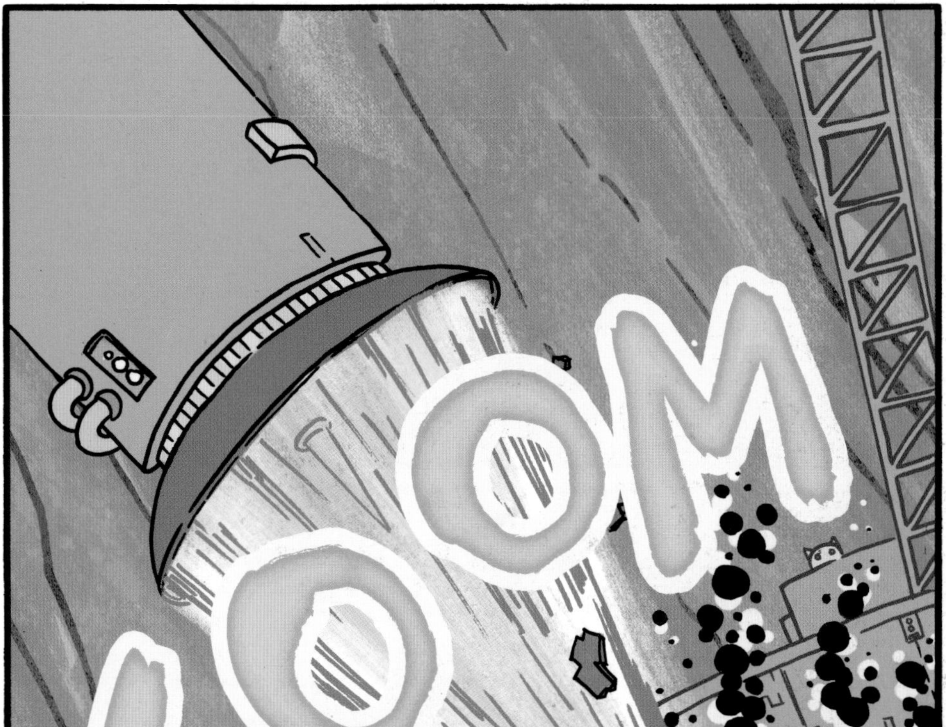
FOOM

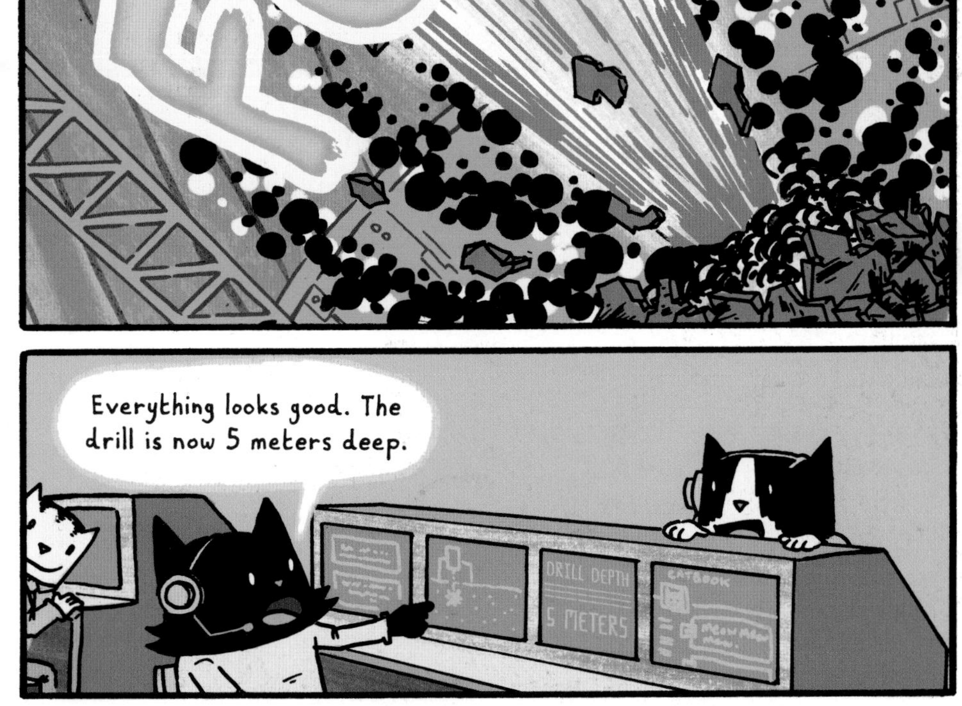
Everything looks good. The drill is now 5 meters deep.
DRILL DEPTH
5 METERS

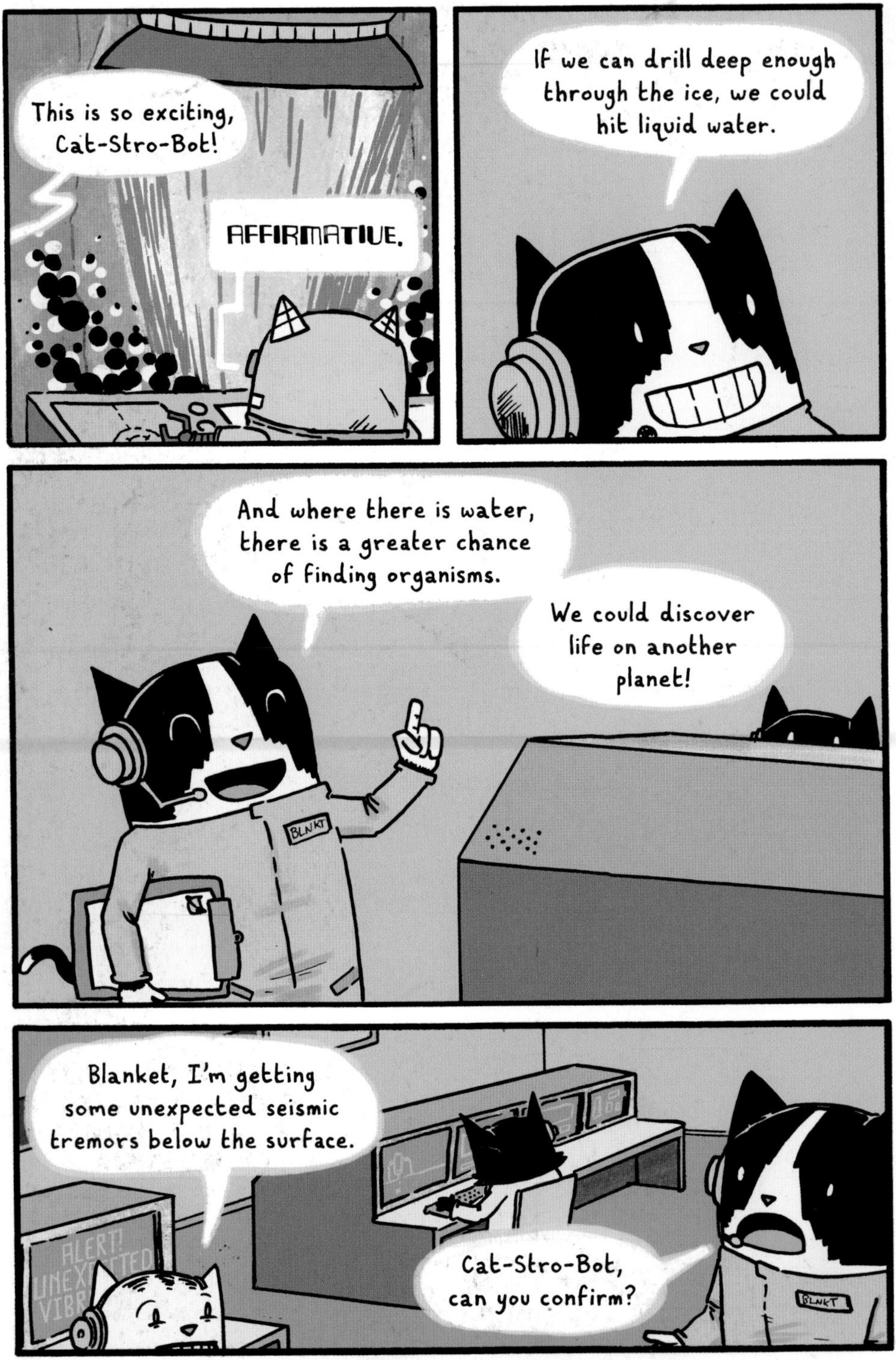
This is so exciting, Cat-Stro-Bot!
AFFIRMATIVE.
If we can drill deep enough through the ice, we could hit liquid water.
And where there is water, there is a greater chance of finding organisms.
We could discover life on another planet!
BLNKT
Blanket, I'm getting some unexpected seismic tremors below the surface.
ALERT! UNEXPECTED VIBR
Cat-Stro-Bot, can you confirm?
BLNKT

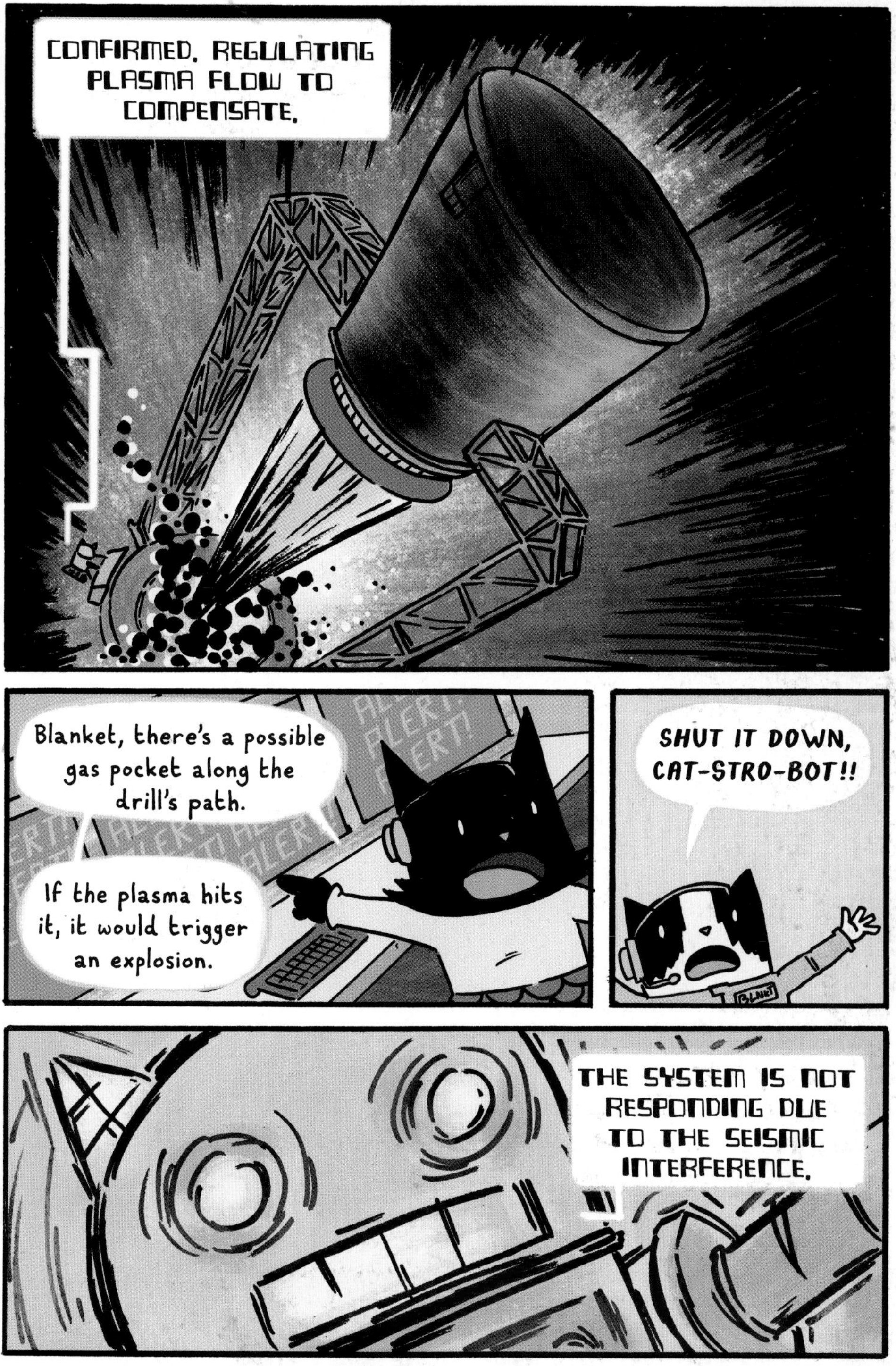
CONFIRMED. REGULATING PLASMA FLOW TO COMPENSATE.
ALERT! ALERT! ALERT!
Blanket, there's a possible gas pocket along the drill's path.
If the plasma hits it, it would trigger an explosion.
SHUT IT DOWN, CAT-STRO-BOT!!
THE SYSTEM IS NOT RESPONDING DUE TO THE SEISMIC INTERFERENCE.

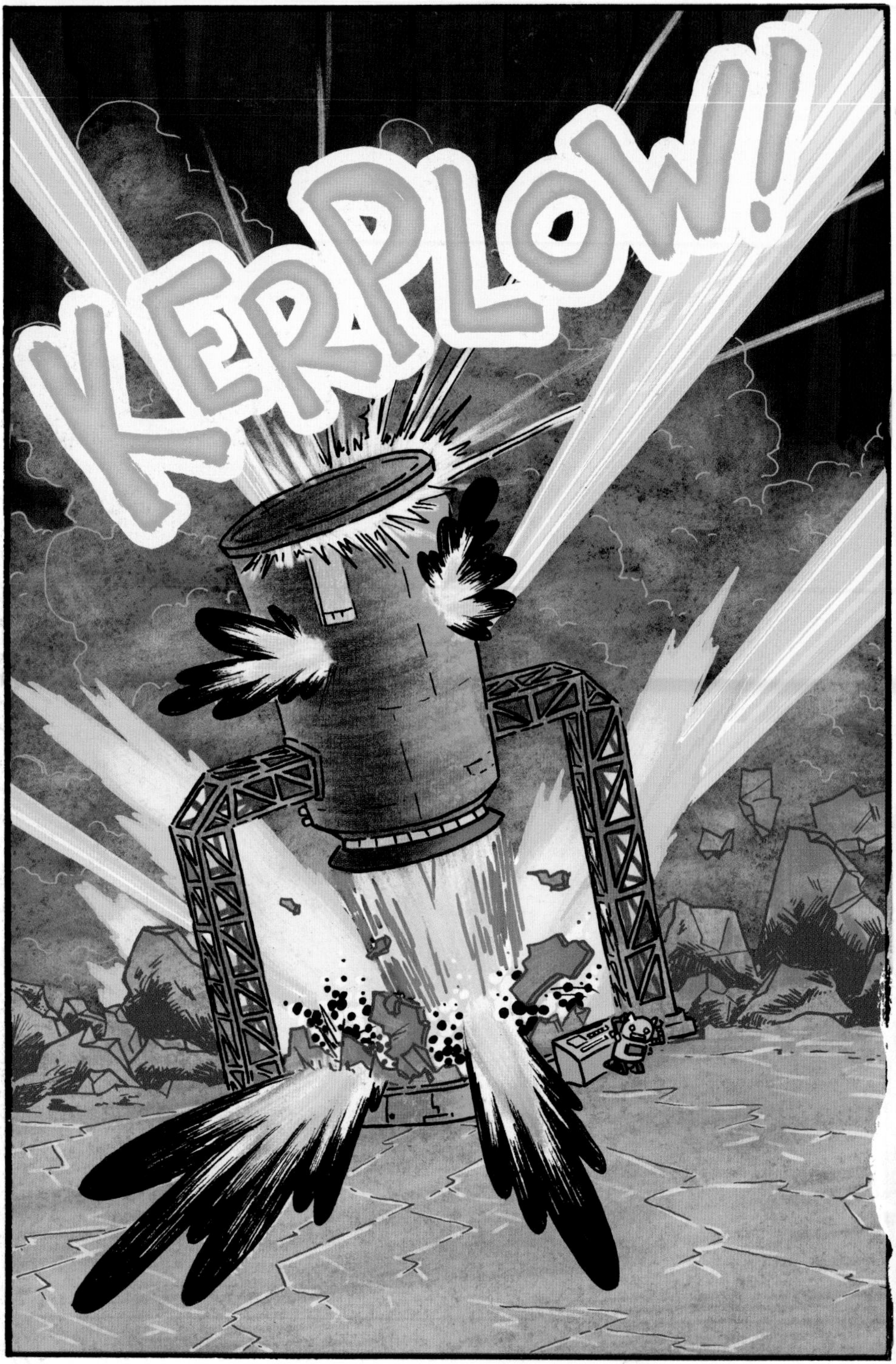
KERPLOW!

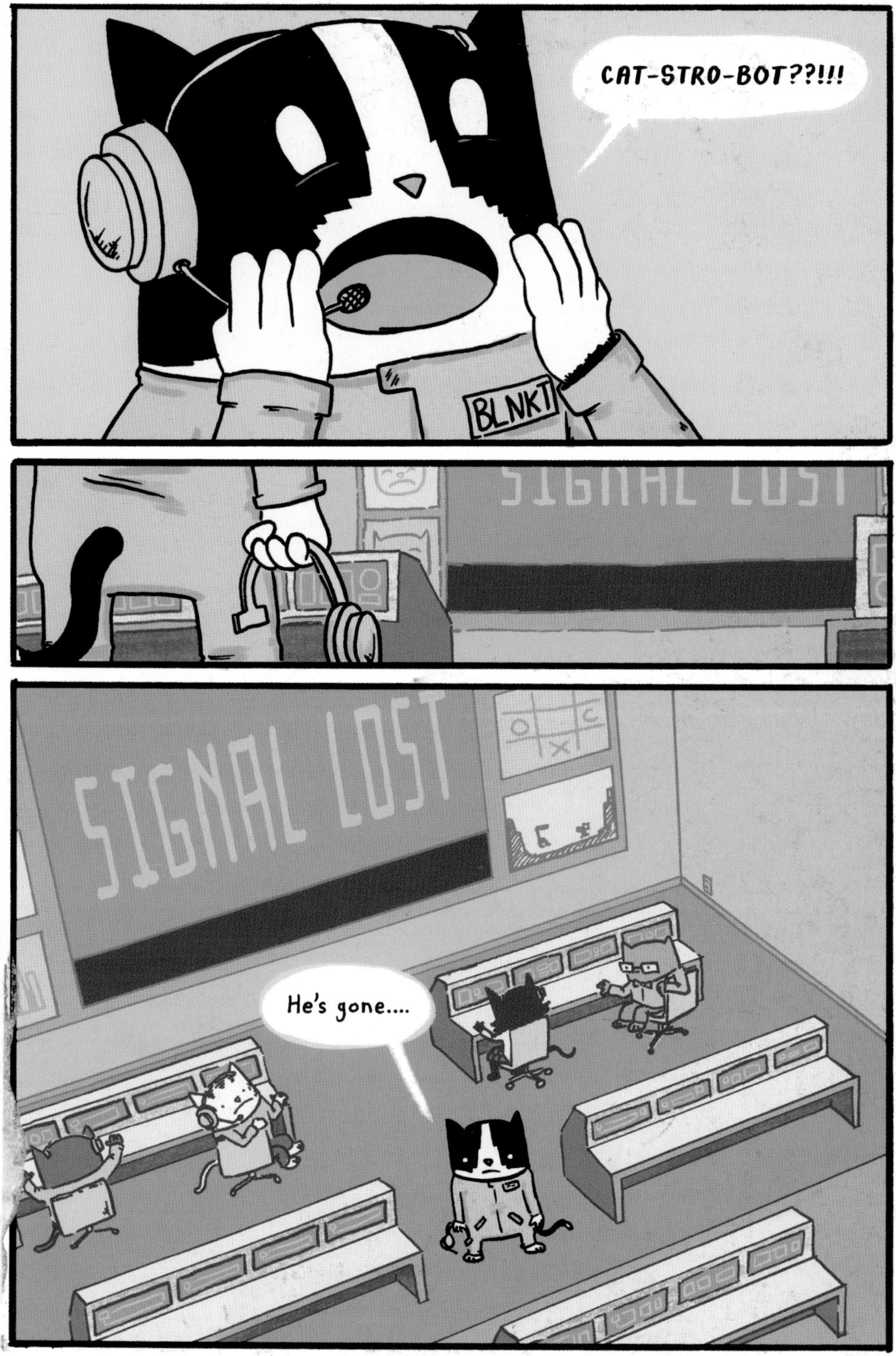
CAT-STRO-BOT??!!!
BLNKT
SIGNAL LOST
SIGNAL LOST
He's gone....

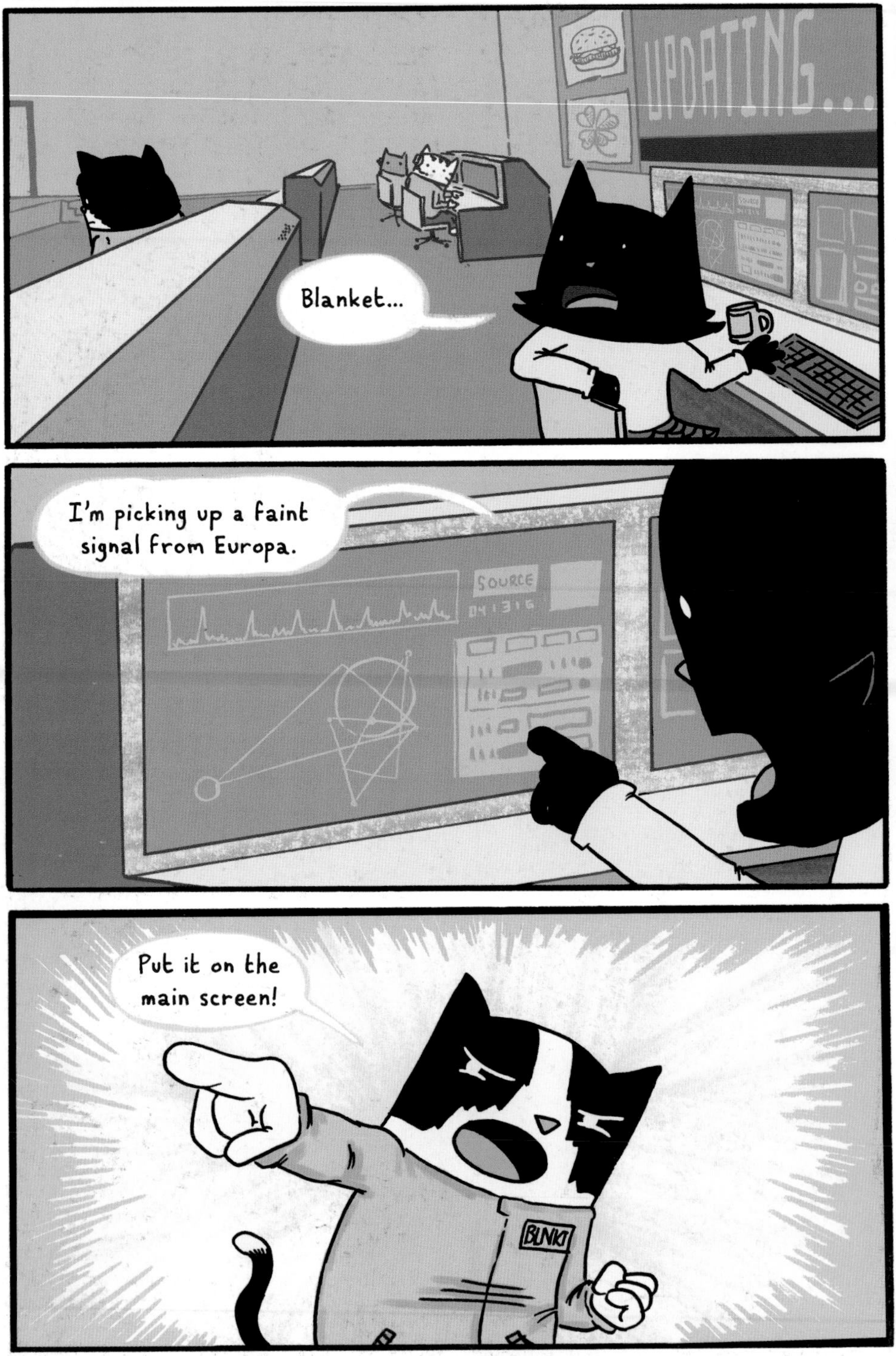

UPDATING...
Blanket...
I'm picking up a faint signal from Europa.
SOURCE
Put it on the main screen!
BLNKT

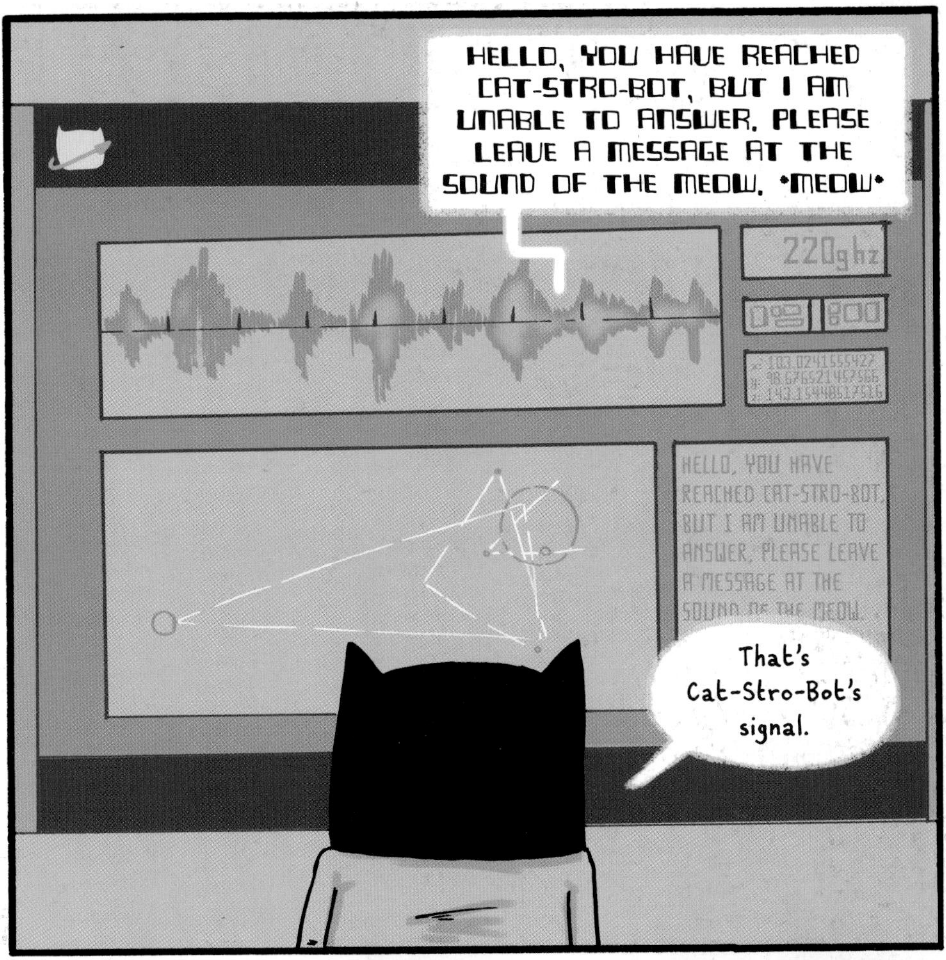
HELLO, YOU HAVE REACHED CAT-STRO-BOT, BUT I AM UNABLE TO ANSWER. PLEASE LEAVE A MESSAGE AT THE SOUND OF THE MEOW. *MEOW*
220ghz
x: 103.0241555427
y: 98.676521457566
z: 143.15448517516
HELLO, YOU HAVE REACHED CAT-STRO-BOT, BUT I AM UNABLE TO ANSWER. PLEASE LEAVE A MESSAGE AT THE SOUND OF THE MEOW.
That's Cat-Stro-Bot's signal.

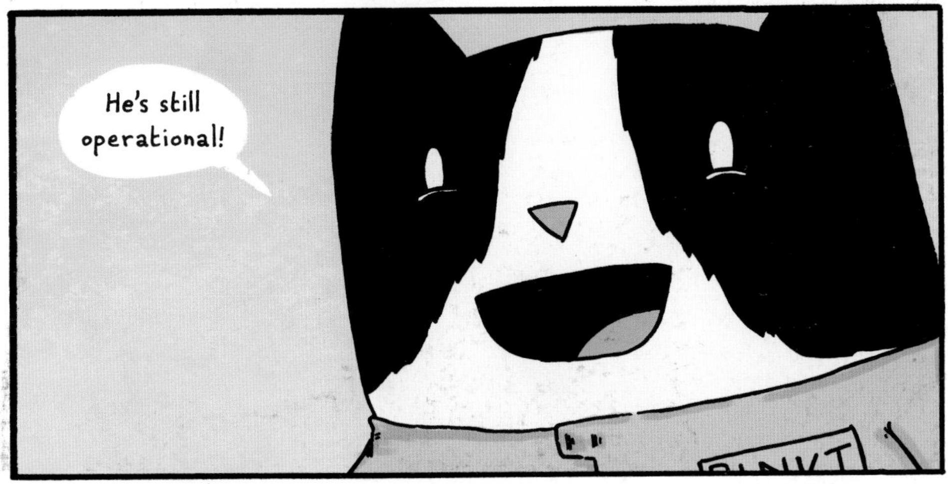
He's still operational!

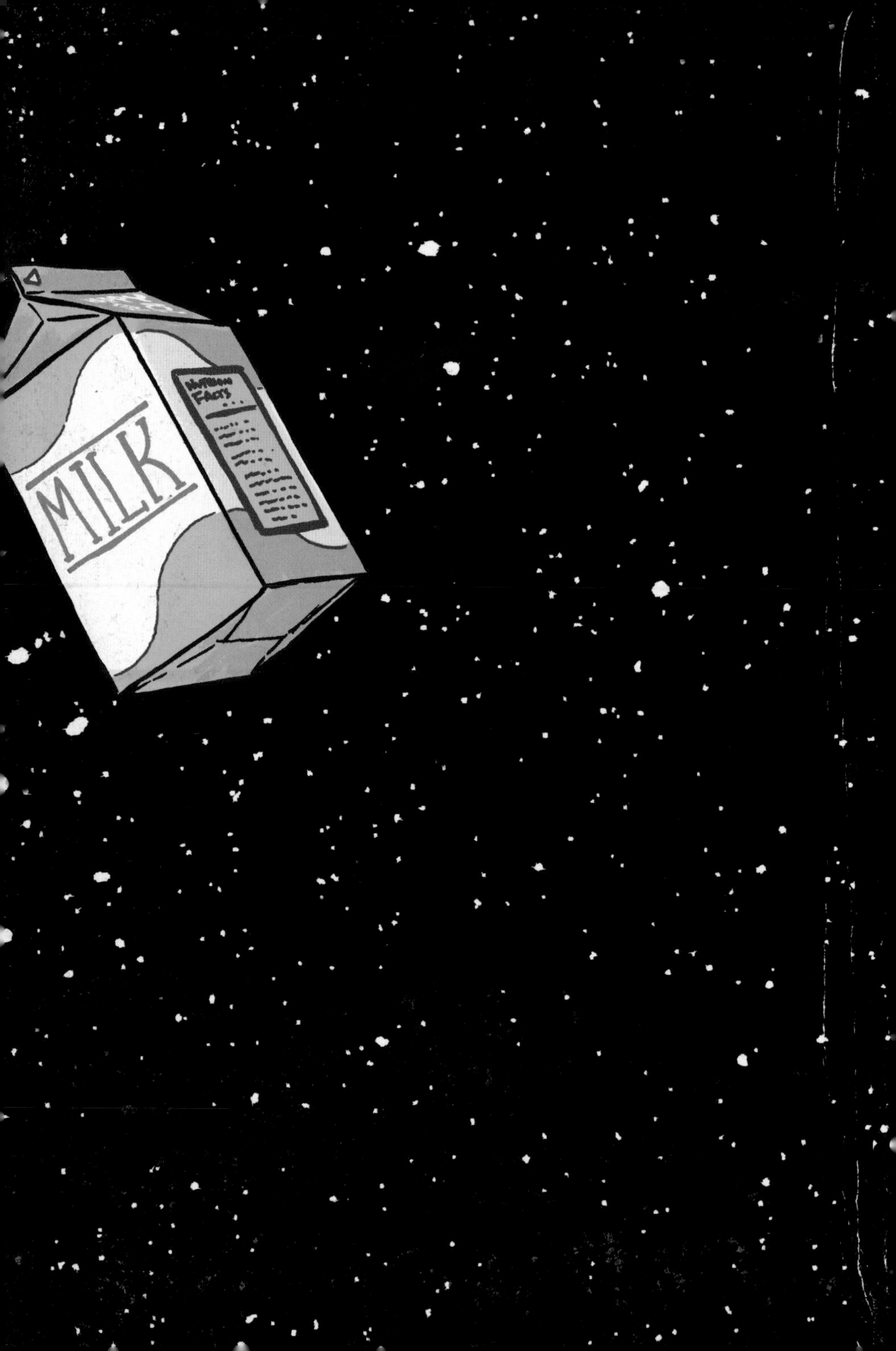
MILK
FACTS

CHAPTER 2

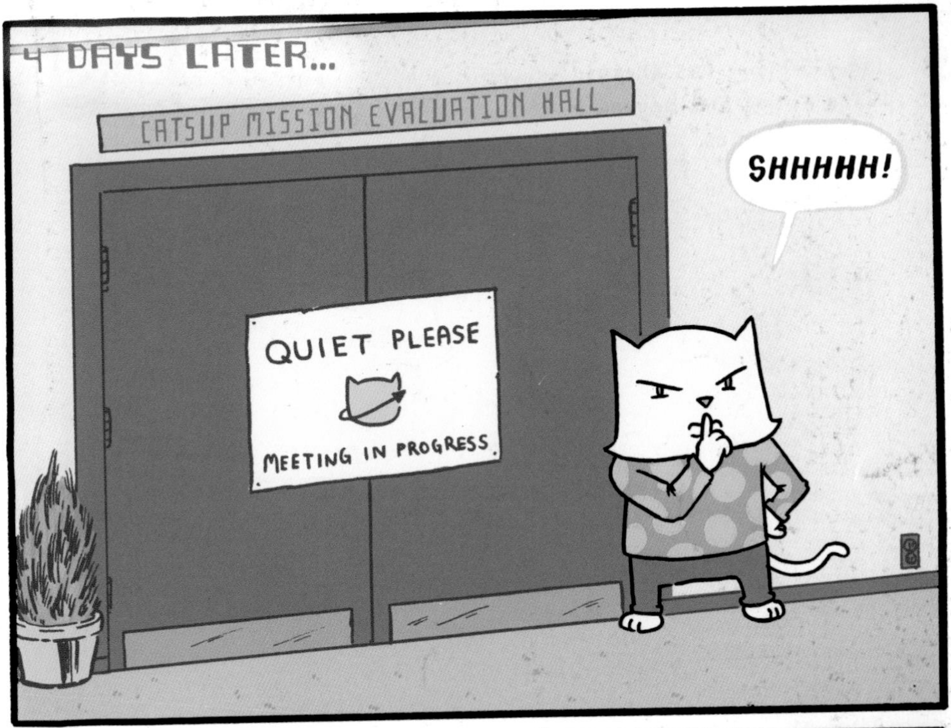
4 DAYS LATER...
CATSUP MISSION EVALUATION HALL
SHHHHH!
QUIET PLEASE
MEETING IN PROGRESS

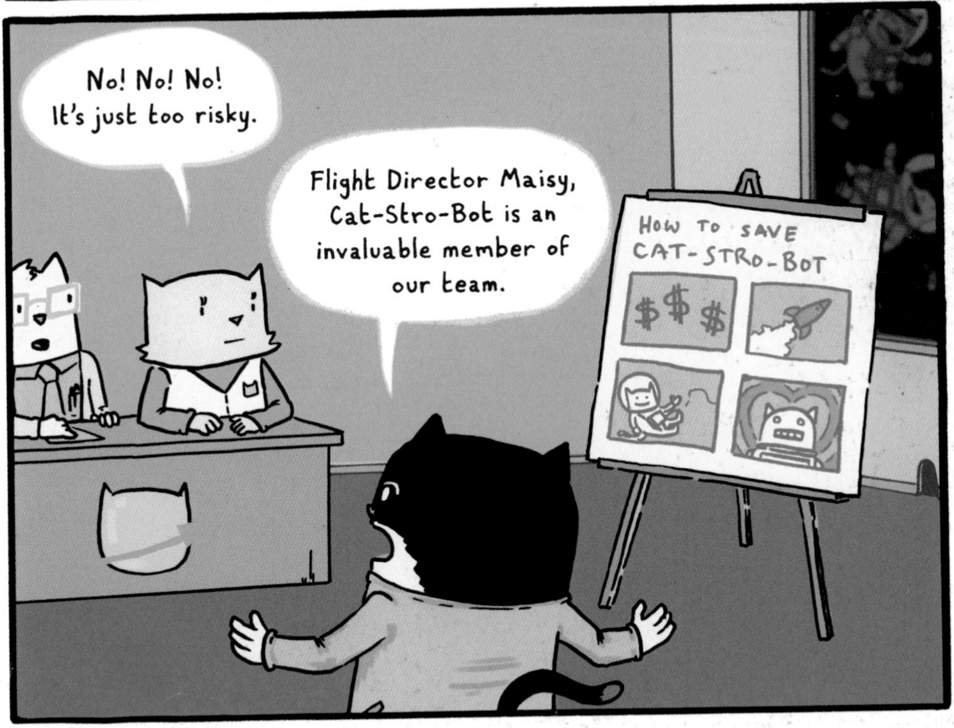
No! No! No!
It's just too risky.
Flight Director Maisy, Cat-Stro-Bot is an invaluable member of our team.
HOW TO SAVE CAT-STRO-BOT
$ $ $

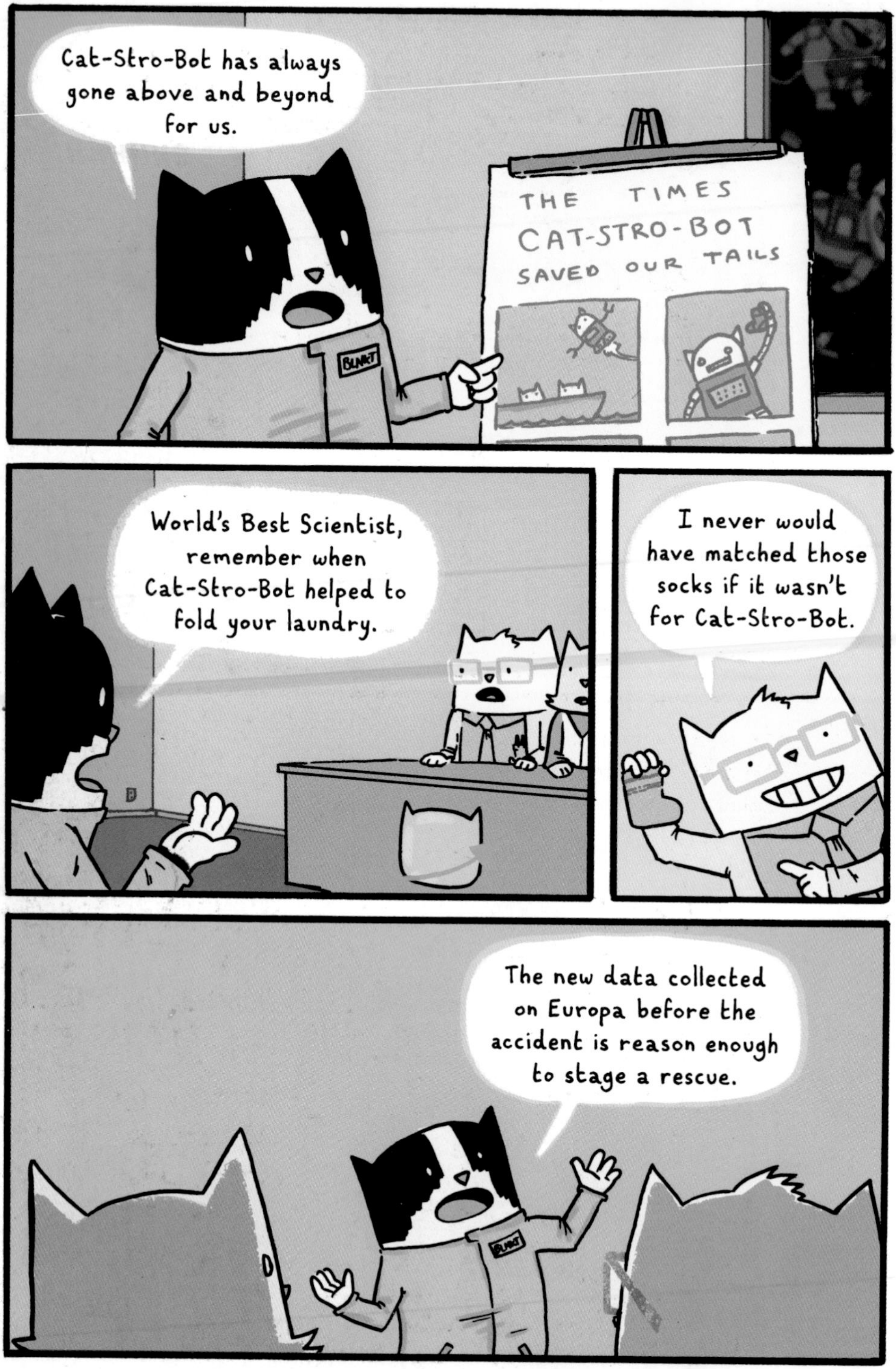
Cat-Stro-Bot has always gone above and beyond for us.
THE TIMES
CAT-STRO-BOT SAVED OUR TAILS
World's Best Scientist, remember when Cat-Stro-Bot helped to fold your laundry.
I never would have matched those socks if it wasn't for Cat-Stro-Bot.
The new data collected on Europa before the accident is reason enough to stage a rescue.

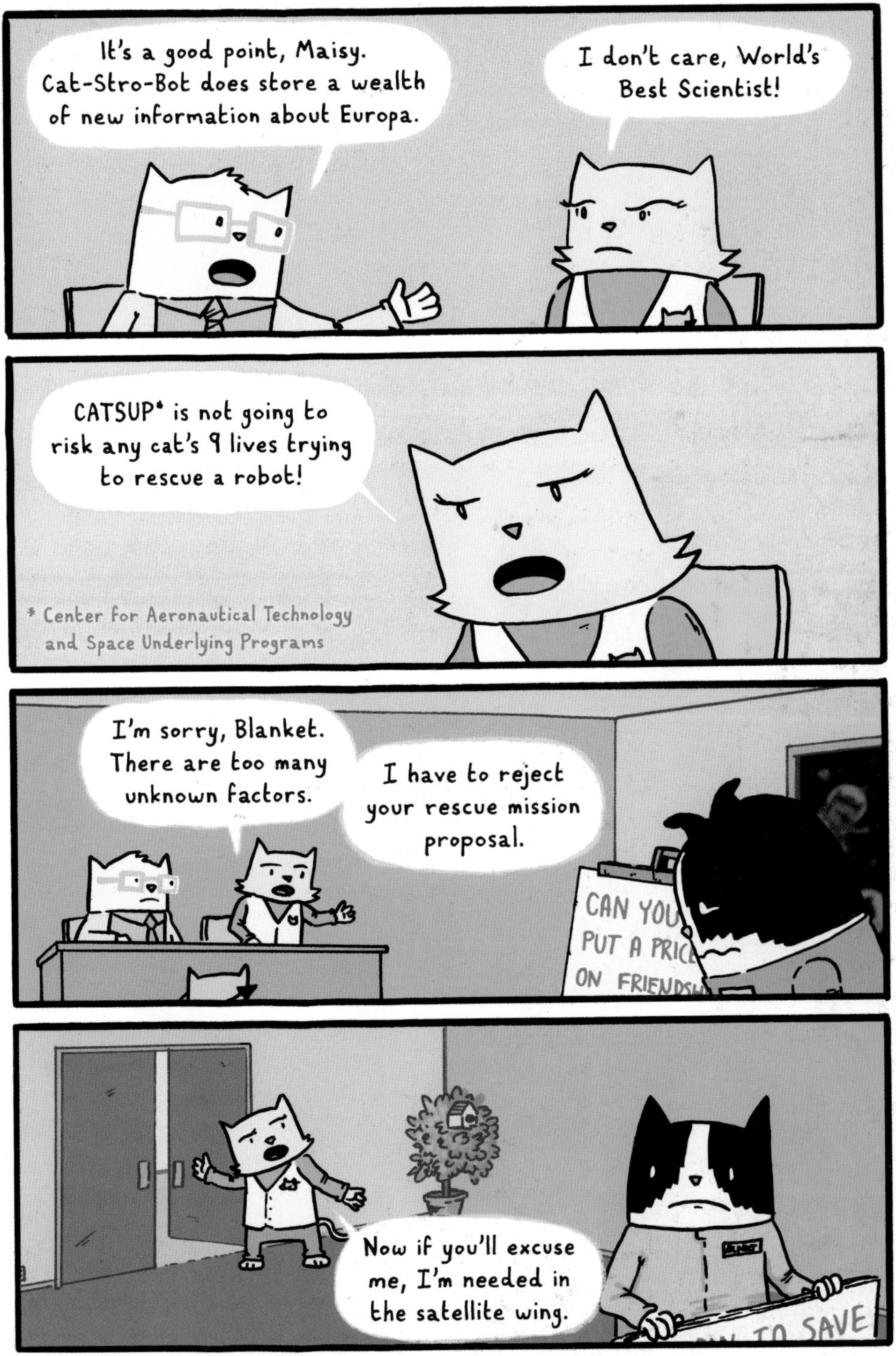
It's a good point, Maisy. Cat-Stro-Bot does store a wealth of new information about Europa.
I don't care, World's Best Scientist!
CATSUP* is not going to risk any cat's 9 lives trying to rescue a robot!
* Center for Aeronautical Technology and Space Underlying Programs
I'm sorry, Blanket. There are too many unknown factors.
I have to reject your rescue mission proposal.
CAN YOU PUT A PRIC ON FRIENDSH
Now if you'll excuse me, I'm needed in the satellite wing.
TO SAVE

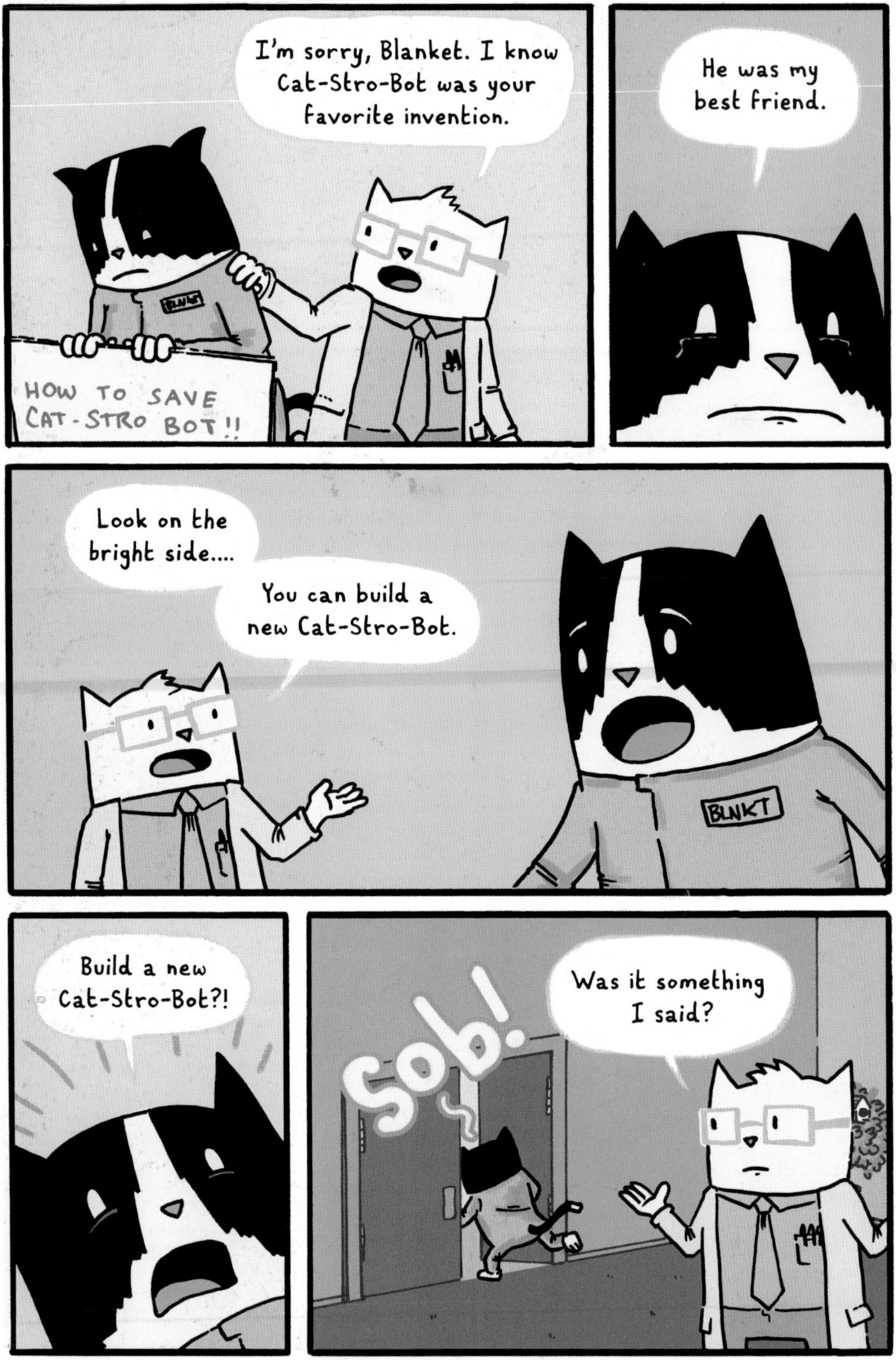
I'm sorry, Blanket. I know Cat-Stro-Bot was your favorite invention.
BLNKT
HOW TO SAVE CAT-STRO BOT!!
He was my best friend.
Look on the bright side....
You can build a new Cat-Stro-Bot.
BLNKT
Build a new Cat-Stro-Bot?!
SOB!
Was it something I said?

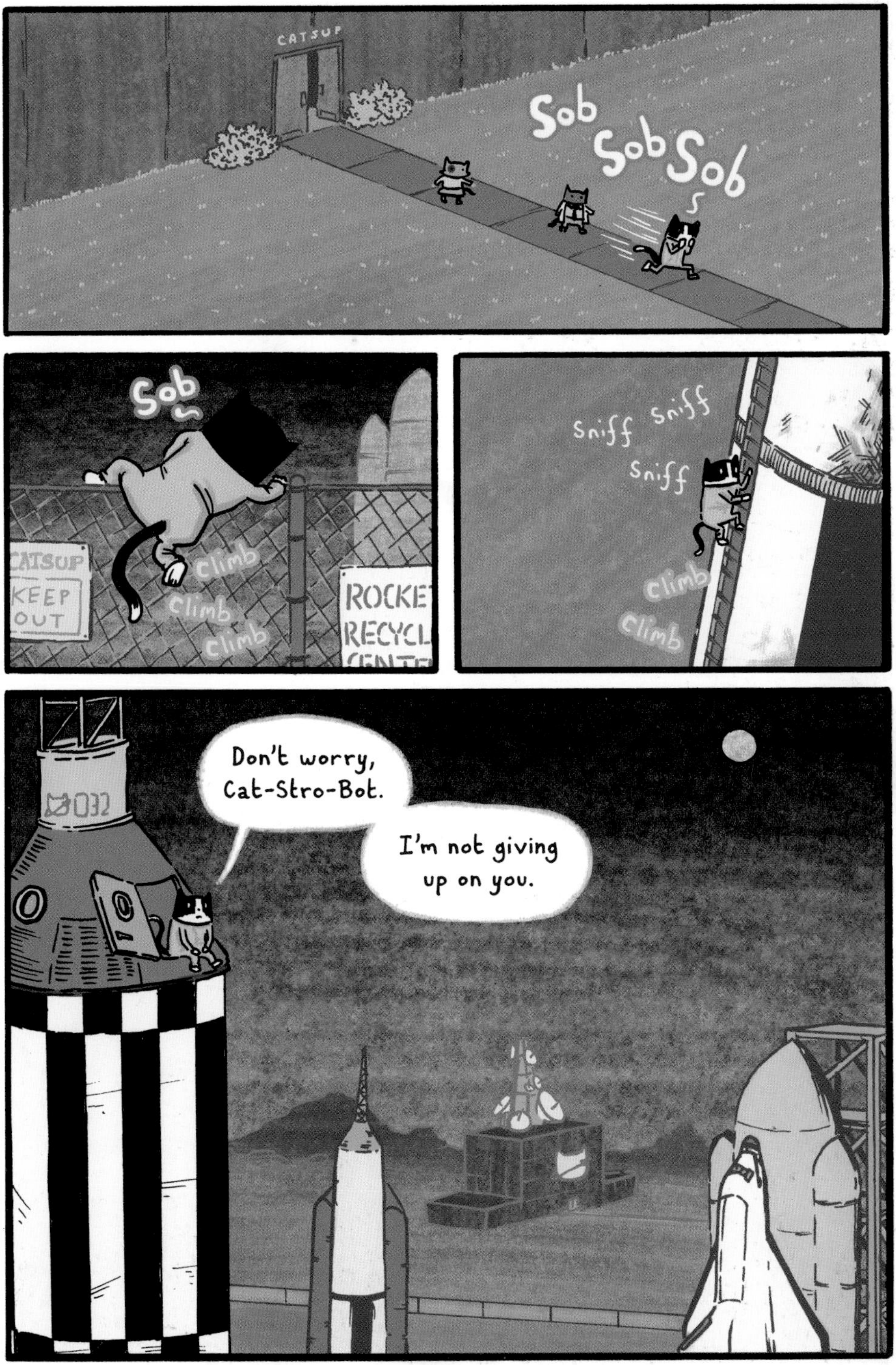
CATSUP
Sob
Sob
Sob
Sob
climb
climb
climb
CATSUP
KEEP OUT
ROCKET RECYCL CENTE
sniff
sniff
sniff
climb
climb
Don't worry, Cat-Stro-Bot.
I'm not giving up on you.

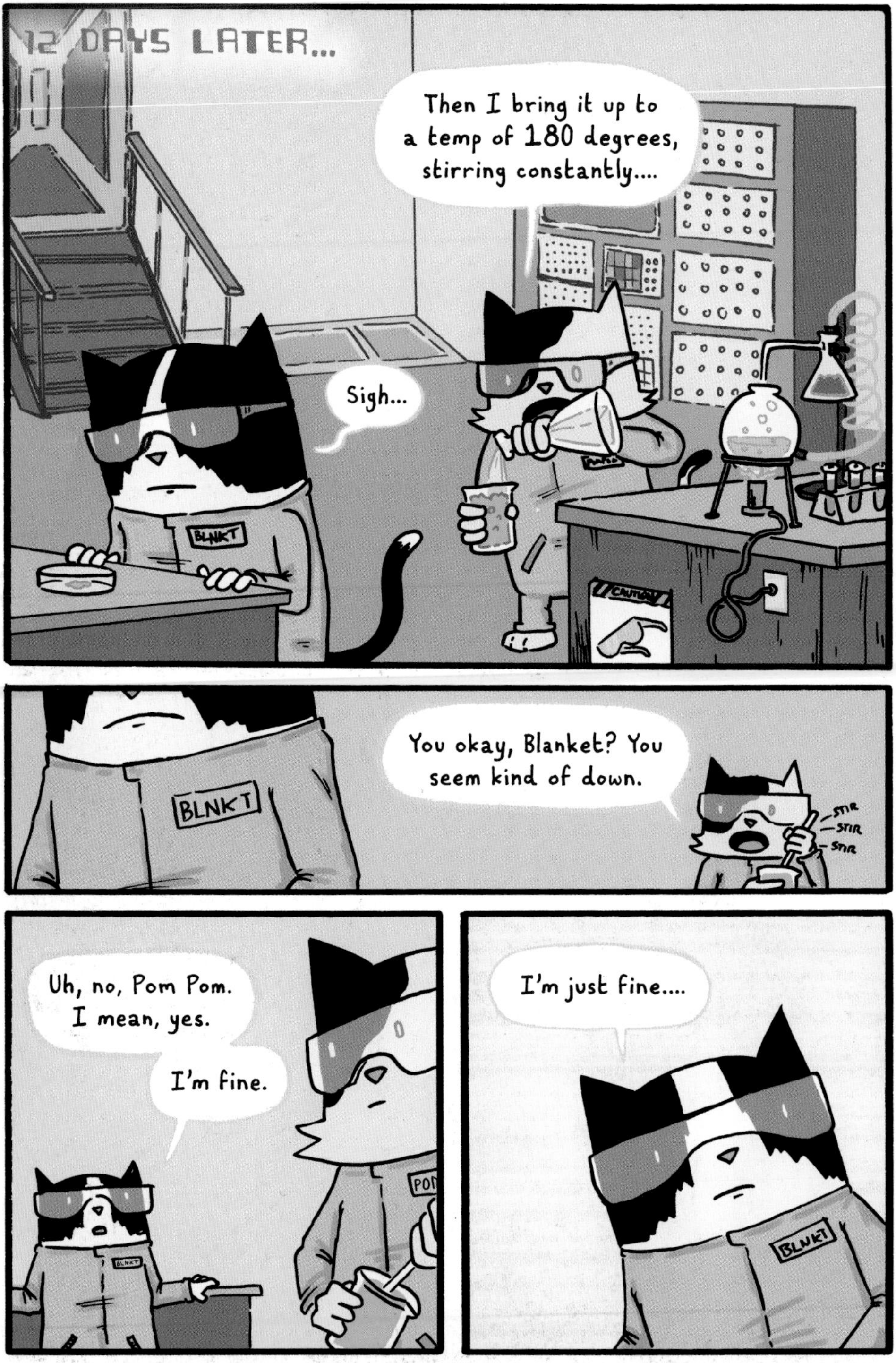
12 DAYS LATER...
Then I bring it up to a temp of 180 degrees, stirring constantly....
Sigh...
CAUTION
BLNKT
You okay, Blanket? You seem kind of down.
STIR
STIR
STIR
BLNKT
Uh, no, Pom Pom. I mean, yes.
I'm fine.
BLNKT
I'm just fine....
BLNKT

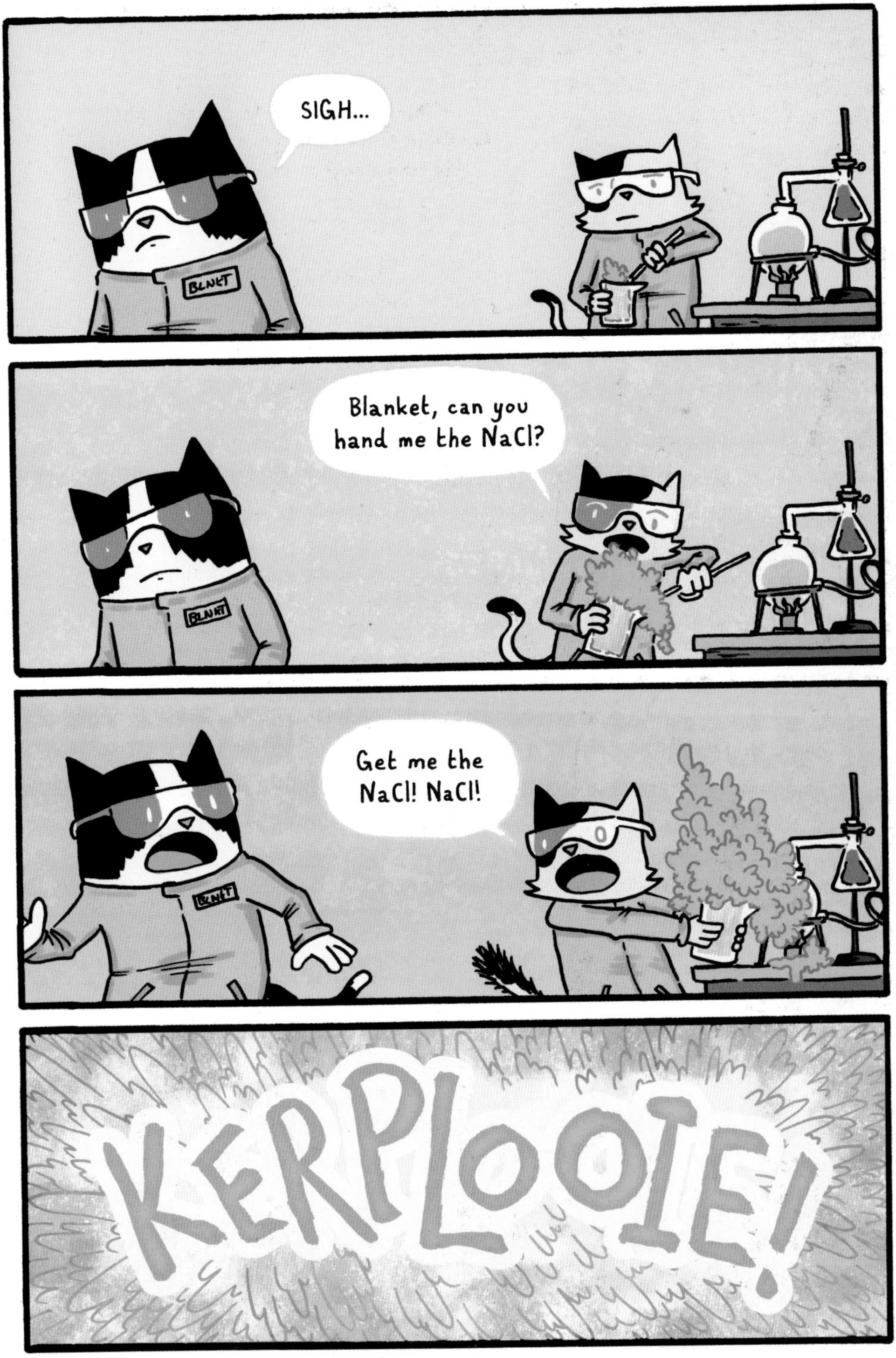
SIGH...
BLNKT
Blanket, can you hand me the NaCl?
BLNKT
Get me the NaCl! NaCl!
BLNKT
KERPLOOIE!

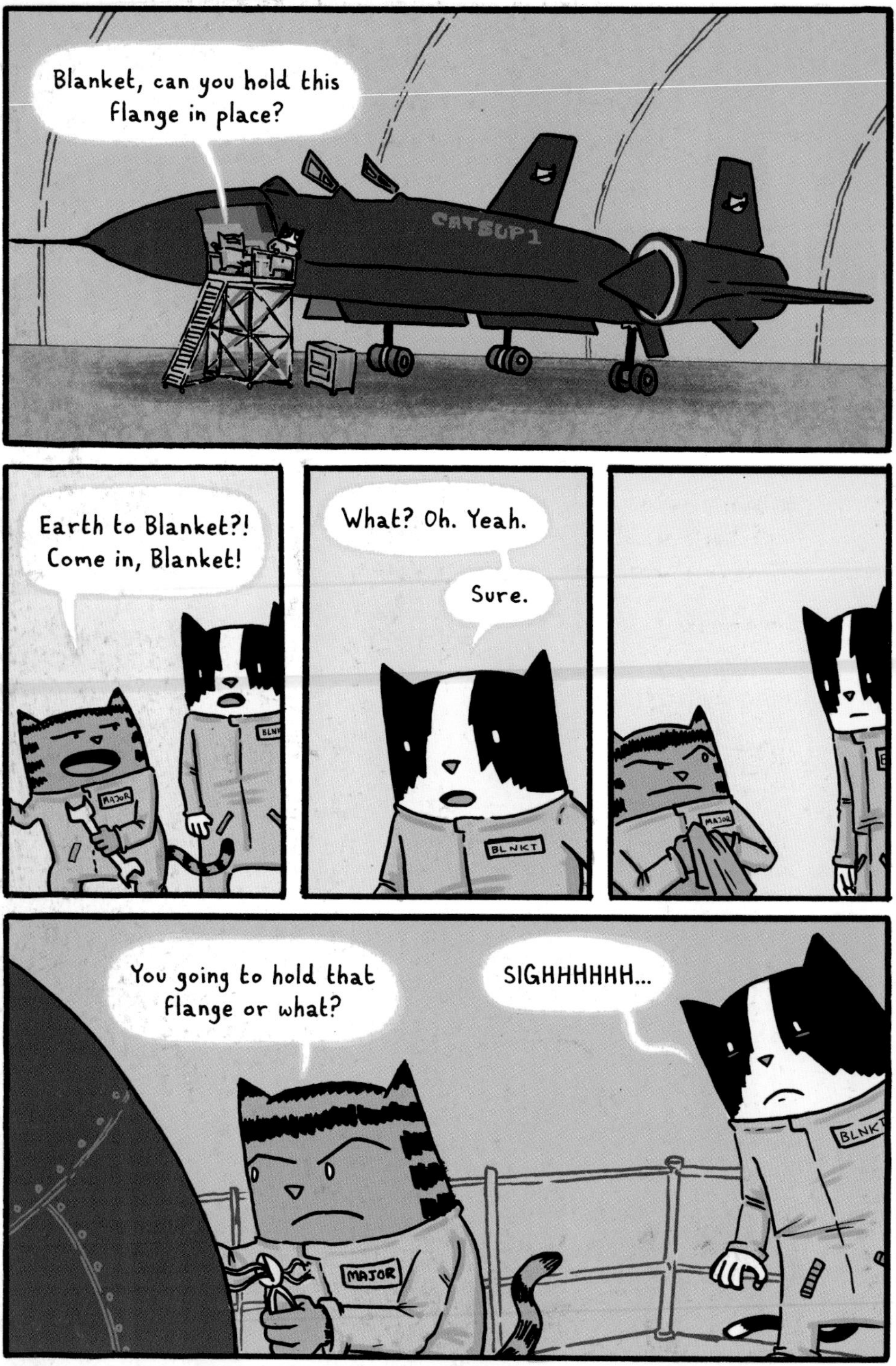
Blanket, can you hold this flange in place?
CATSUP 1
Earth to Blanket?! Come in, Blanket!
MAJOR
BLNK
What? Oh. Yeah.
Sure.
BLNKT
MAJOR
You going to hold that flange or what?
SIGHHHHHH...
MAJOR
BLNK

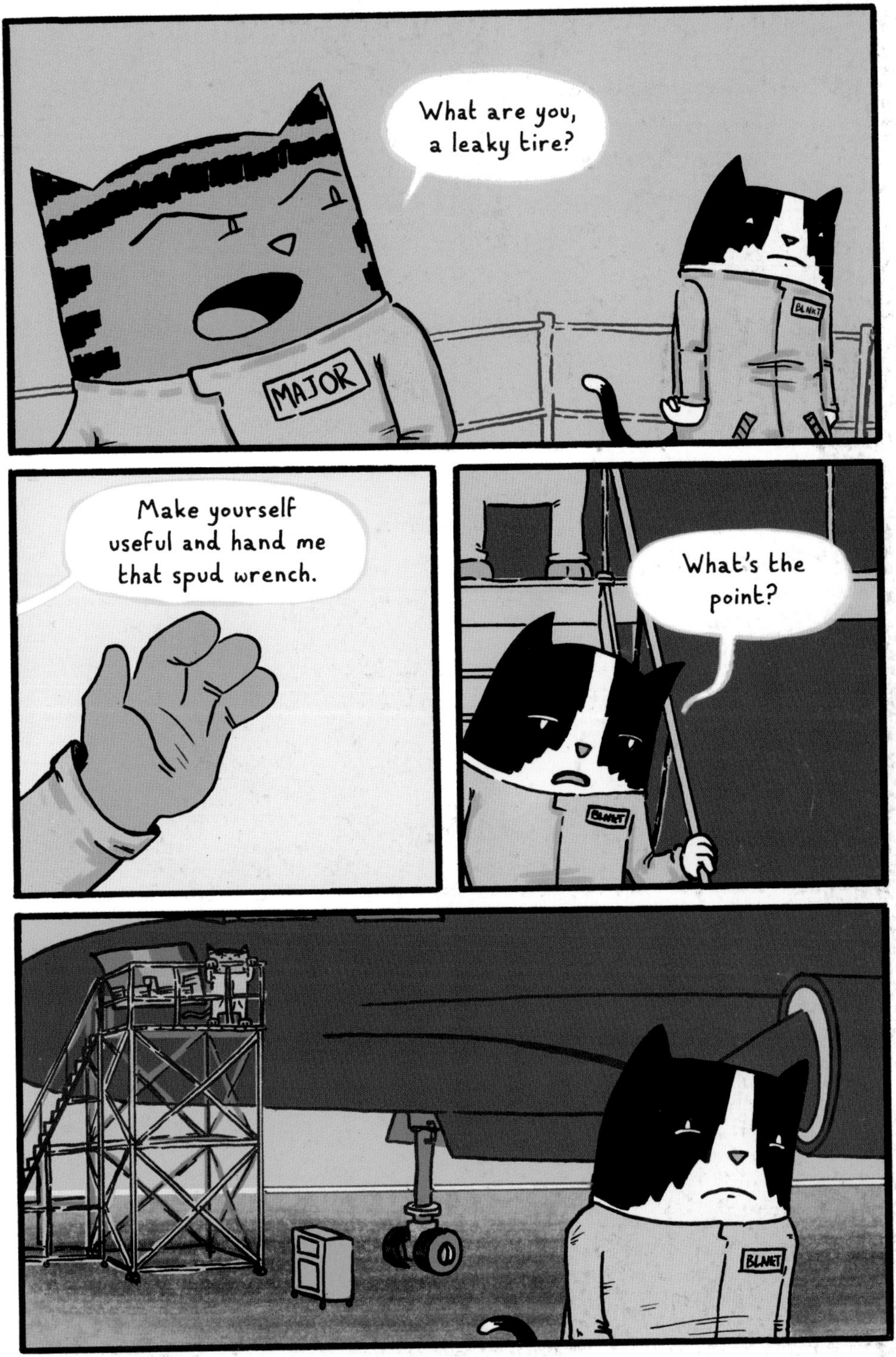
What are you, a leaky tire?
MAJOR
BLNKT
Make yourself useful and hand me that spud wrench.
What's the point?
BLNKT

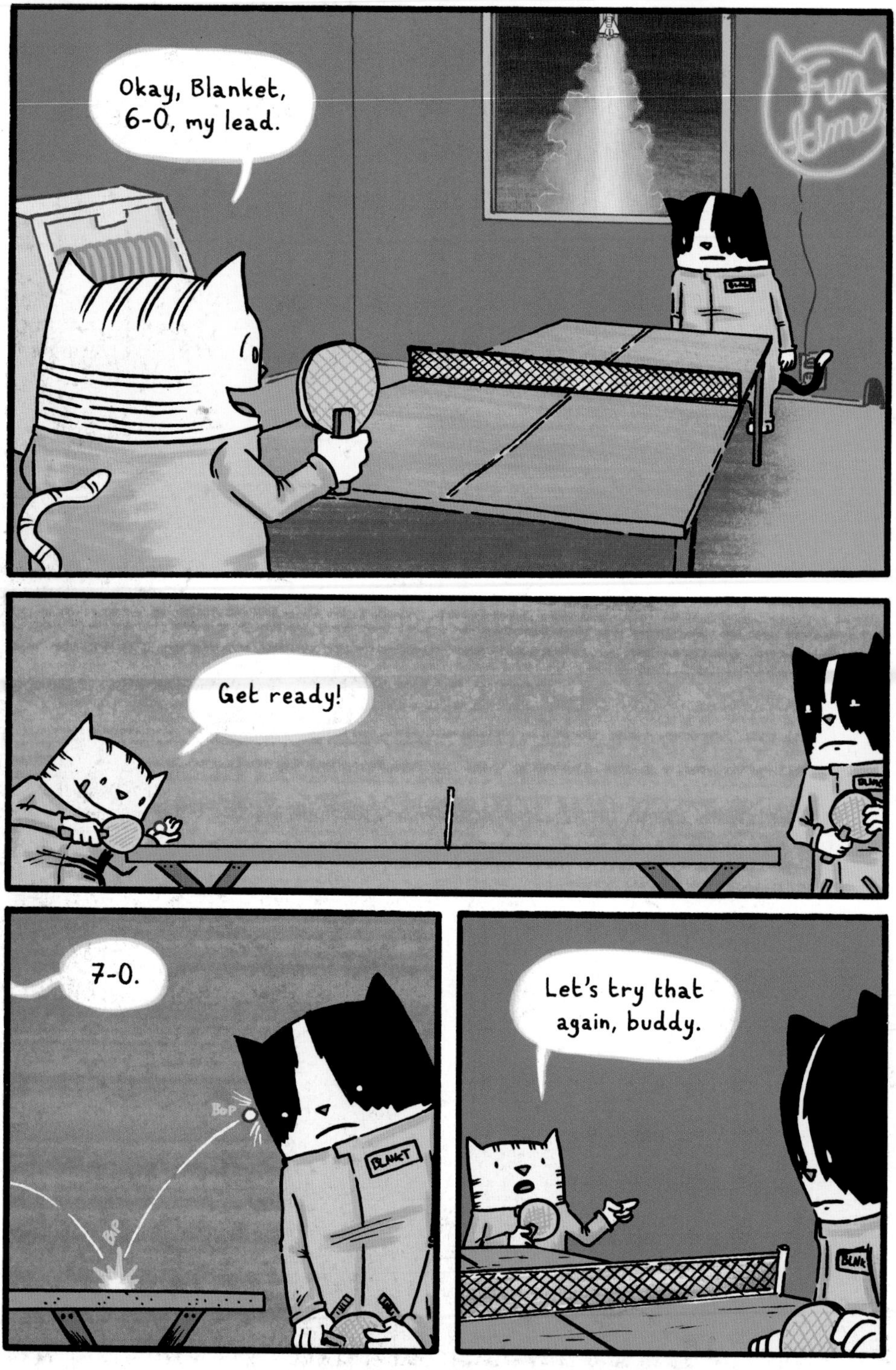
Okay, Blanket, 6-0, my lead.
Get ready!
7-0.
Let's try that again, buddy.

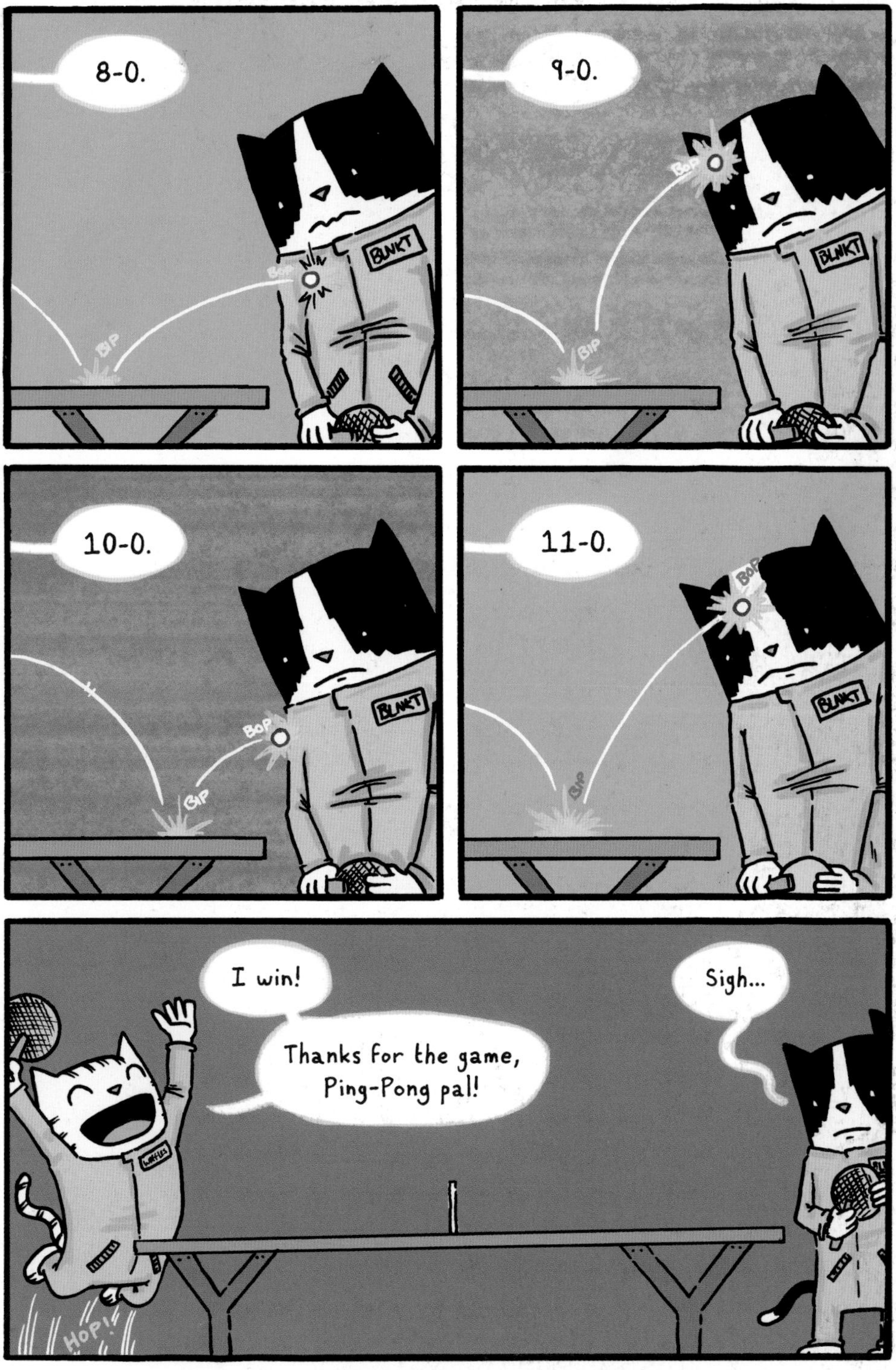
8-0.
BOP
BIP
BLNKT
9-0.
BOP
BIP
BLNKT
10-0.
BOP
BIP
BLNKT
11-0.
BOP
BIP
BLNKT
I win!
Thanks for the game, Ping-Pong pal!
Sigh...
HOP!

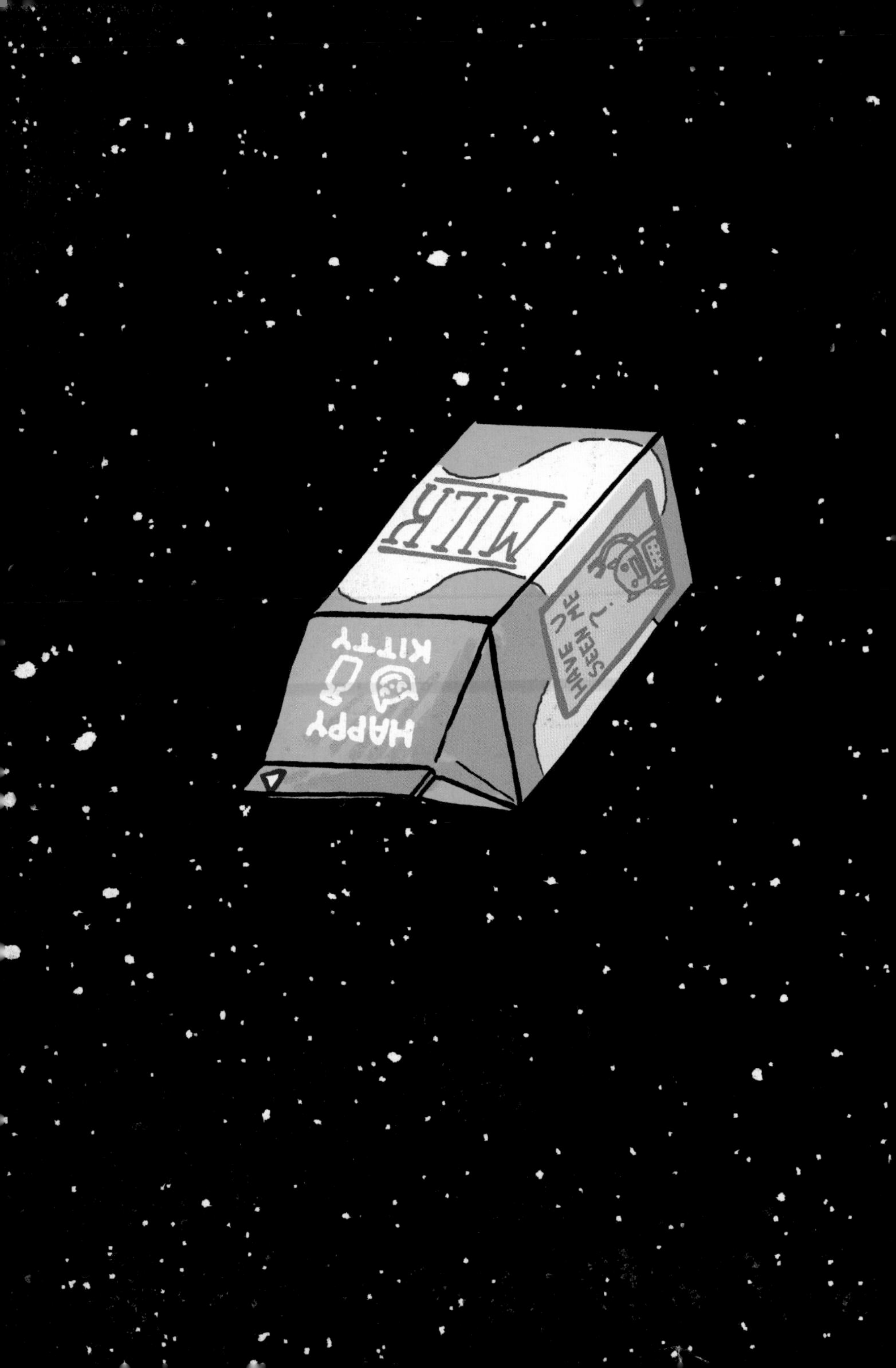
MILK
HAPPY KITTY
HAVE U SEEN ME ?

CHAPTER 3

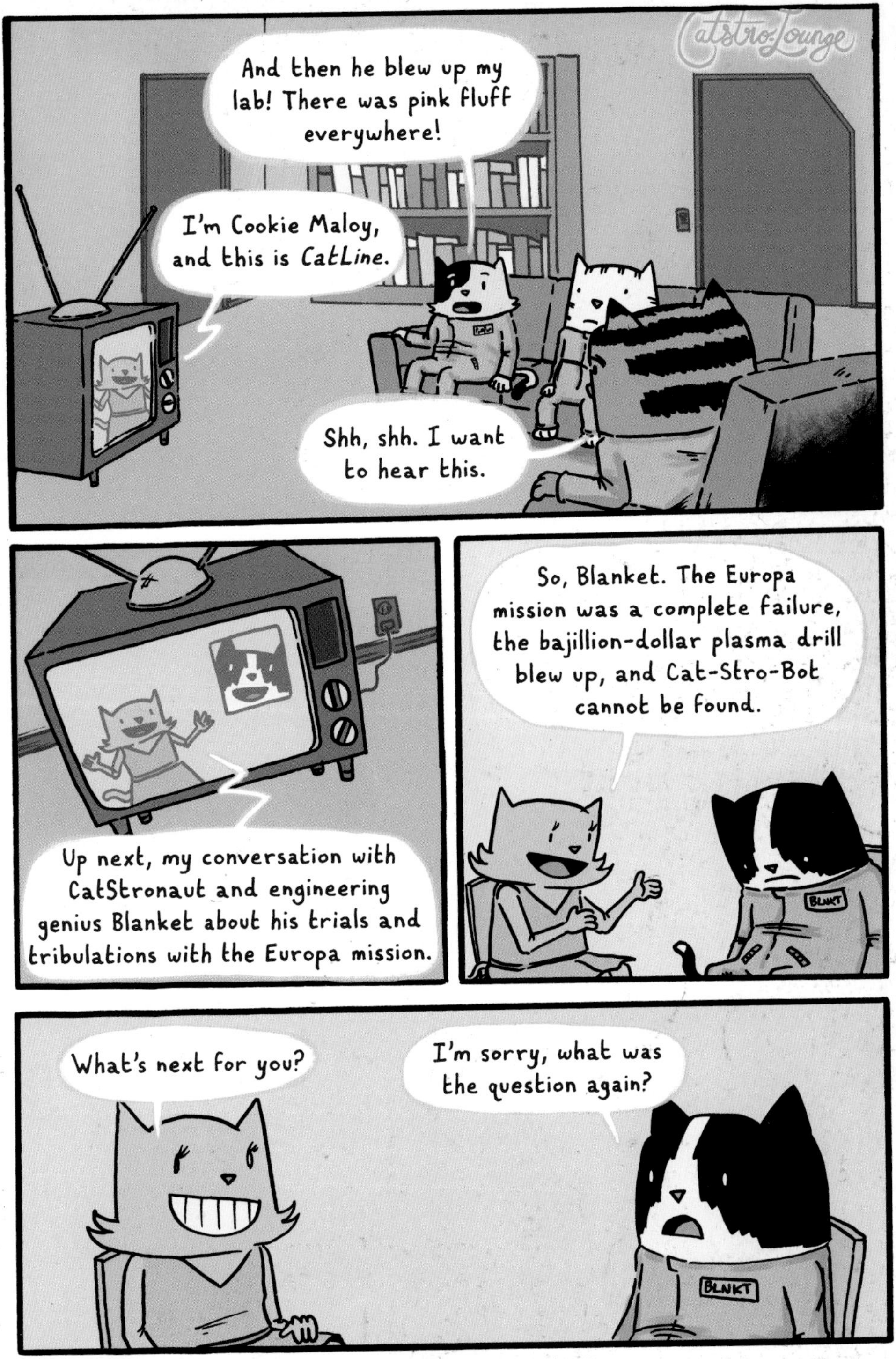
Catstro-Lounge
And then he blew up my lab! There was pink fluff everywhere!
I'm Cookie Maloy, and this is *CatLine*.
Shh, shh. I want to hear this.
Up next, my conversation with CatStronaut and engineering genius Blanket about his trials and tribulations with the Europa mission.
So, Blanket. The Europa mission was a complete failure, the bajillion-dollar plasma drill blew up, and Cat-Stro-Bot cannot be found.
BLNKT
What's next for you?
I'm sorry, what was the question again?
BLNKT

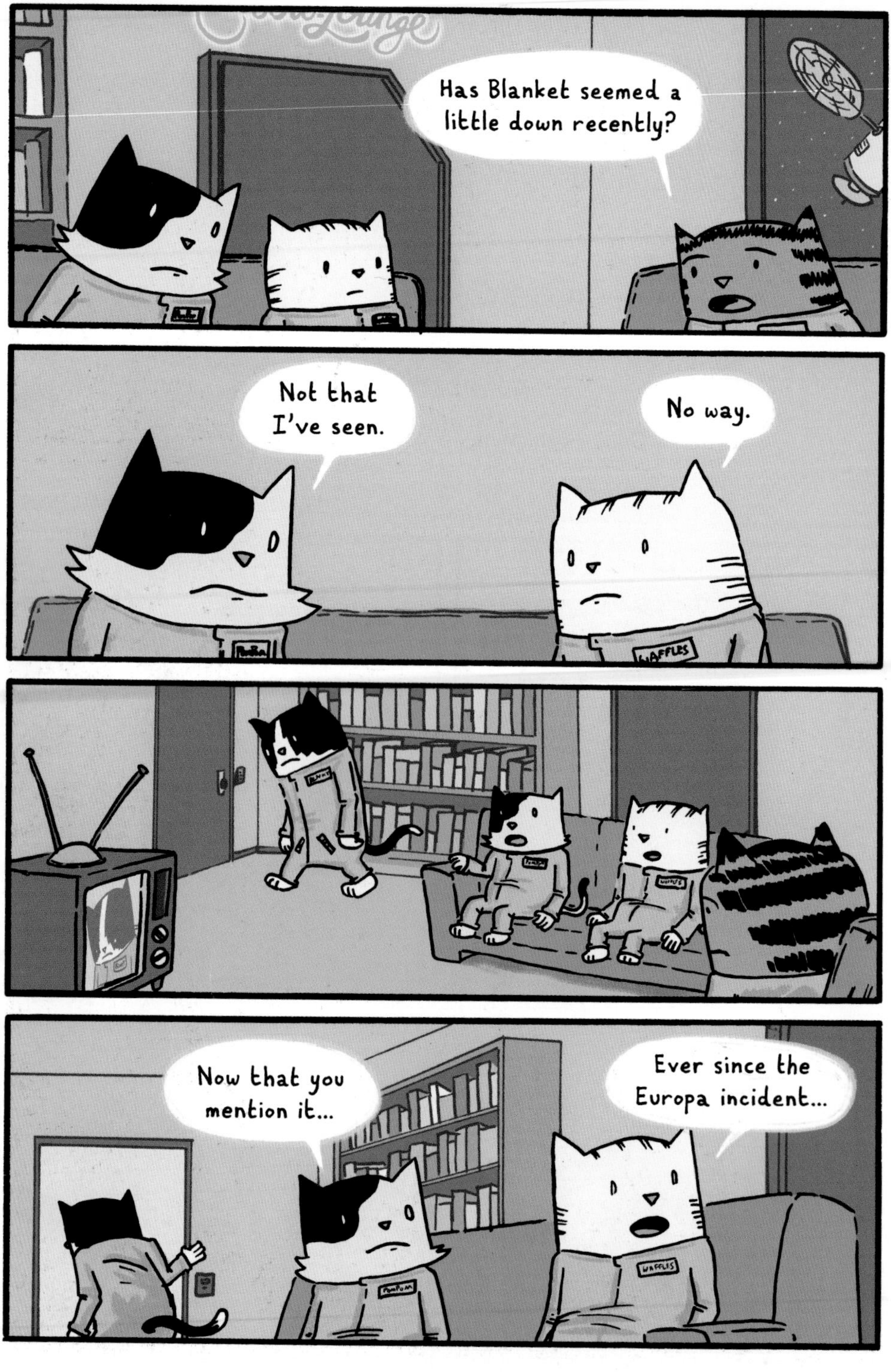
Has Blanket seemed a little down recently?
Not that I've seen.
No way.
Now that you mention it...
Ever since the Europa incident...

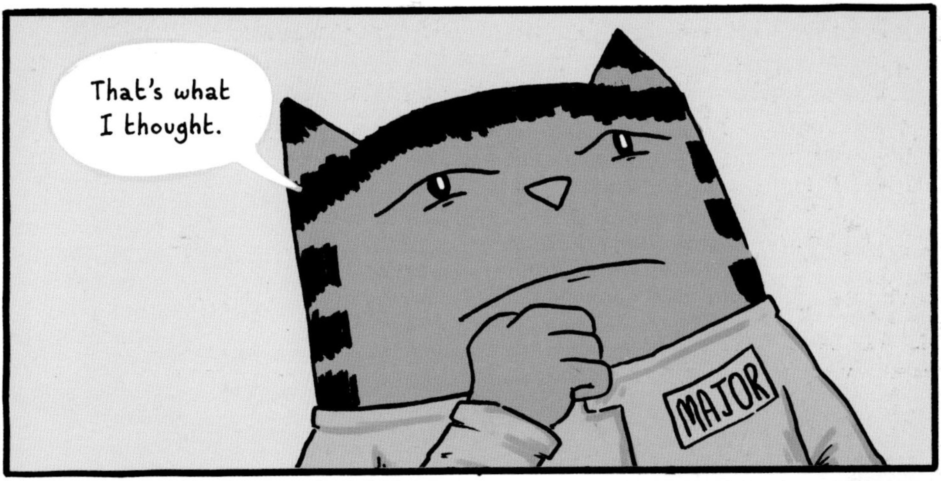
That's what I thought.
MAJOR

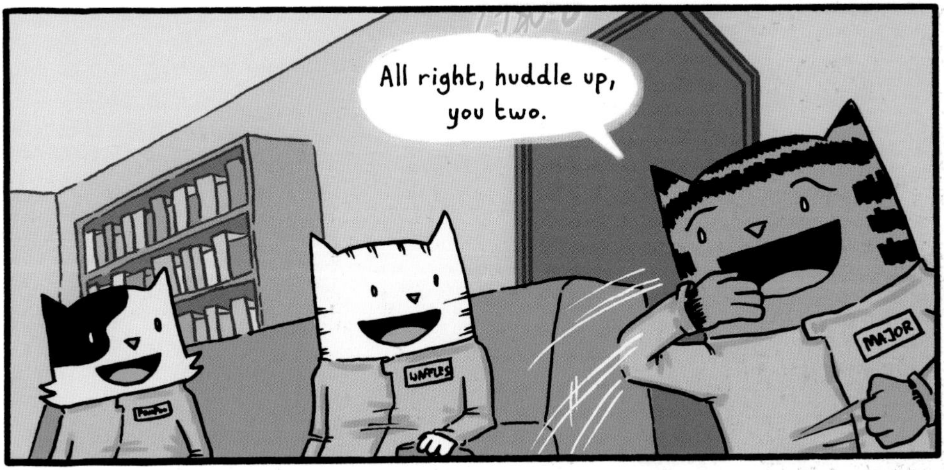
All right, huddle up, you two.
MAJOR

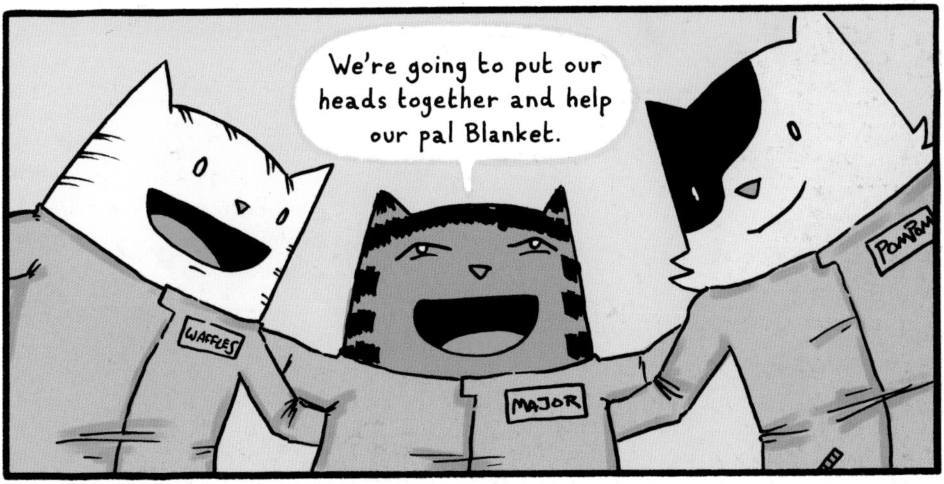
We're going to put our heads together and help our pal Blanket.
WAFFLES
MAJOR

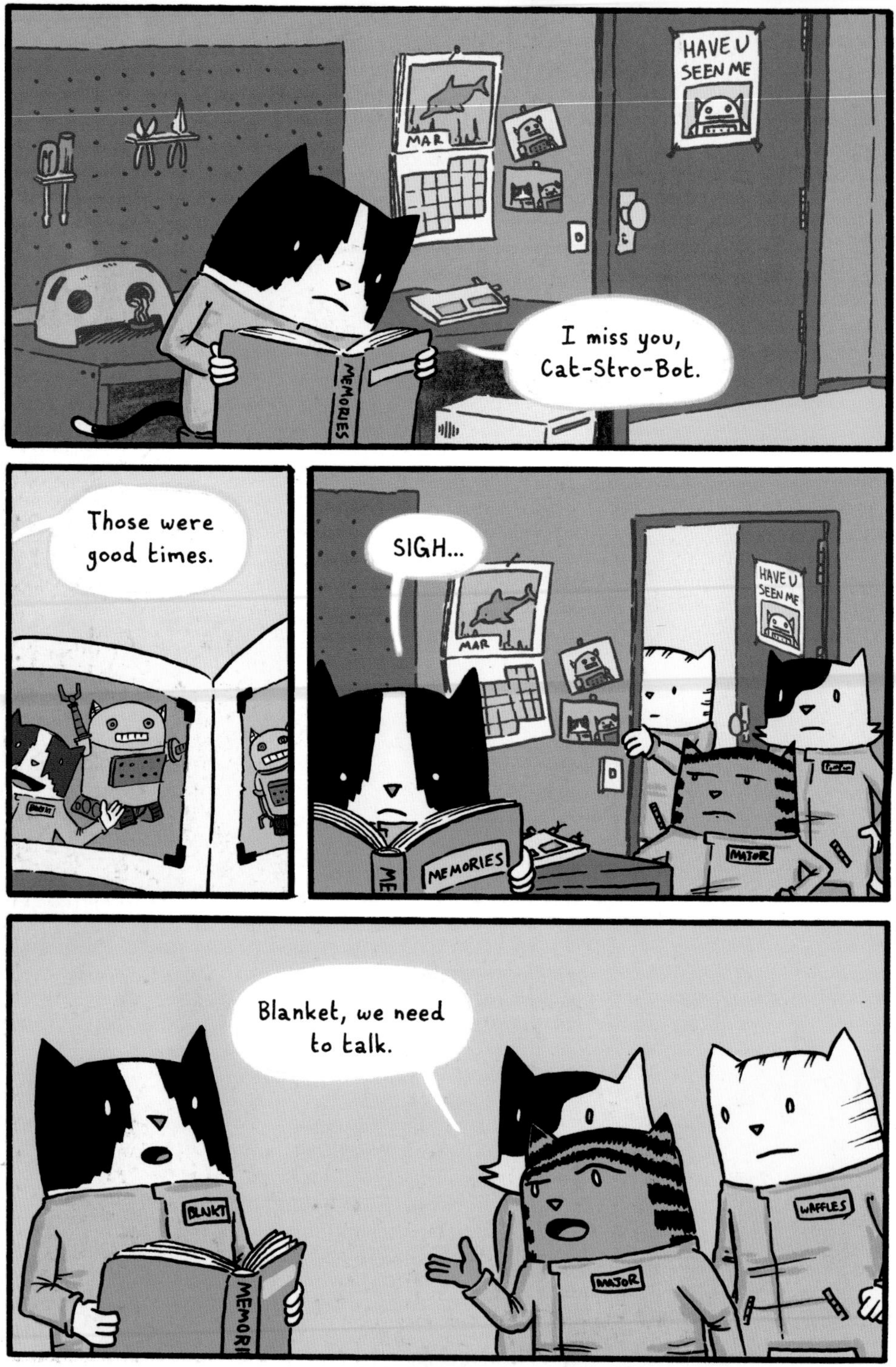
HAVE U SEEN ME
MAR
MEMORIES
I miss you, Cat-Stro-Bot.
Those were good times.
SIGH...
HAVE U SEEN ME
MAR
MEMORIES
MAJOR
Blanket, we need to talk.
BLNKT
MEMORI
MAJOR
WAFFLES

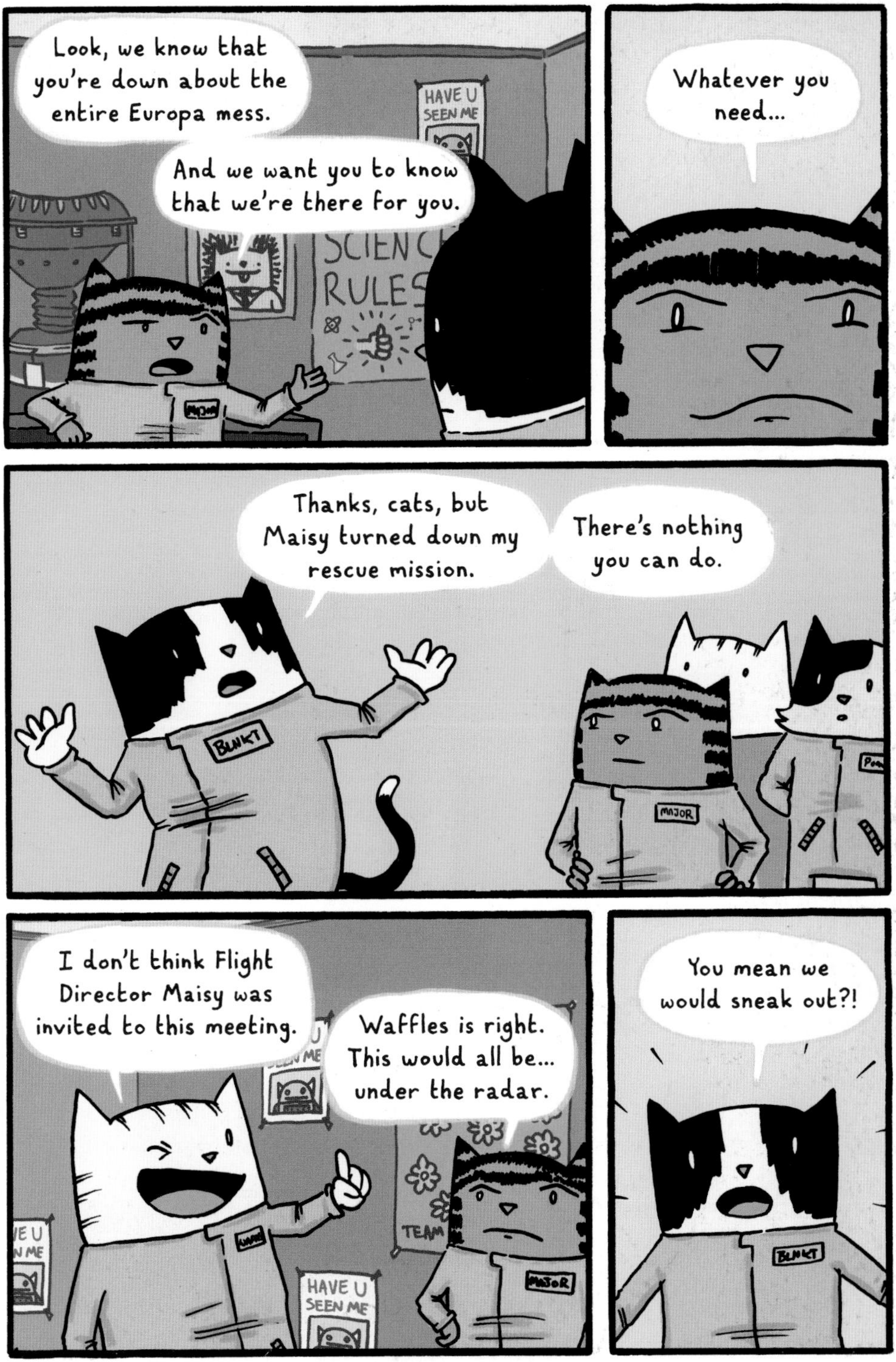
Look, we know that you're down about the entire Europa mess.
And we want you to know that we're there for you.
HAVE U SEEN ME
SCIENCE RULES
MAJOR
Whatever you need...
Thanks, cats, but Maisy turned down my rescue mission.
There's nothing you can do.
BLNKT
MAJOR
I don't think Flight Director Maisy was invited to this meeting.
Waffles is right. This would all be... under the radar.
HAVE U SEEN ME
TEAM
MAJOR
You mean we would sneak out?!
BLNKT

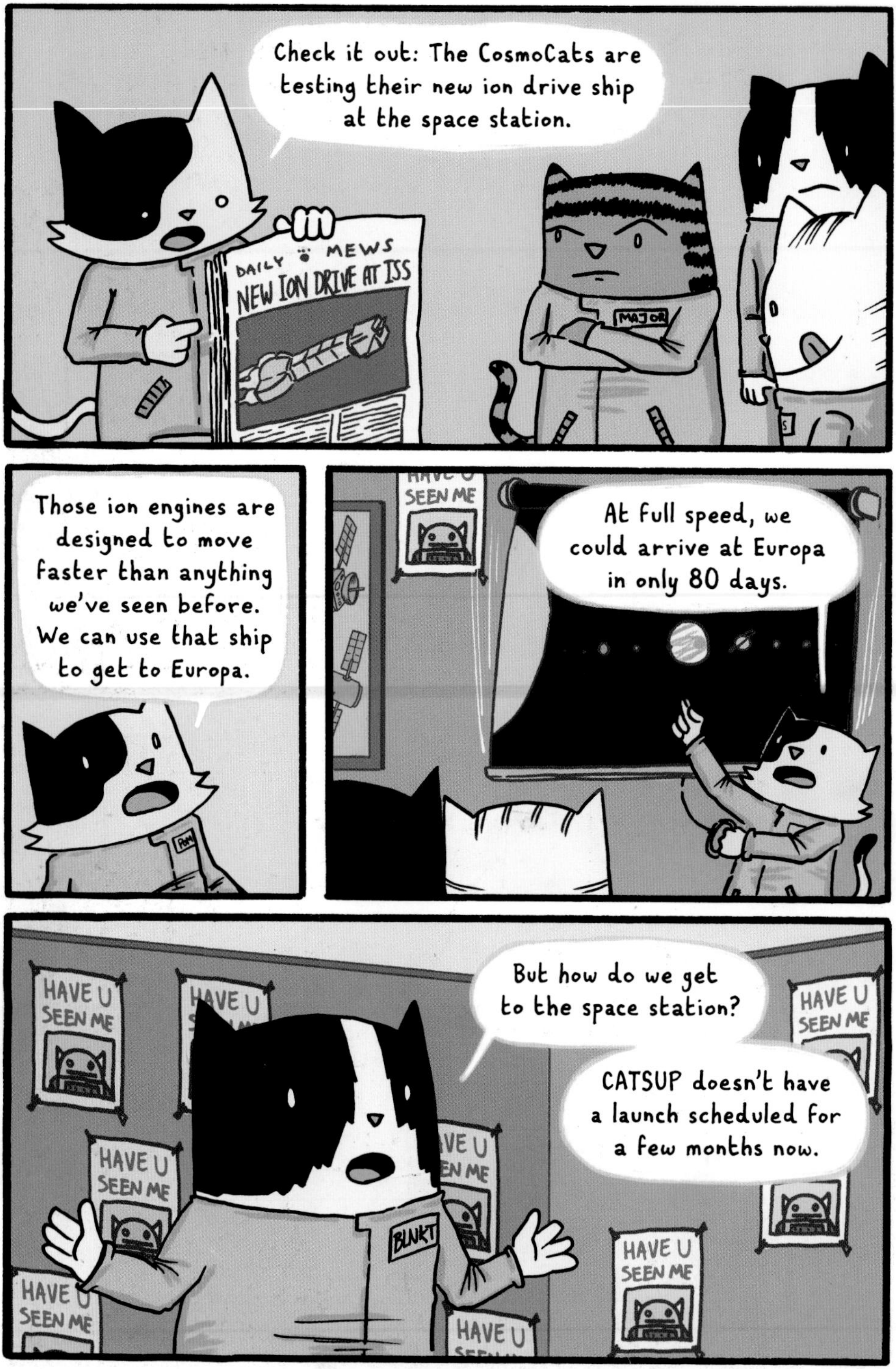
Check it out: The CosmoCats are testing their new ion drive ship at the space station.
DAILY MEWS
NEW ION DRIVE AT ISS
MAJOR
Those ion engines are designed to move faster than anything we've seen before. We can use that ship to get to Europa.
HAVE U SEEN ME
At full speed, we could arrive at Europa in only 80 days.
HAVE U SEEN ME
But how do we get to the space station?
CATSUP doesn't have a launch scheduled for a few months now.
BLNKT

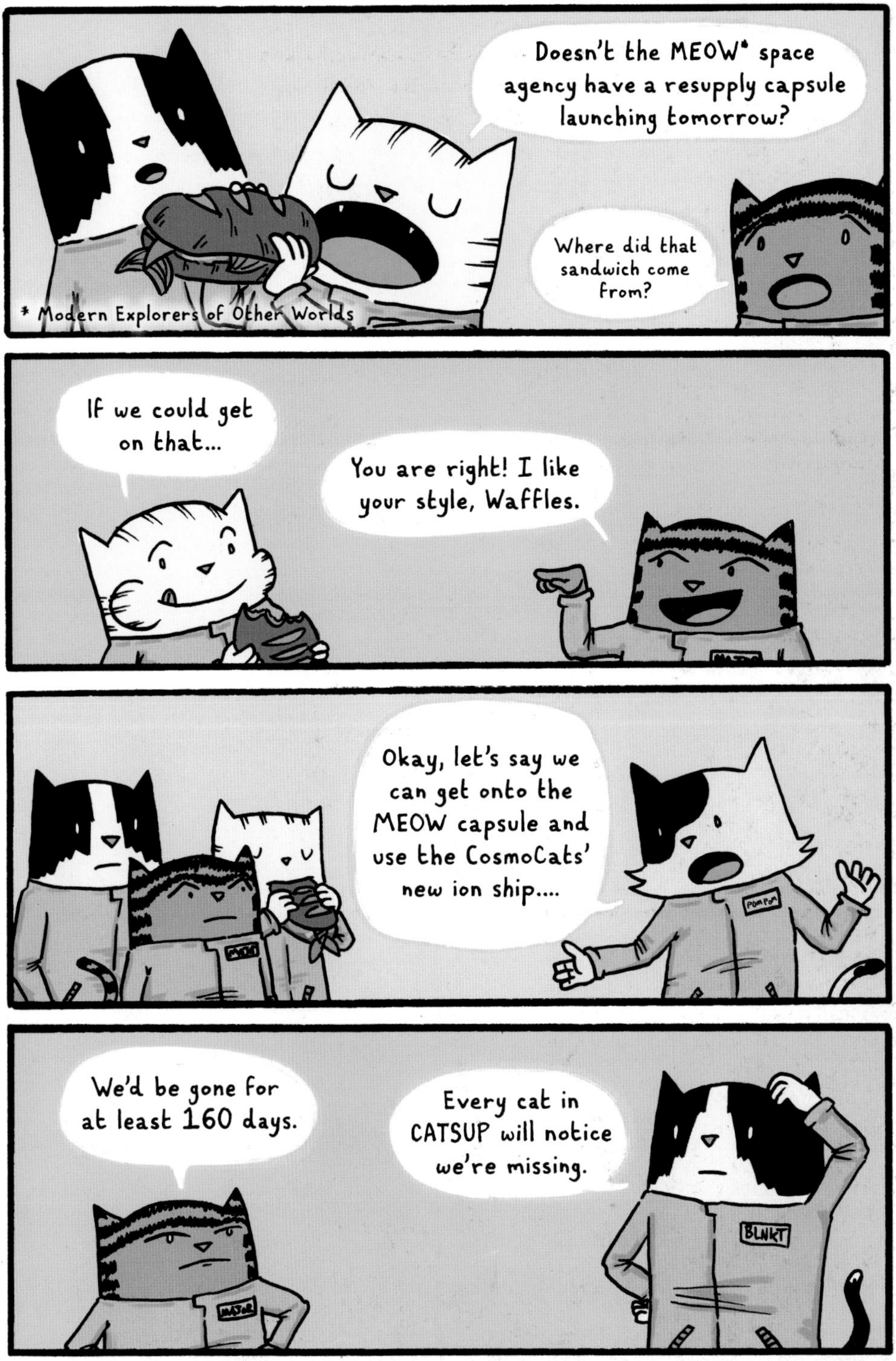
Doesn't the MEOW* space agency have a resupply capsule launching tomorrow?
Where did that sandwich come from?
* Modern Explorers of Other Worlds
If we could get on that...
You are right! I like your style, Waffles.
Okay, let's say we can get onto the MEOW capsule and use the CosmoCats' new ion ship....
POM POM
We'd be gone for at least 160 days.
MAJOR
Every cat in CATSUP will notice we're missing.
BLNKT

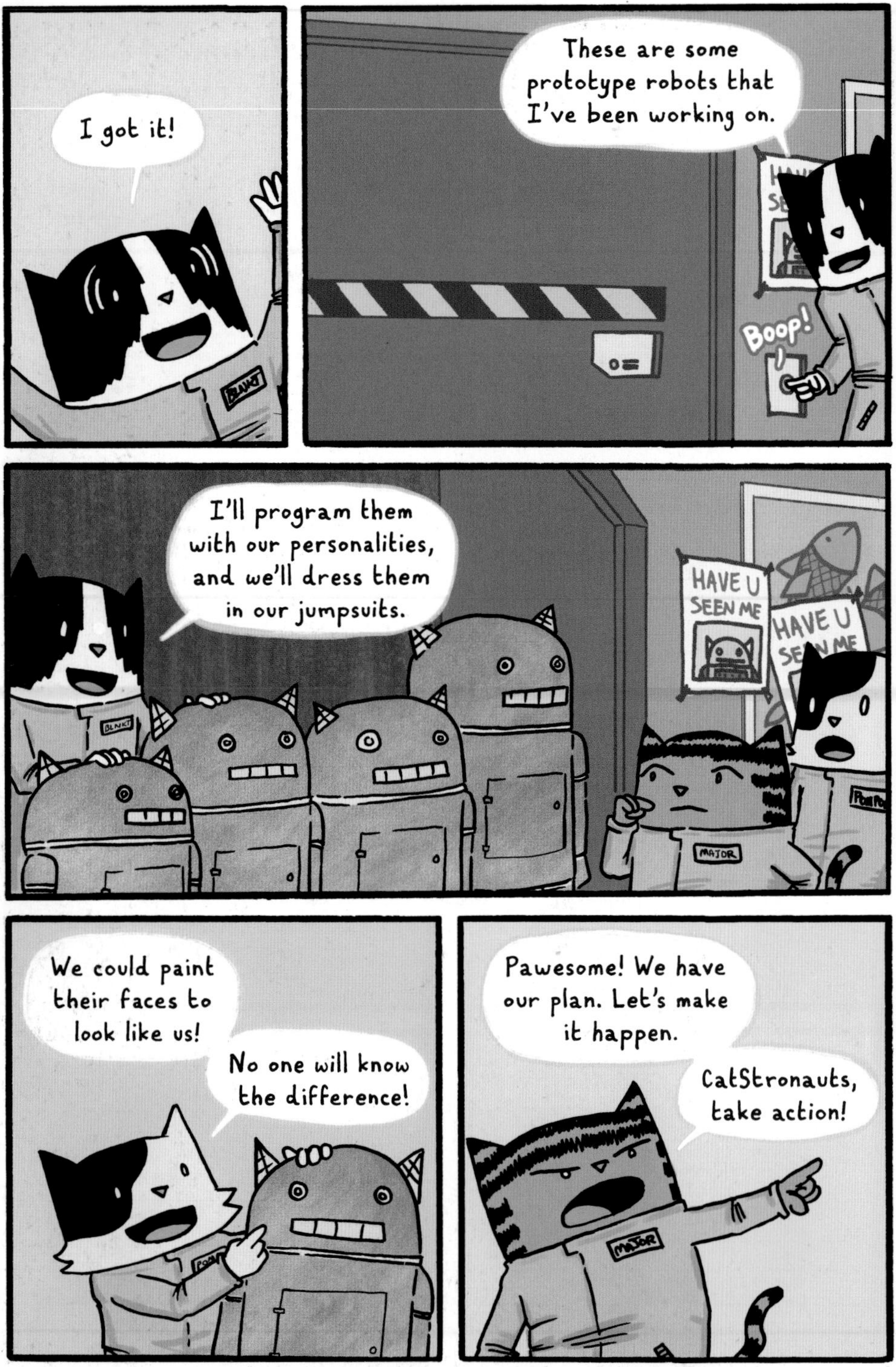
I got it!
These are some prototype robots that I've been working on.
HAVE U SEEN ME
BOOP!
BLNKT
I'll program them with our personalities, and we'll dress them in our jumpsuits.
HAVE U SEEN ME
HAVE U SEEN ME
MAJOR
We could paint their faces to look like us!
No one will know the difference!
Pawesome! We have our plan. Let's make it happen.
CatStronauts, take action!
MAJOR

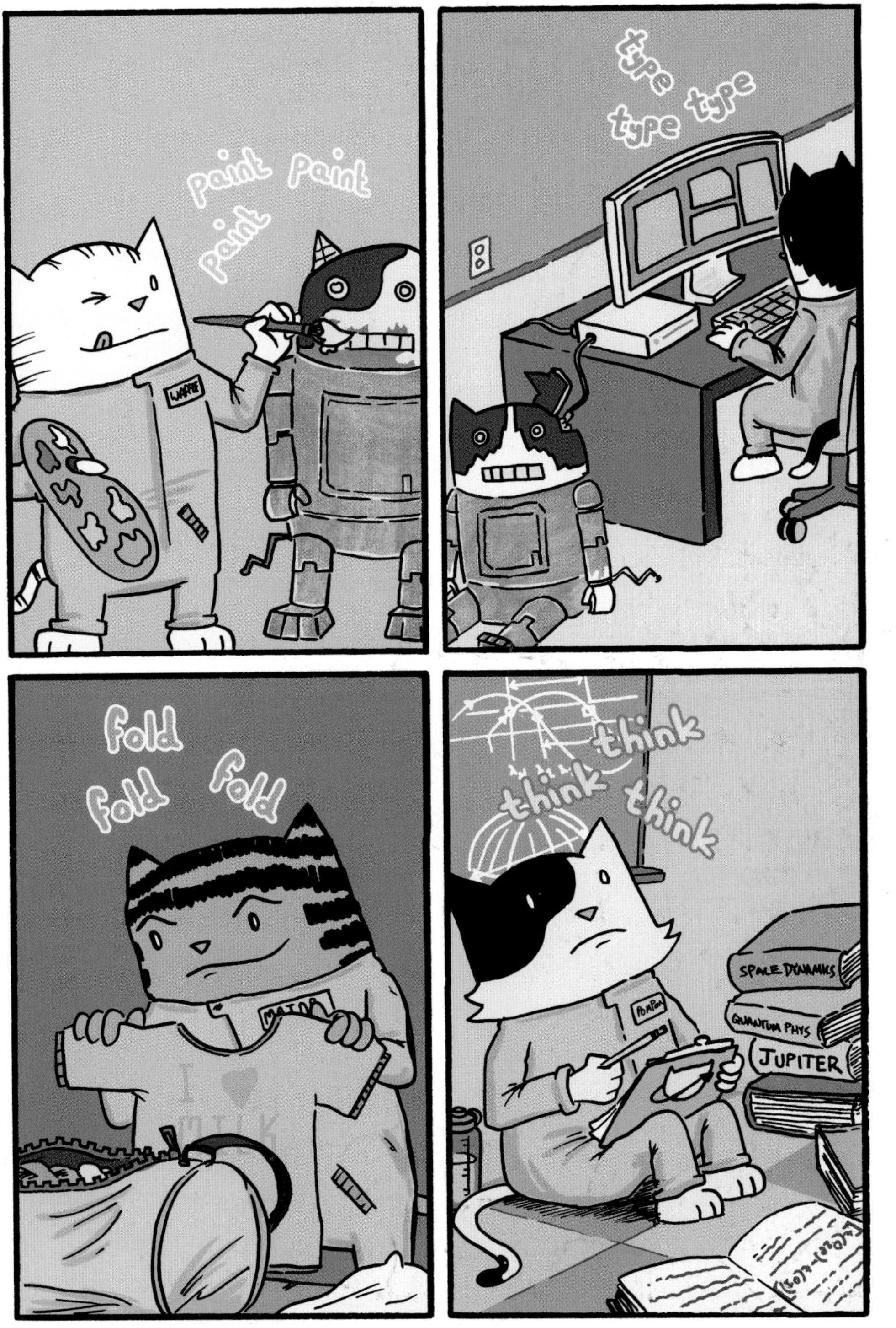
paint paint
paint
type
type type
fold
fold fold
MAJOR
I ♥ MILK
think
think think
POMPOM
SPACE DYNAMICS
QUANTUM PHYS
JUPITER

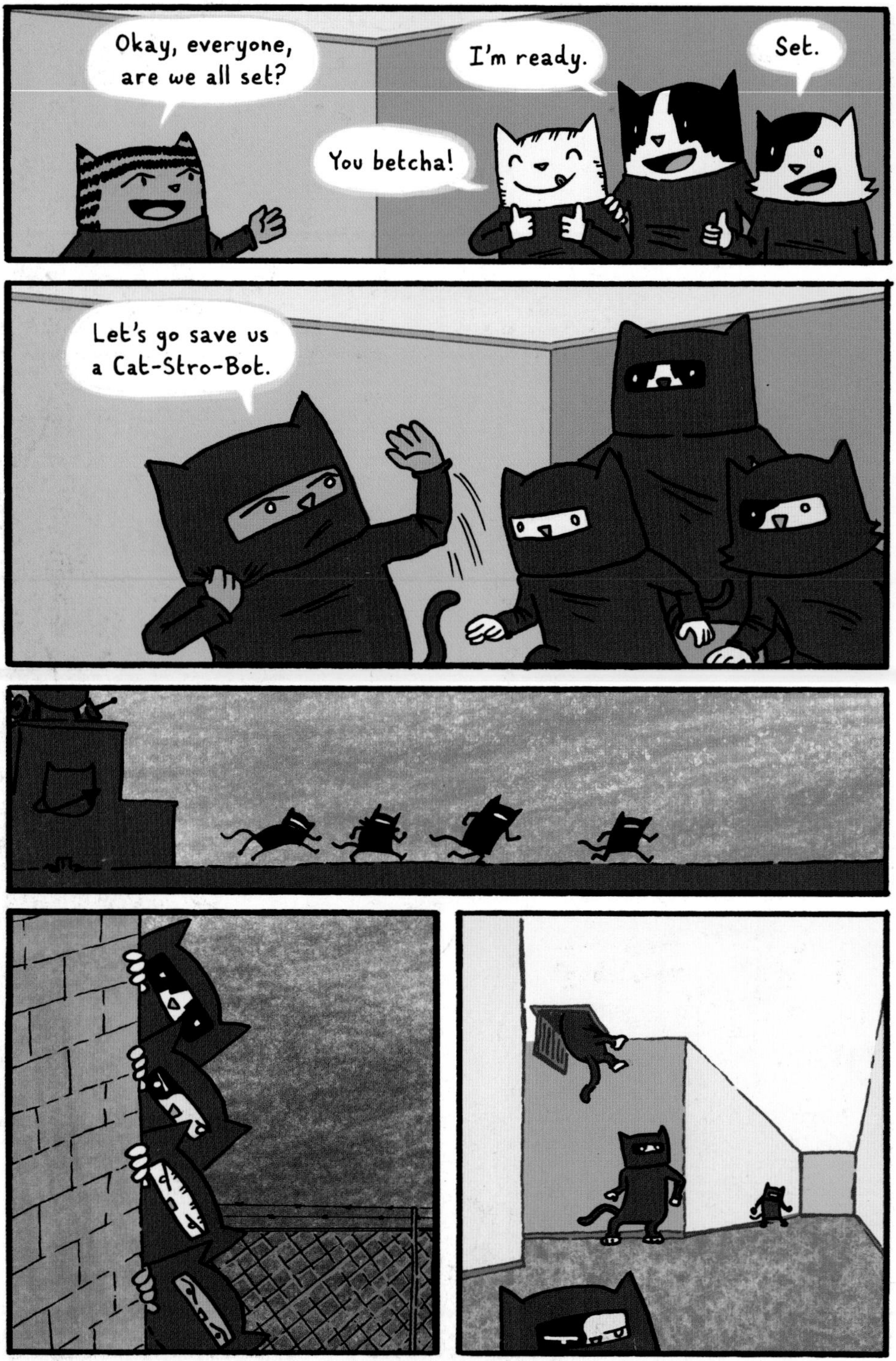
Okay, everyone, are we all set?
You betcha!
I'm ready.
Set.
Let's go save us a Cat-Stro-Bot.

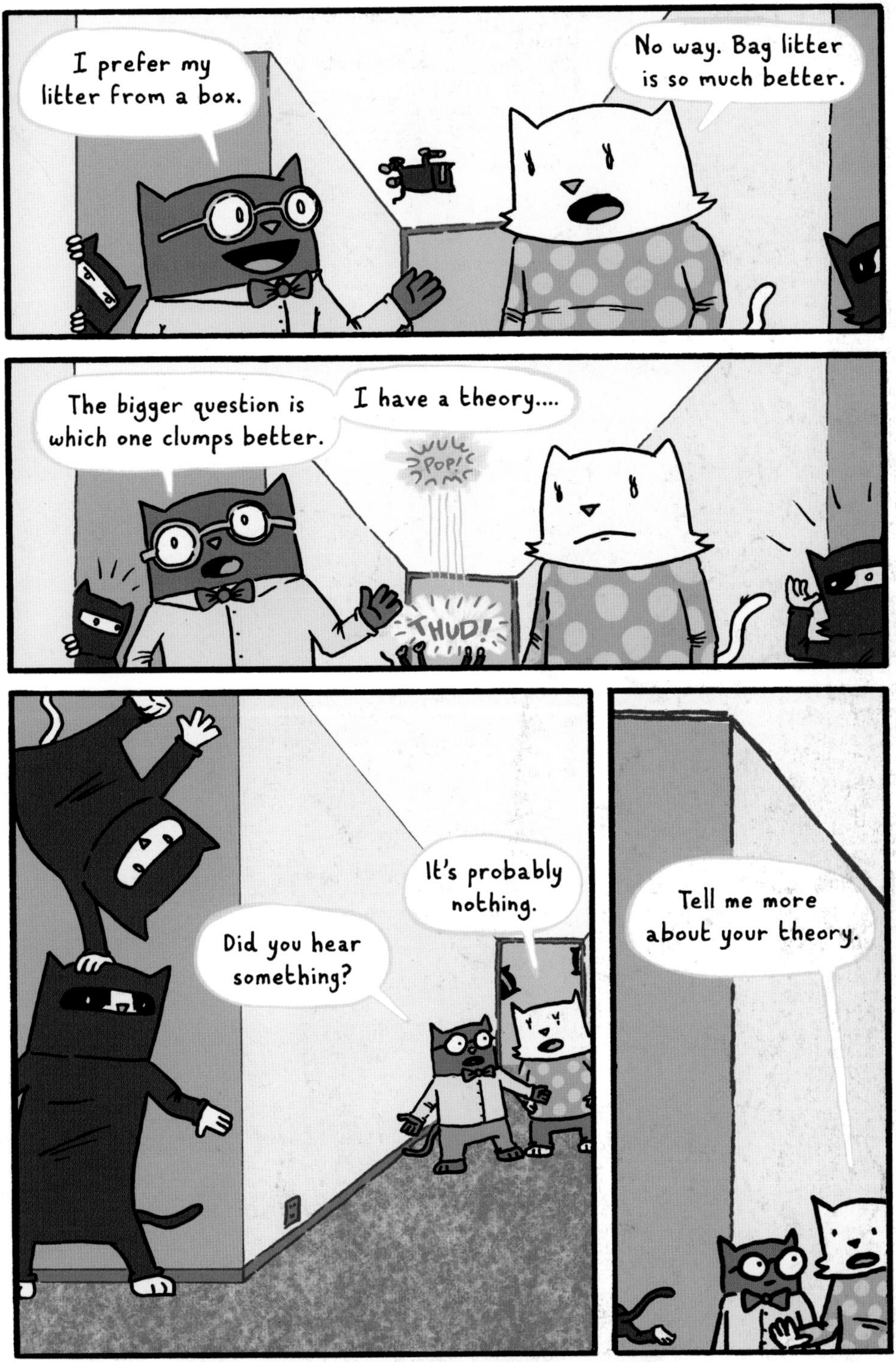
I prefer my litter from a box.
No way. Bag litter is so much better.
The bigger question is which one clumps better.
I have a theory....
POP!
THUD!
Did you hear something?
It's probably nothing.
Tell me more about your theory.

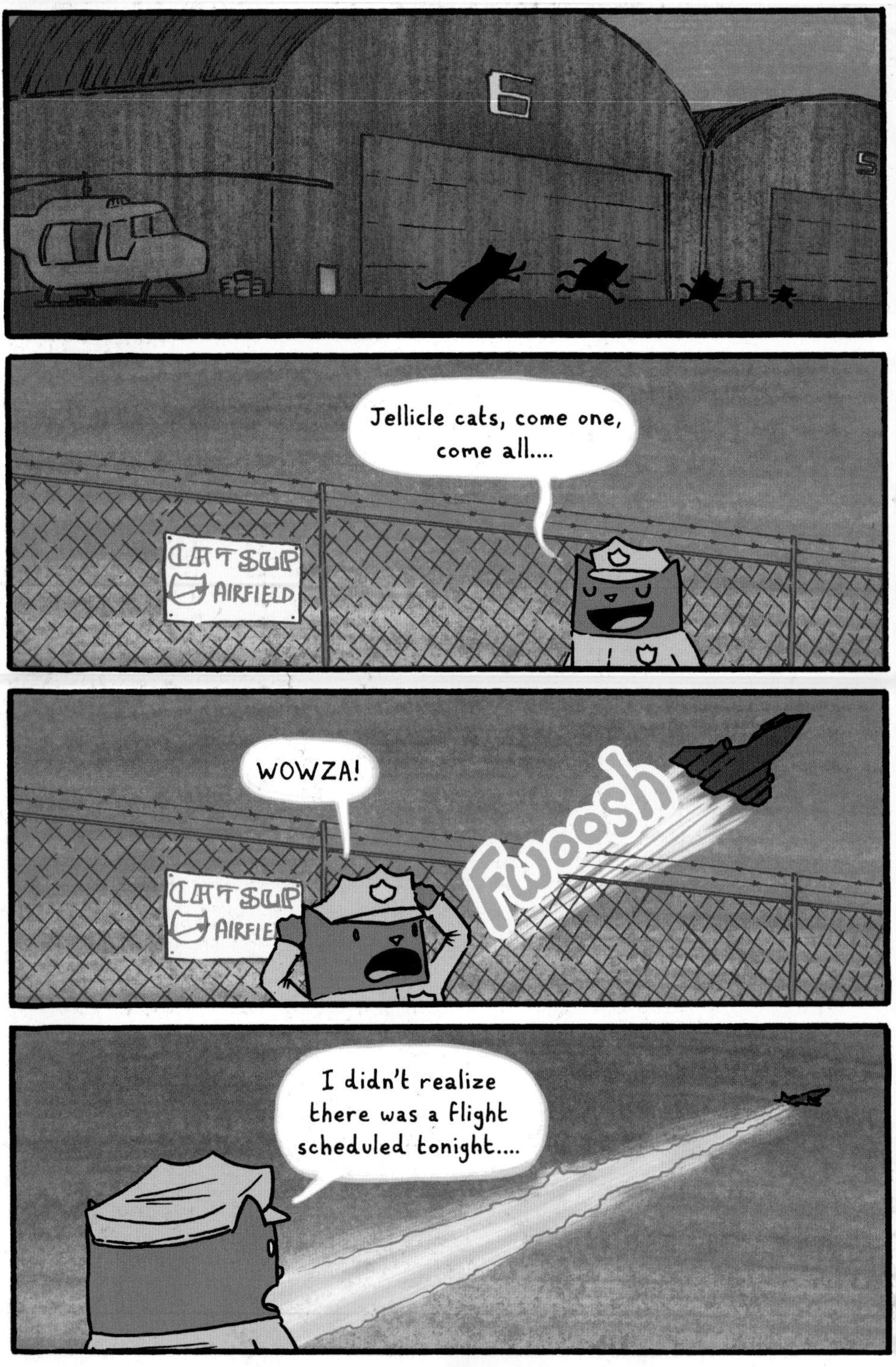

6
5
Jellicle cats, come one, come all....
CATSUP AIRFIELD
WOWZA!
Fwoosh
CATSUP AIRFIE
I didn't realize there was a flight scheduled tonight....

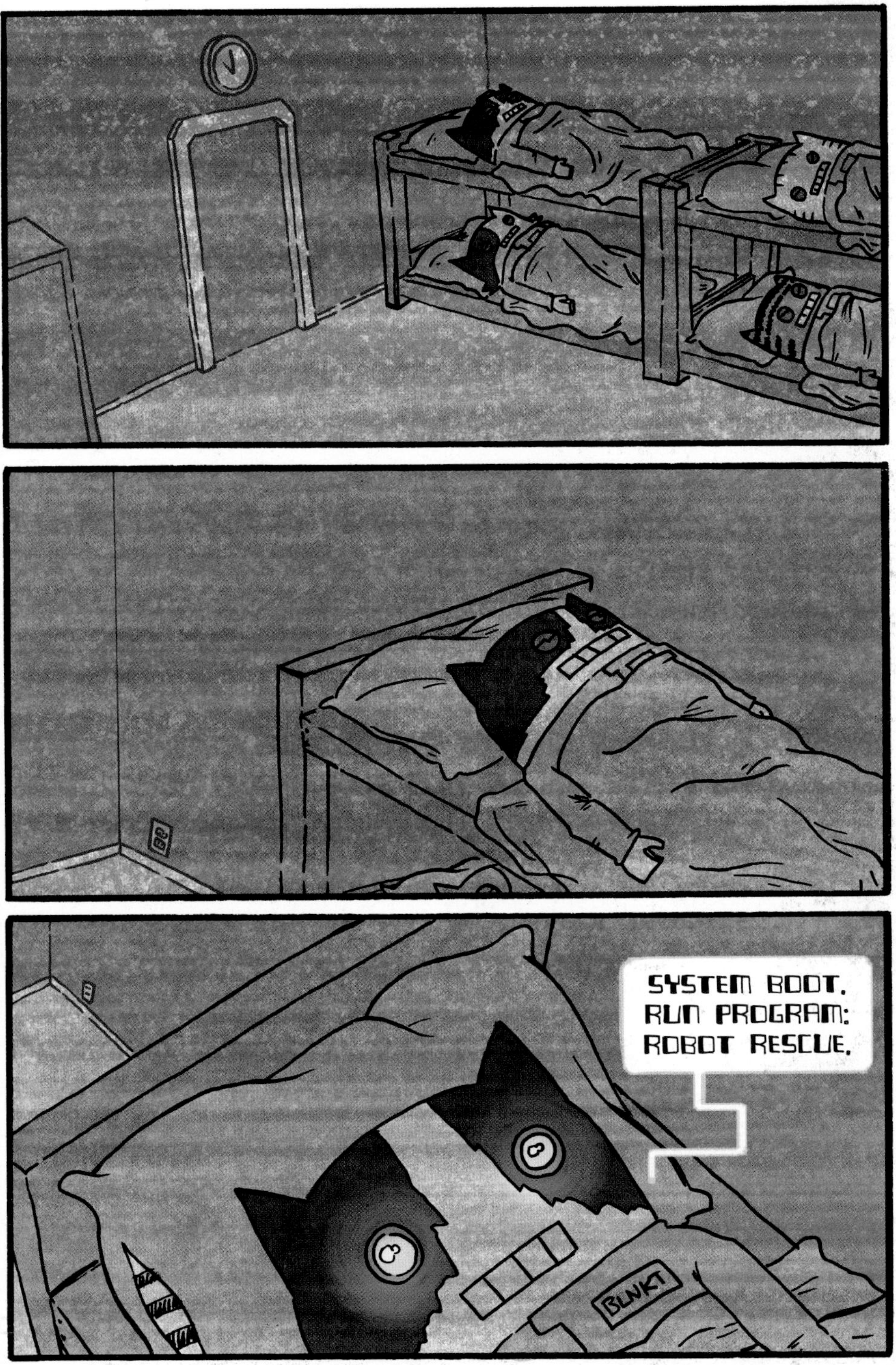
SYSTEM BOOT. RUN PROGRAM: ROBOT RESCUE.
BLNKT

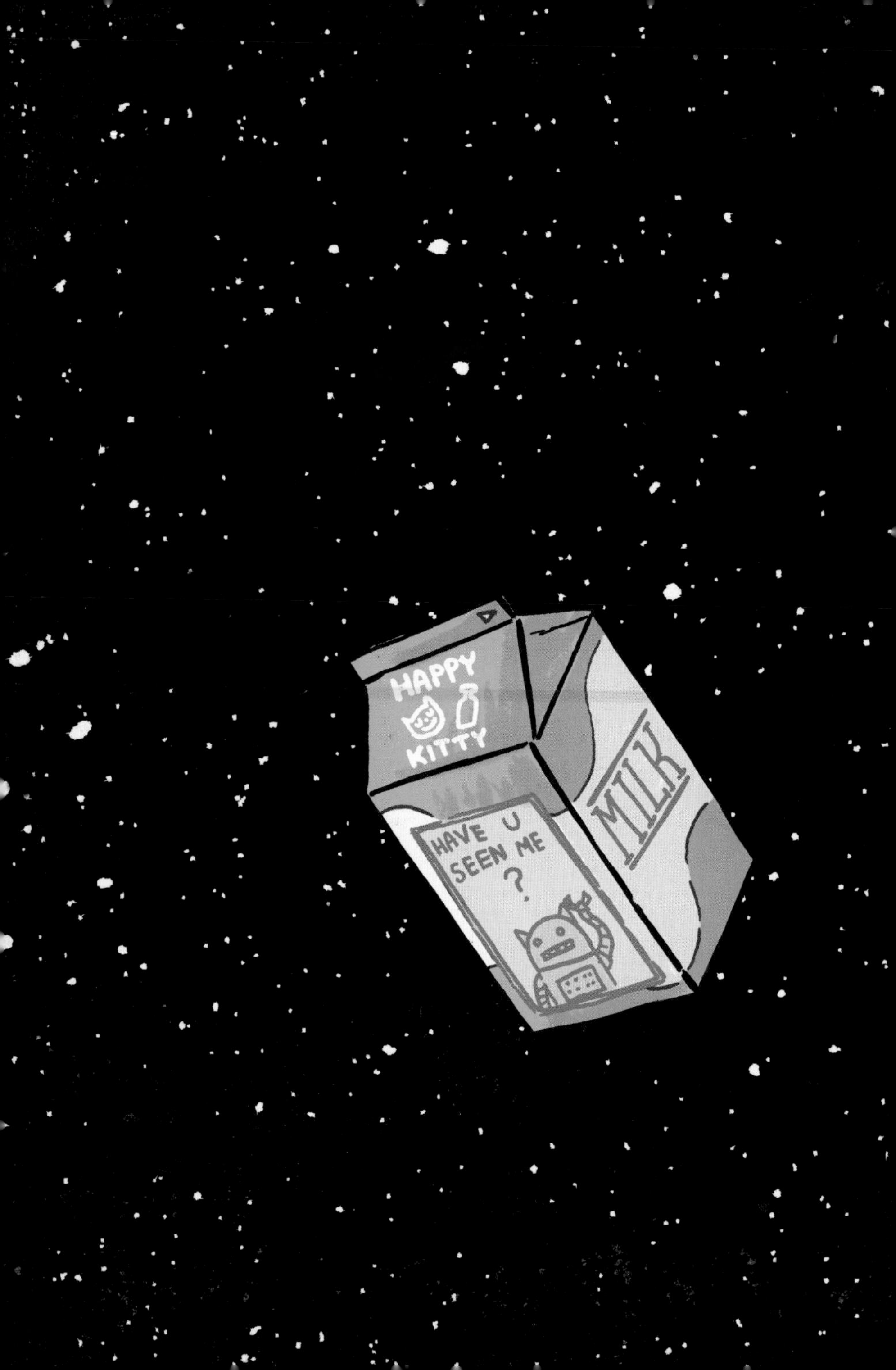
HAPPY
KITTY
MILK
HAVE U
SEEN ME
?

CHAPTER 4

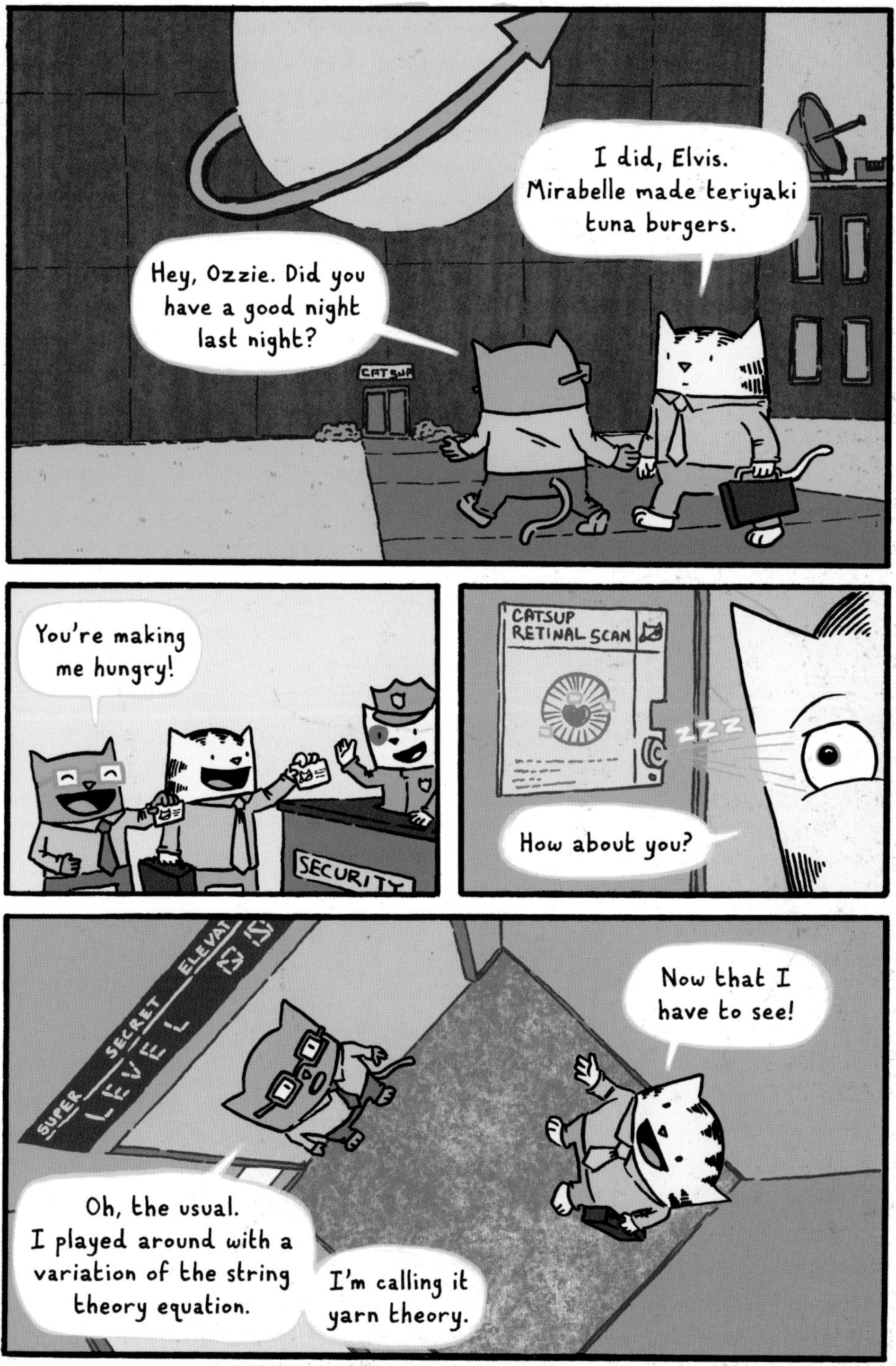
CATSUP
Hey, Ozzie. Did you have a good night last night?
I did, Elvis. Mirabelle made teriyaki tuna burgers.
You're making me hungry!
SECURITY
CATSUP RETINAL SCAN
How about you?
SUPER SECRET LEVEL
Oh, the usual. I played around with a variation of the string theory equation.
I'm calling it yarn theory.
Now that I have to see!

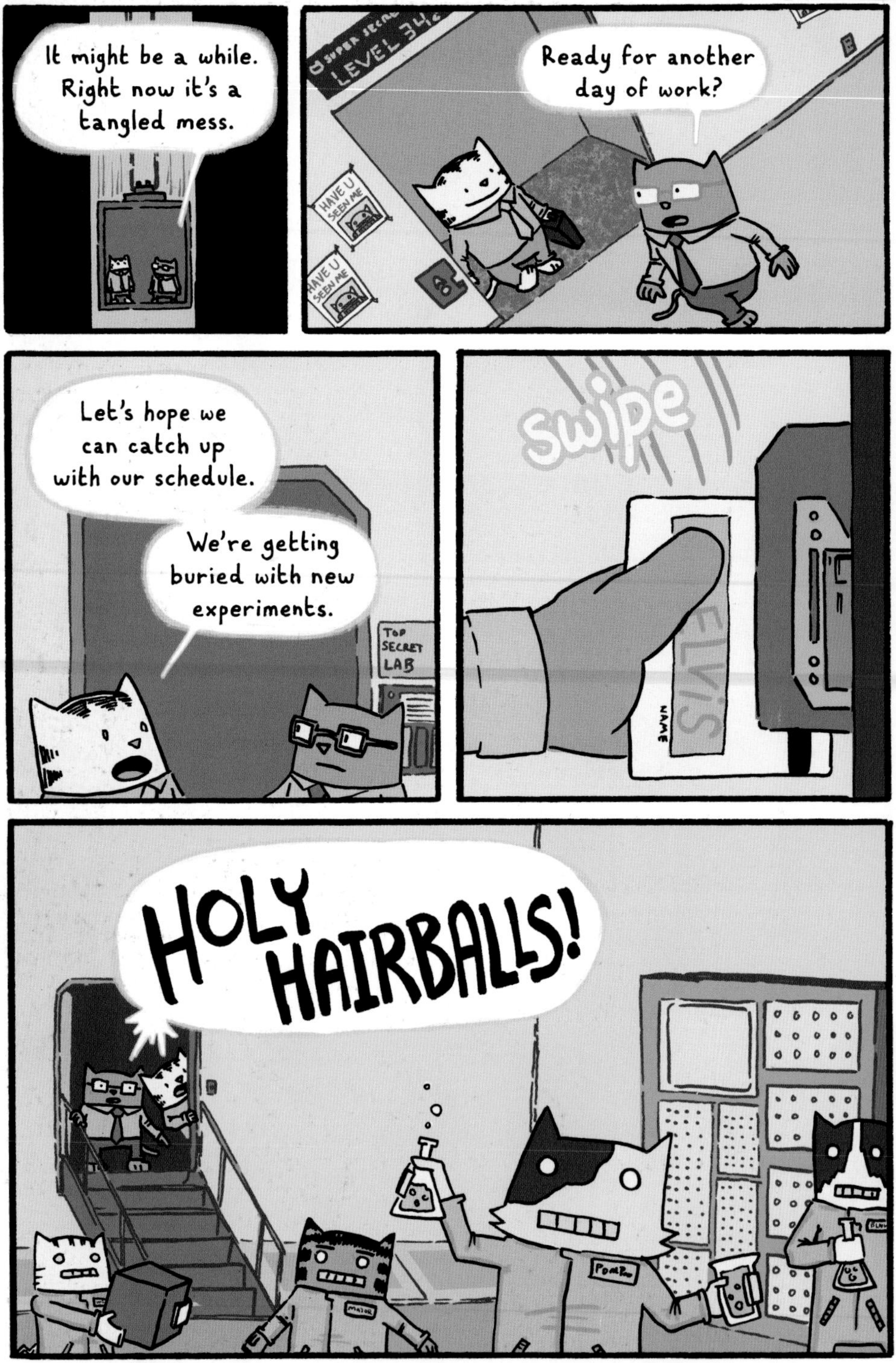

It might be a while. Right now it's a tangled mess.
LEVEL 34
Ready for another day of work?
HAVE U SEEN ME
HAVE U SEEN ME
Let's hope we can catch up with our schedule.
We're getting buried with new experiments.
TOP SECRET LAB
swipe
ELVIS
NAME
HOLY HAIRBALLS!

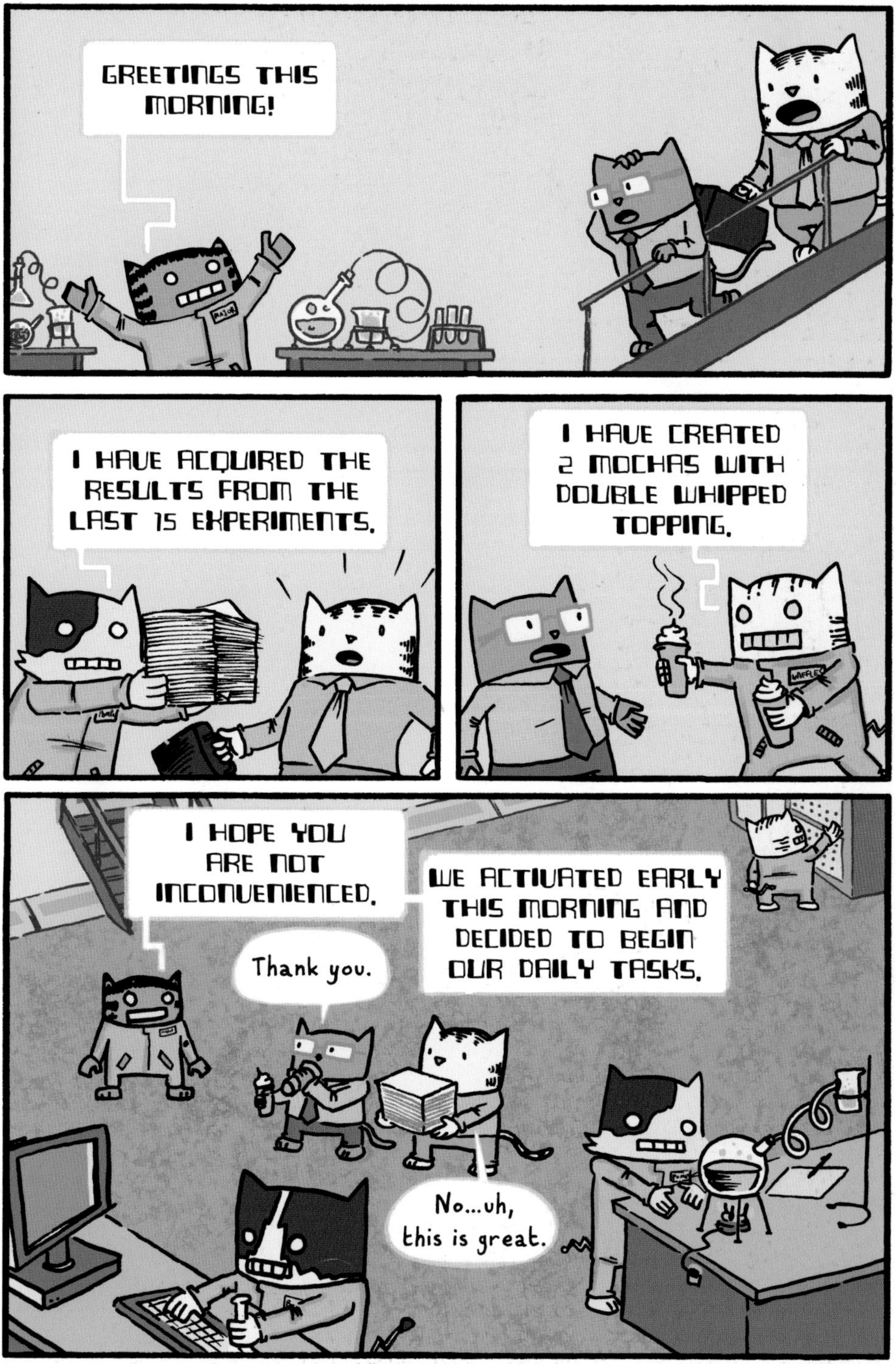
GREETINGS THIS MORNING!
I HAVE ACQUIRED THE RESULTS FROM THE LAST 15 EXPERIMENTS.
I HAVE CREATED 2 MOCHAS WITH DOUBLE WHIPPED TOPPING.
I HOPE YOU ARE NOT INCONVENIENCED.
WE ACTIVATED EARLY THIS MORNING AND DECIDED TO BEGIN OUR DAILY TASKS.
Thank you.
No...uh, this is great.

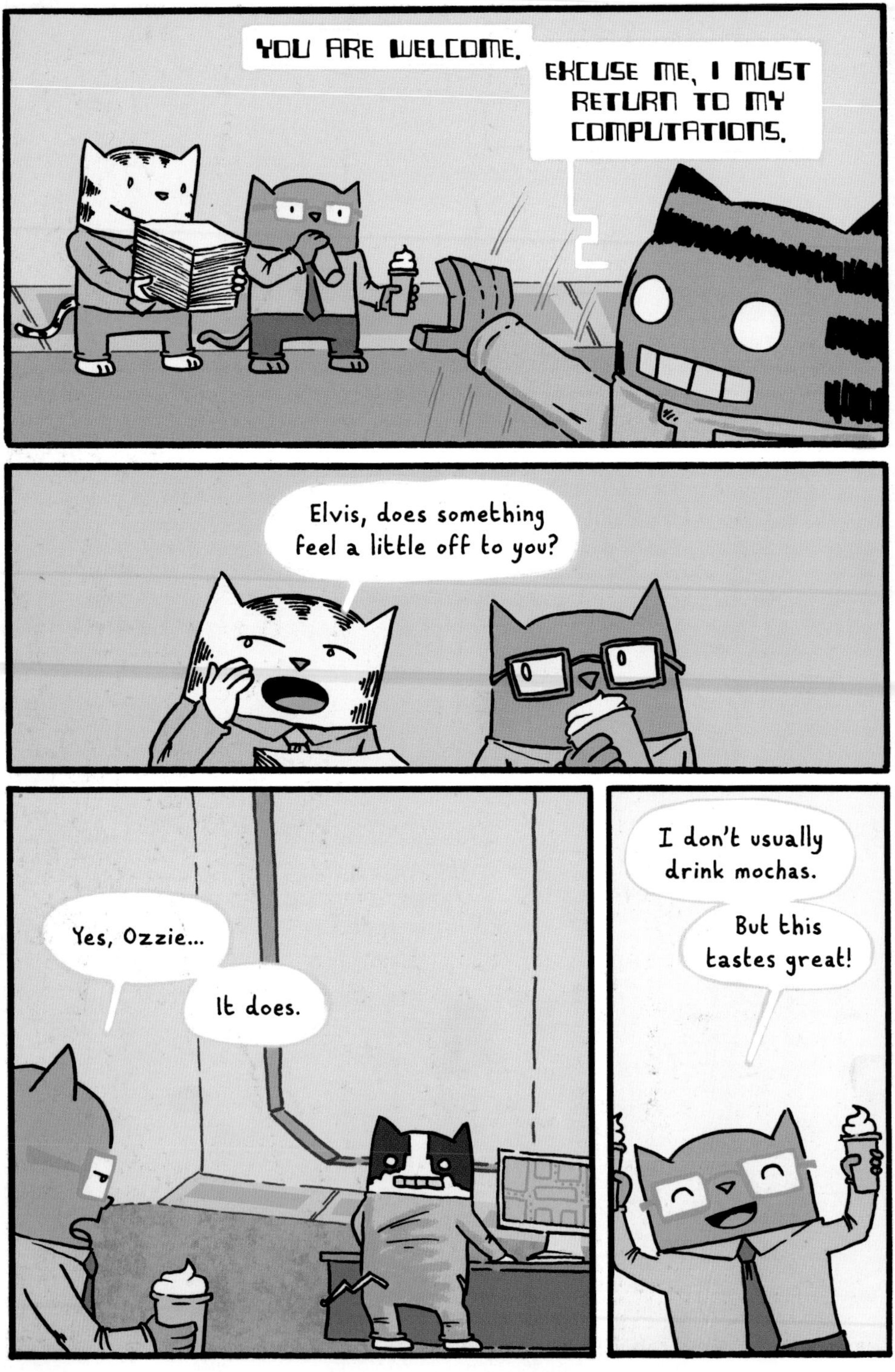
YOU ARE WELCOME.
EXCUSE ME, I MUST RETURN TO MY COMPUTATIONS.
Elvis, does something feel a little off to you?
Yes, Ozzie...
It does.
I don't usually drink mochas.
But this tastes great!

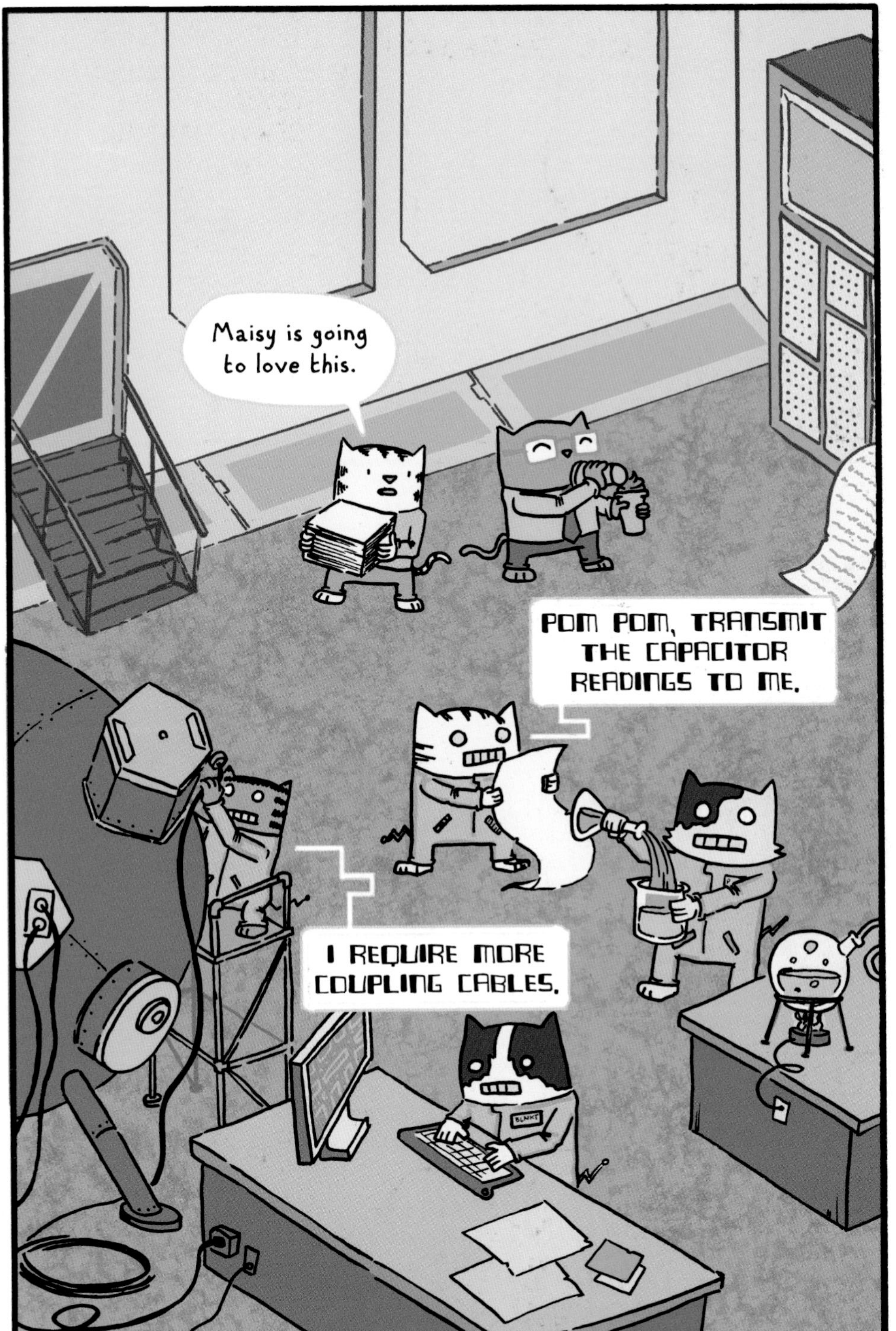
Maisy is going to love this.
POM POM, TRANSMIT THE CAPACITOR READINGS TO ME.
I REQUIRE MORE COUPLING CABLES.

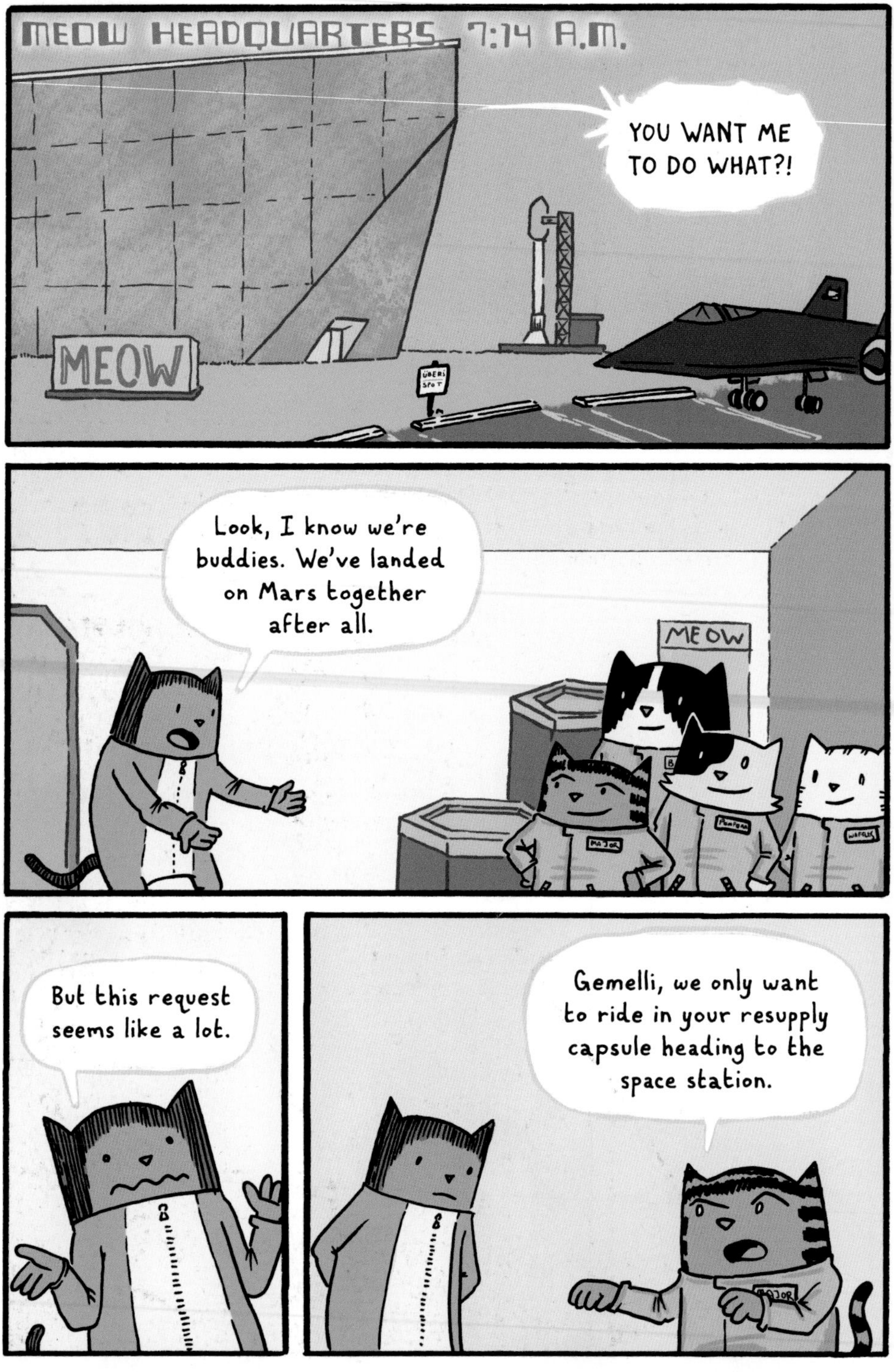
MEOW HEADQUARTERS, 7:14 A.M.
YOU WANT ME TO DO WHAT?!
MEOW
Look, I know we're buddies. We've landed on Mars together after all.
MEOW
MAJOR
But this request seems like a lot.
Gemelli, we only want to ride in your resupply capsule heading to the space station.
MAJOR

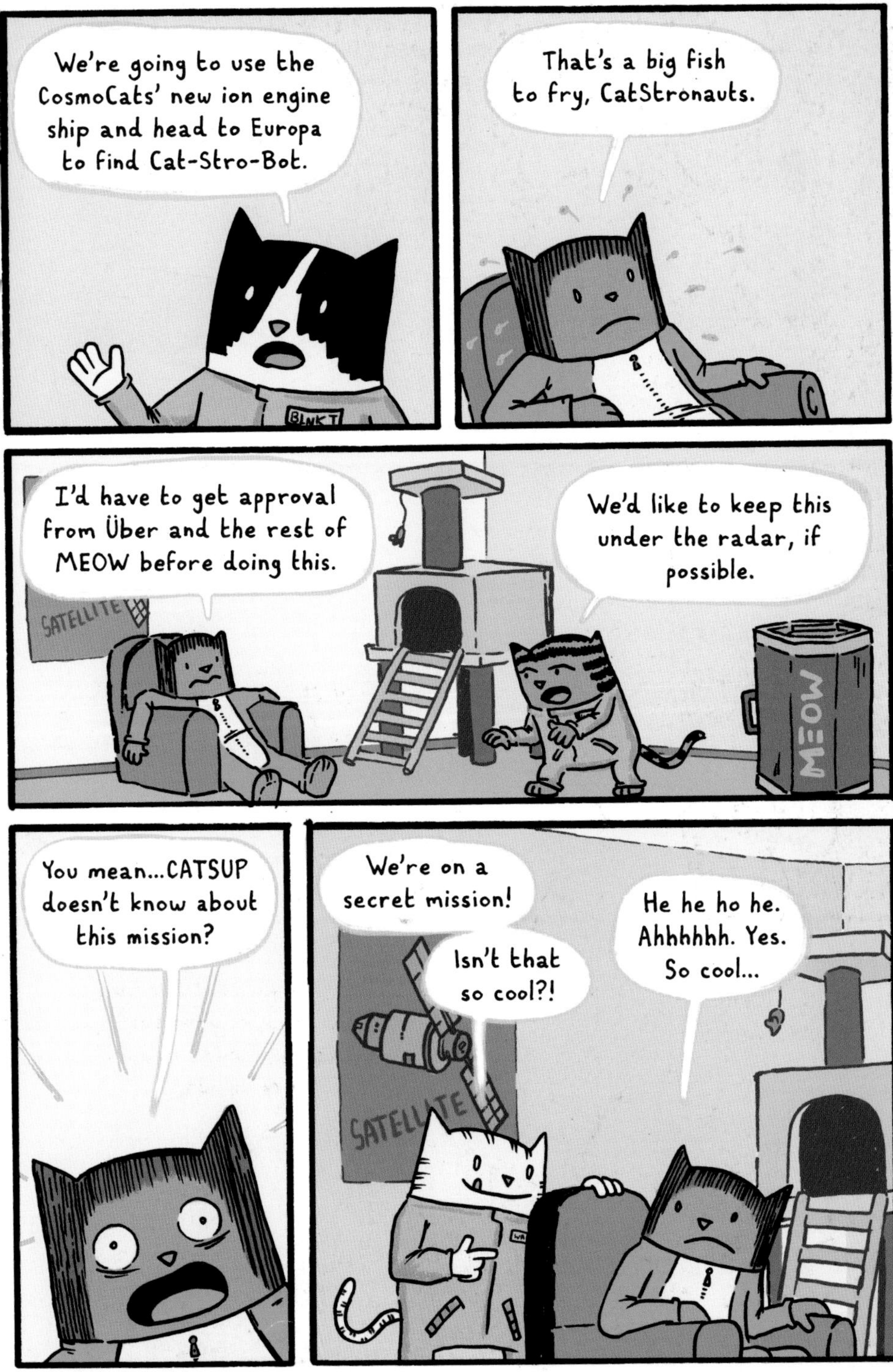
We're going to use the CosmoCats' new ion engine ship and head to Europa to find Cat-Stro-Bot.
BLNKT
That's a big fish to fry, CatStronauts.
I'd have to get approval from Über and the rest of MEOW before doing this.
SATELLITE
We'd like to keep this under the radar, if possible.
MEOW
You mean...CATSUP doesn't know about this mission?
We're on a secret mission!
Isn't that so cool?!
SATELLITE
He he ho he. Ahhhhhh. Yes. So cool...

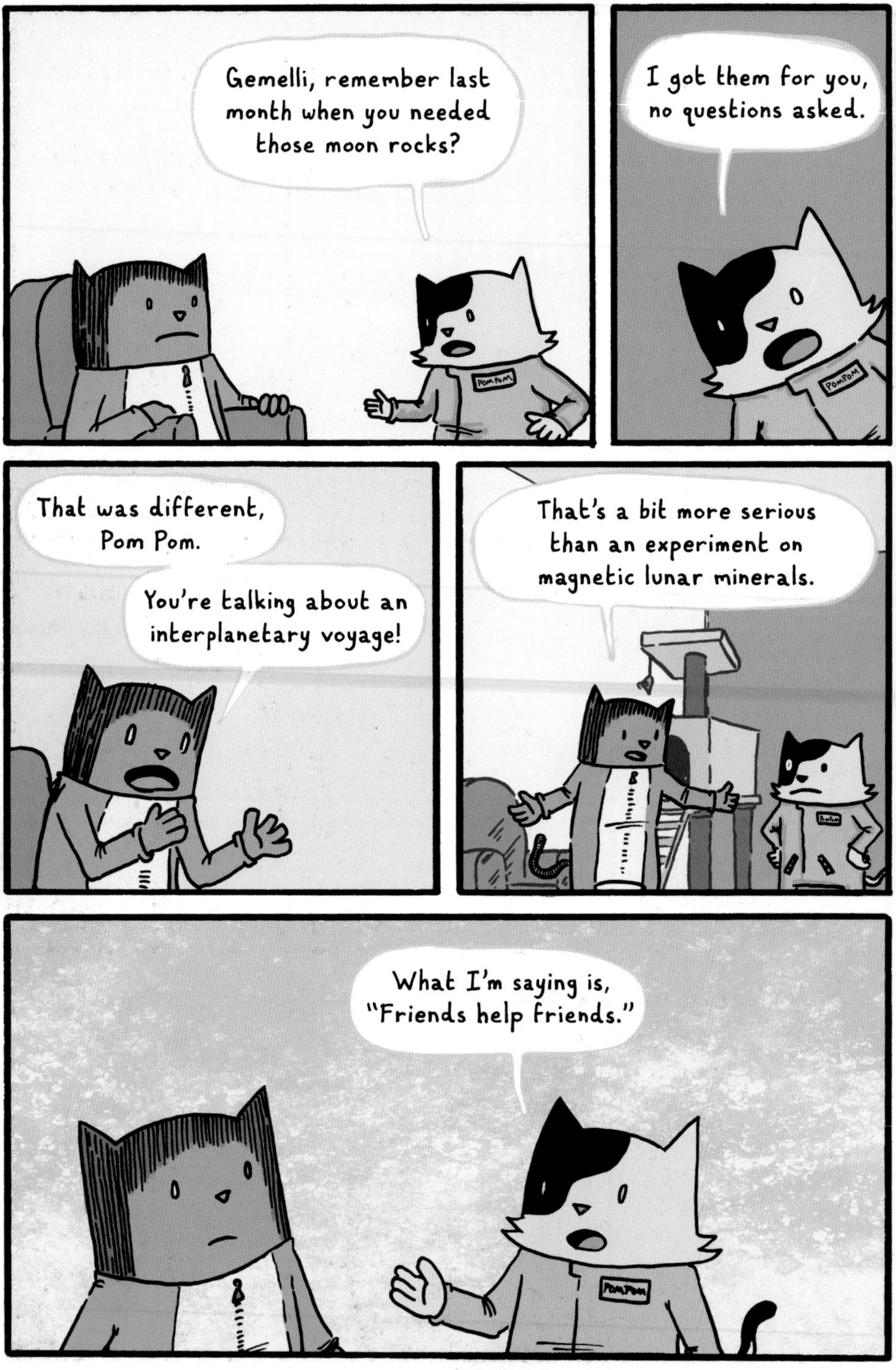
Gemelli, remember last month when you needed those moon rocks?
I got them for you, no questions asked.
POM POM
That was different, Pom Pom.
You're talking about an interplanetary voyage!
That's a bit more serious than an experiment on magnetic lunar minerals.
What I'm saying is, "Friends help friends."
POM POM

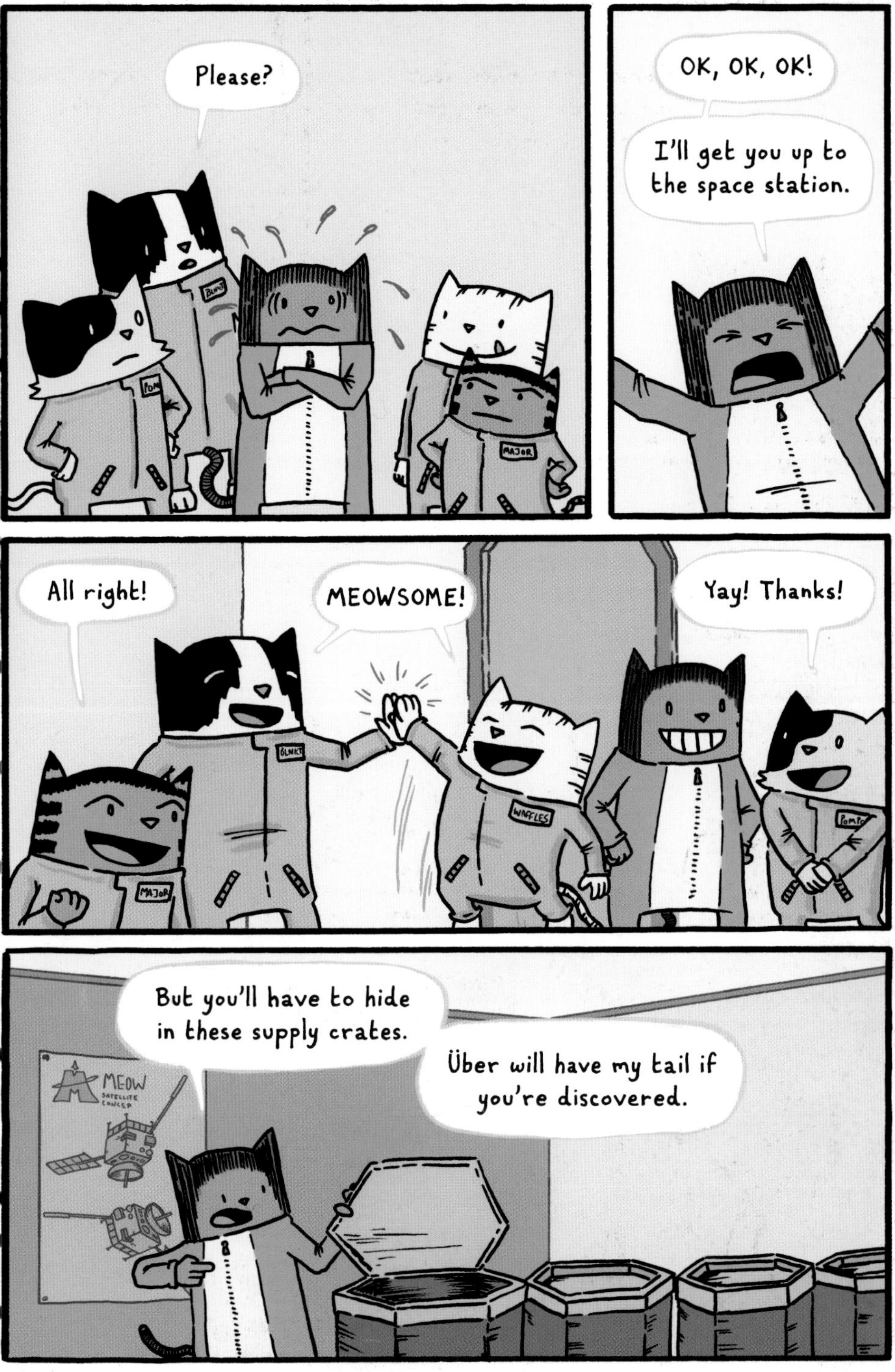
Please?
OK, OK, OK!
I'll get you up to the space station.
All right!
MEOWSOME!
Yay! Thanks!
But you'll have to hide in these supply crates.
Über will have my tail if you're discovered.
MEOW

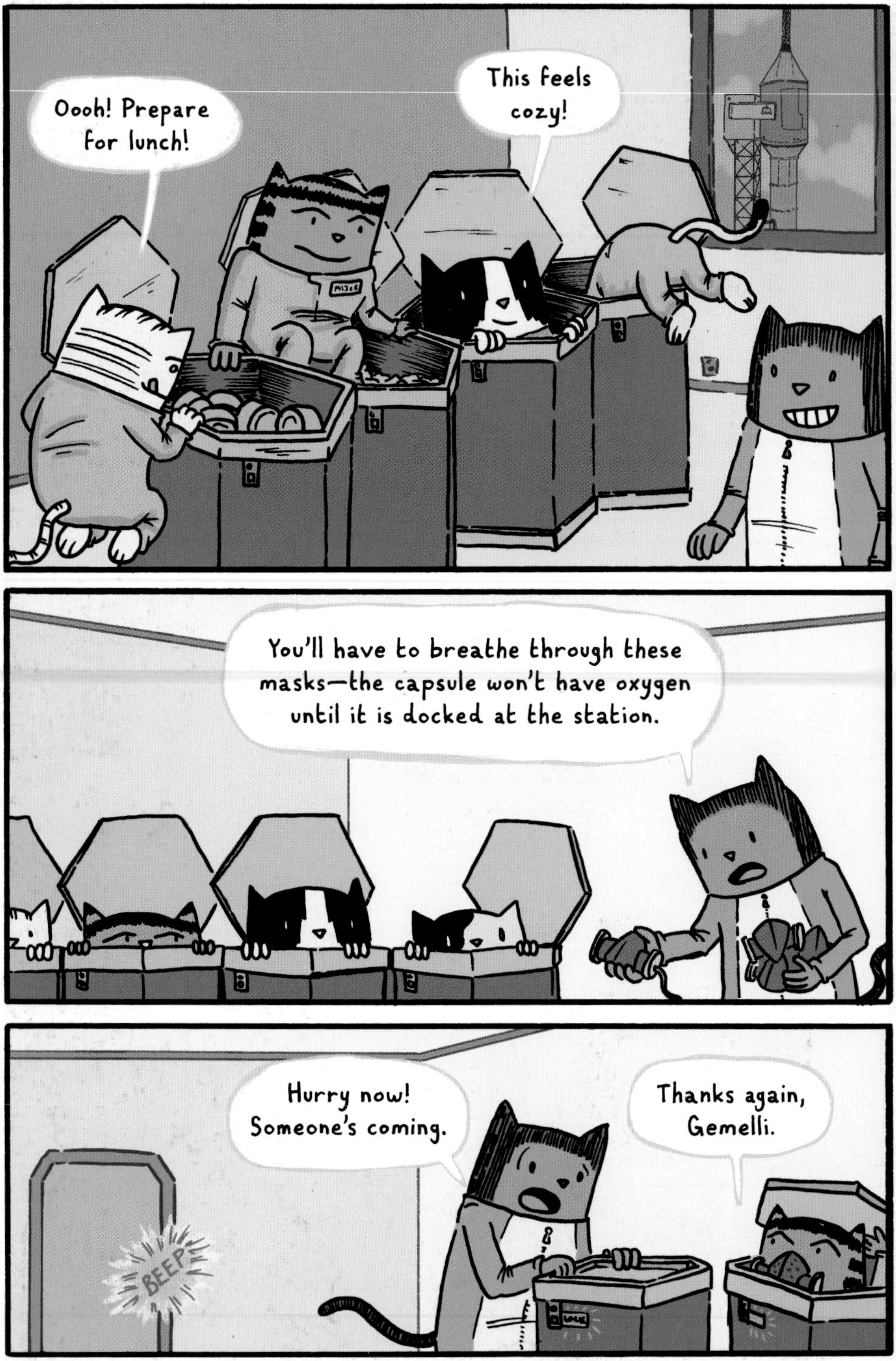
Oooh! Prepare for lunch!
This feels cozy!
MAJOR
You'll have to breathe through these masks—the capsule won't have oxygen until it is docked at the station.
Hurry now! Someone's coming.
Thanks again, Gemelli.
BEEP

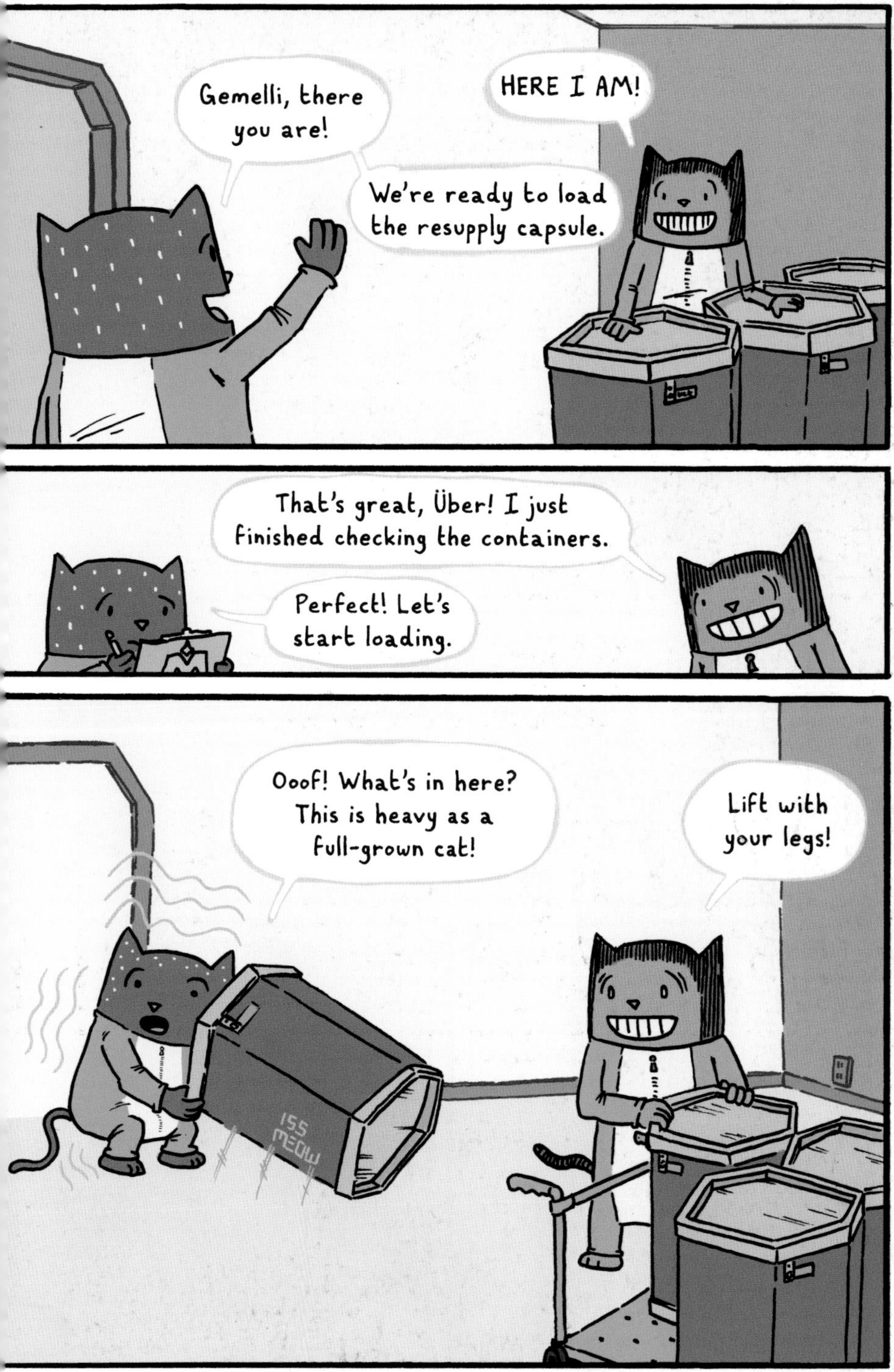
Gemelli, there you are!
HERE I AM!
We're ready to load the resupply capsule.
That's great, Über! I just finished checking the containers.
Perfect! Let's start loading.
Ooof! What's in here? This is heavy as a full-grown cat!
Lift with your legs!
ISS MEOW

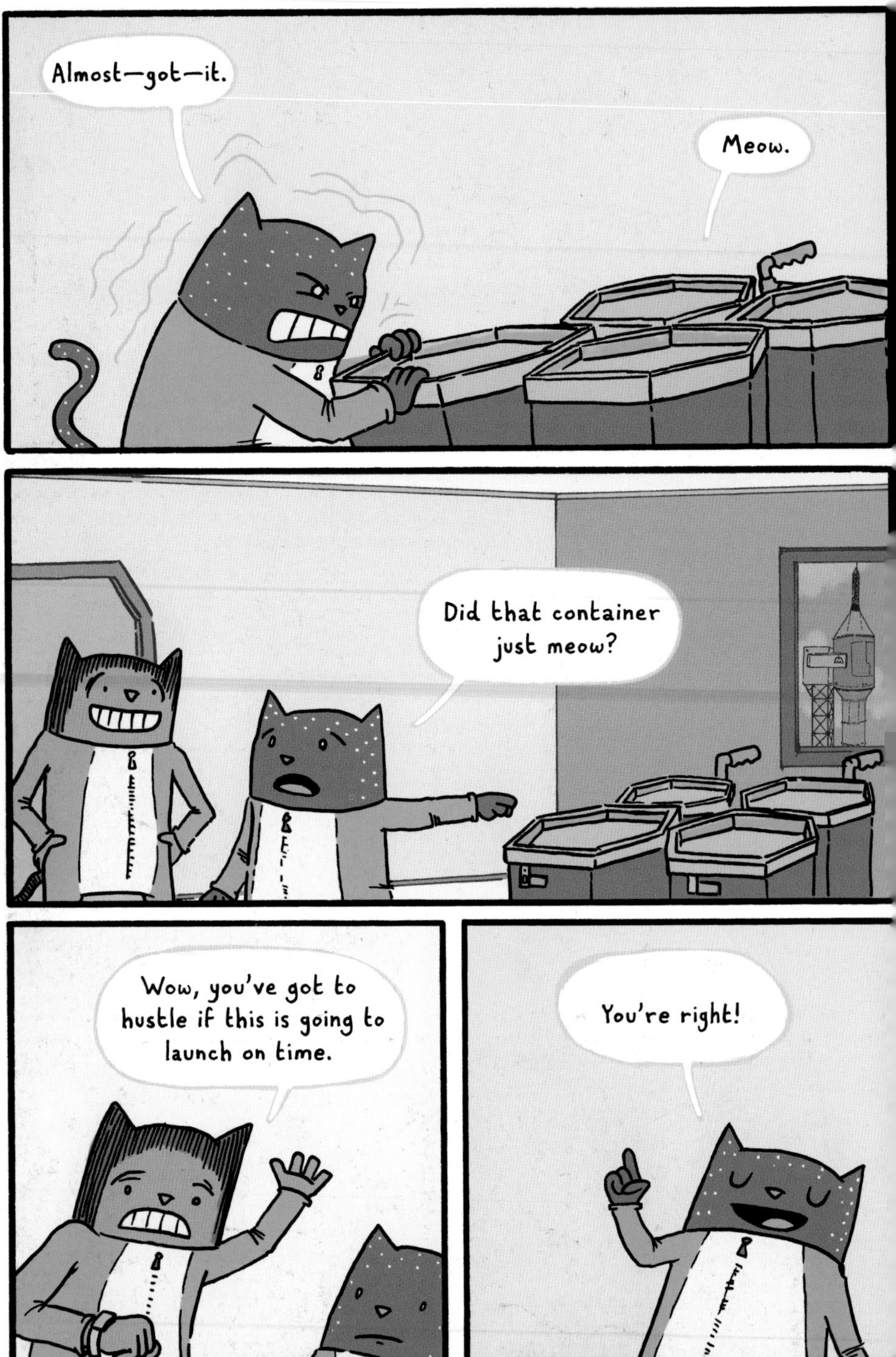
Almost—got—it.
Meow.
Did that container just meow?
Wow, you've got to hustle if this is going to launch on time.
You're right!

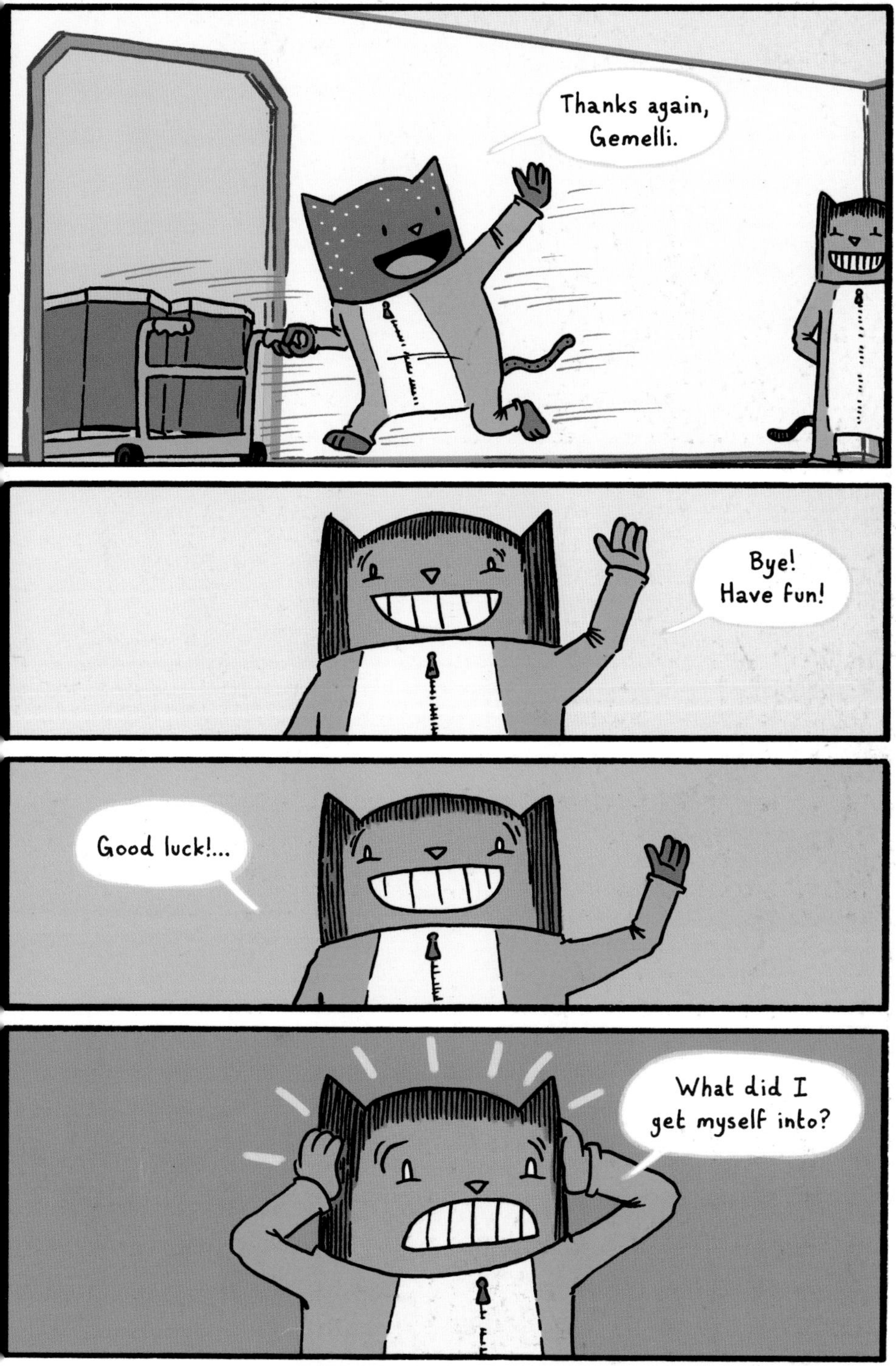
Thanks again, Gemelli.
Bye! Have fun!
Good luck!...
What did I get myself into?

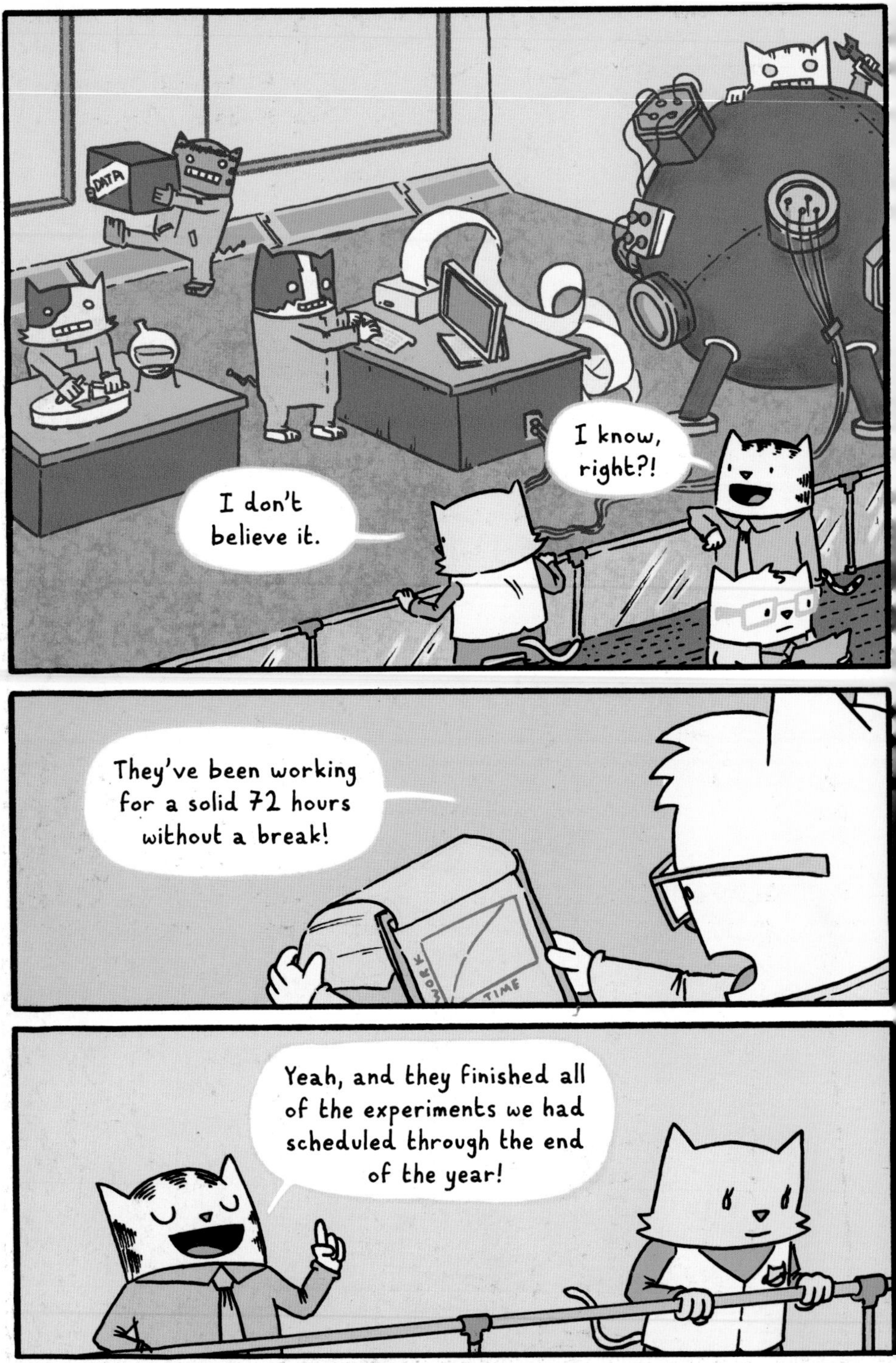
DATA
I don't believe it.
I know, right?!
They've been working for a solid 72 hours without a break!
WORK
TIME
Yeah, and they finished all of the experiments we had scheduled through the end of the year!

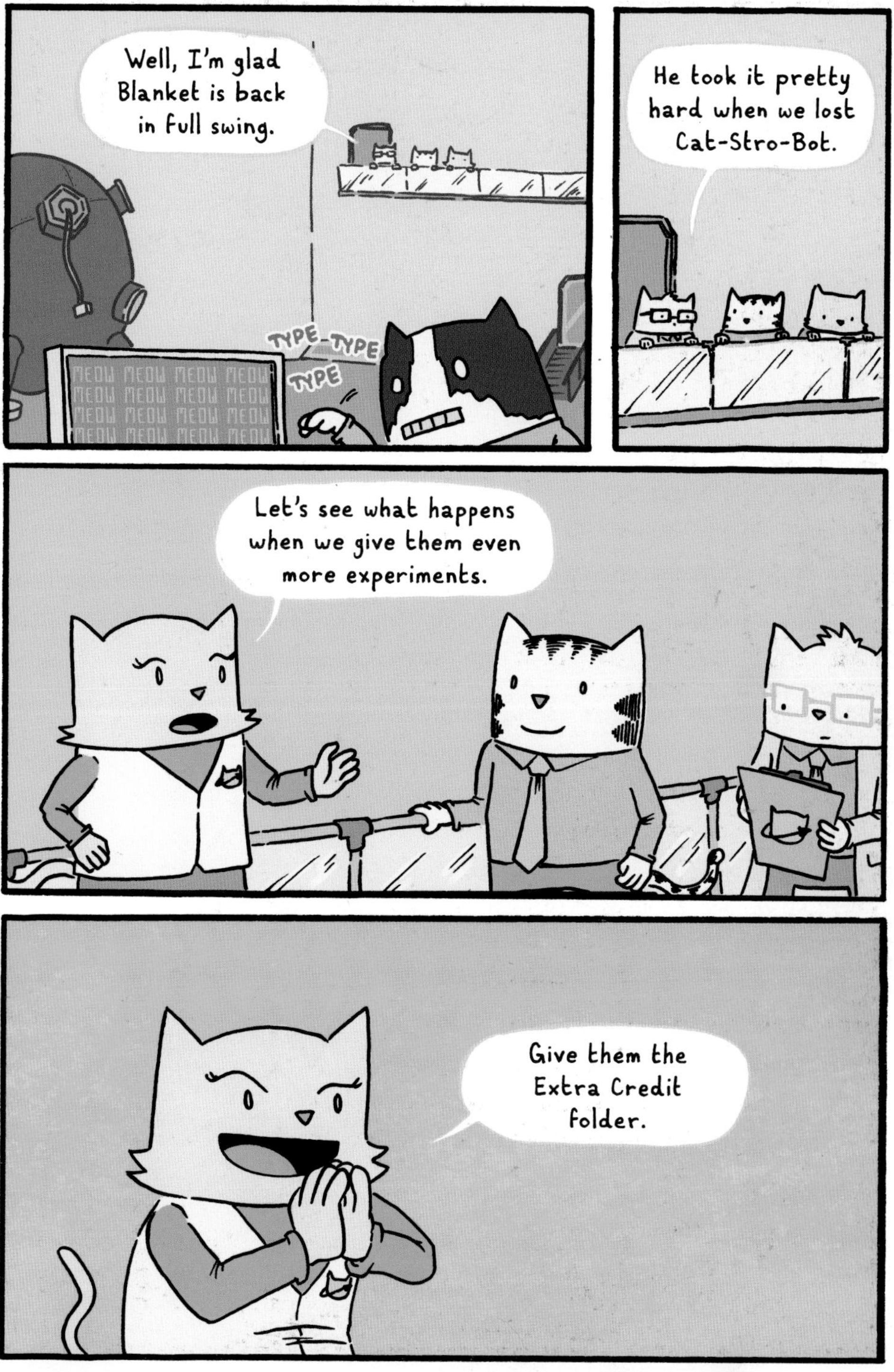
Well, I'm glad Blanket is back in full swing.
TYPE TYPE
TYPE
MEOW MEOW MEOW MEOW
MEOW MEOW MEOW MEOW
MEOW MEOW MEOW MEOW
MEOW MEOW MEOW MEOW
He took it pretty hard when we lost Cat-Stro-Bot.
Let's see what happens when we give them even more experiments.
Give them the Extra Credit folder.

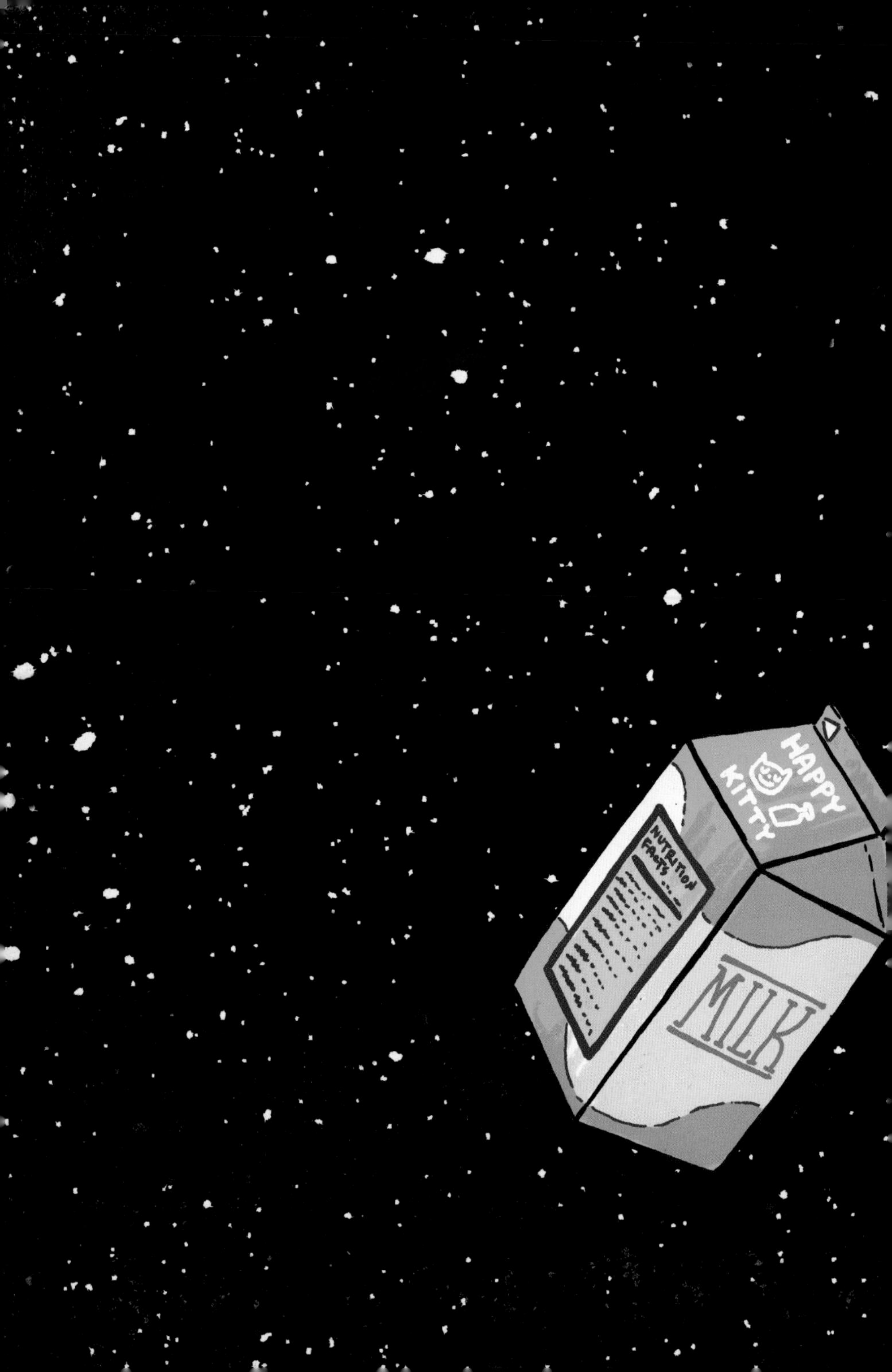
HAPPY KITTY
NUTRITION FACTS
MILK

CHAPTER 5

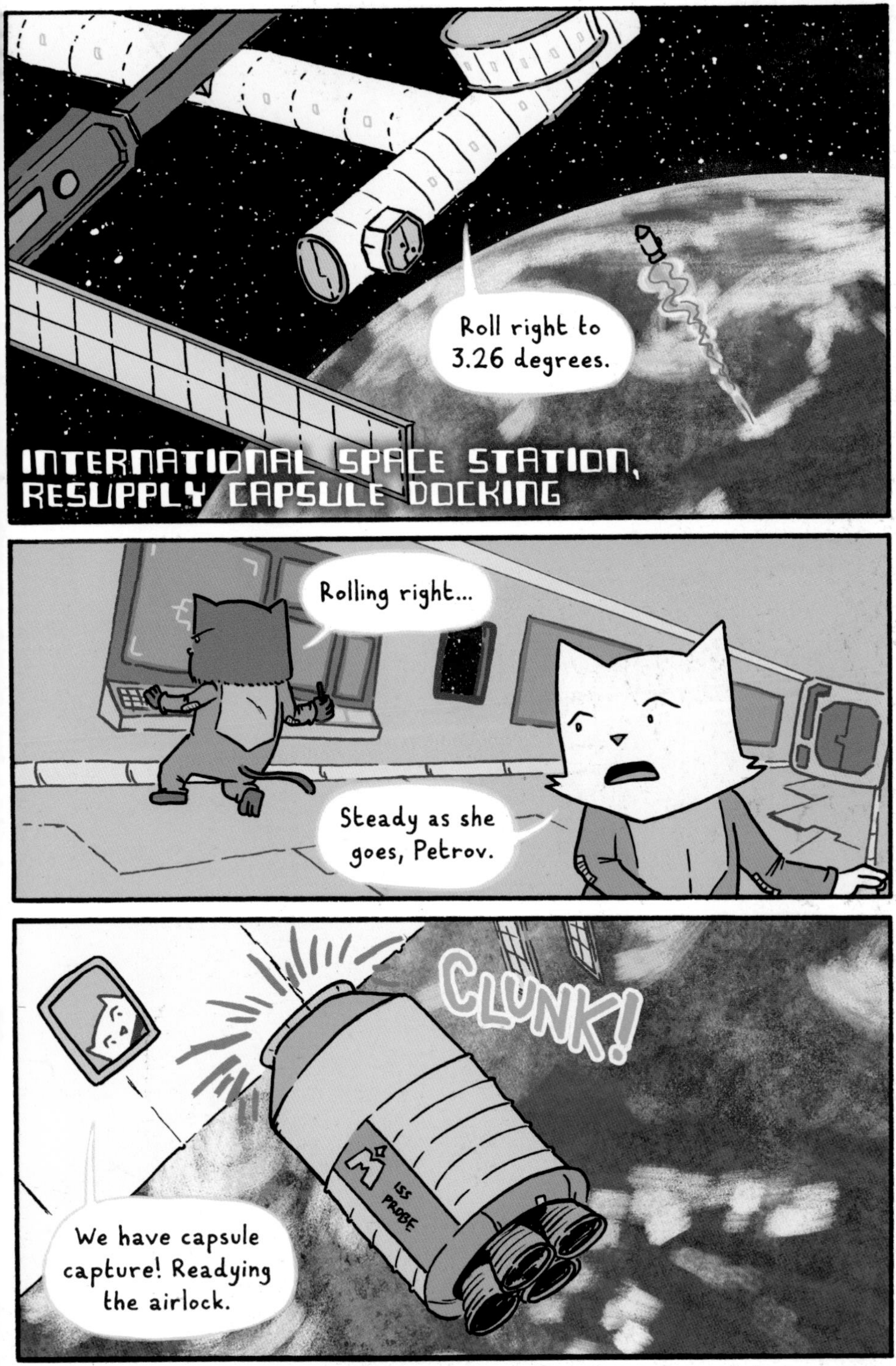
Roll right to 3.26 degrees.
INTERNATIONAL SPACE STATION, RESUPPLY CAPSULE DOCKING
Rolling right...
Steady as she goes, Petrov.
CLUNK!
ISS PROBE
We have capsule capture! Readying the airlock.

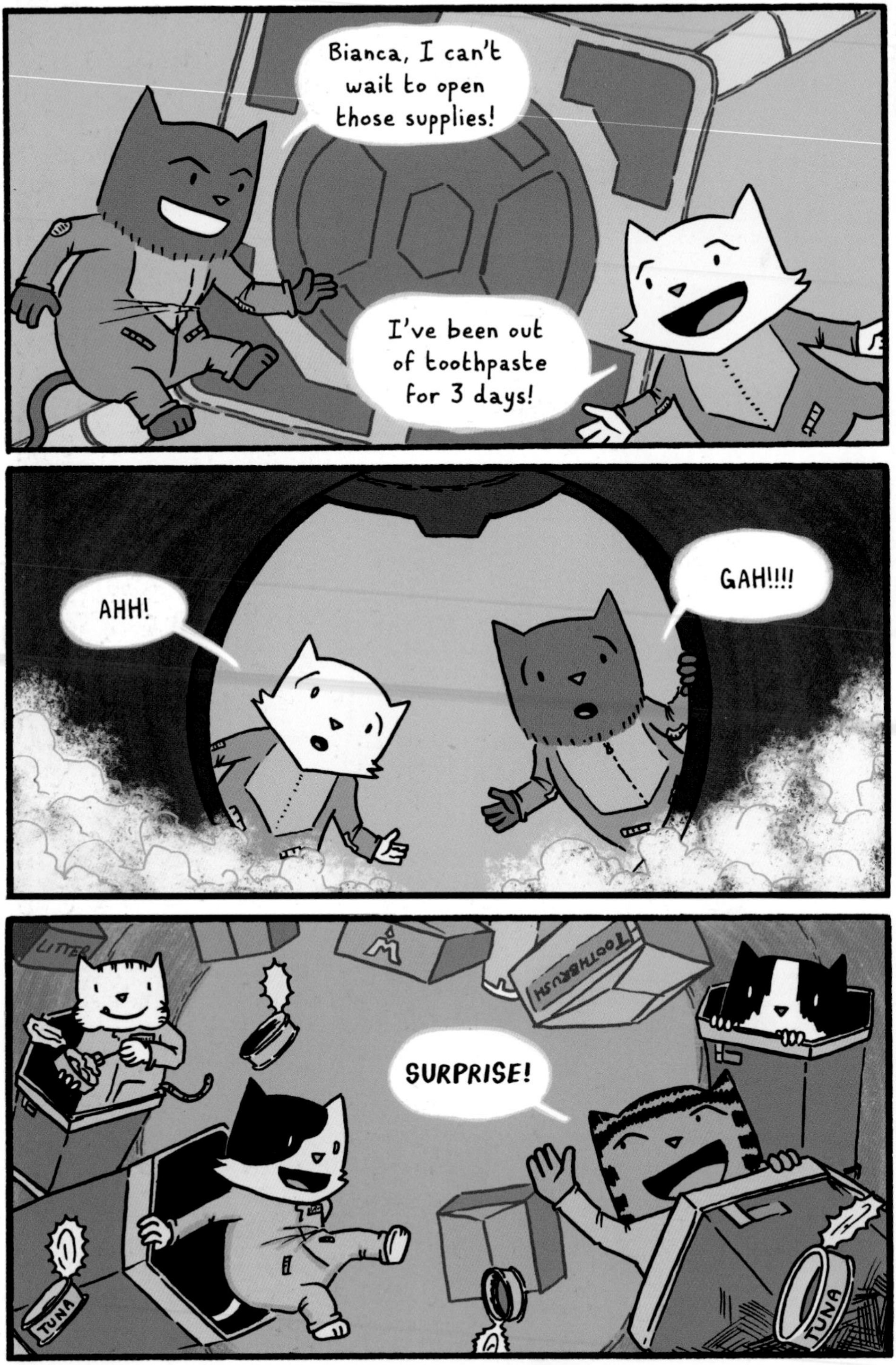
Bianca, I can't wait to open those supplies!
I've been out of toothpaste for 3 days!
AHH!
GAH!!!!
LITTER
TOOTHBRUSH
SURPRISE!
TUNA
TUNA

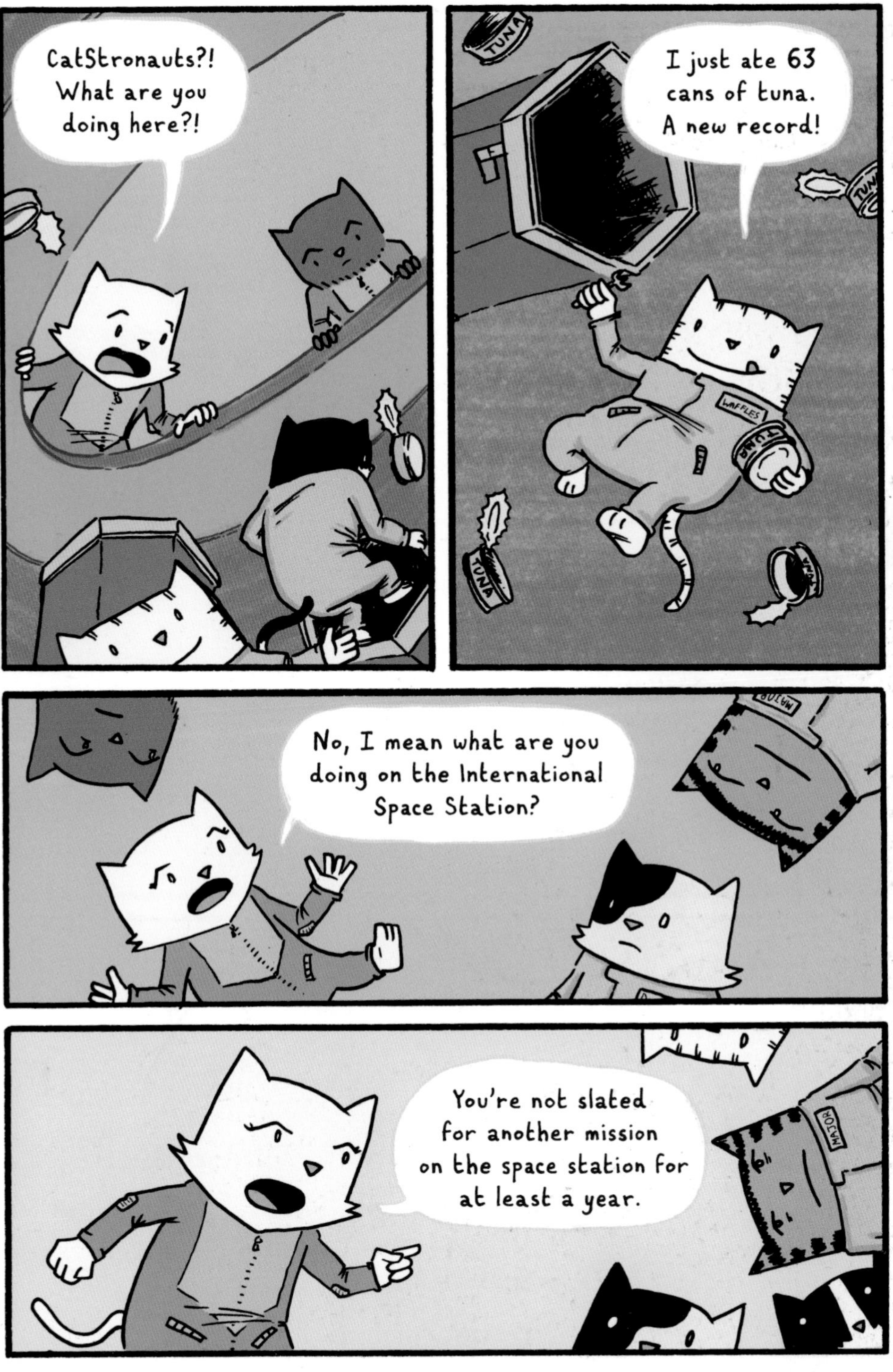
CatStronauts?! What are you doing here?!
TUNA
I just ate 63 cans of tuna. A new record!
WAFFLES
TUNA
No, I mean what are you doing on the International Space Station?
MAJOR
You're not slated for another mission on the space station for at least a year.
MAJOR

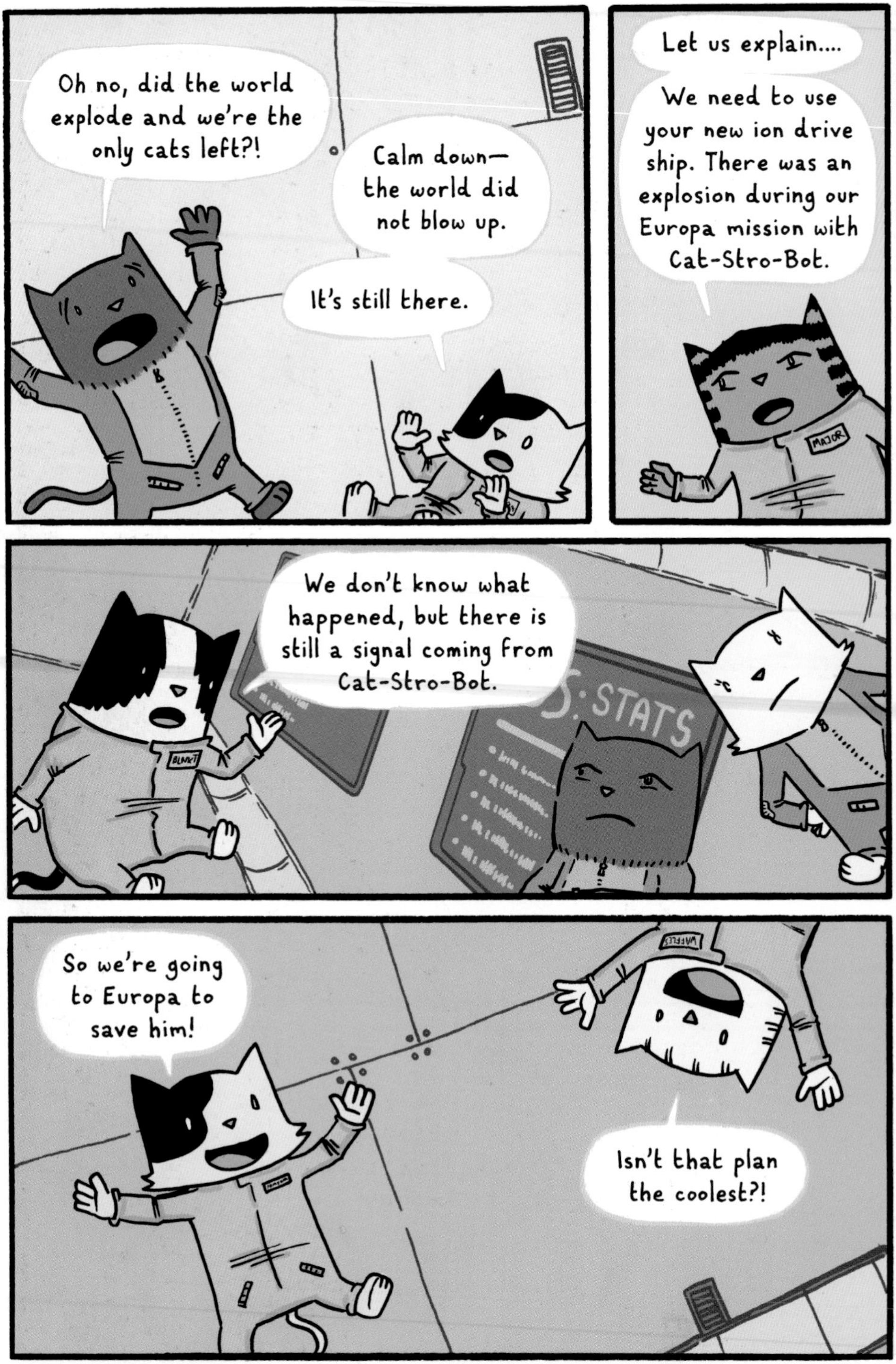
Oh no, did the world explode and we're the only cats left?!
Calm down— the world did not blow up.
It's still there.
Let us explain....
We need to use your new ion drive ship. There was an explosion during our Europa mission with Cat-Stro-Bot.
MAJOR
We don't know what happened, but there is still a signal coming from Cat-Stro-Bot.
STATS
So we're going to Europa to save him!
Isn't that plan the coolest?!

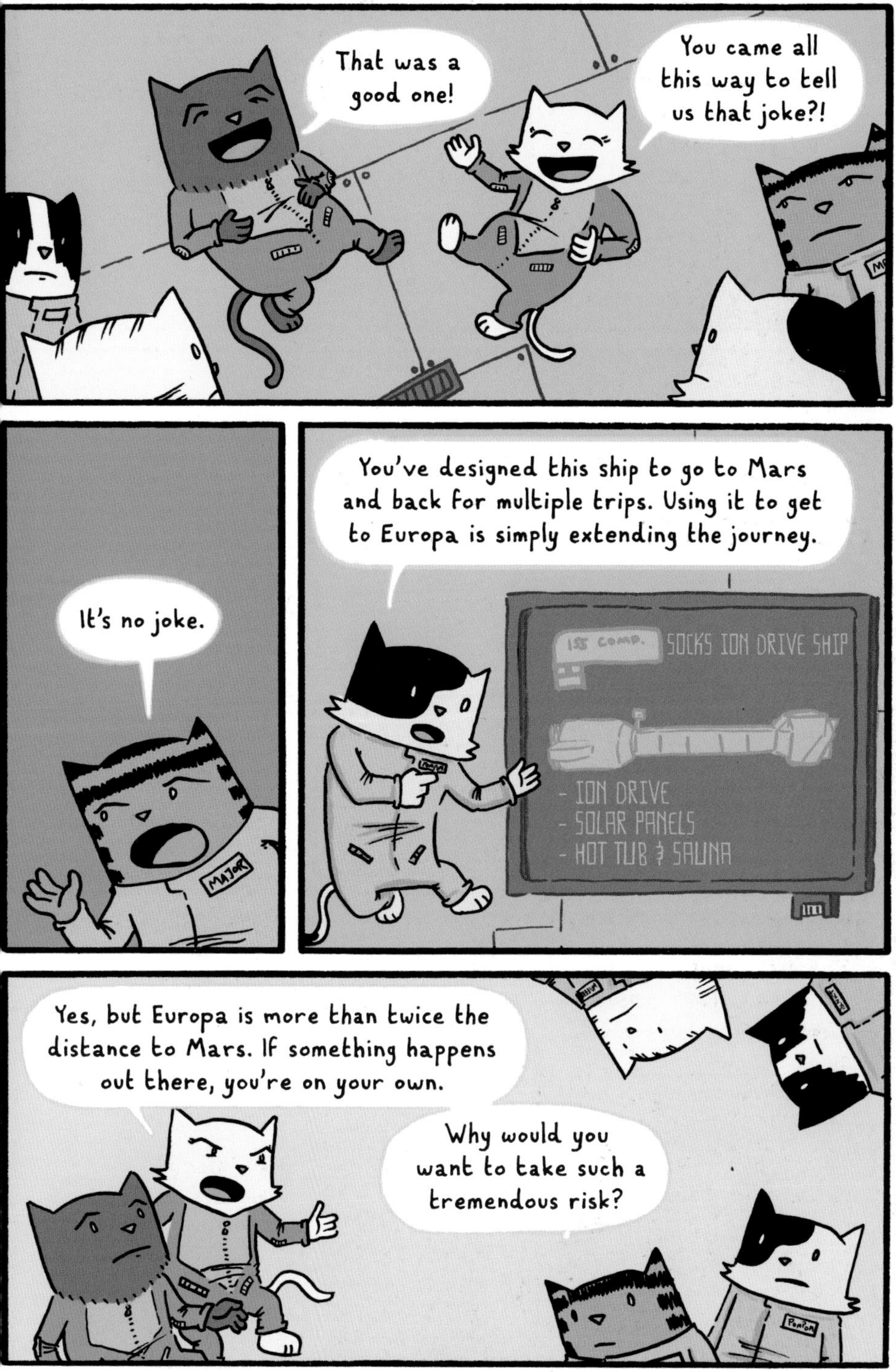
That was a good one!
You came all this way to tell us that joke?!
It's no joke.
You've designed this ship to go to Mars and back for multiple trips. Using it to get to Europa is simply extending the journey.
ISS COMP.
SOCKS ION DRIVE SHIP
- ION DRIVE
- SOLAR PANELS
- HOT TUB & SAUNA
MAJOR
Yes, but Europa is more than twice the distance to Mars. If something happens out there, you're on your own.
Why would you want to take such a tremendous risk?
POMPOM

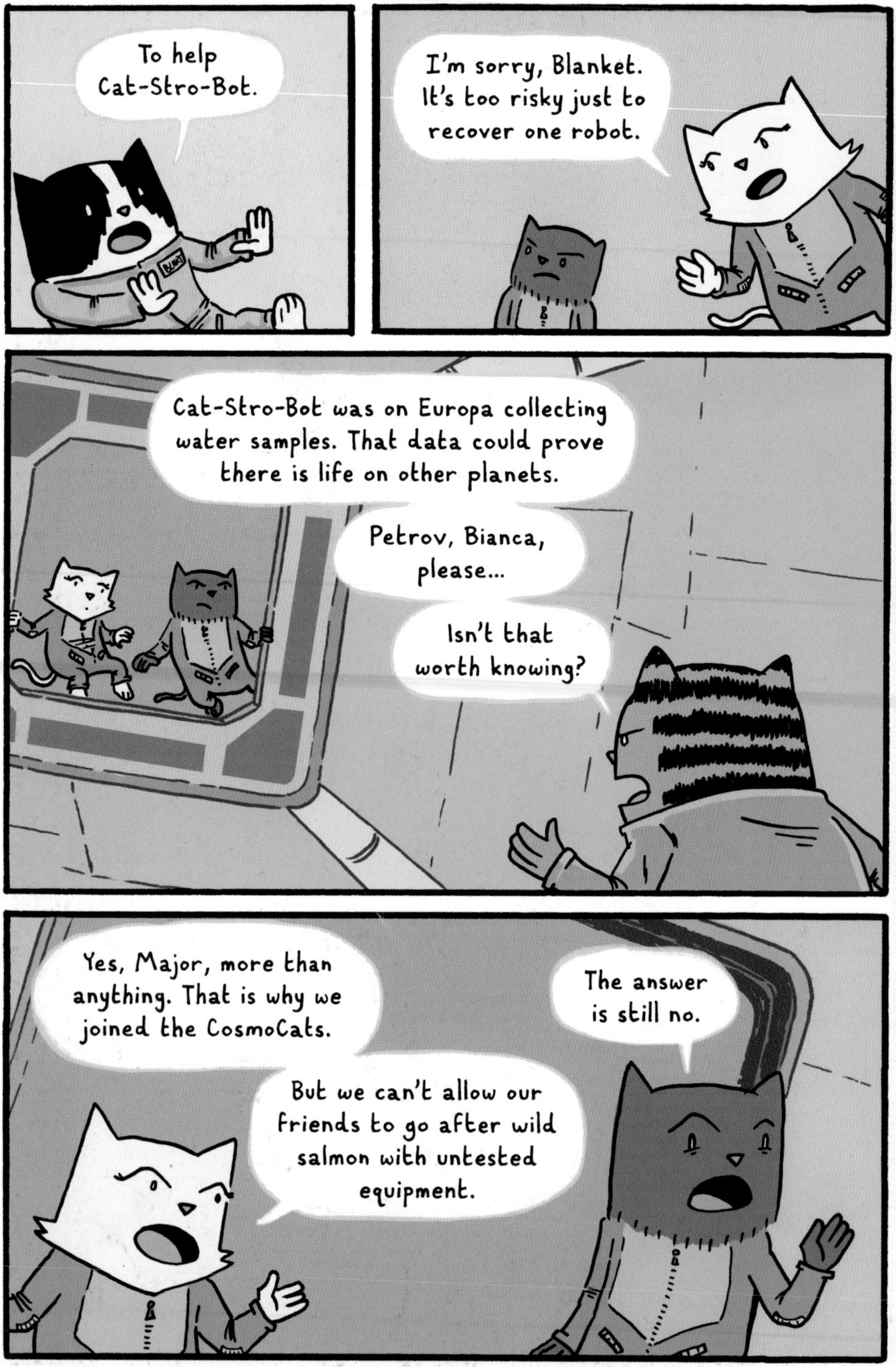
To help Cat-Stro-Bot.
I'm sorry, Blanket. It's too risky just to recover one robot.
Cat-Stro-Bot was on Europa collecting water samples. That data could prove there is life on other planets.
Petrov, Bianca, please...
Isn't that worth knowing?
Yes, Major, more than anything. That is why we joined the CosmoCats.
But we can't allow our friends to go after wild salmon with untested equipment.
The answer is still no.

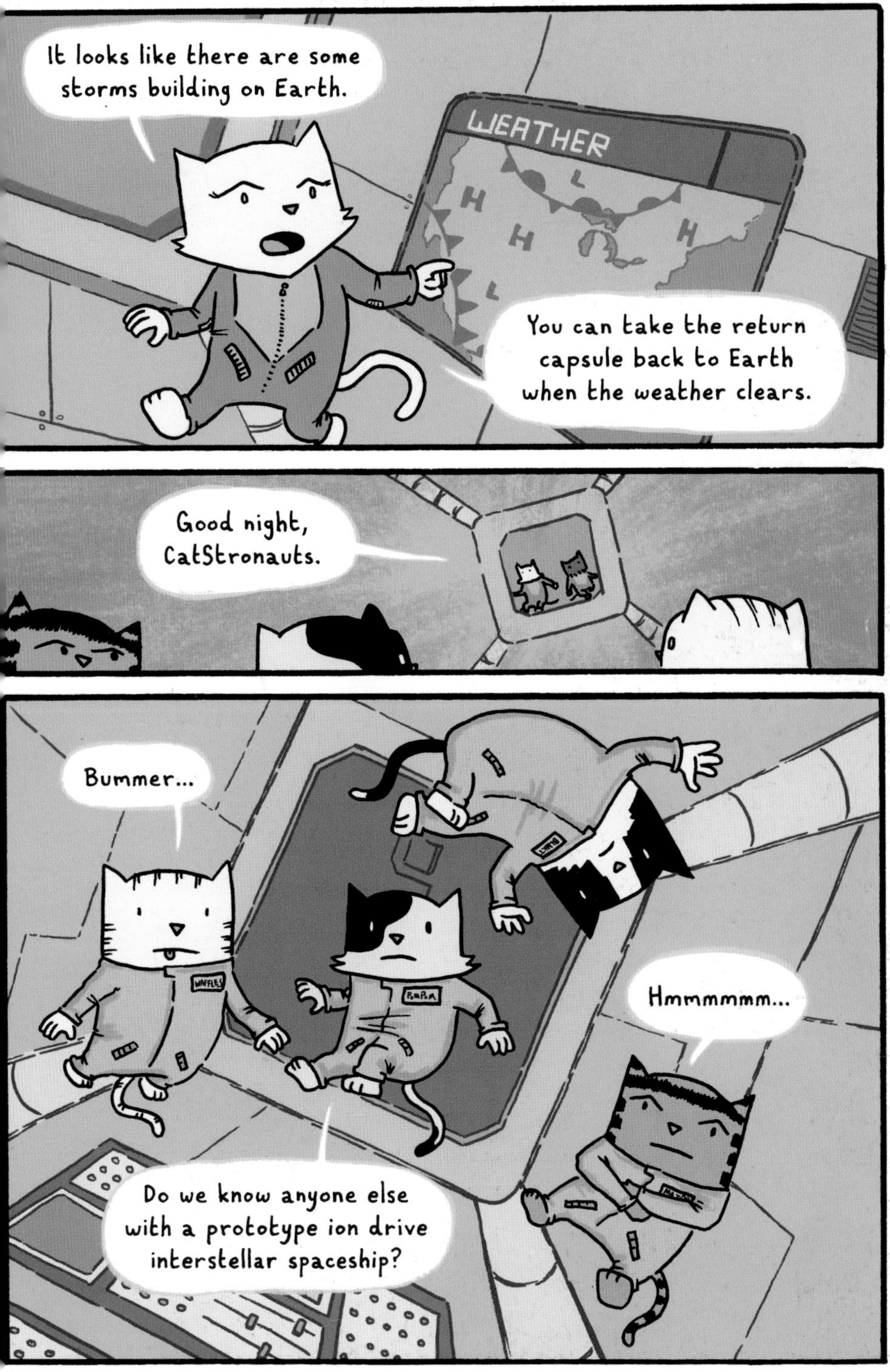
It looks like there are some storms building on Earth.
WEATHER
You can take the return capsule back to Earth when the weather clears.
Good night, CatStronauts.
Bummer...
Hmmmmmm...
Do we know anyone else with a prototype ion drive interstellar spaceship?

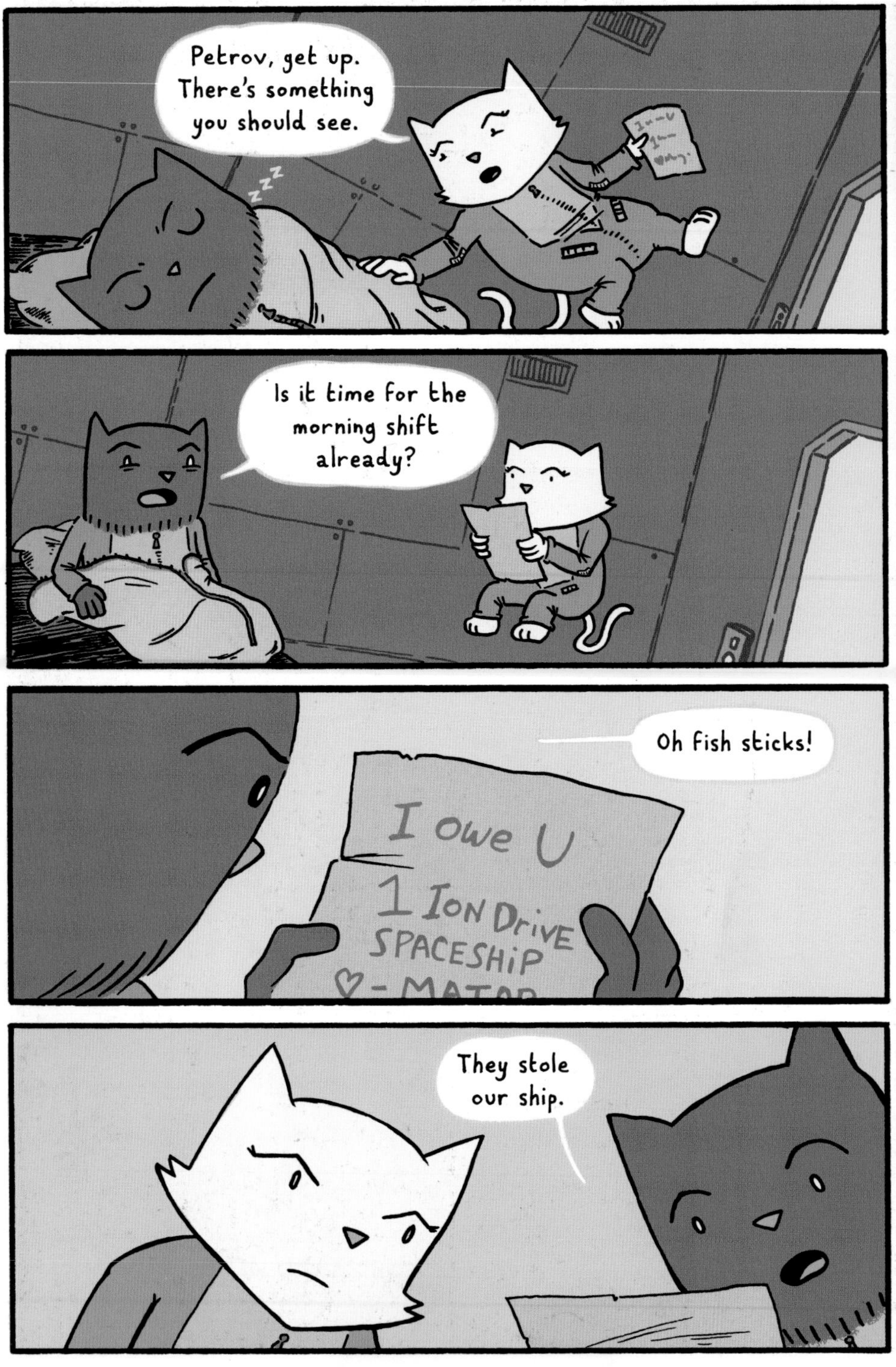
Petrov, get up. There's something you should see.
Is it time for the morning shift already?
Oh fish sticks!
I owe U
1 Ion Drive
SPACESHIP
They stole our ship.

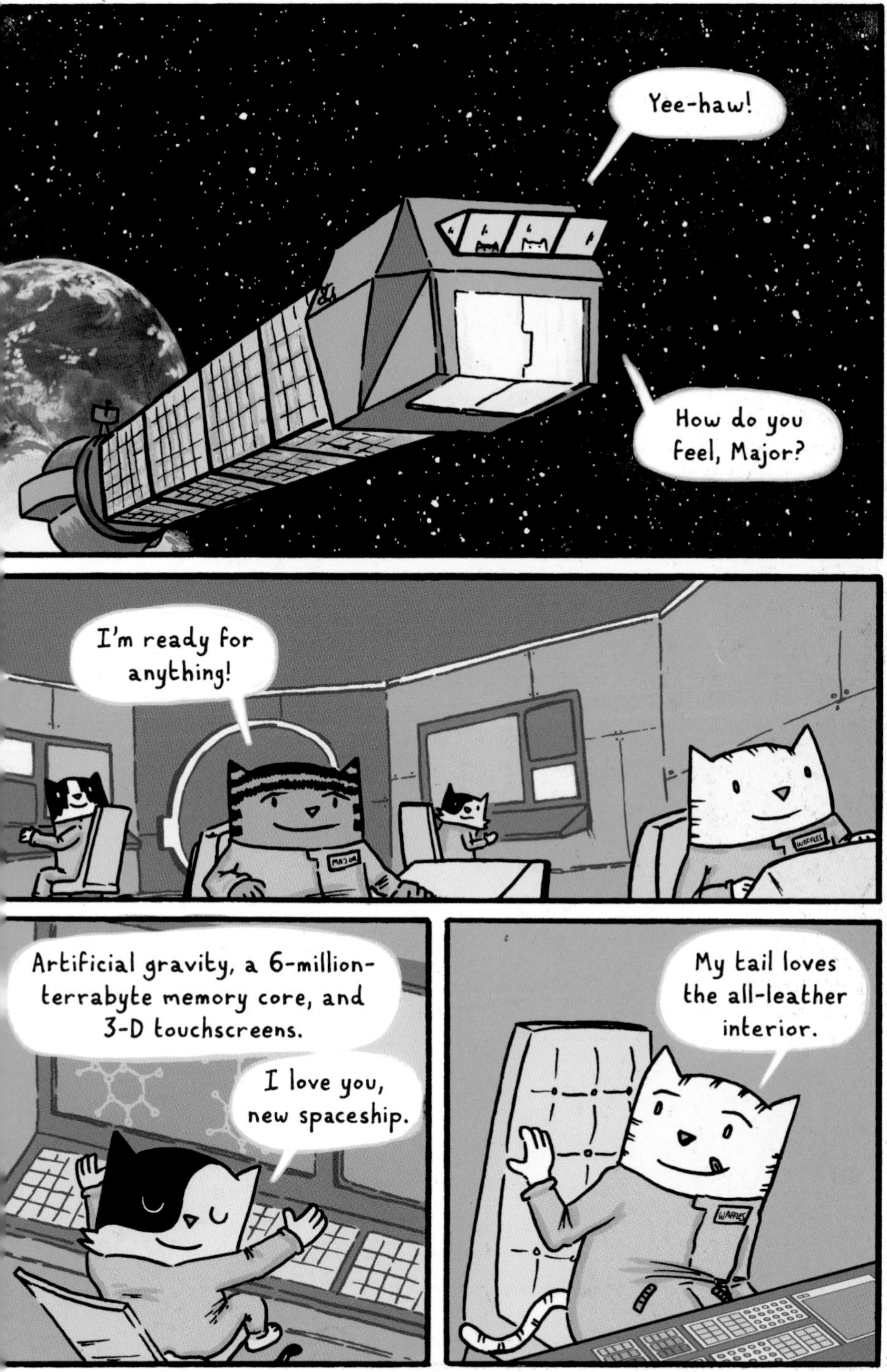
Yee-haw!
How do you feel, Major?
I'm ready for anything!
MAJOR
WAFFLES
Artificial gravity, a 6-million-terrabyte memory core, and 3-D touchscreens.
I love you, new spaceship.
My tail loves the all-leather interior.
WAFFLES

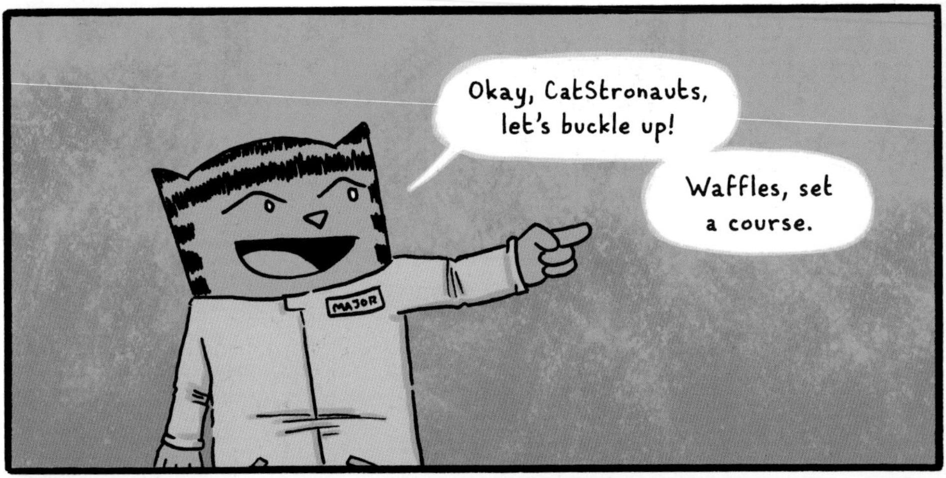
Okay, CatStronauts, let's buckle up!
Waffles, set a course.
MAJOR

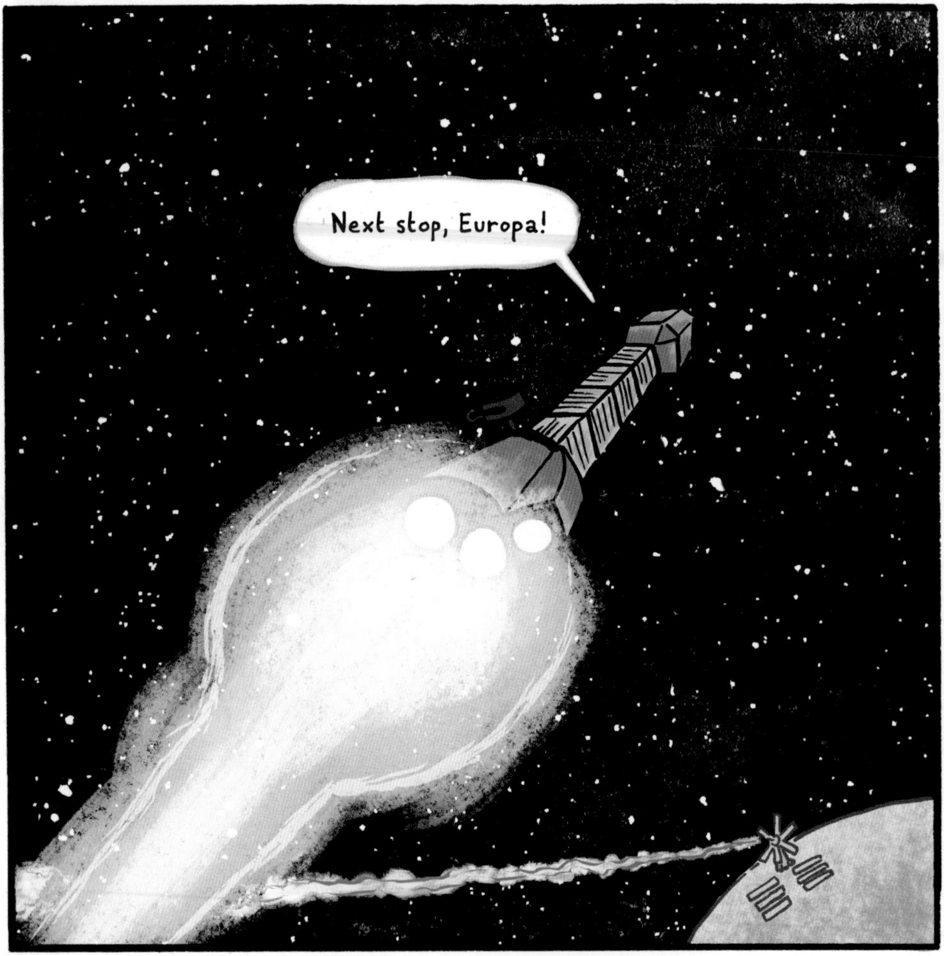
Next stop, Europa!

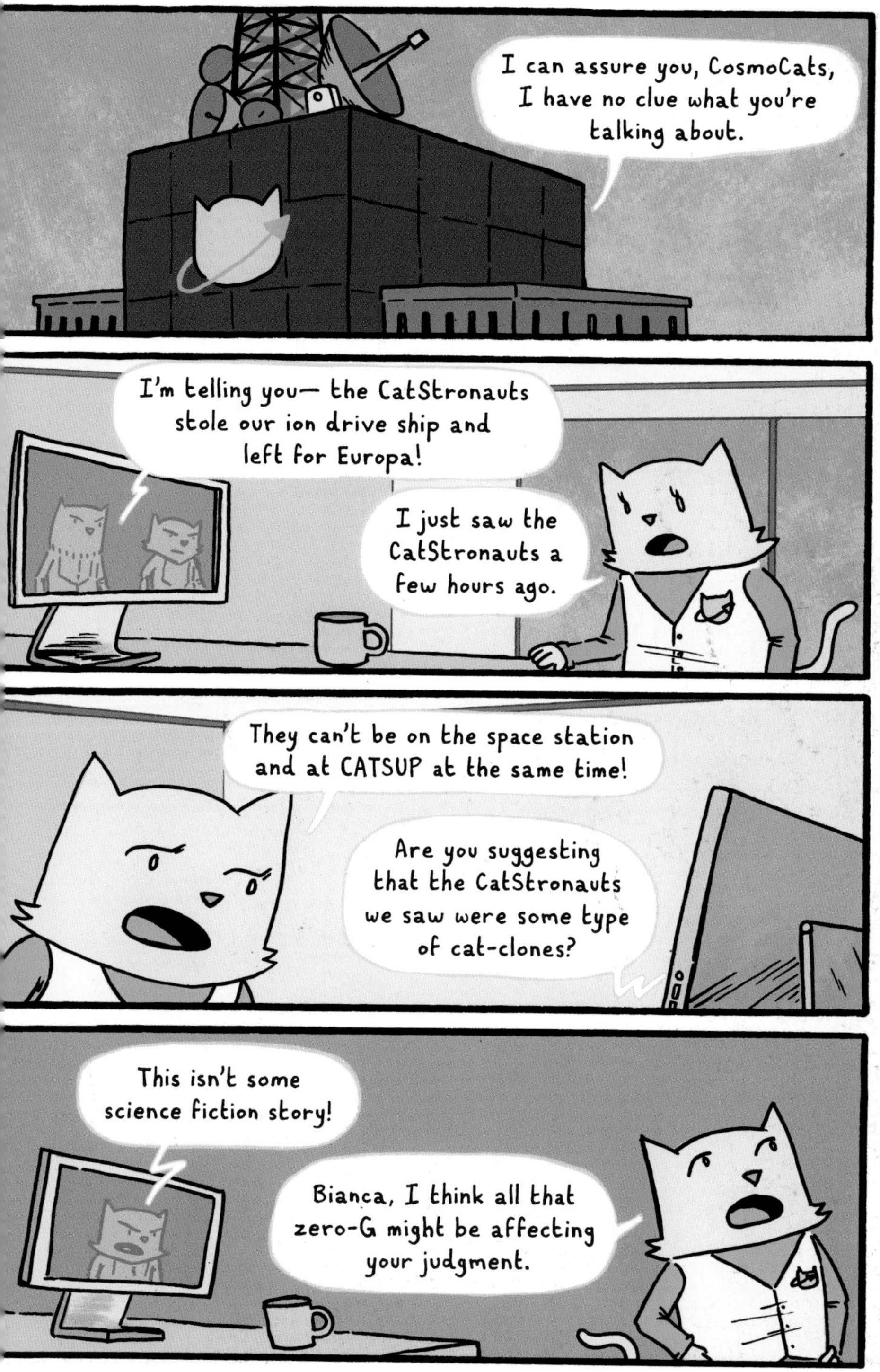
I can assure you, CosmoCats, I have no clue what you're talking about.
I'm telling you— the CatStronauts stole our ion drive ship and left for Europa!
I just saw the CatStronauts a few hours ago.
They can't be on the space station and at CATSUP at the same time!
Are you suggesting that the CatStronauts we saw were some type of cat-clones?
This isn't some science fiction story!
Bianca, I think all that zero-G might be affecting your judgment.

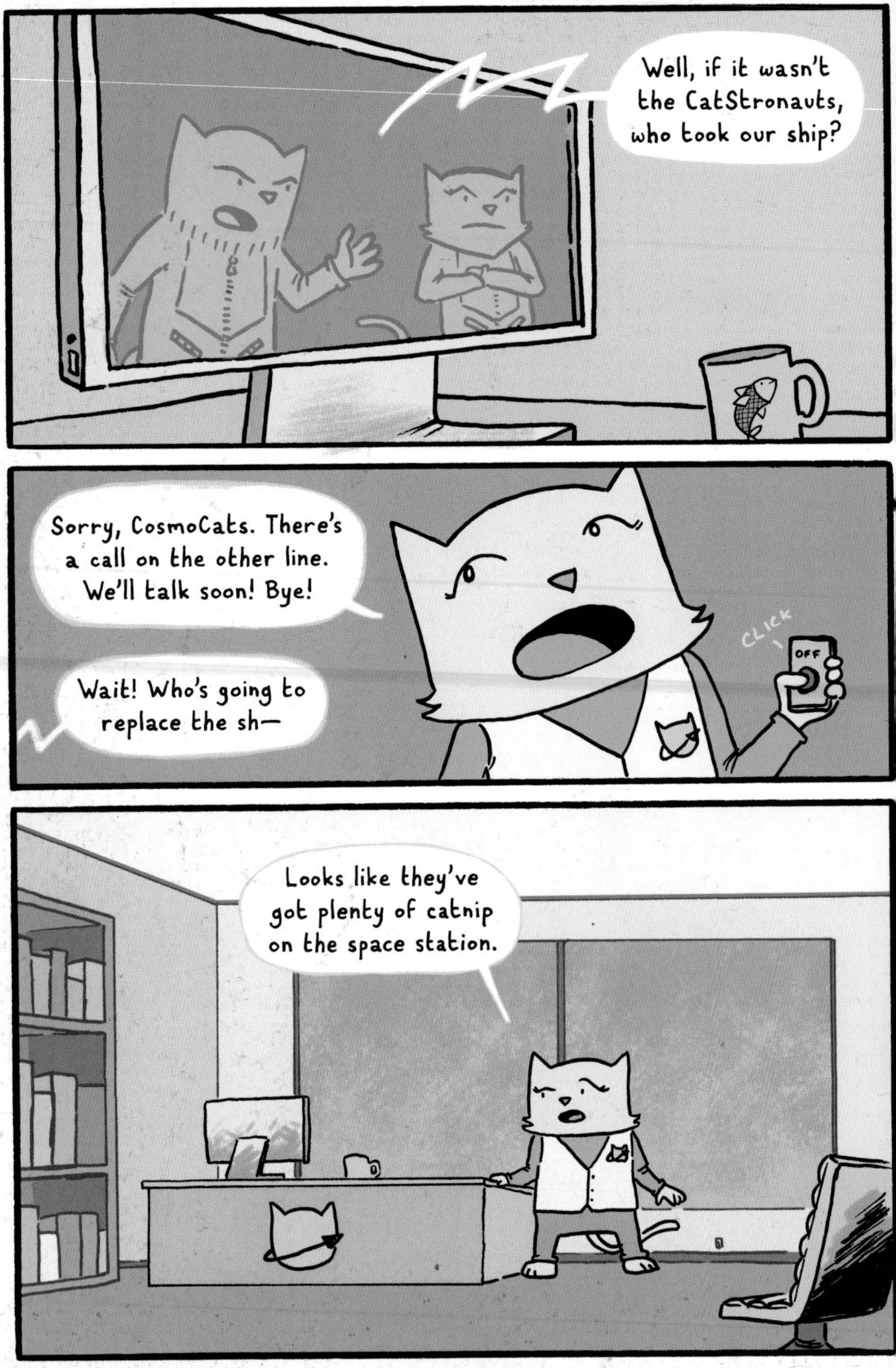
Well, if it wasn't the CatStronauts, who took our ship?
Sorry, CosmoCats. There's a call on the other line. We'll talk soon! Bye!
Wait! Who's going to replace the sh—
CLICK
OFF
Looks like they've got plenty of catnip on the space station.

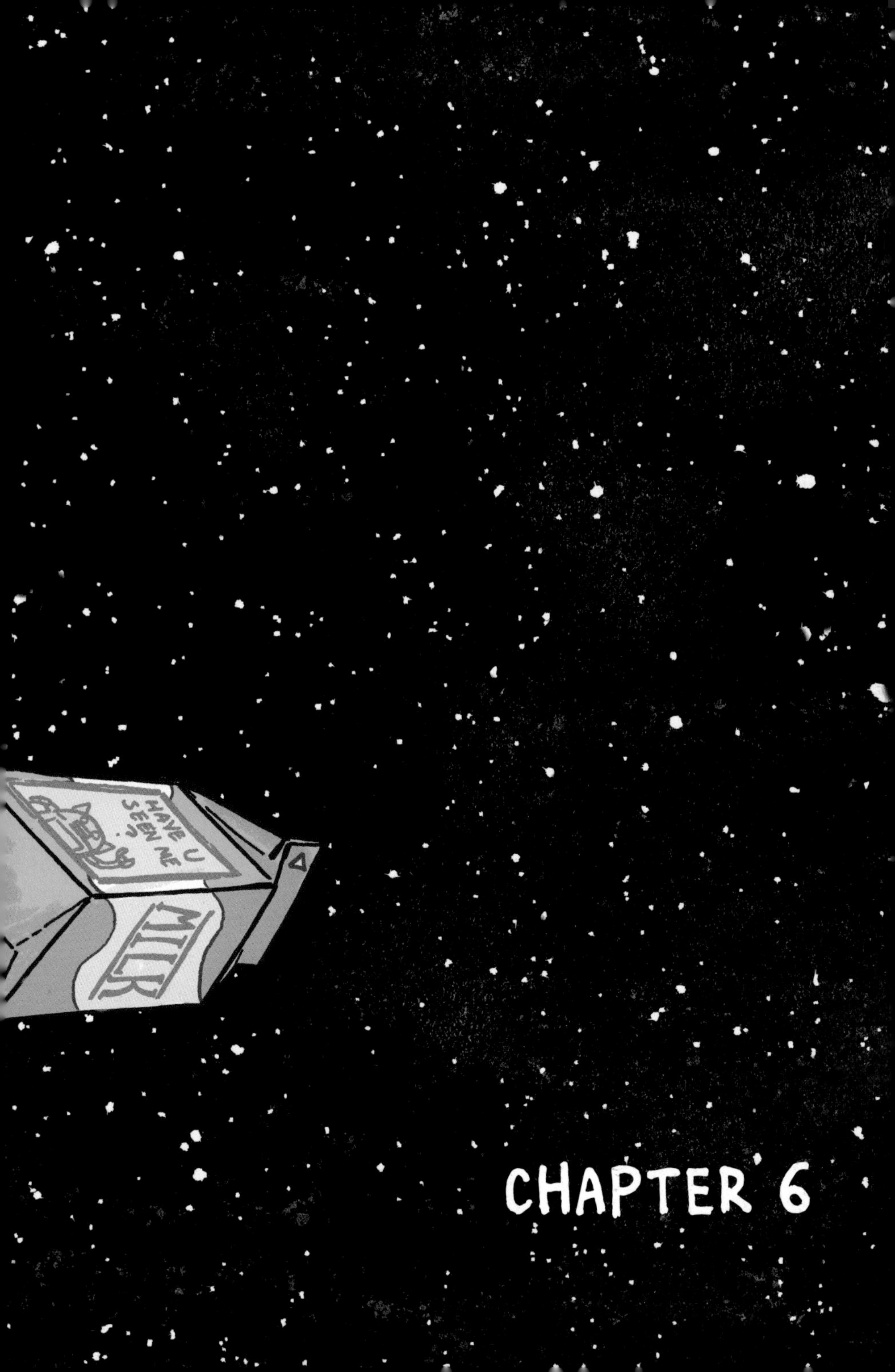
HAVE U SEEN ME ?
MILK

CHAPTER 6

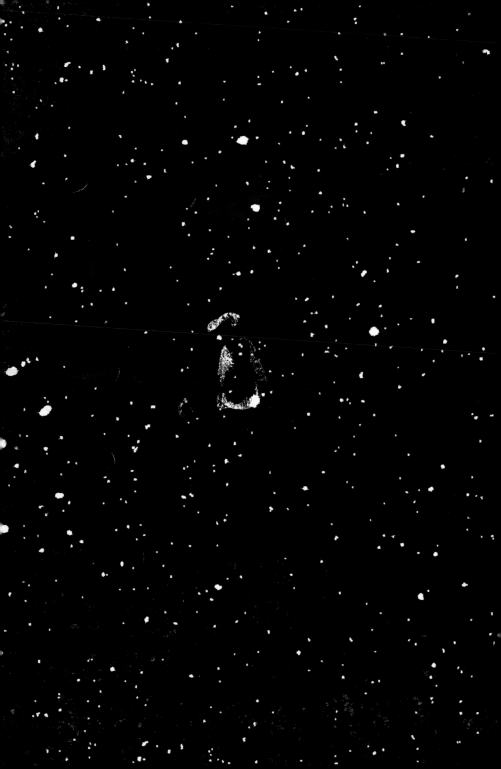

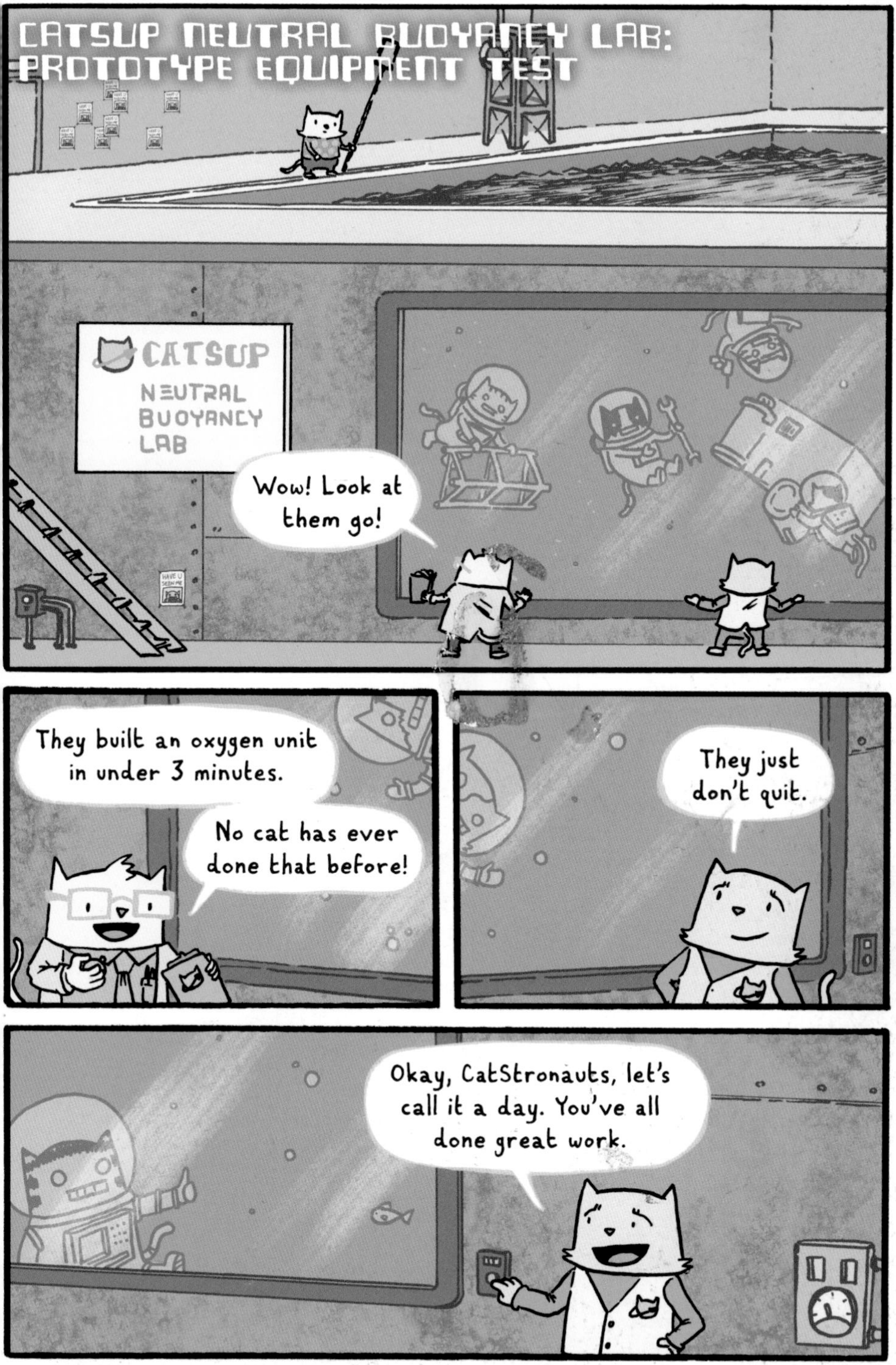
CATSUP NEUTRAL BUOYANCY LAB:
PROTOTYPE EQUIPMENT TEST
CATSUP
NEUTRAL
BUOYANCY
LAB
Wow! Look at them go!
They built an oxygen unit in under 3 minutes.
No cat has ever done that before!
They just don't quit.
Okay, CatStronauts, let's call it a day. You've all done great work.

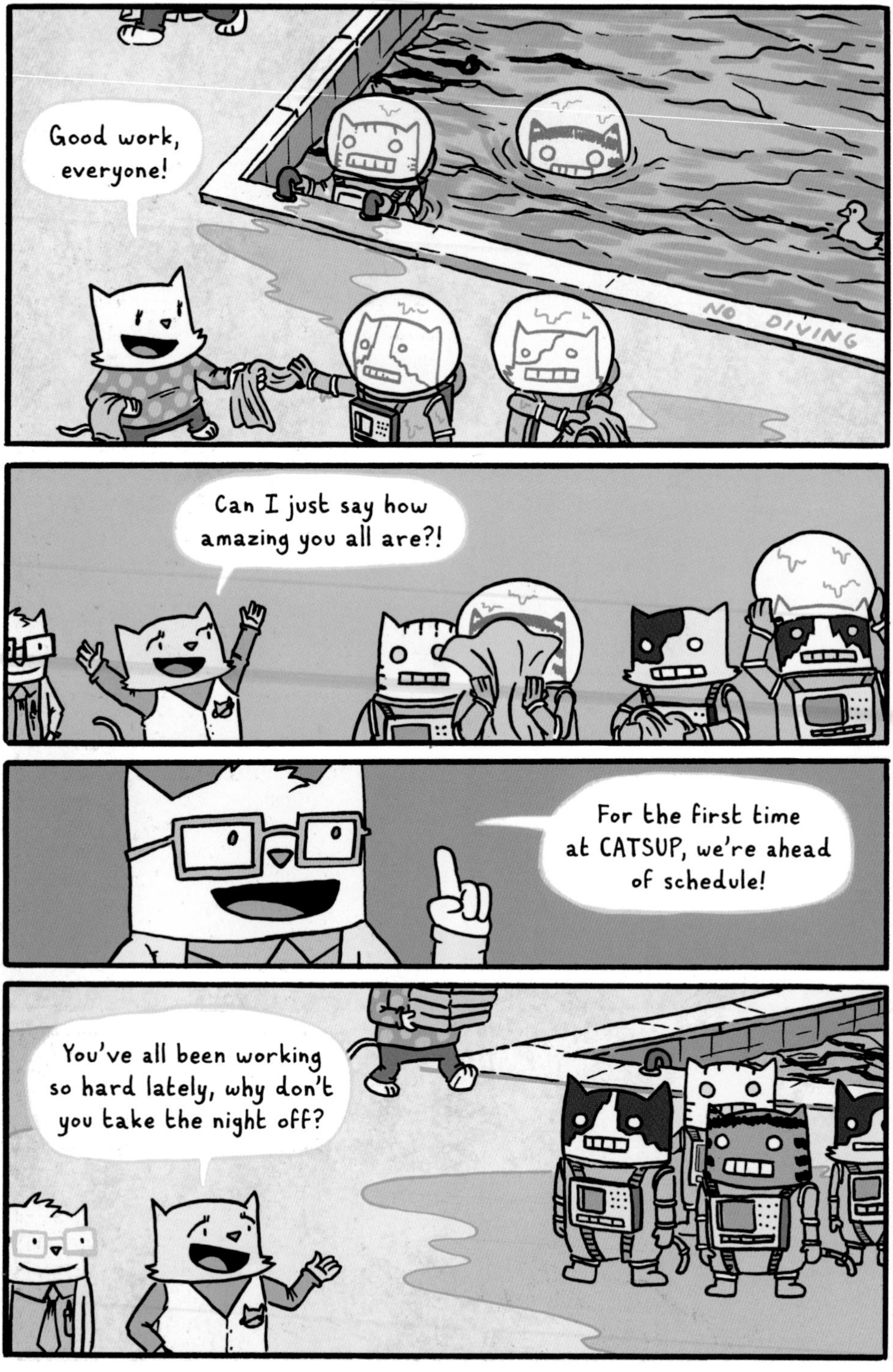
Good work, everyone!
NO DIVING
Can I just say how amazing you all are?!
For the first time at CATSUP, we're ahead of schedule!
You've all been working so hard lately, why don't you take the night off?

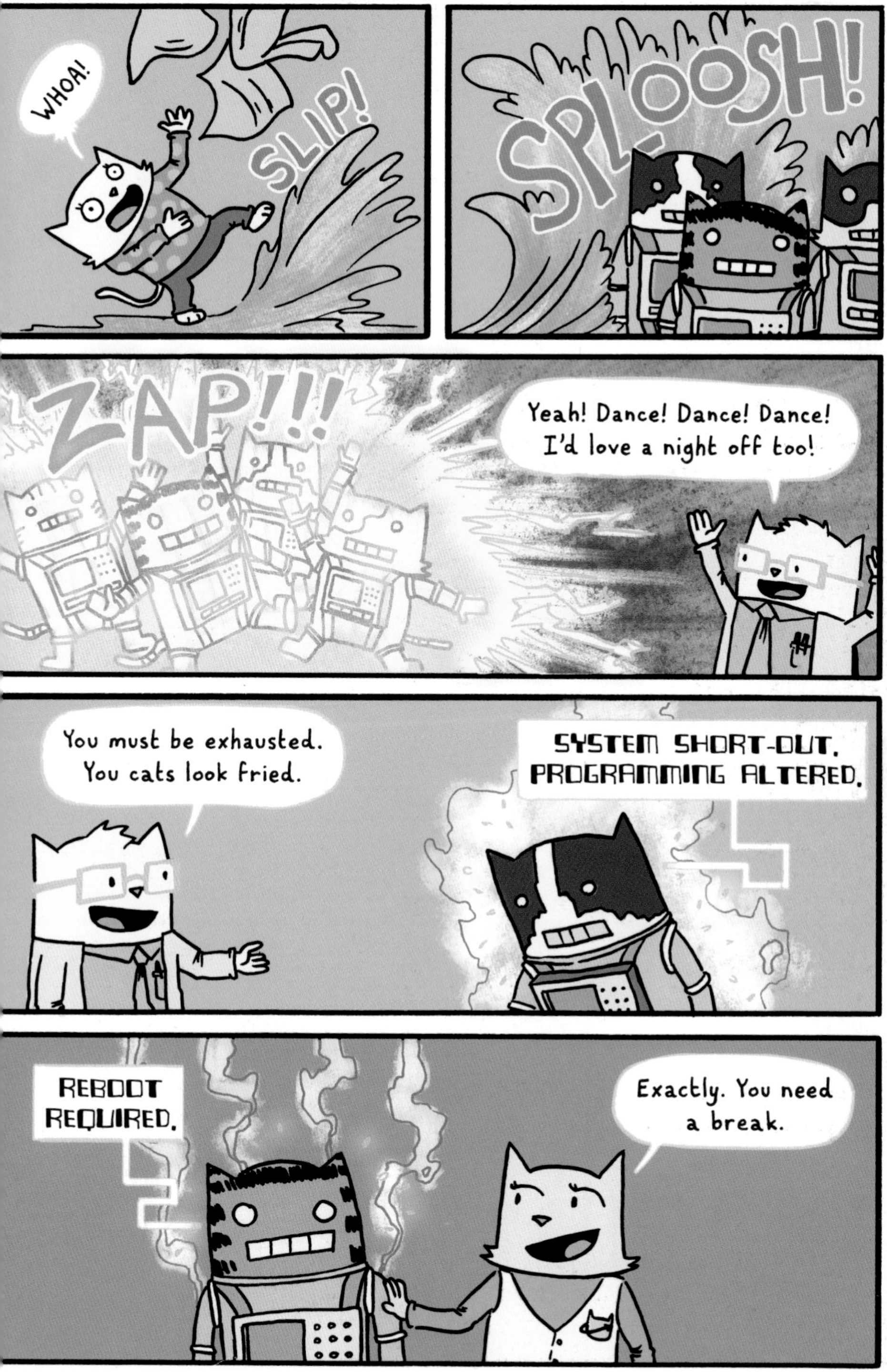
WHOA!
SLIP!
SPLOOSH!
ZAP!!!
Yeah! Dance! Dance! Dance! I'd love a night off too!
You must be exhausted. You cats look fried.
SYSTEM SHORT-OUT. PROGRAMMING ALTERED.
REBOOT REQUIRED.
Exactly. You need a break.

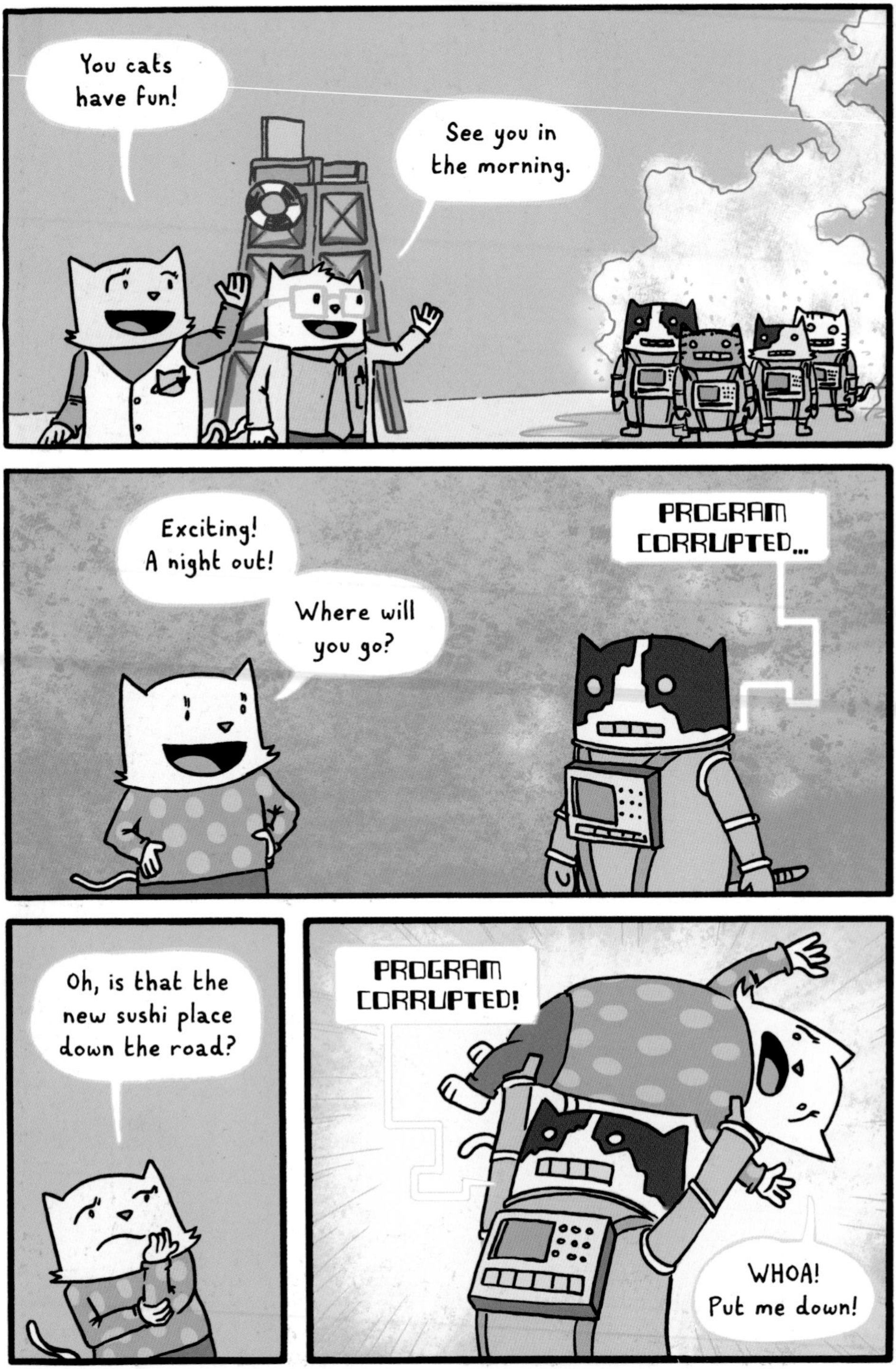
You cats have fun!
See you in the morning.
Exciting! A night out!
Where will you go?
PROGRAM CORRUPTED...
Oh, is that the new sushi place down the road?
PROGRAM CORRUPTED!
WHOA! Put me down!

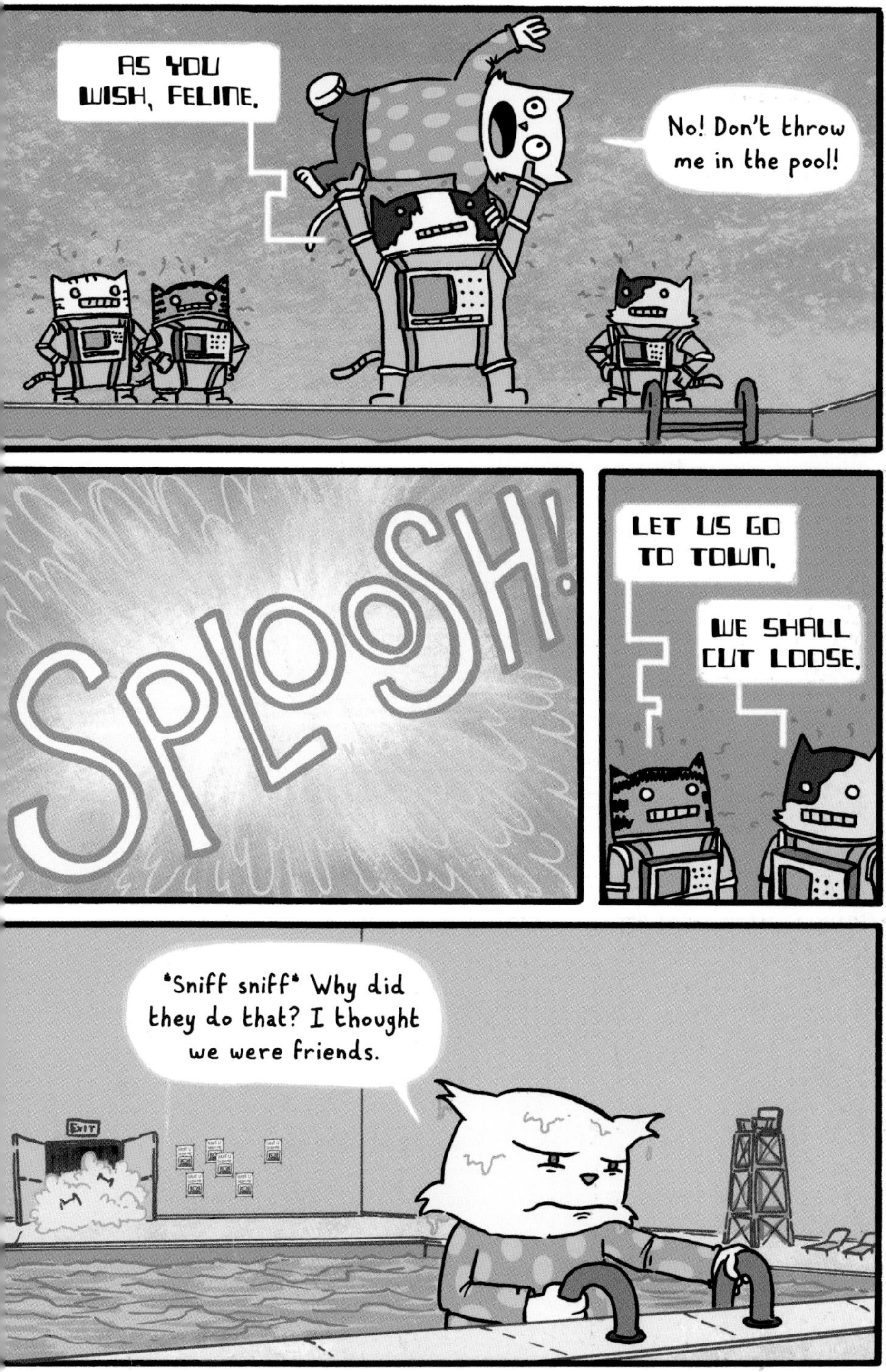
AS YOU WISH, FELINE.
No! Don't throw me in the pool!
SPLOOSH!
LET US GO TO TOWN.
WE SHALL CUT LOOSE.
Sniff sniff Why did they do that? I thought we were friends.
EXIT

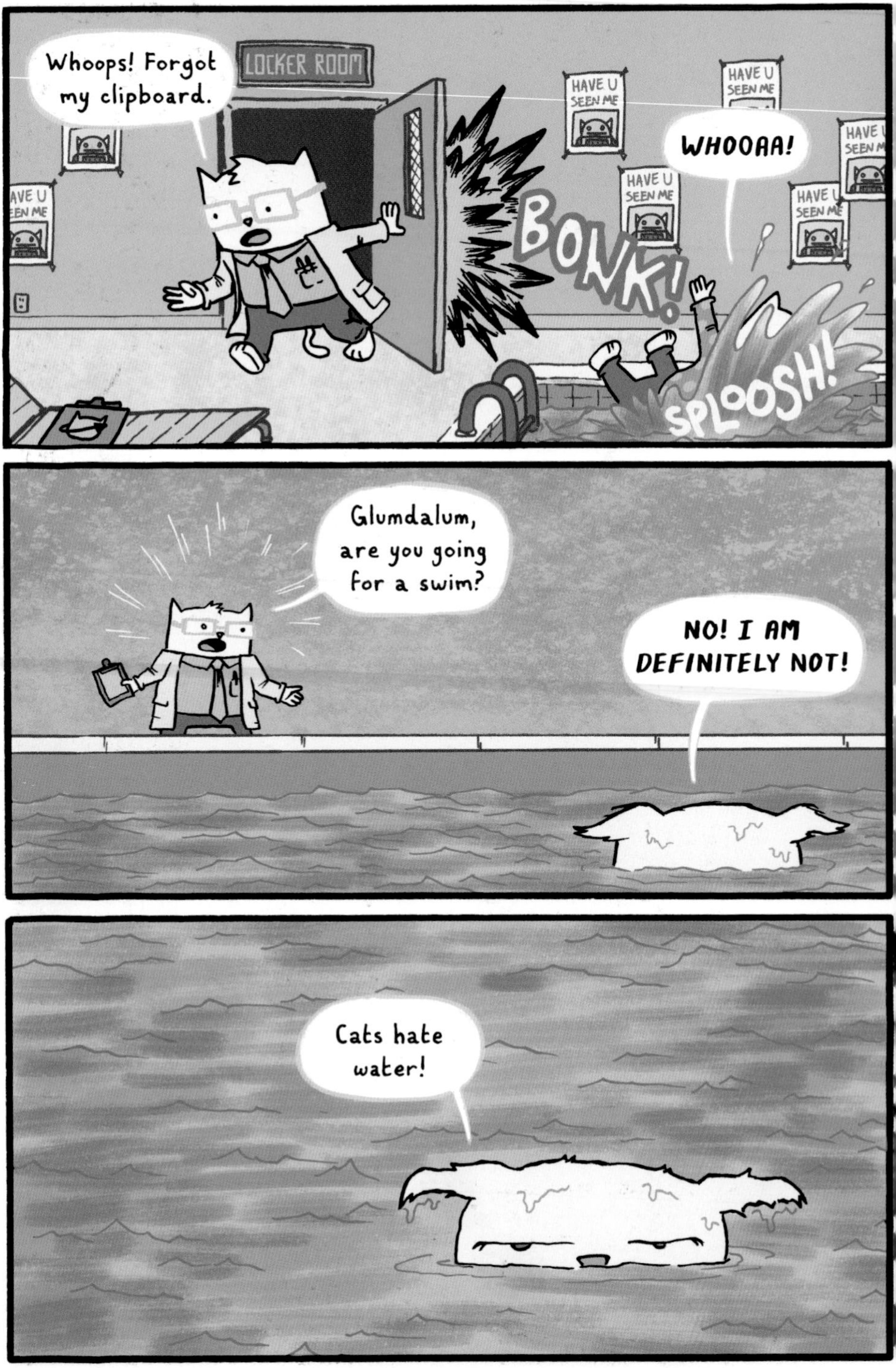
Whoops! Forgot my clipboard.
LOCKER ROOM
HAVE U SEEN ME
BONK!
WHOOAA!
SPLOOSH!
Glumdalum, are you going for a swim?
NO! I AM DEFINITELY NOT!
Cats hate water!

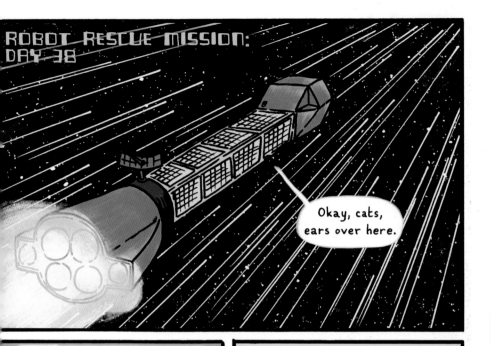

ROBOT RESCUE MISSION: DAY 38

Okay, cats, ears over here.

I just finished the inventory of our supplies, and if we stick to this rationing schedule, we'll have enough of everything to last until we get back to Earth.

One can of tuna a day?!

But my record is 63!

I'm sorry, Waffles. We're all making sacrifices.

Just look at me. I'm wasting away.

Only two trips to the litter box a day?!

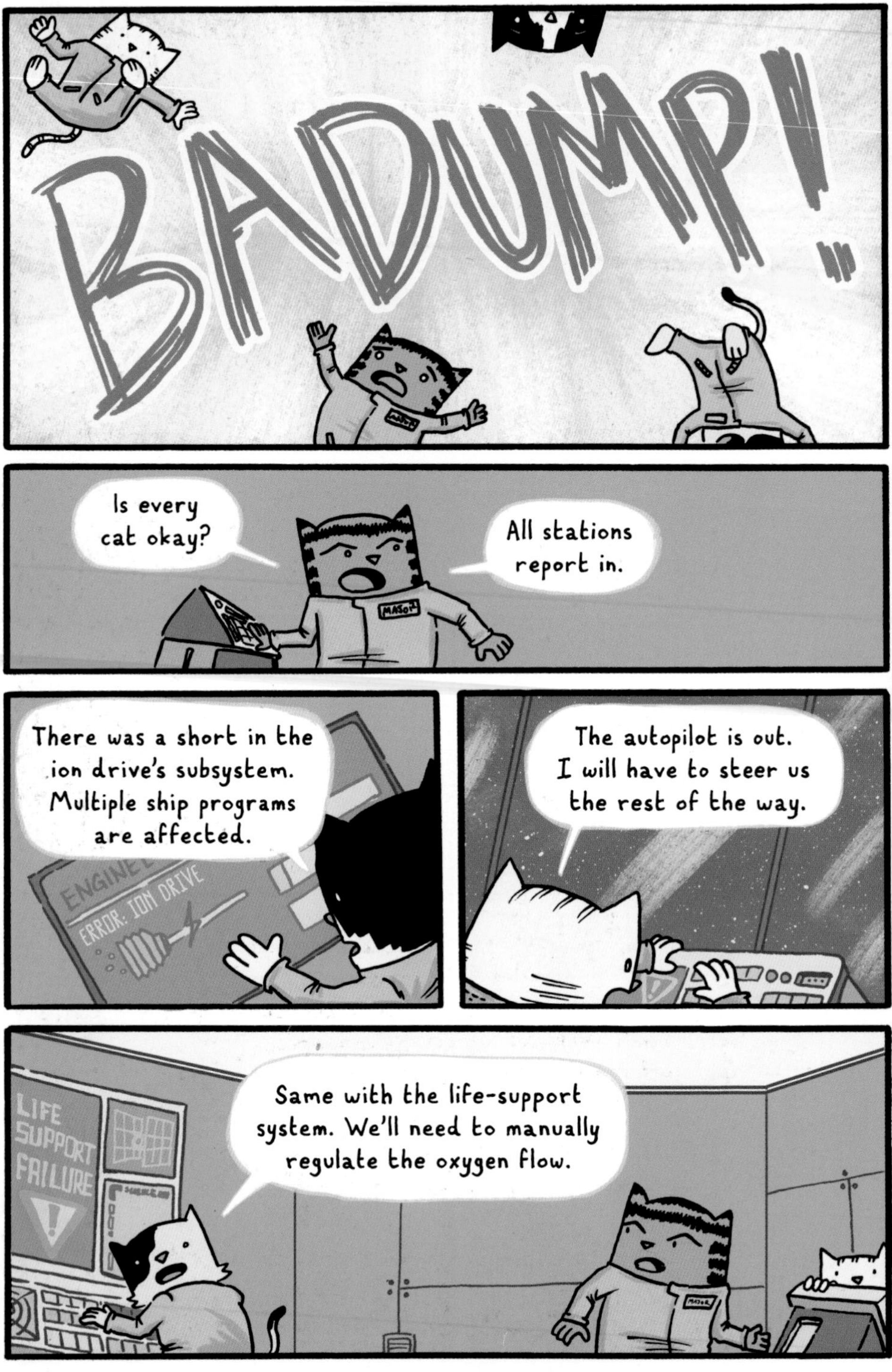
BADUMP!
Is every cat okay?
All stations report in.
There was a short in the ion drive's subsystem. Multiple ship programs are affected.
ENGINE
ERROR: ION DRIVE
The autopilot is out. I will have to steer us the rest of the way.
LIFE SUPPORT FAILURE
Same with the life-support system. We'll need to manually regulate the oxygen flow.

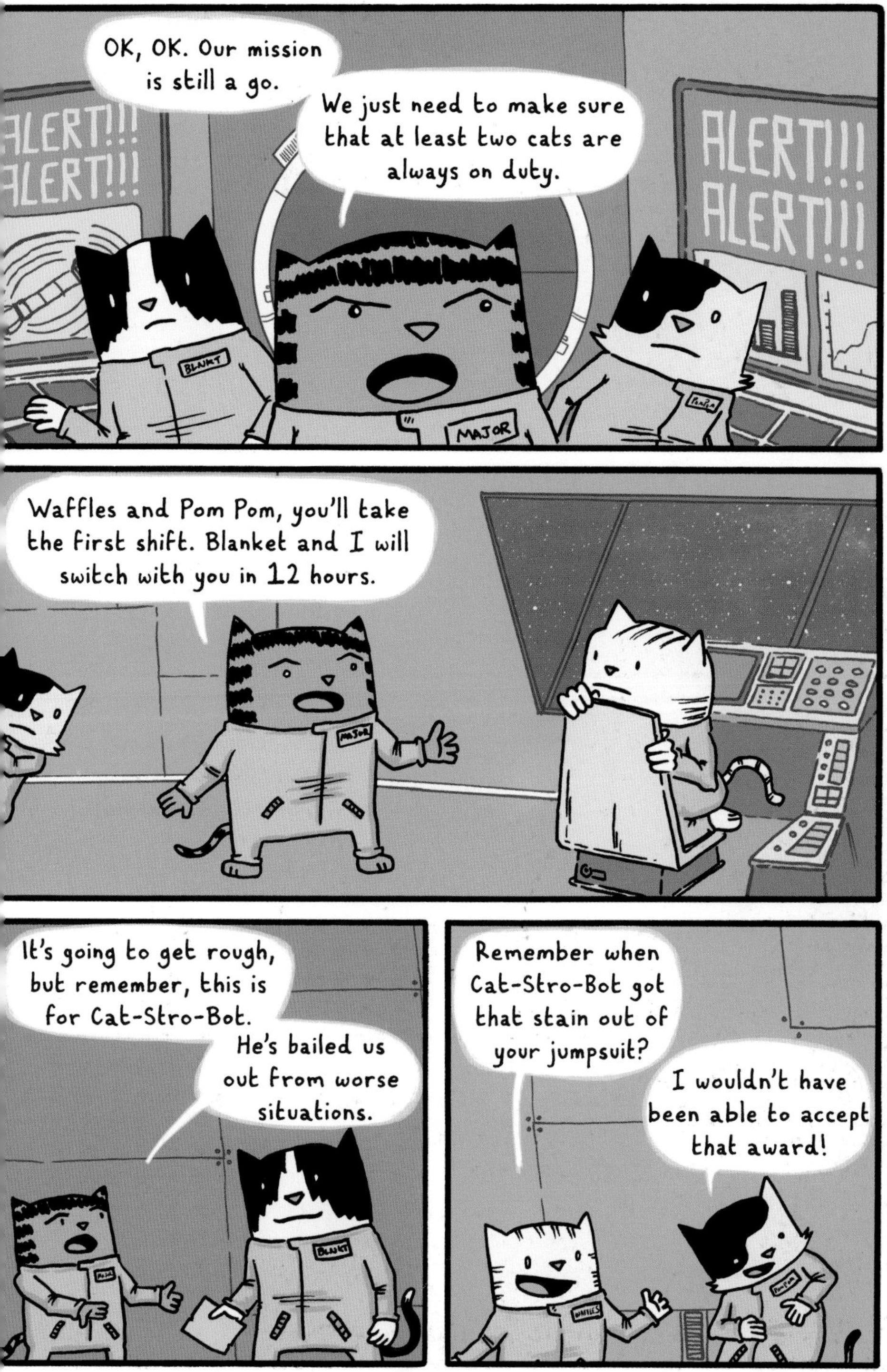
OK, OK. Our mission is still a go.
We just need to make sure that at least two cats are always on duty.
ALERT!!! ALERT!!!
ALERT!!! ALERT!!!
BLNKT
MAJOR
Waffles and Pom Pom, you'll take the first shift. Blanket and I will switch with you in 12 hours.
MAJOR
It's going to get rough, but remember, this is for Cat-Stro-Bot.
He's bailed us out from worse situations.
BLNKT
Remember when Cat-Stro-Bot got that stain out of your jumpsuit?
I wouldn't have been able to accept that award!
WAFFLES

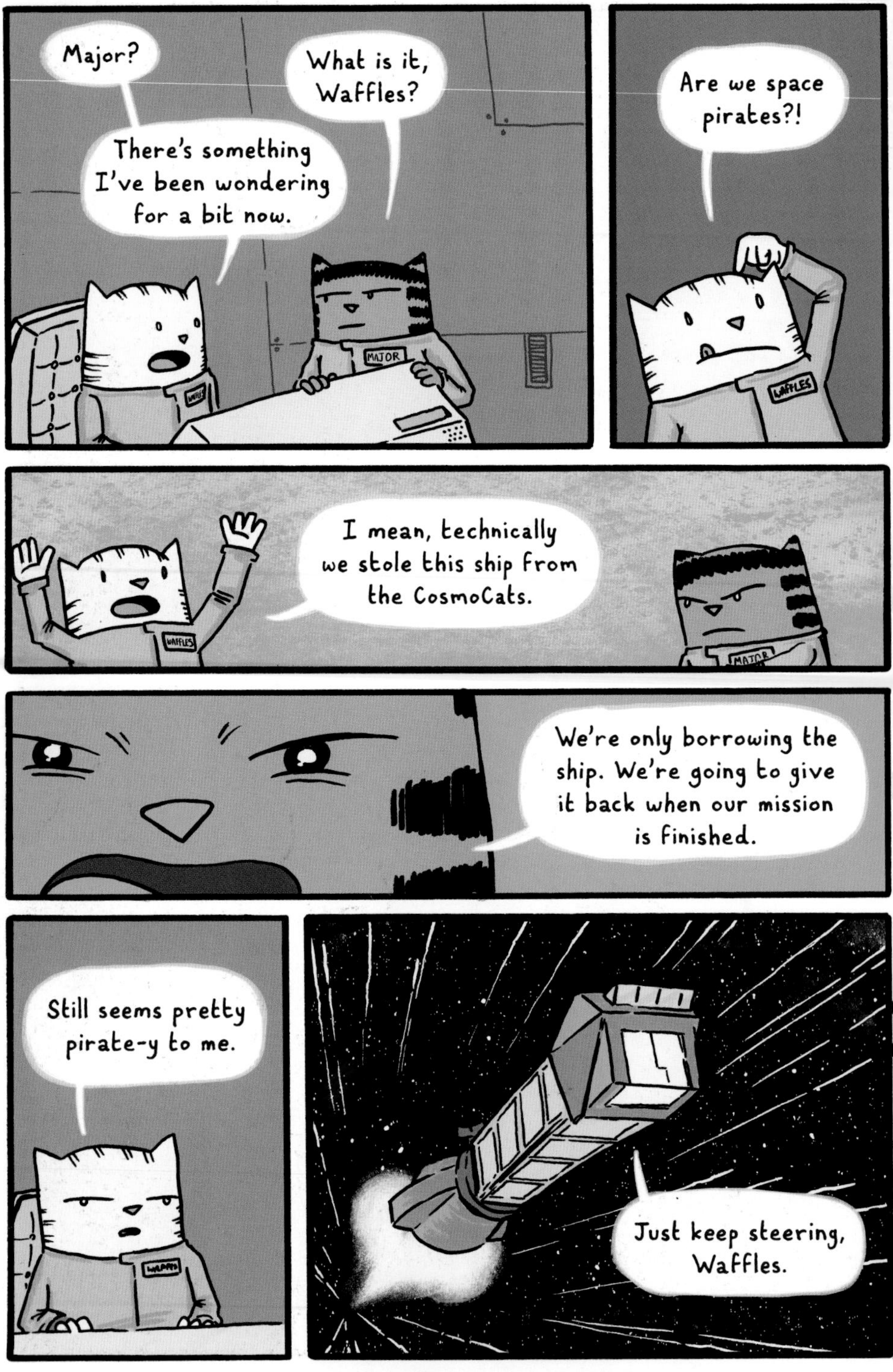
Major?
What is it, Waffles?
There's something I've been wondering for a bit now.
MAJOR
WAFFLES
Are we space pirates?!
WAFFLES
I mean, technically we stole this ship from the CosmoCats.
WAFFLES
We're only borrowing the ship. We're going to give it back when our mission is finished.
Still seems pretty pirate-y to me.
Just keep steering, Waffles.

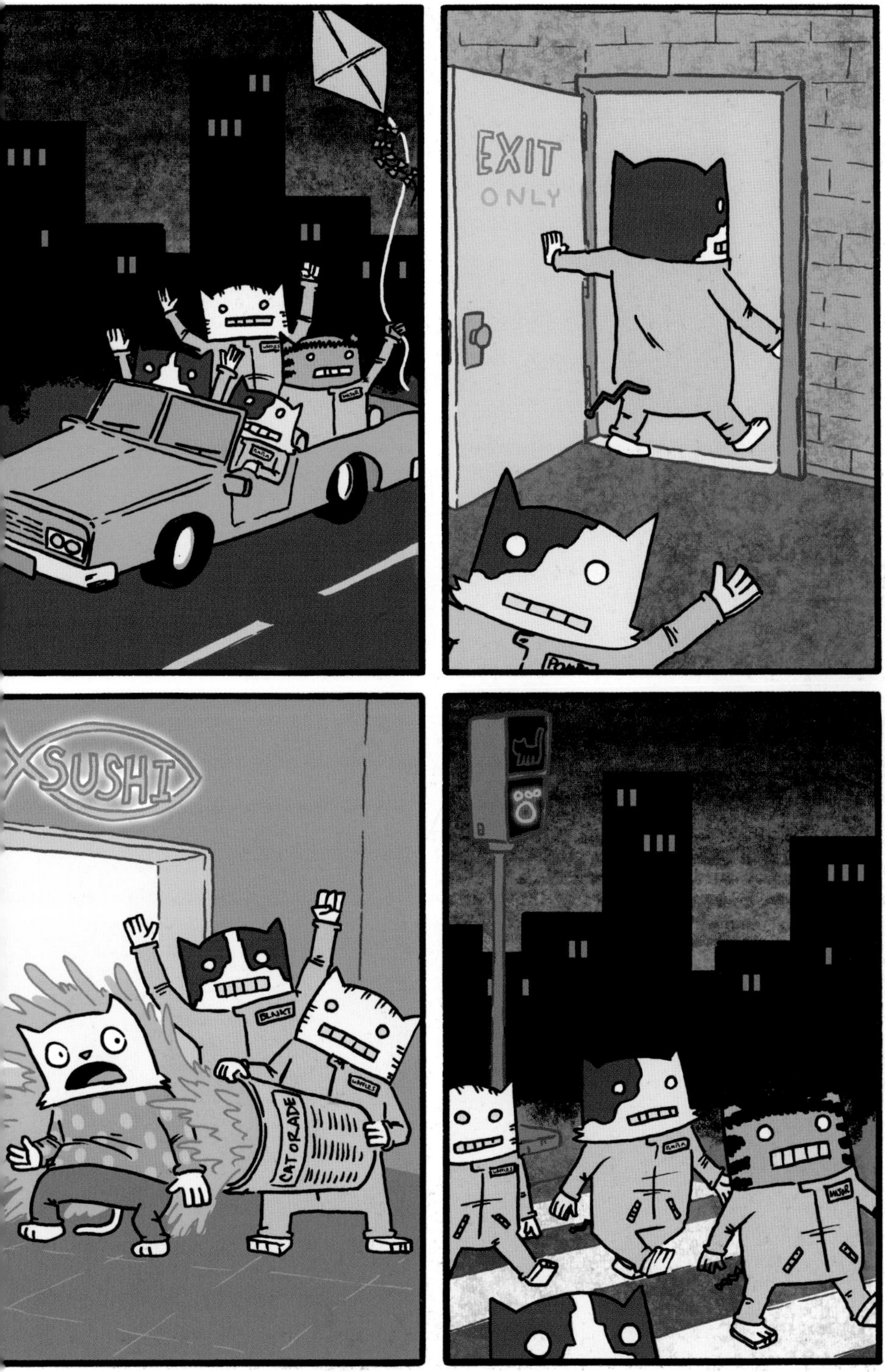
EXIT
ONLY
SUSHI
CATORADE

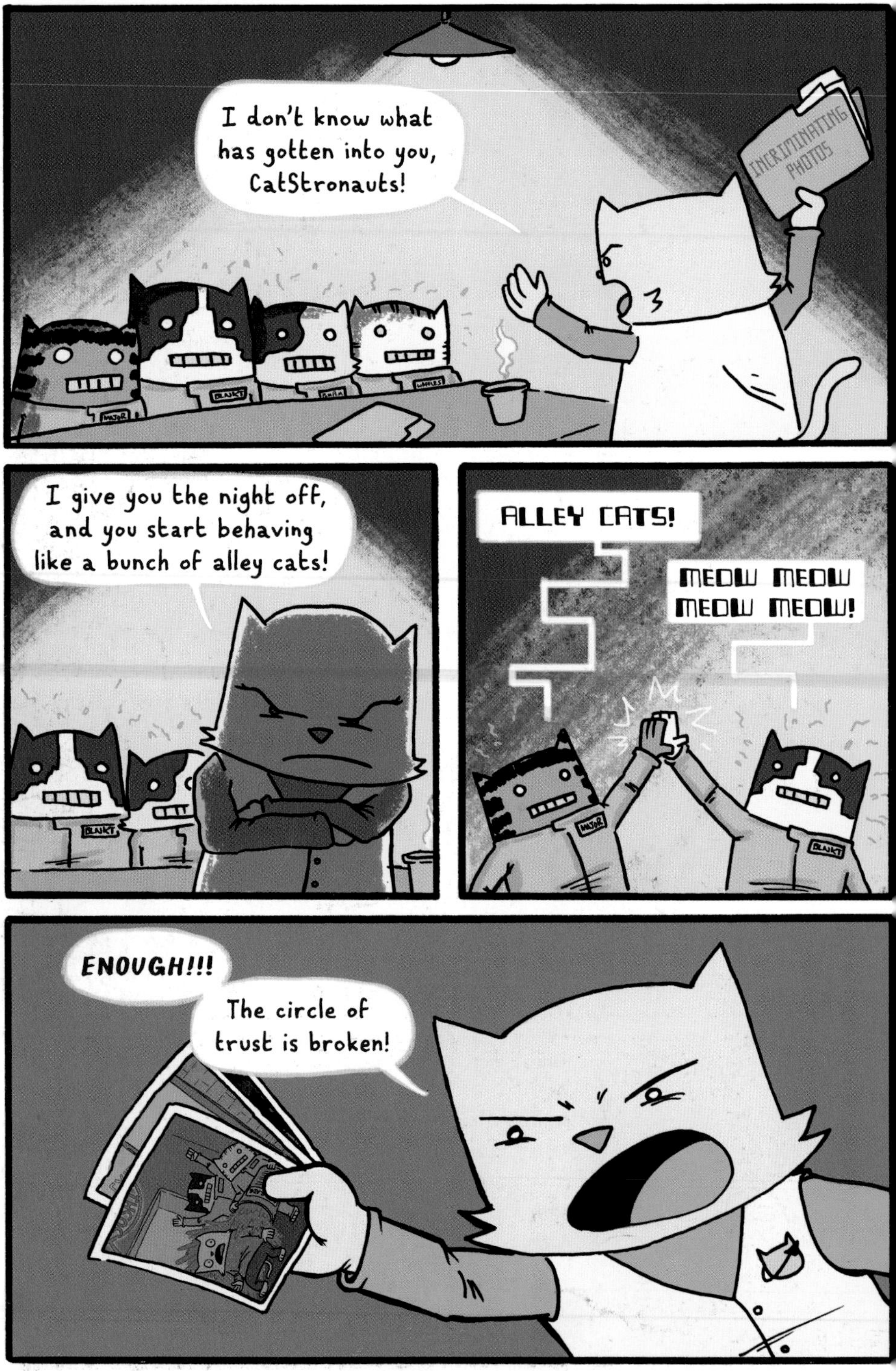
I don't know what has gotten into you, CatStronauts!
INCRIMINATING PHOTOS
I give you the night off, and you start behaving like a bunch of alley cats!
ALLEY CATS!
MEOW MEOW MEOW MEOW!
ENOUGH!!!
The circle of trust is broken!

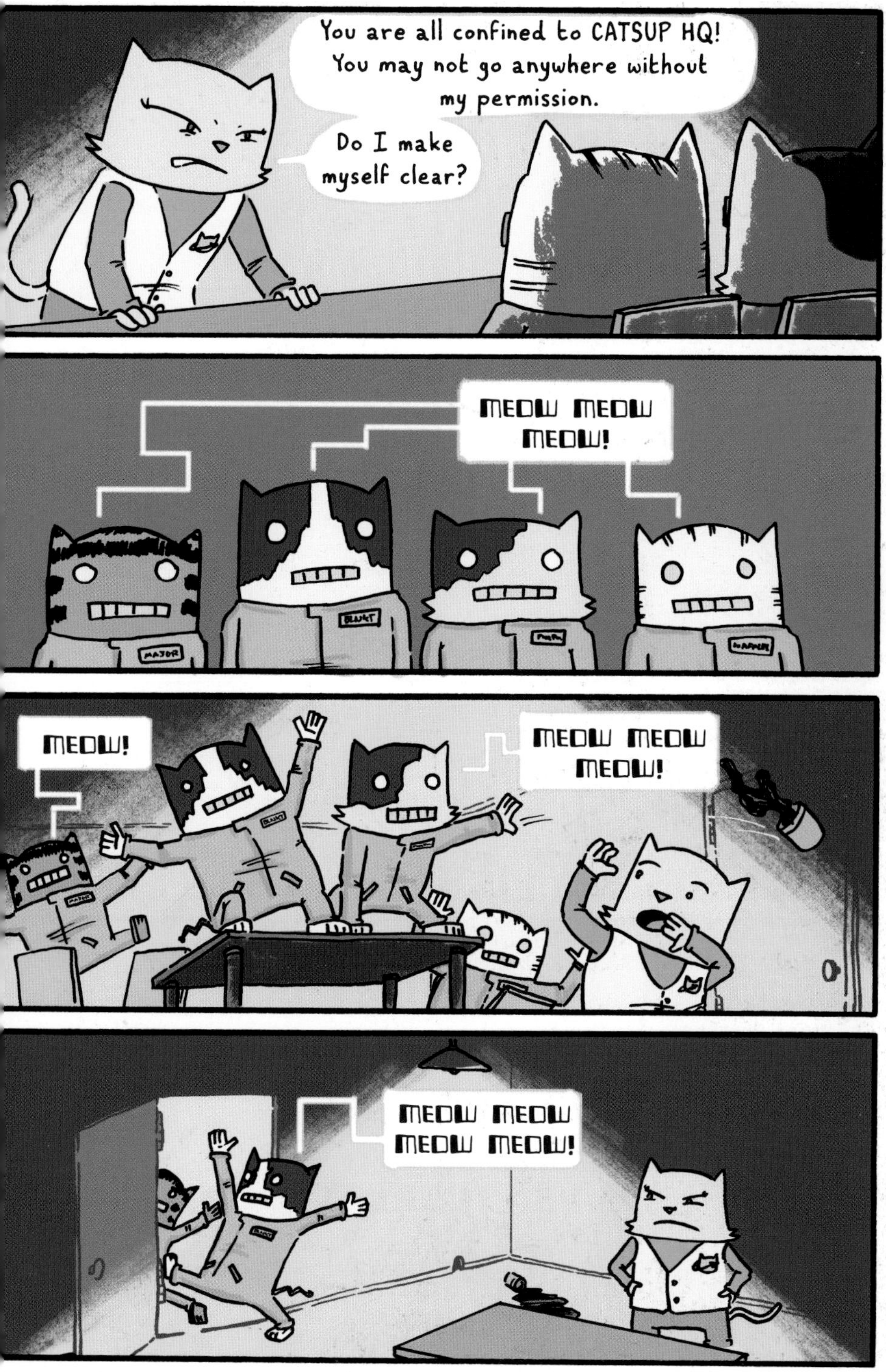
You are all confined to CATSUP HQ! You may not go anywhere without my permission.
Do I make myself clear?
MEOW MEOW MEOW!
MEOW!
MEOW MEOW MEOW!
MEOW MEOW MEOW MEOW!

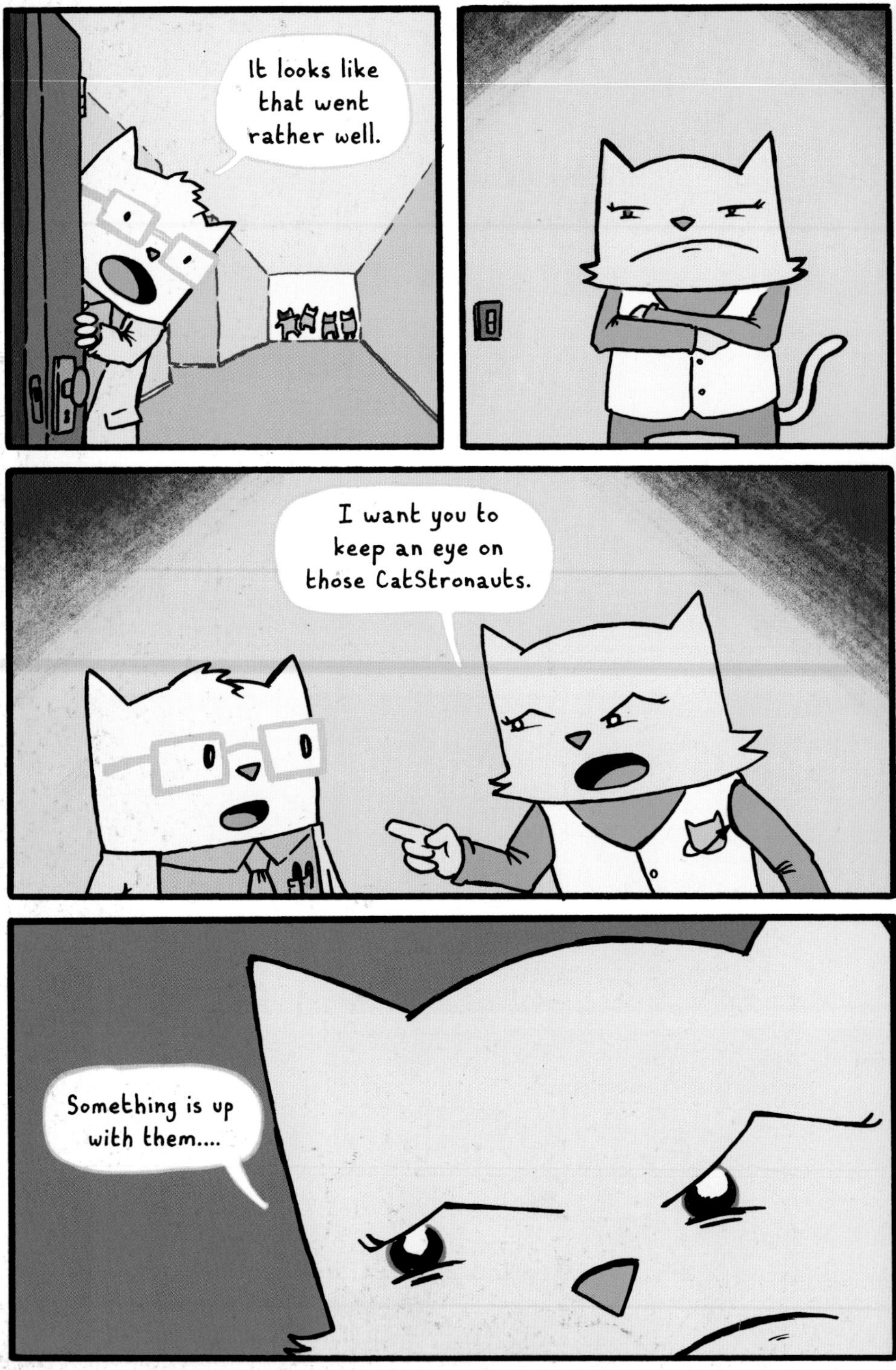
It looks like that went rather well.
I want you to keep an eye on those CatStronauts.
Something is up with them....

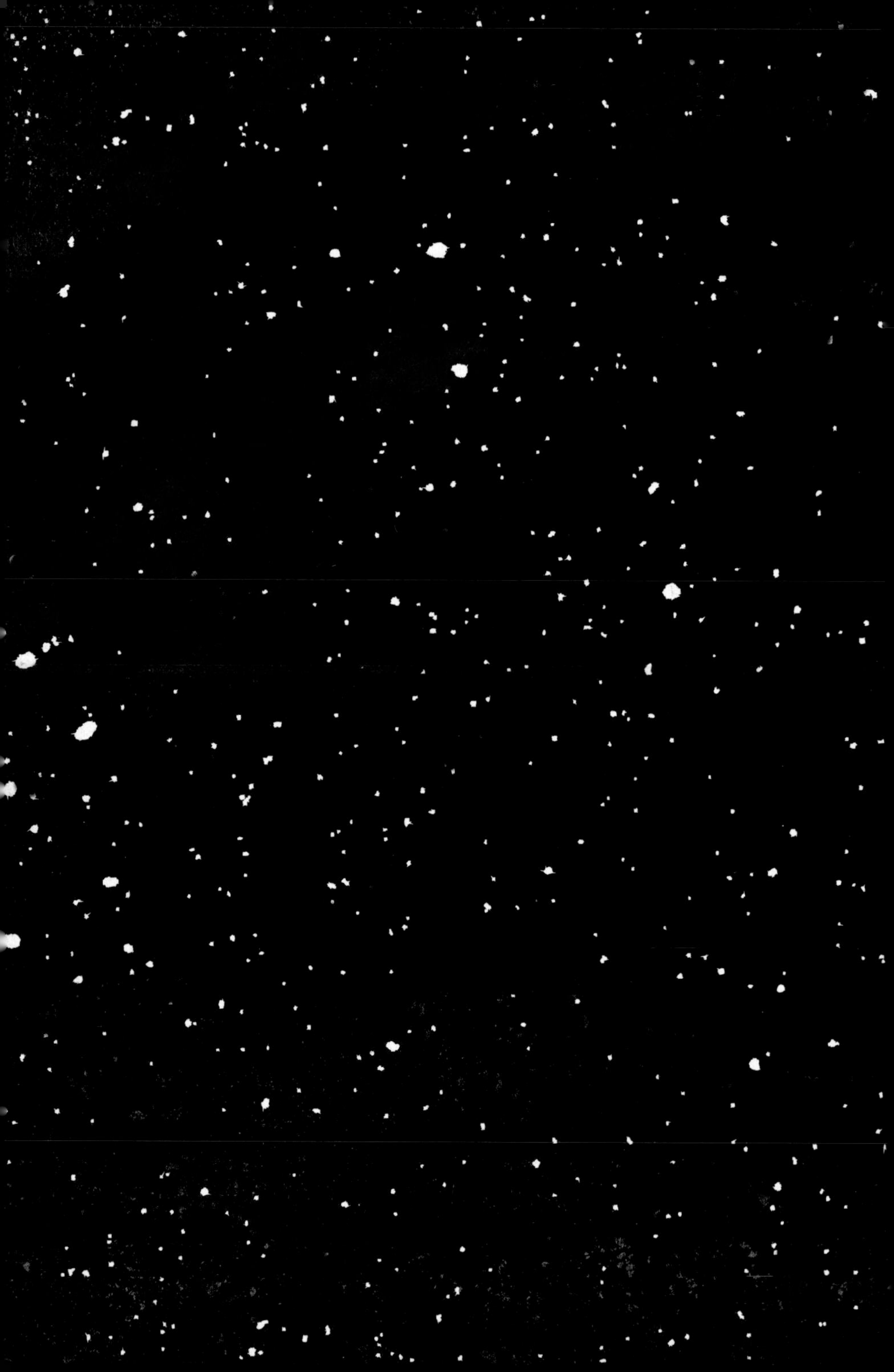

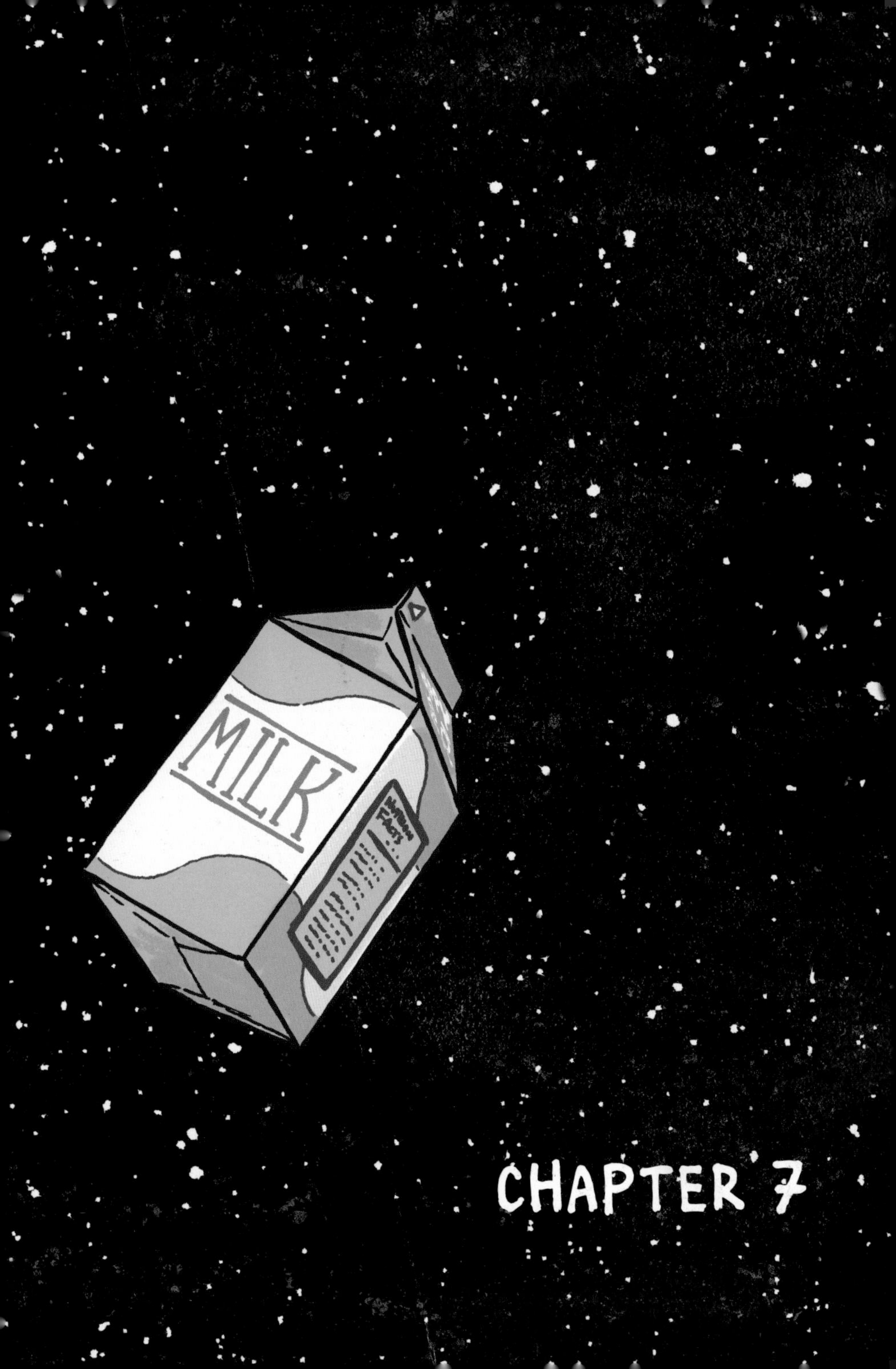
MILK

CHAPTER 7

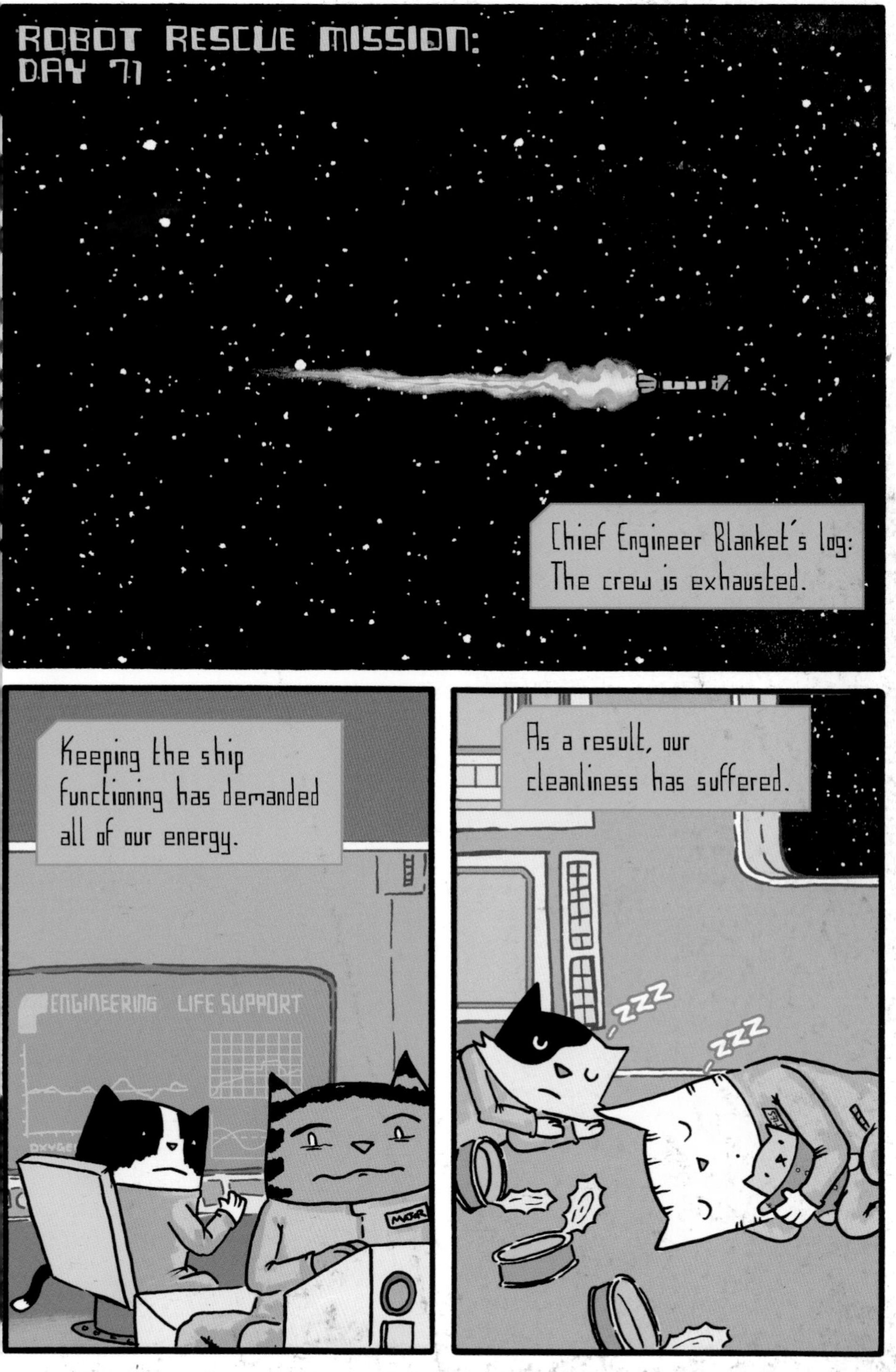
ROBOT RESCUE MISSION:
DAY 71
Chief Engineer Blanket's log:
The crew is exhausted.
Keeping the ship functioning has demanded all of our energy.
ENGINEERING LIFE SUPPORT
As a result, our cleanliness has suffered.
ZZZ
ZZZ

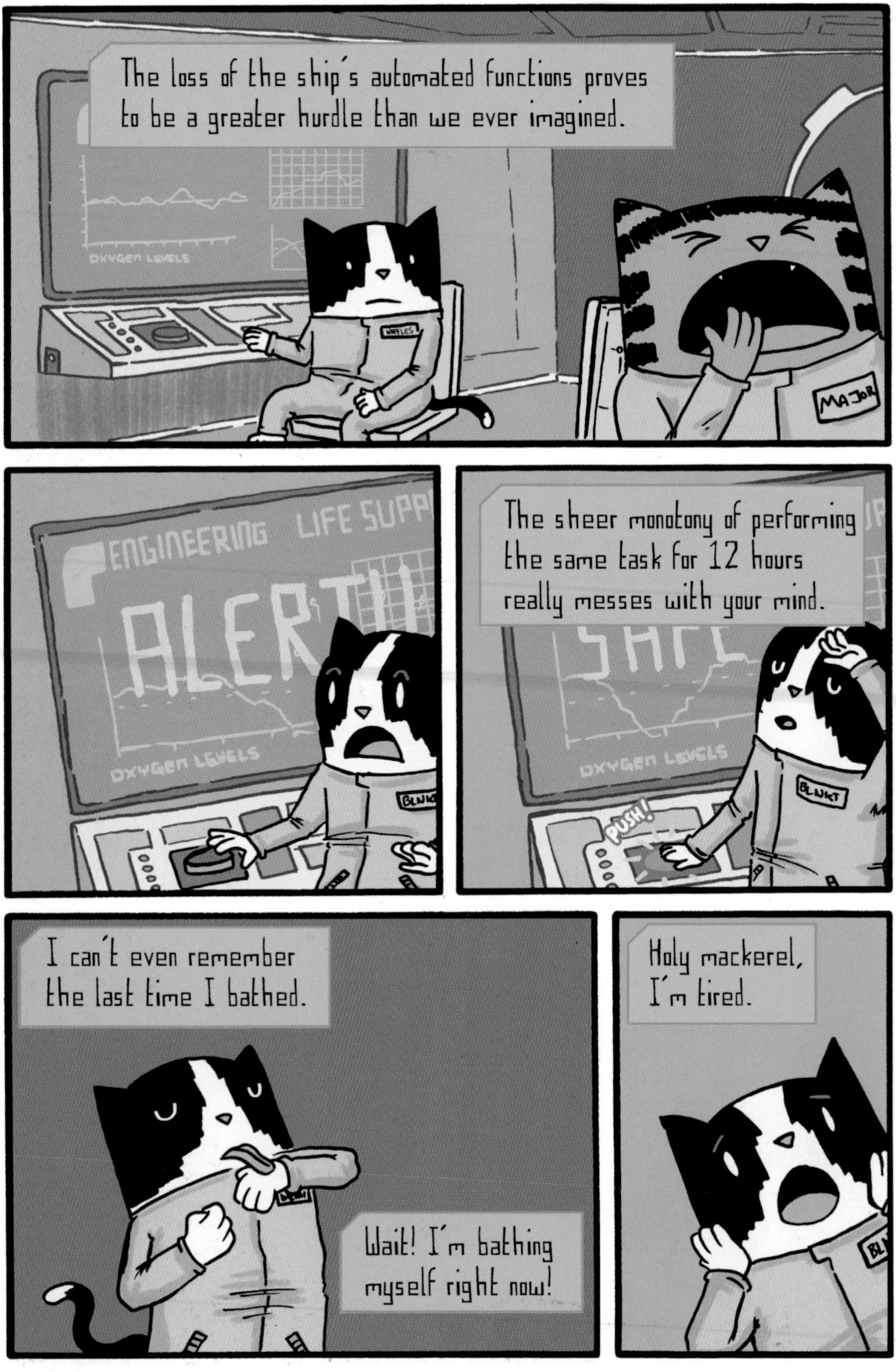
The loss of the ship's automated functions proves to be a greater hurdle than we ever imagined.
OXYGEN LEVELS
WAFFLES
MAJOR
ENGINEERING
LIFE SUPP
ALERT!!
OXYGEN LEVELS
BLNKT
The sheer monotony of performing the same task for 12 hours really messes with your mind.
OXYGEN LEVELS
PUSH!
BLNKT
I can't even remember the last time I bathed.
Wait! I'm bathing myself right now!
Holy mackerel, I'm tired.

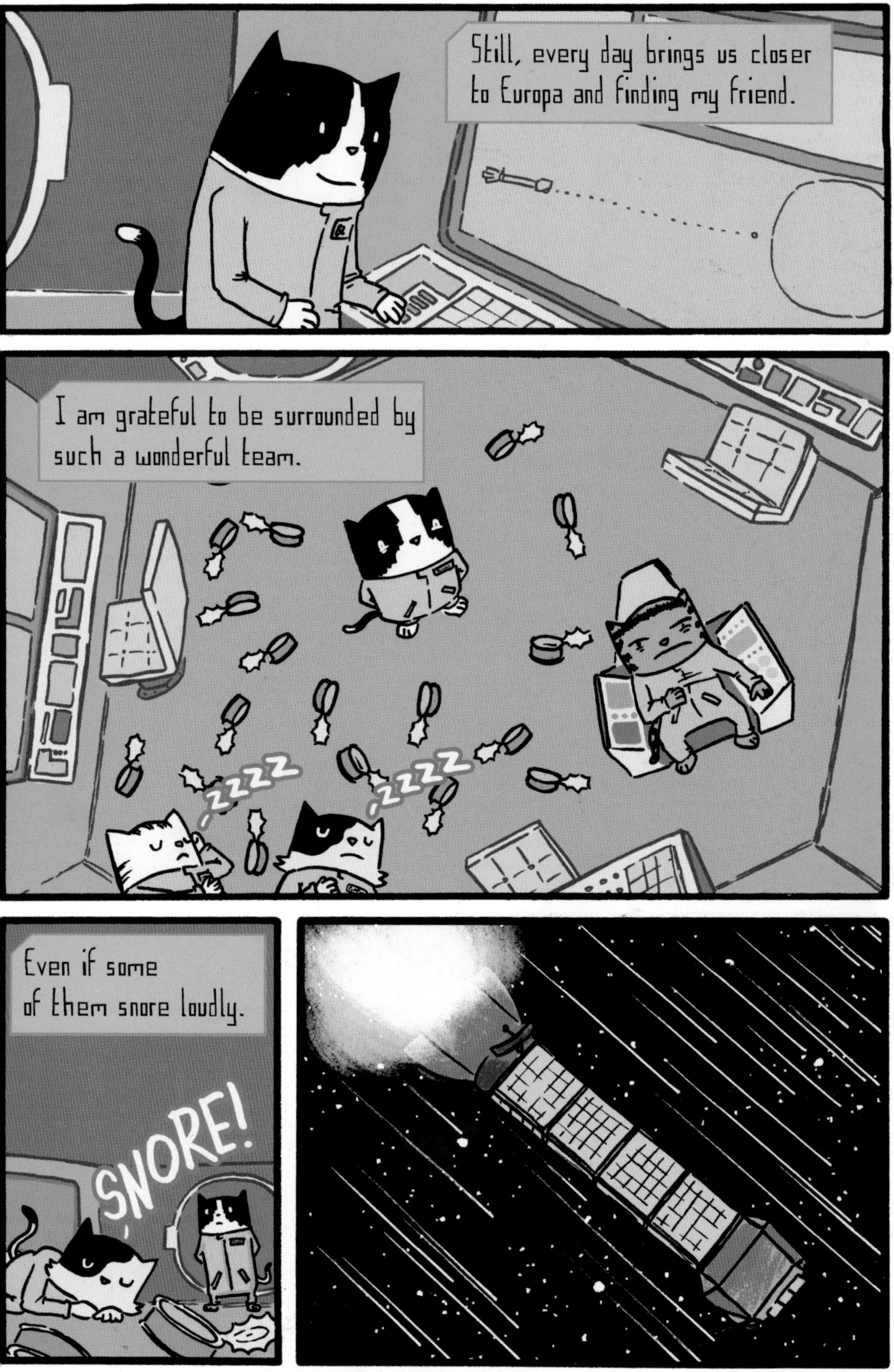

Still, every day brings us closer to Europa and finding my friend.
I am grateful to be surrounded by such a wonderful team.
ZZZZ
ZZZZ
Even if some of them snore loudly.
SNORE!

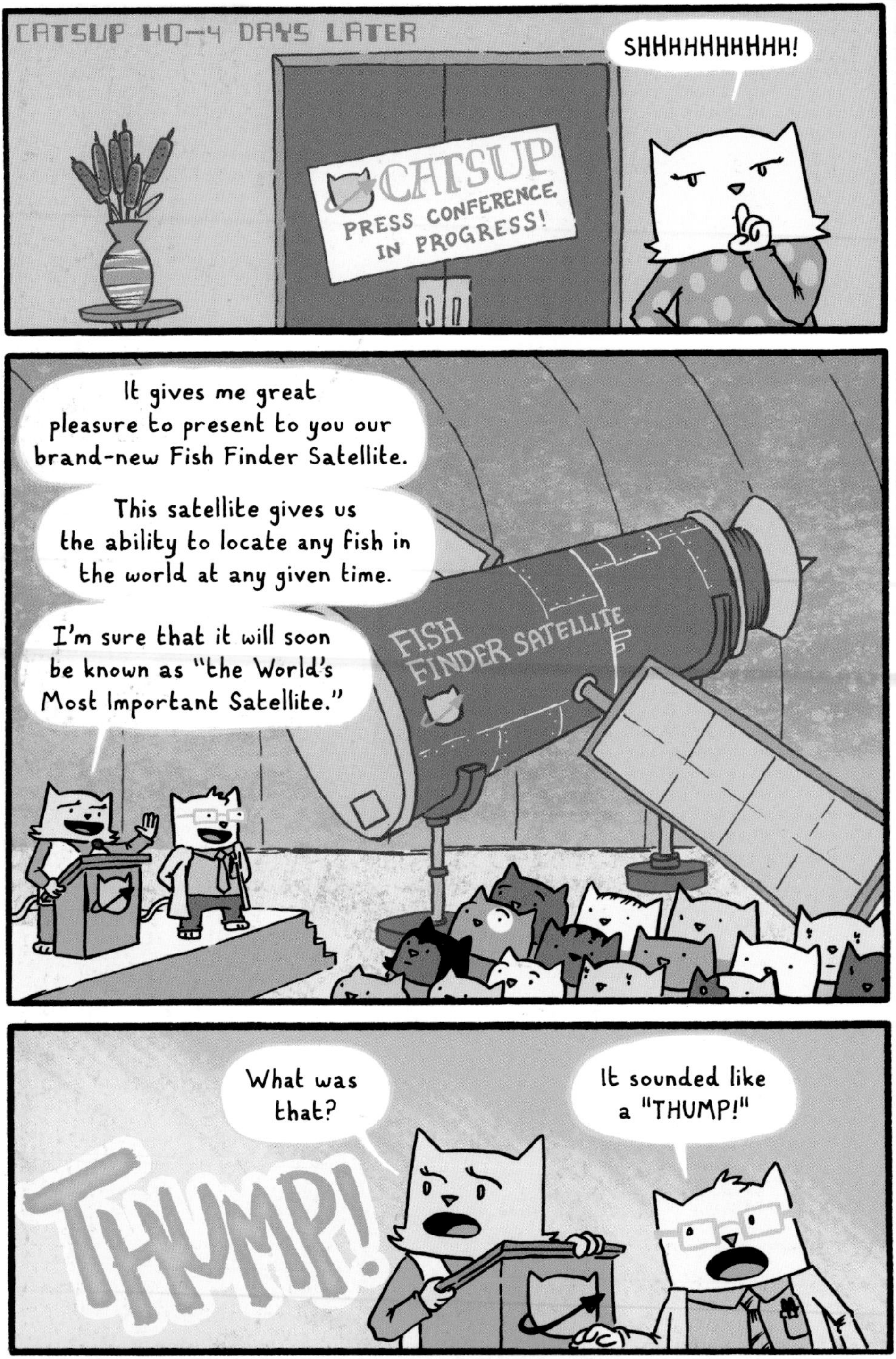
CATSUP HQ—4 DAYS LATER
SHHHHHHHHHH!
CATSUP
PRESS CONFERENCE IN PROGRESS!
It gives me great pleasure to present to you our brand-new Fish Finder Satellite.
This satellite gives us the ability to locate any fish in the world at any given time.
I'm sure that it will soon be known as "the World's Most Important Satellite."
FISH FINDER SATELLITE
THUMP!
What was that?
It sounded like a "THUMP!"

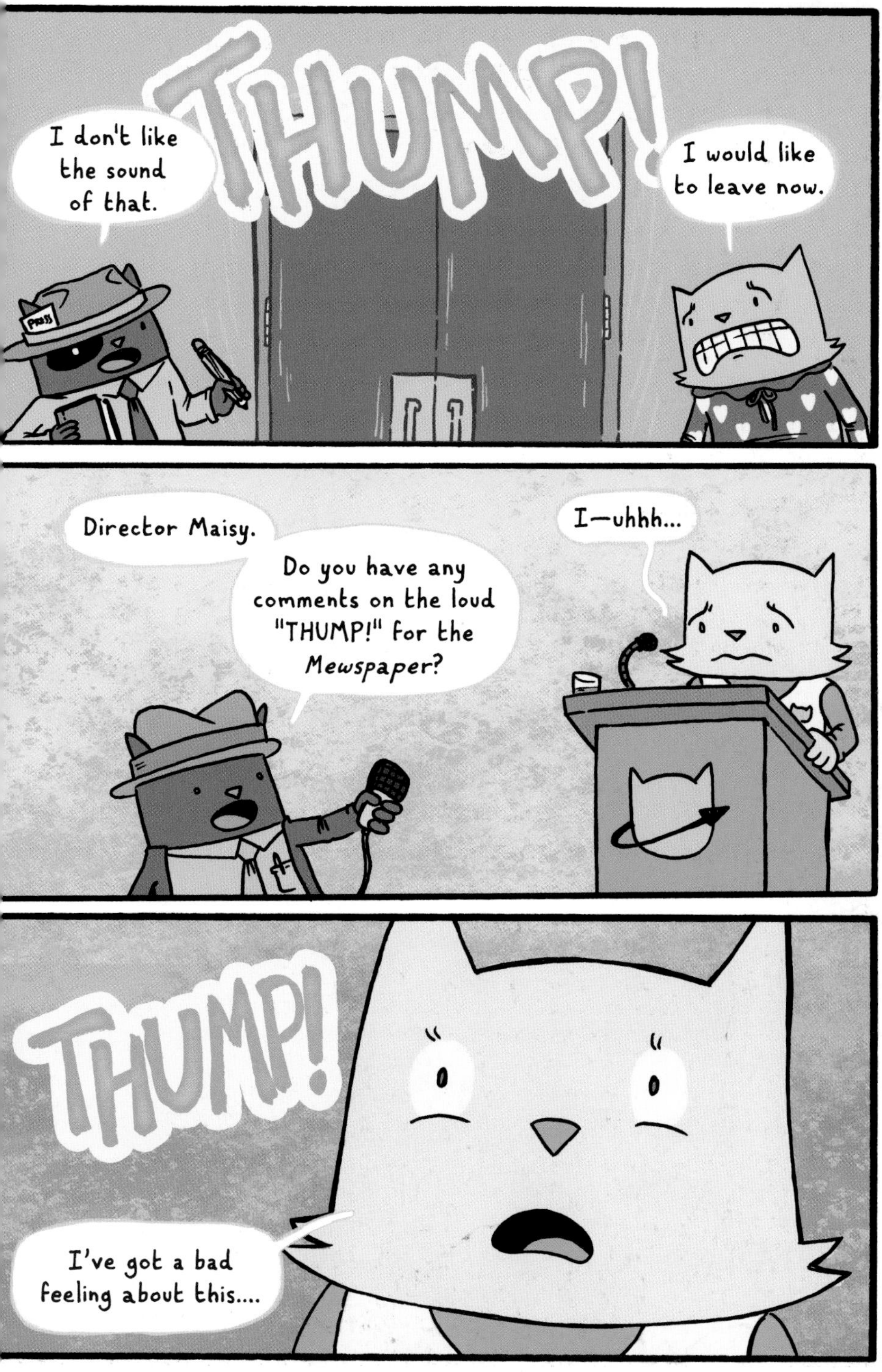
THUMP!
I don't like the sound of that.
I would like to leave now.
PRESS
Director Maisy.
Do you have any comments on the loud "THUMP!" for the *Mewspaper*?
I—uhhh...
THUMP!
I've got a bad feeling about this....

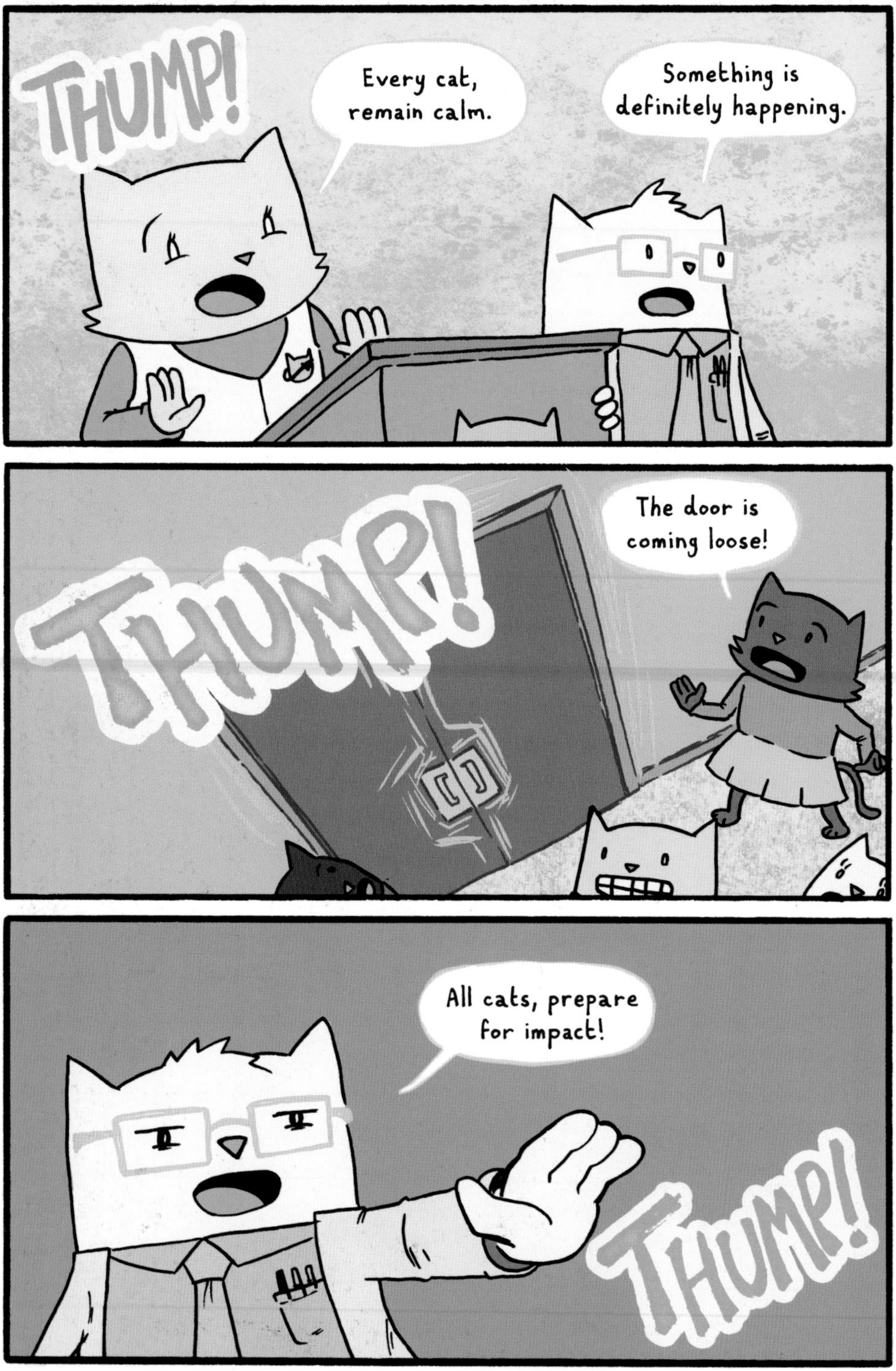
THUMP!
Every cat, remain calm.
Something is definitely happening.
THUMP!
The door is coming loose!
All cats, prepare for impact!
THUMP!

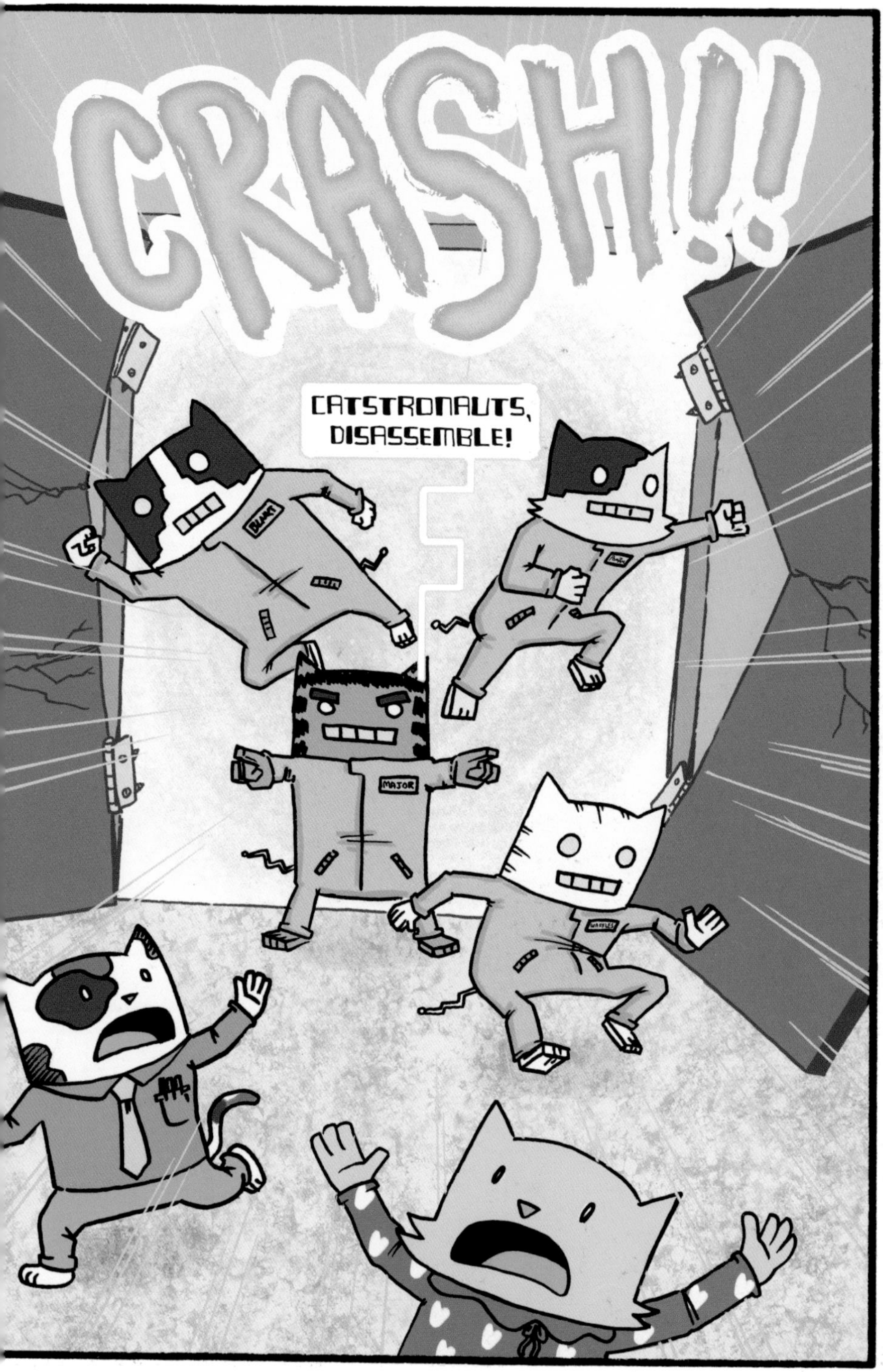
CRASH!!
CATSTRONAUTS, DISASSEMBLE!
MAJOR

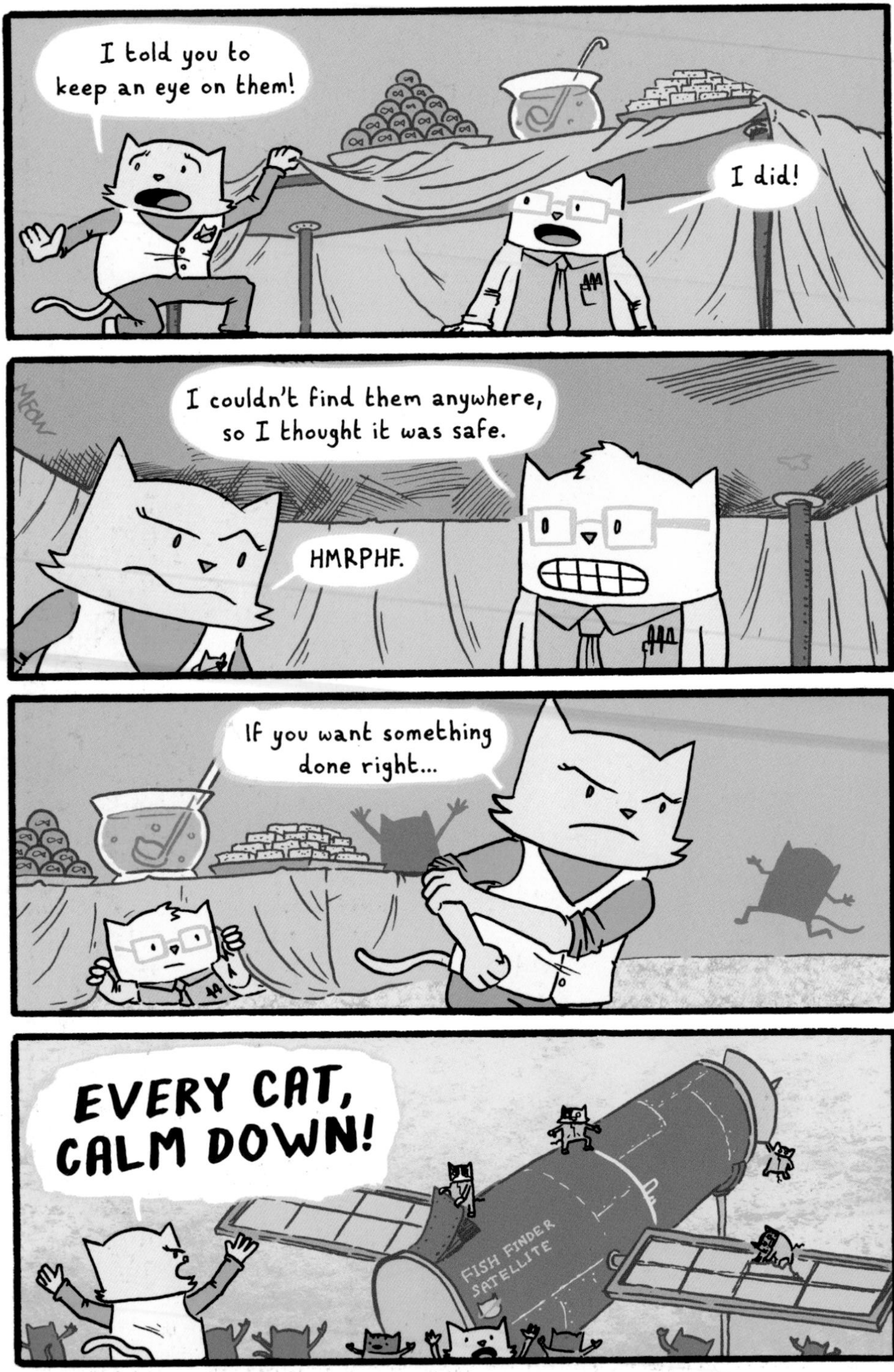
I told you to keep an eye on them!
I did!
I couldn't find them anywhere, so I thought it was safe.
HMRPHF.
If you want something done right...
EVERY CAT, CALM DOWN!
FISH FINDER SATELLITE

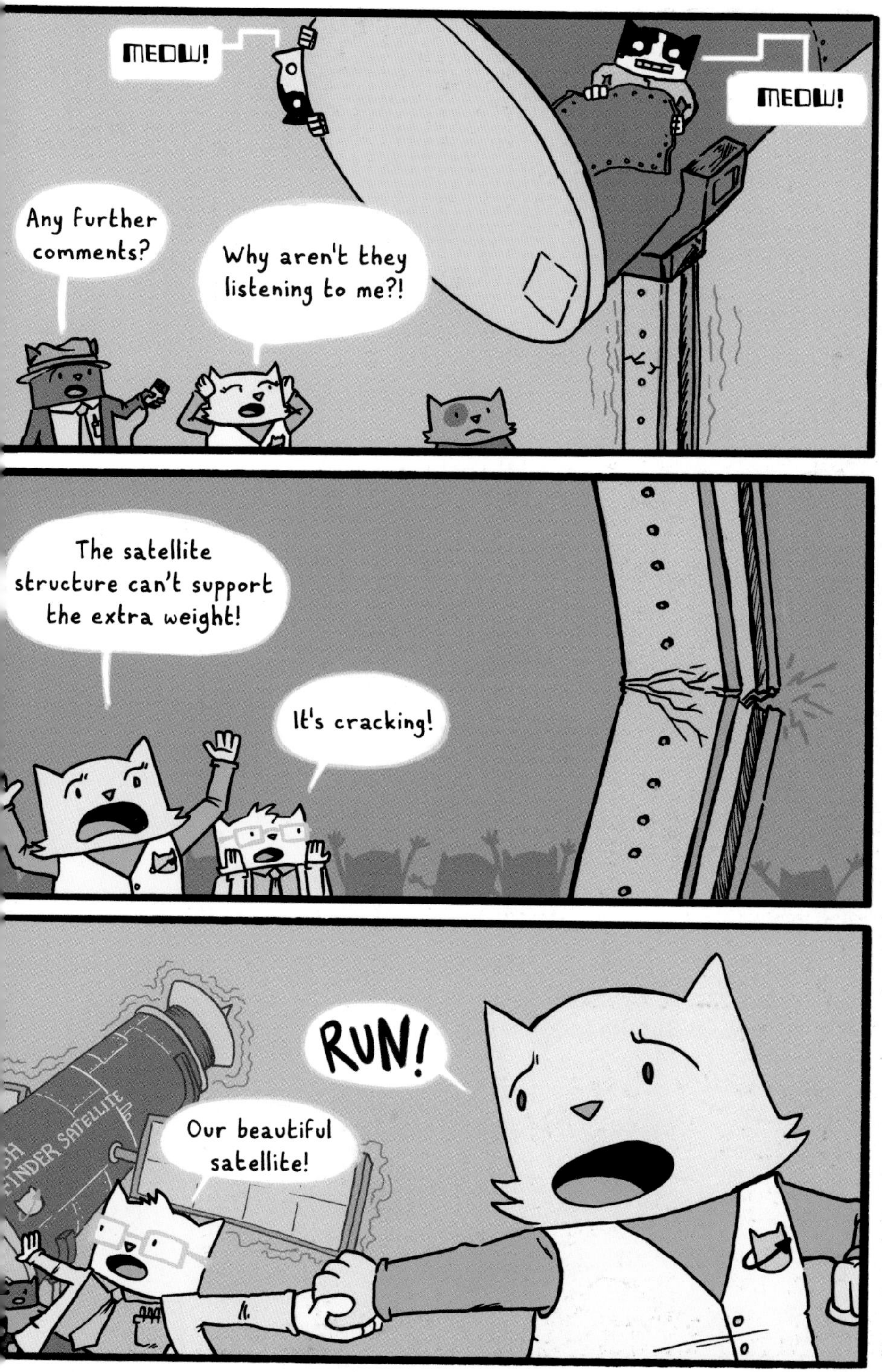
MEOW!
MEOW!
Any further comments?
Why aren't they listening to me?!
The satellite structure can't support the extra weight!
It's cracking!
RUN!
Our beautiful satellite!
FINDER SATELLITE

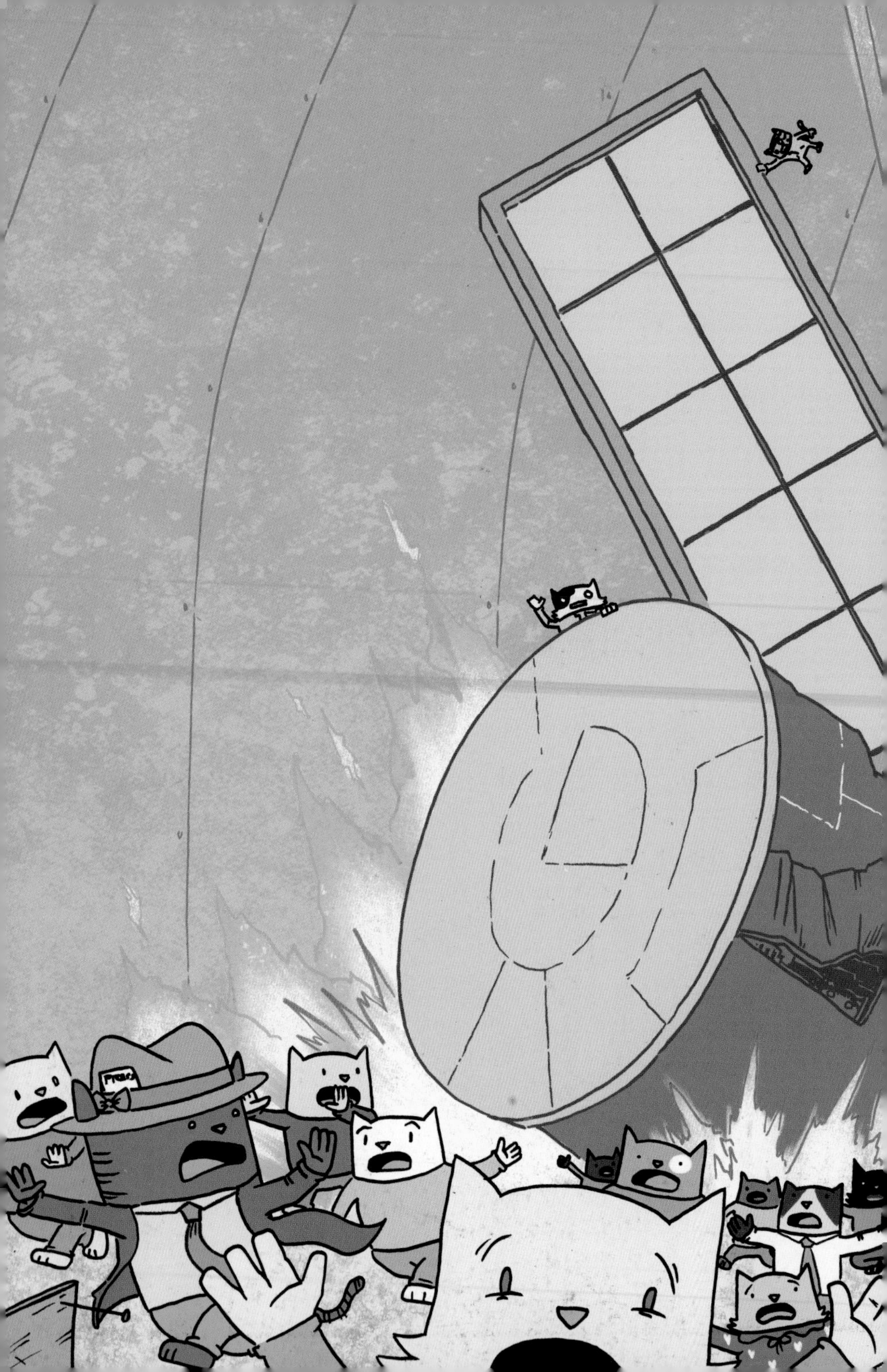

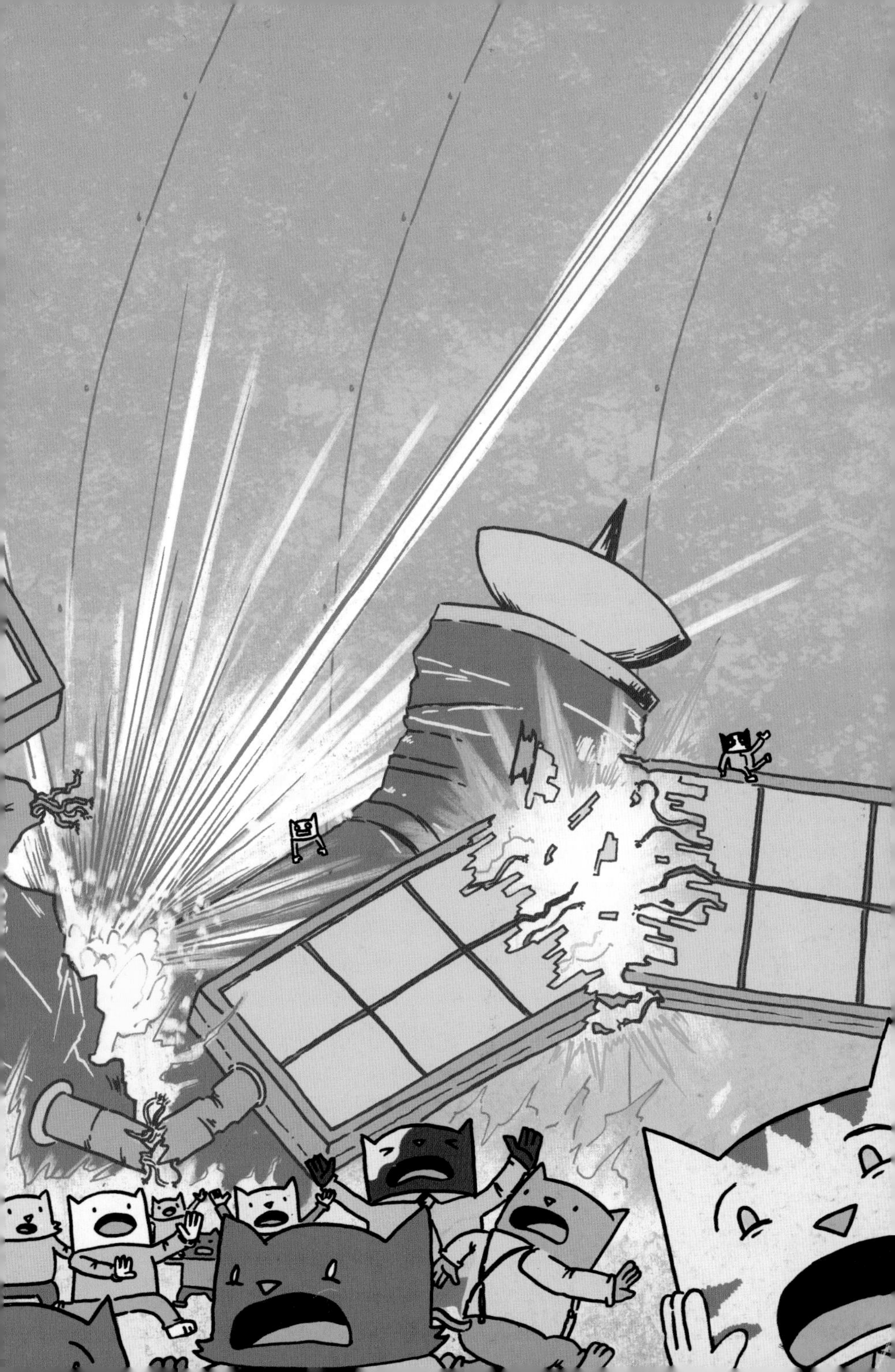

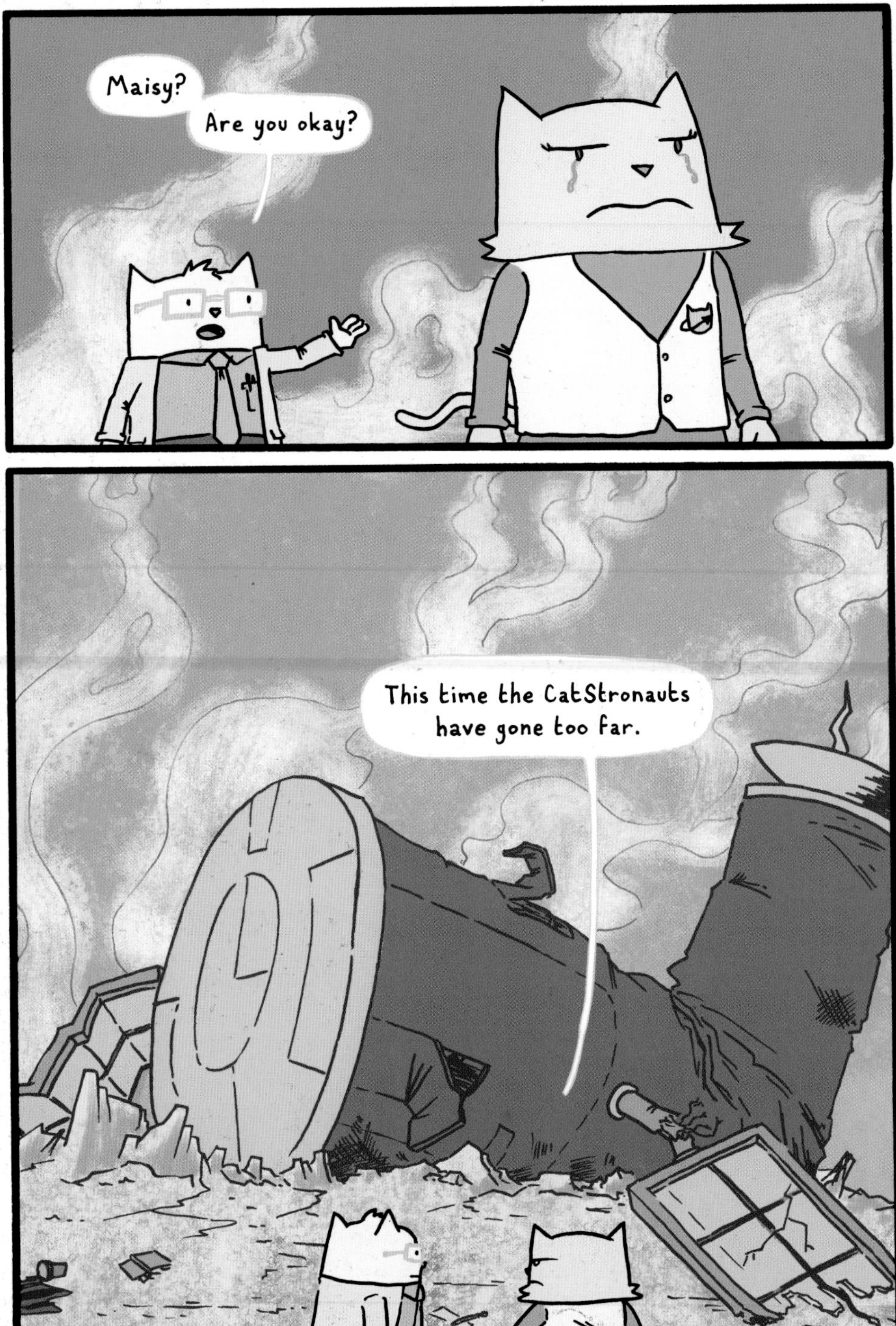
Maisy?
Are you okay?
This time the CatStronauts have gone too far.

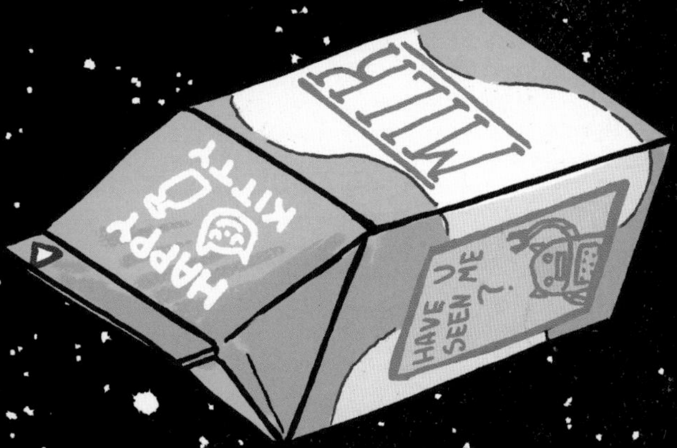
MILK
HAPPY KITTY
HAVE U SEEN ME ?

CHAPTER 8

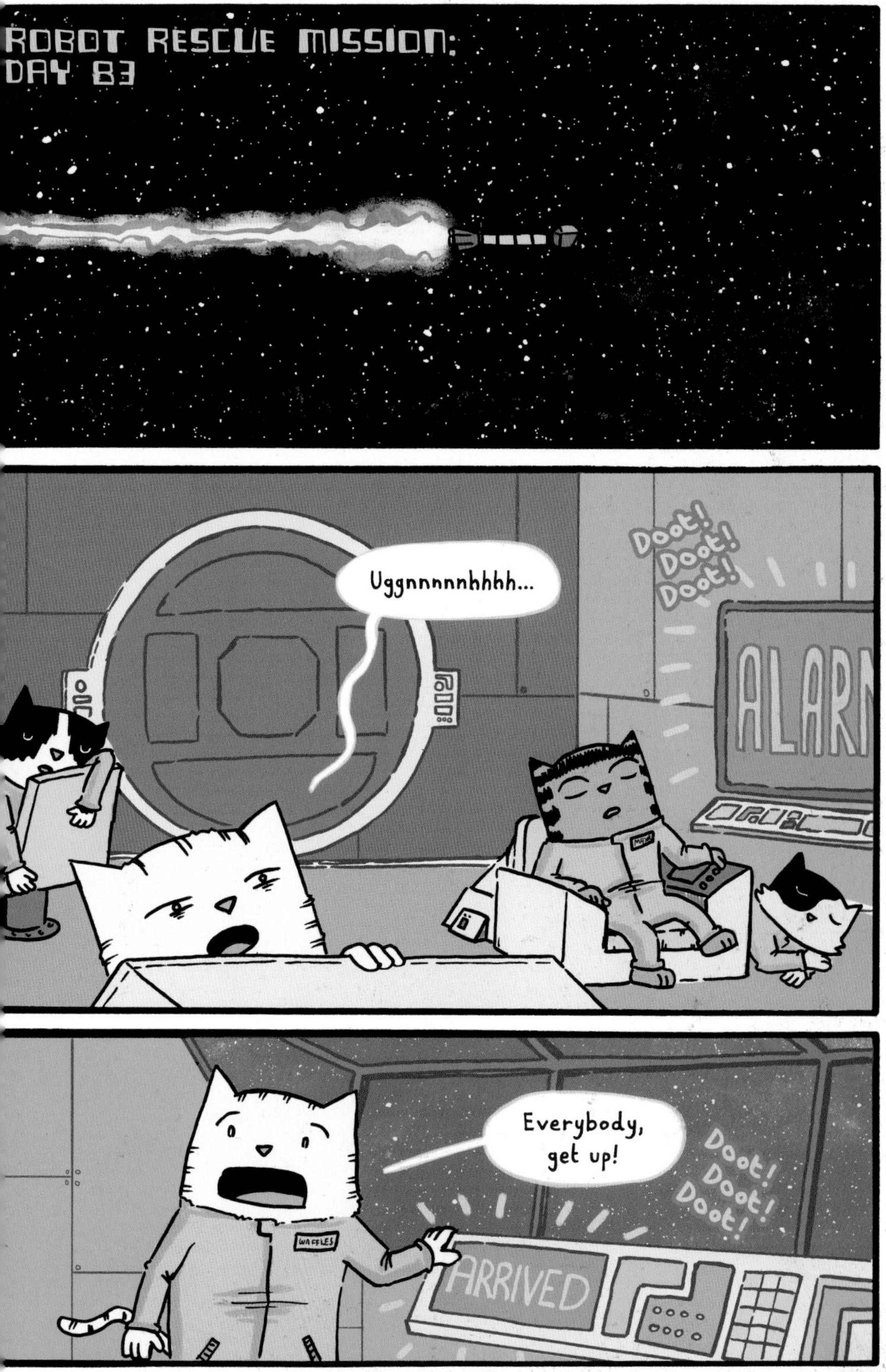
ROBOT RESCUE MISSION:
DAY 83
Uggnnnnnhhhh...
Doot! Doot! Doot!
ALARM
Everybody, get up!
Doot! Doot! Doot!
WAFFLES
ARRIVED

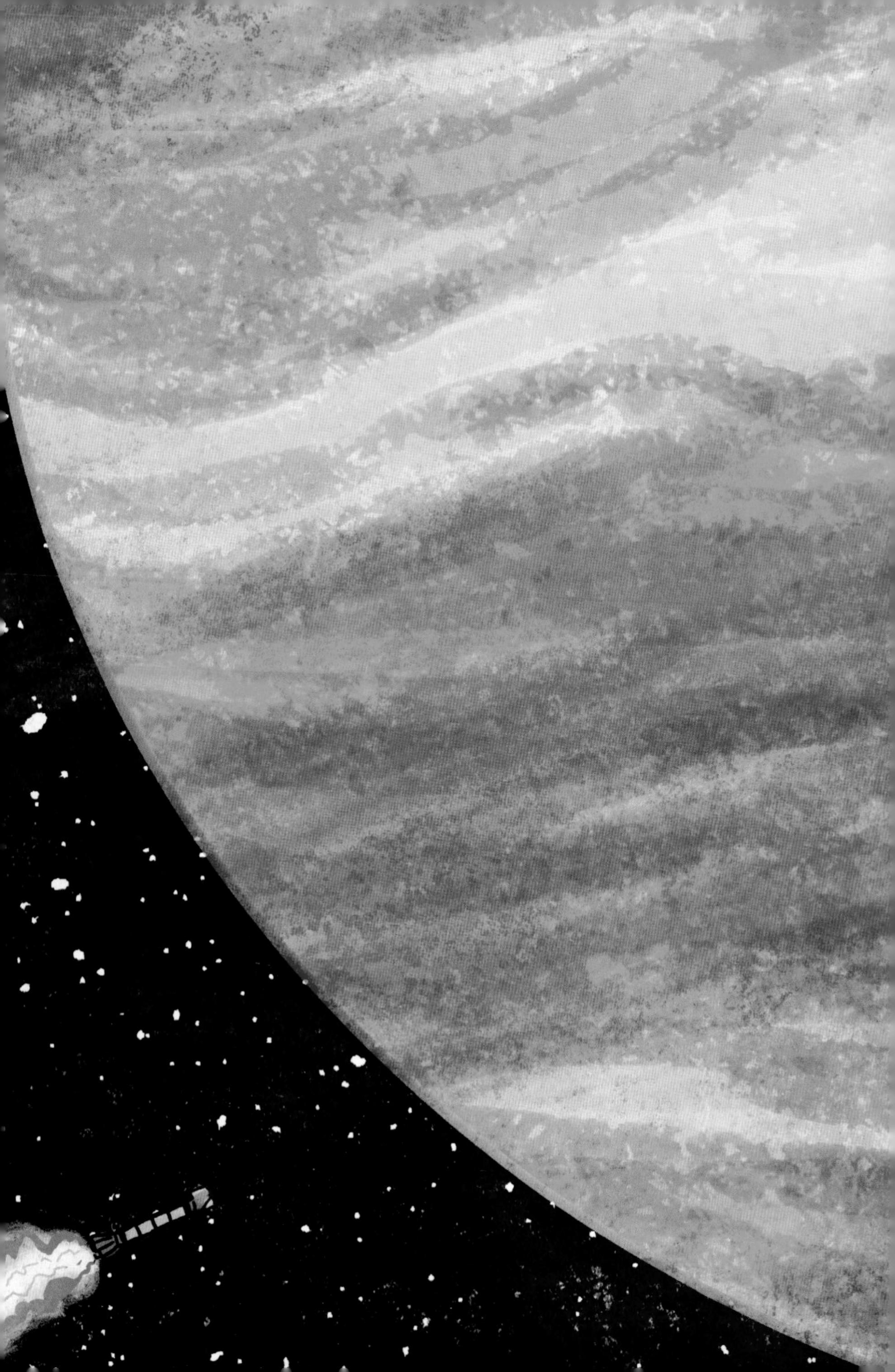

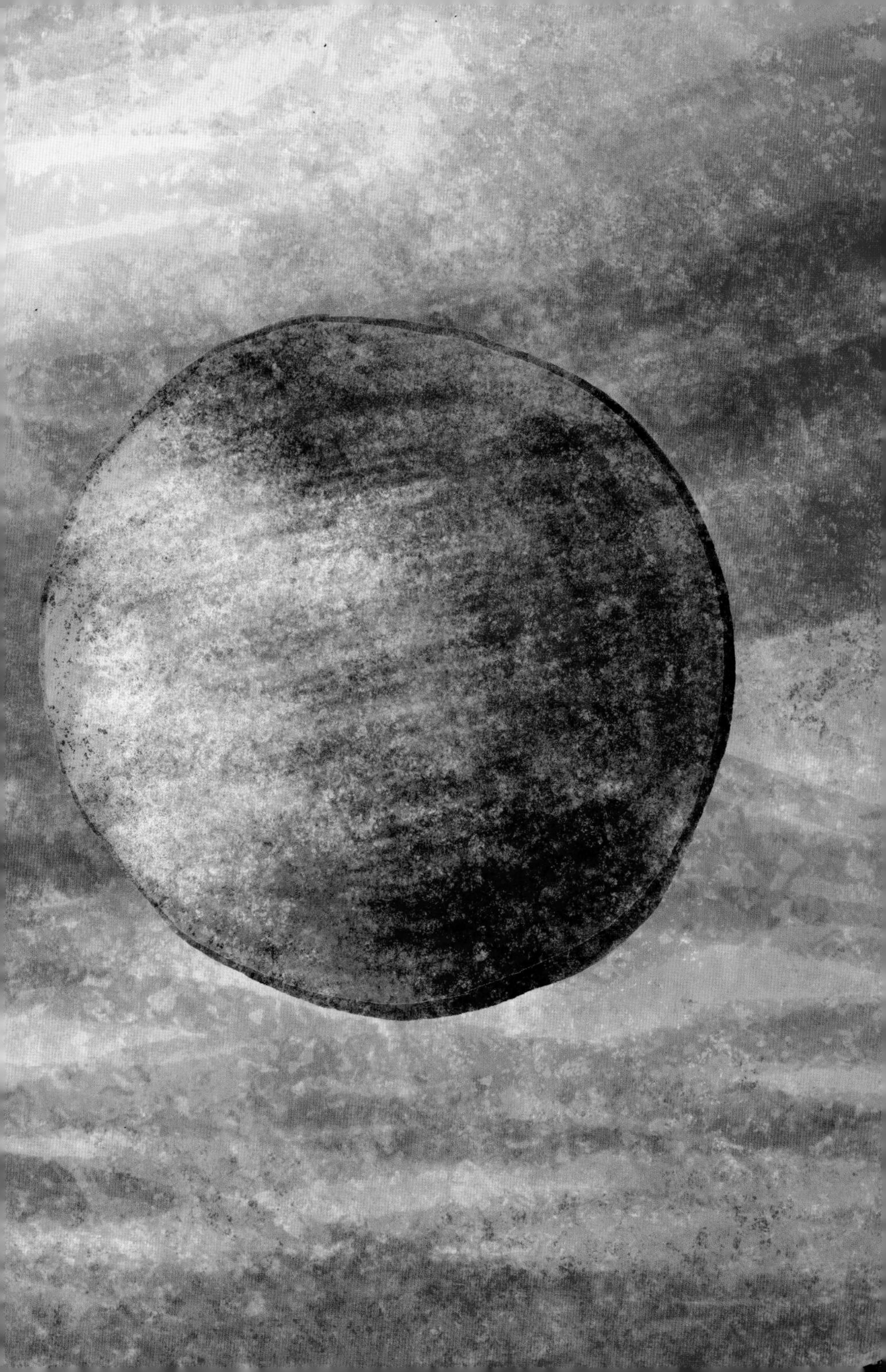

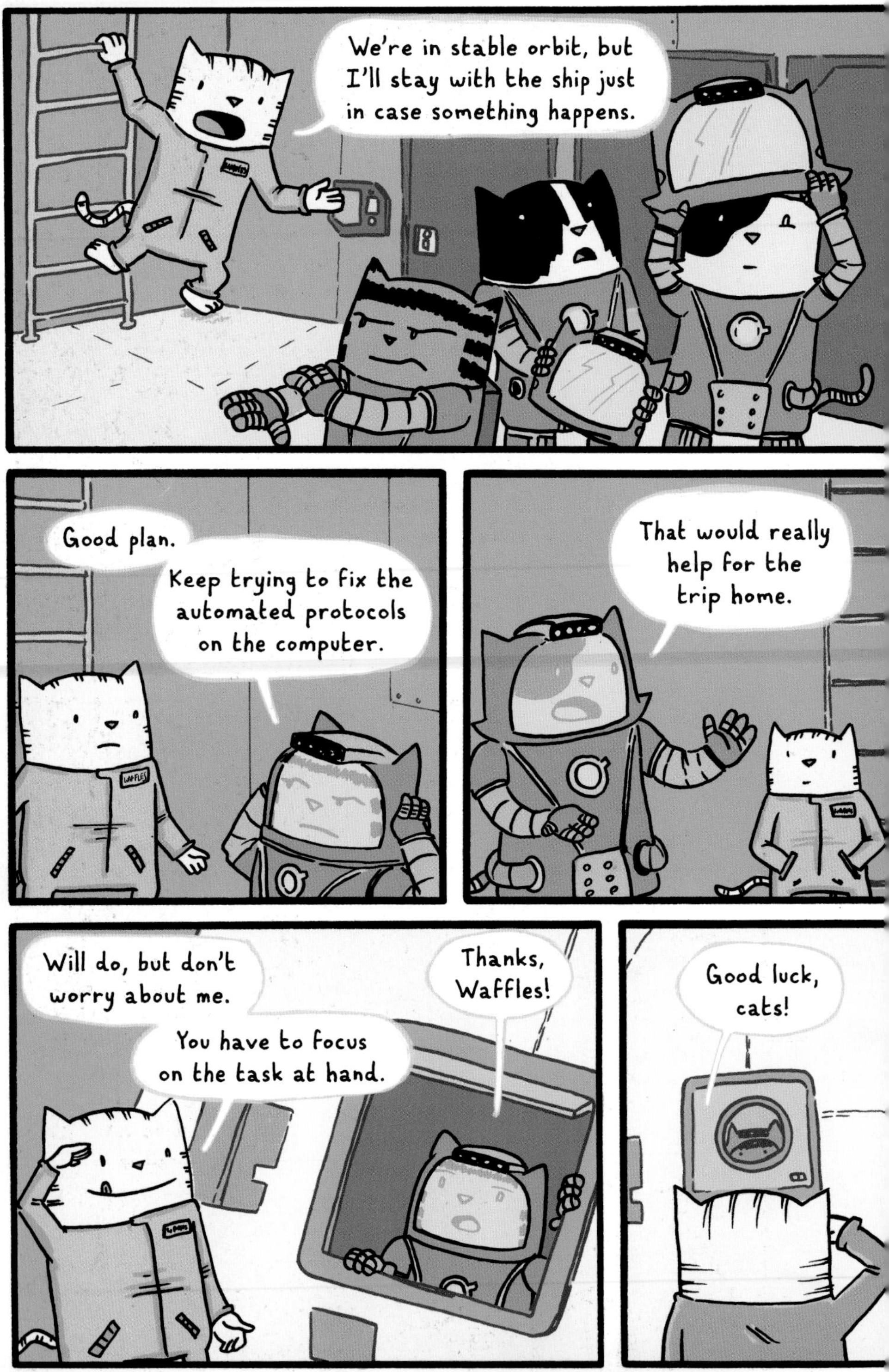

We're in stable orbit, but I'll stay with the ship just in case something happens.
Good plan.
Keep trying to fix the automated protocols on the computer.
That would really help for the trip home.
Will do, but don't worry about me.
You have to focus on the task at hand.
Thanks, Waffles!
Good luck, cats!

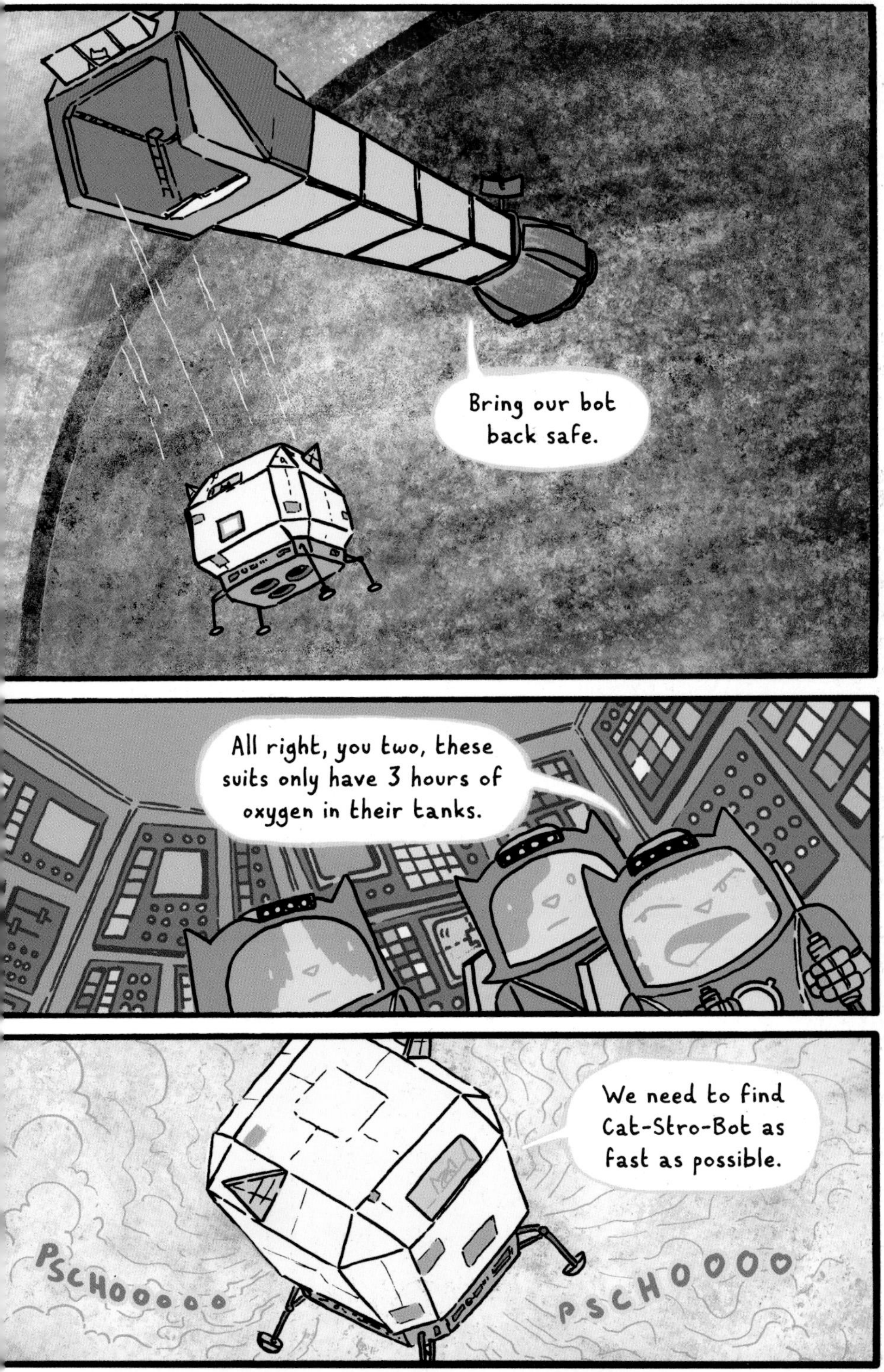
Bring our bot back safe.
All right, you two, these suits only have 3 hours of oxygen in their tanks.
We need to find Cat-Stro-Bot as fast as possible.
PSCHOOOOOO
PSCHOOOOO

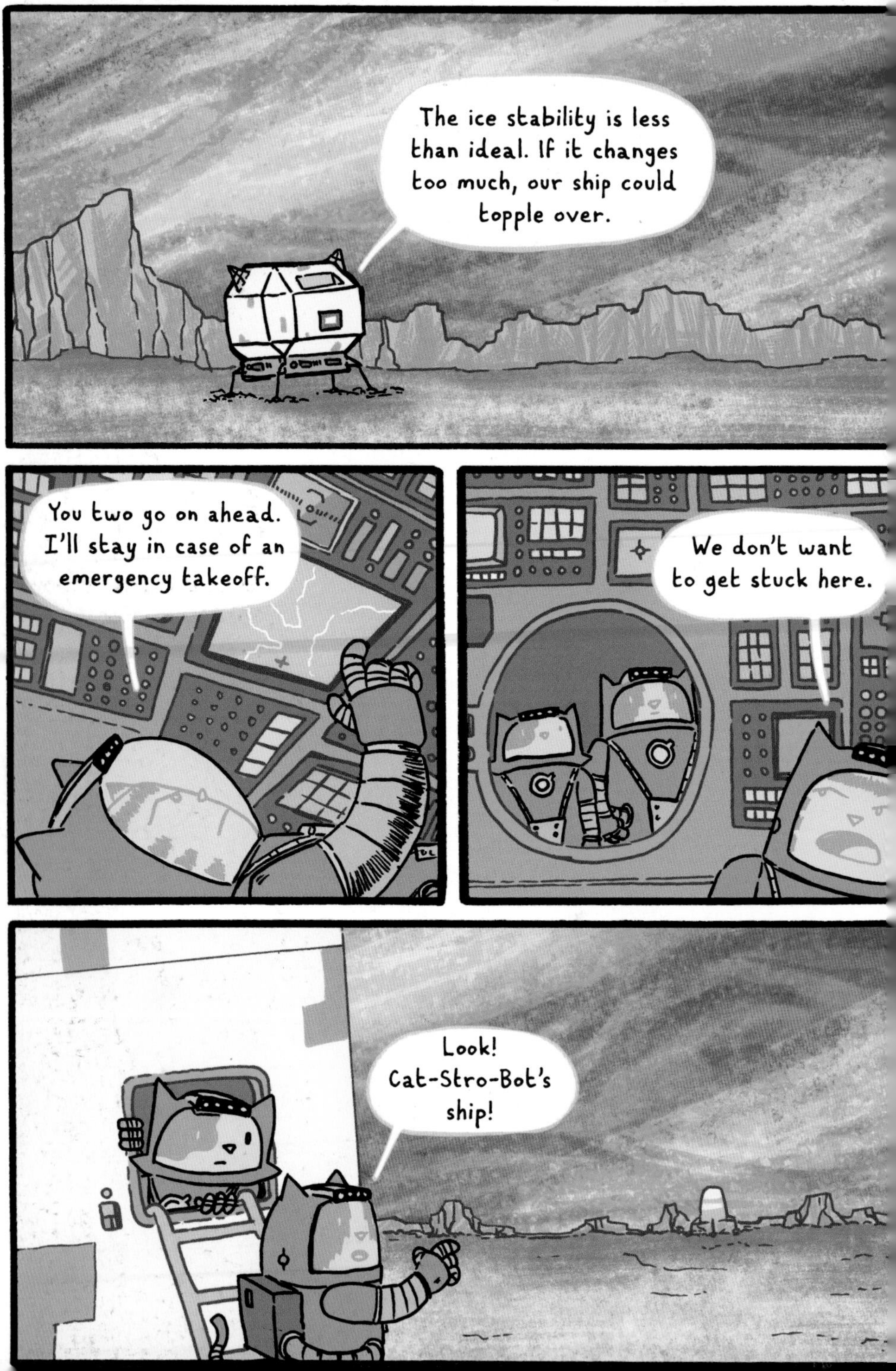
The ice stability is less than ideal. If it changes too much, our ship could topple over.
You two go on ahead. I'll stay in case of an emergency takeoff.
We don't want to get stuck here.
Look! Cat-Stro-Bot's ship!

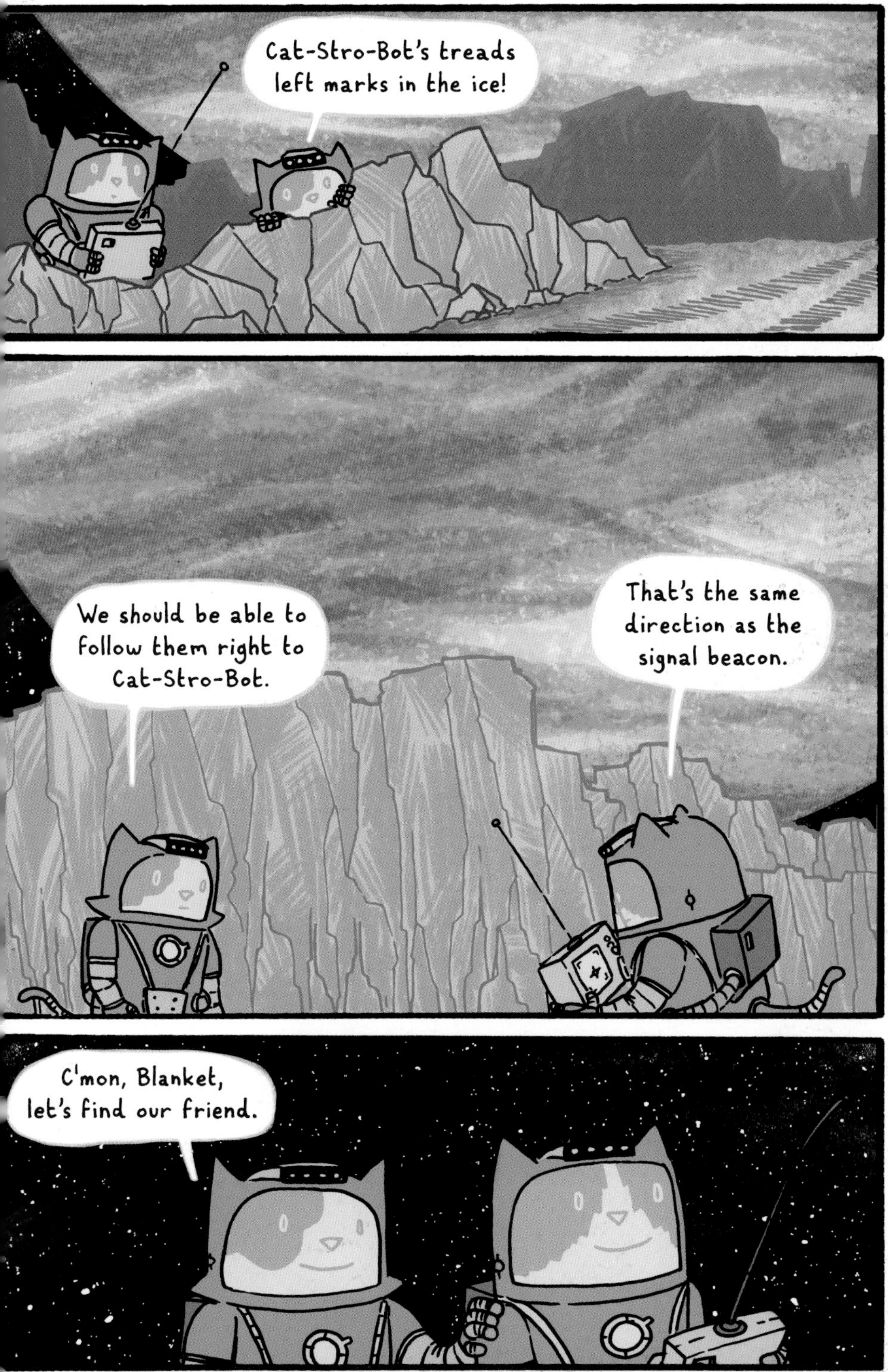
Cat-Stro-Bot's treads left marks in the ice!
We should be able to follow them right to Cat-Stro-Bot.
That's the same direction as the signal beacon.
C'mon, Blanket, let's find our friend.

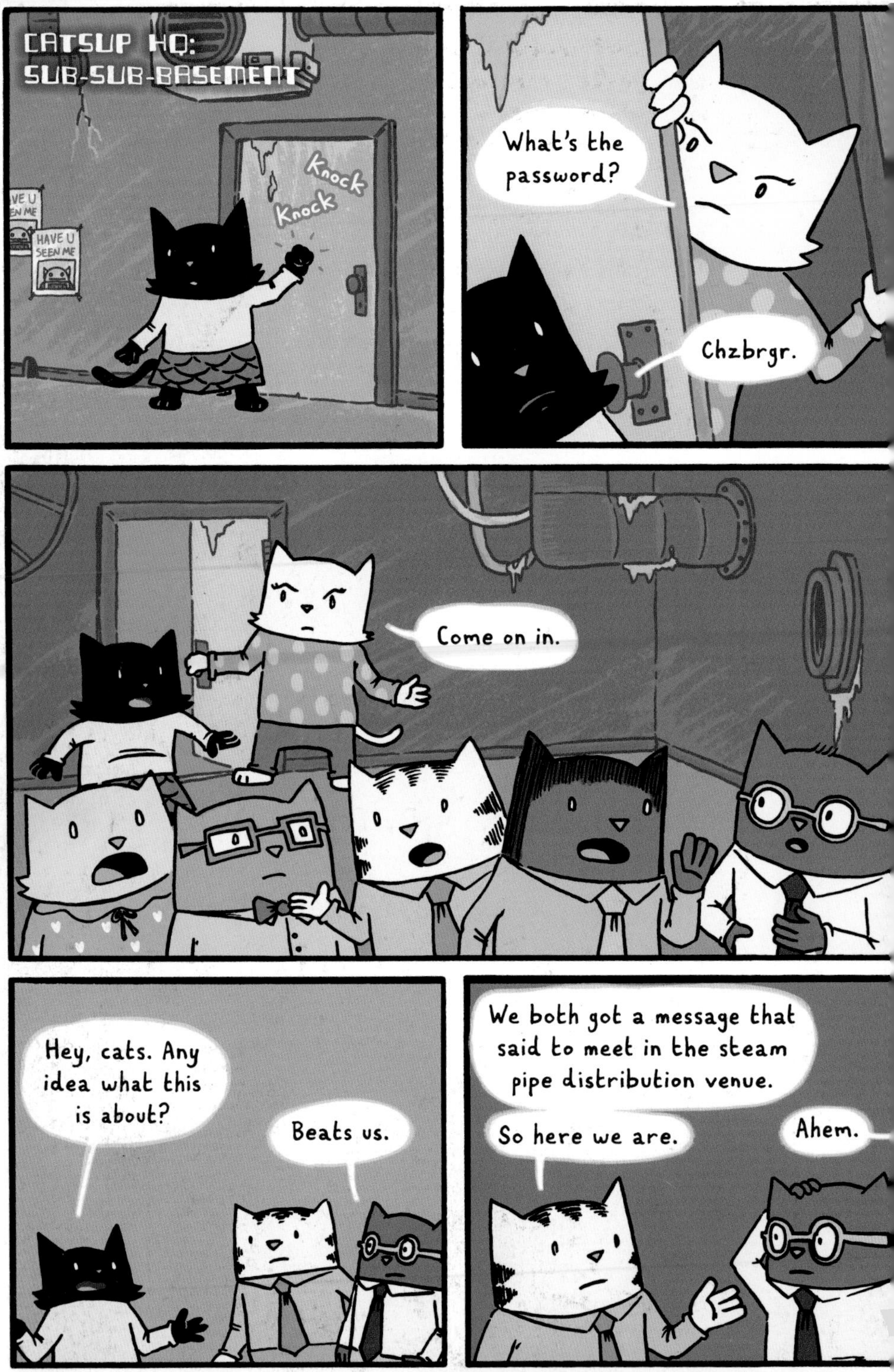
CATSUP HQ:
SUB-SUB-BASEMENT
HAVE U SEEN ME
Knock
Knock
What's the password?
Chzbrgr.
Come on in.
Hey, cats. Any idea what this is about?
Beats us.
We both got a message that said to meet in the steam pipe distribution venue.
So here we are.
Ahem.

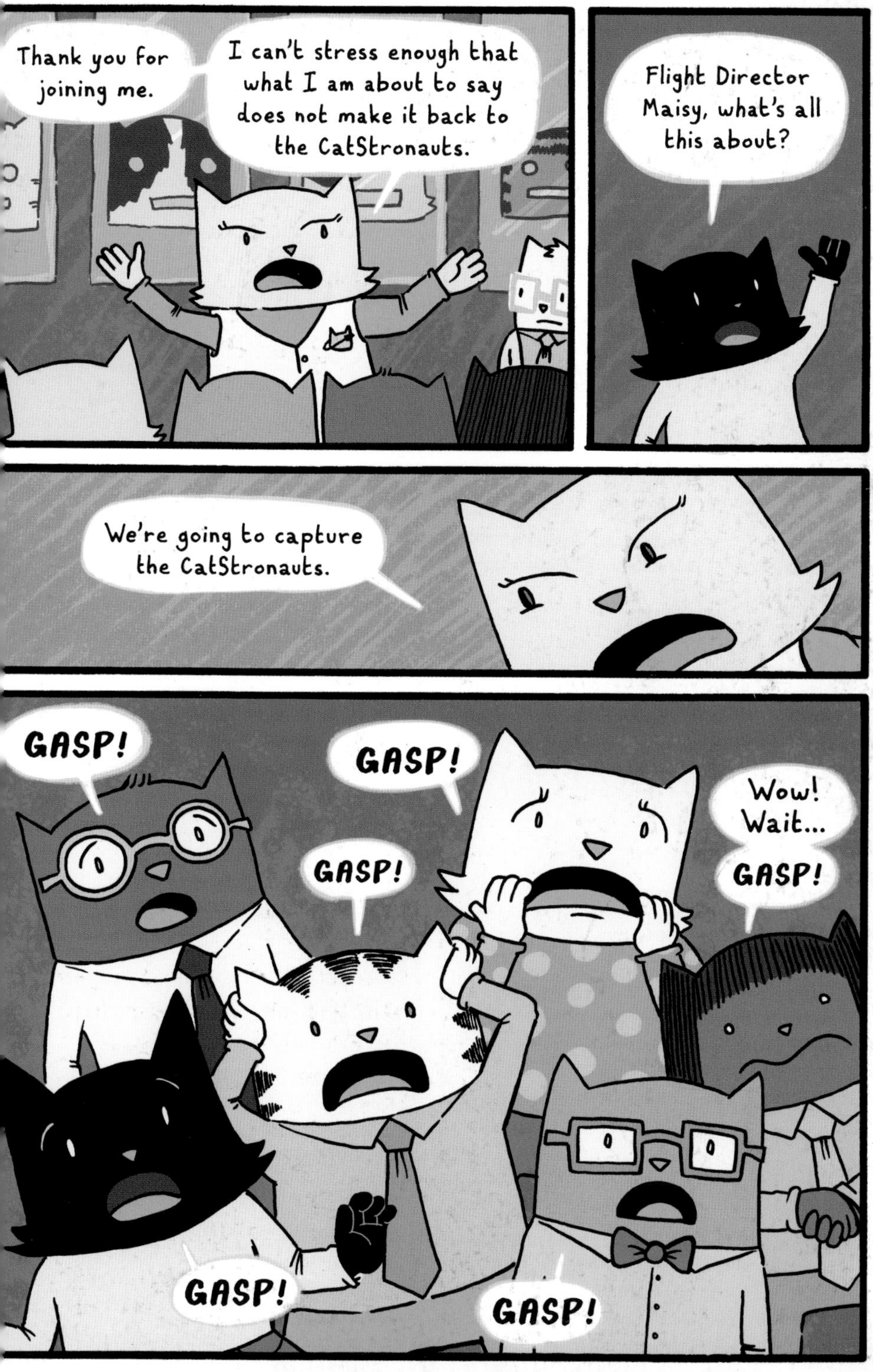
Thank you for joining me.
I can't stress enough that what I am about to say does not make it back to the CatStronauts.
Flight Director Maisy, what's all this about?
We're going to capture the CatStronauts.
GASP!
GASP!
Wow! Wait...
GASP!
GASP!
GASP!
GASP!

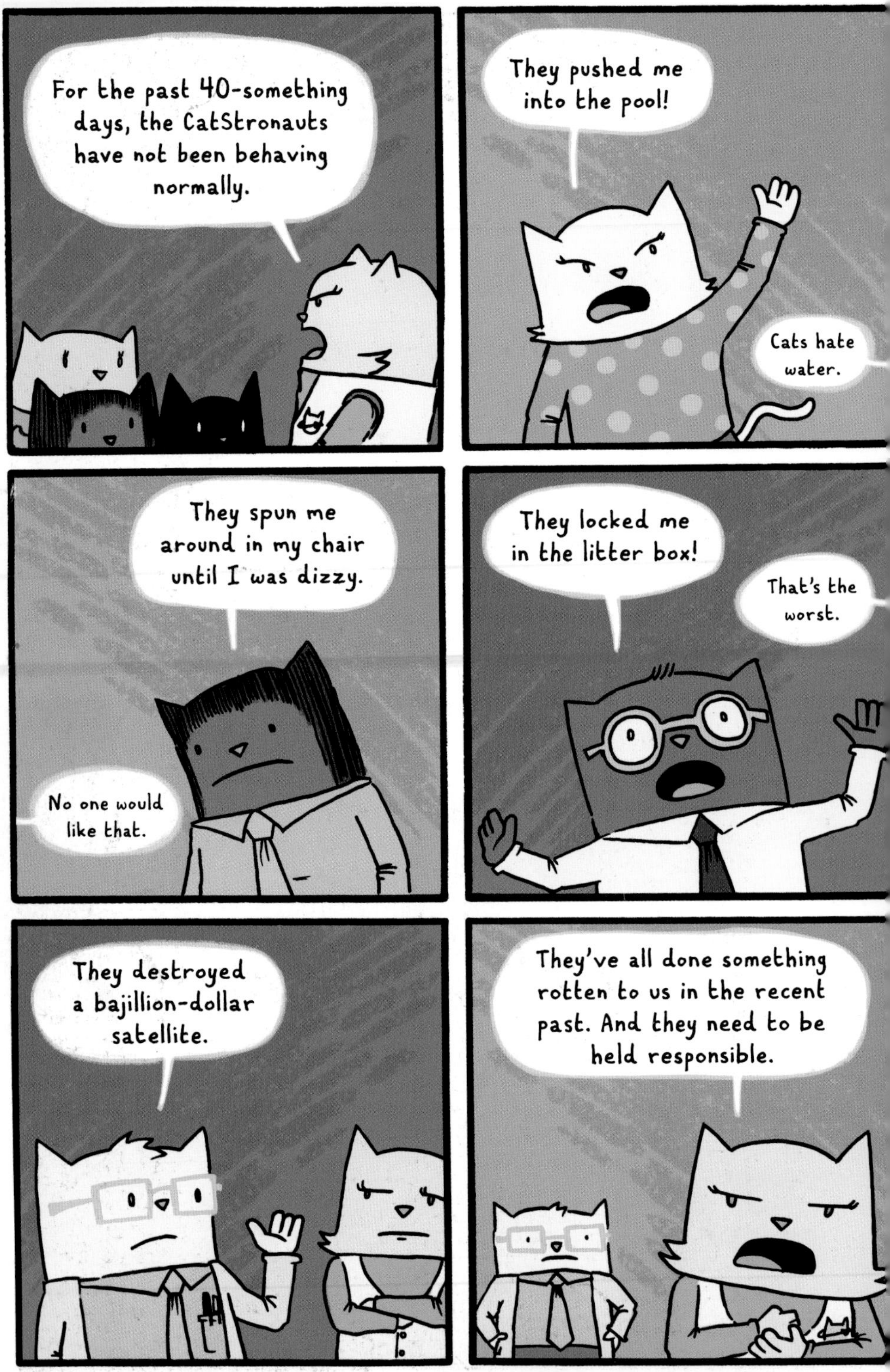
For the past 40-something days, the CatStronauts have not been behaving normally.
They pushed me into the pool!
Cats hate water.
They spun me around in my chair until I was dizzy.
No one would like that.
They locked me in the litter box!
That's the worst.
They destroyed a bajillion-dollar satellite.
They've all done something rotten to us in the recent past. And they need to be held responsible.

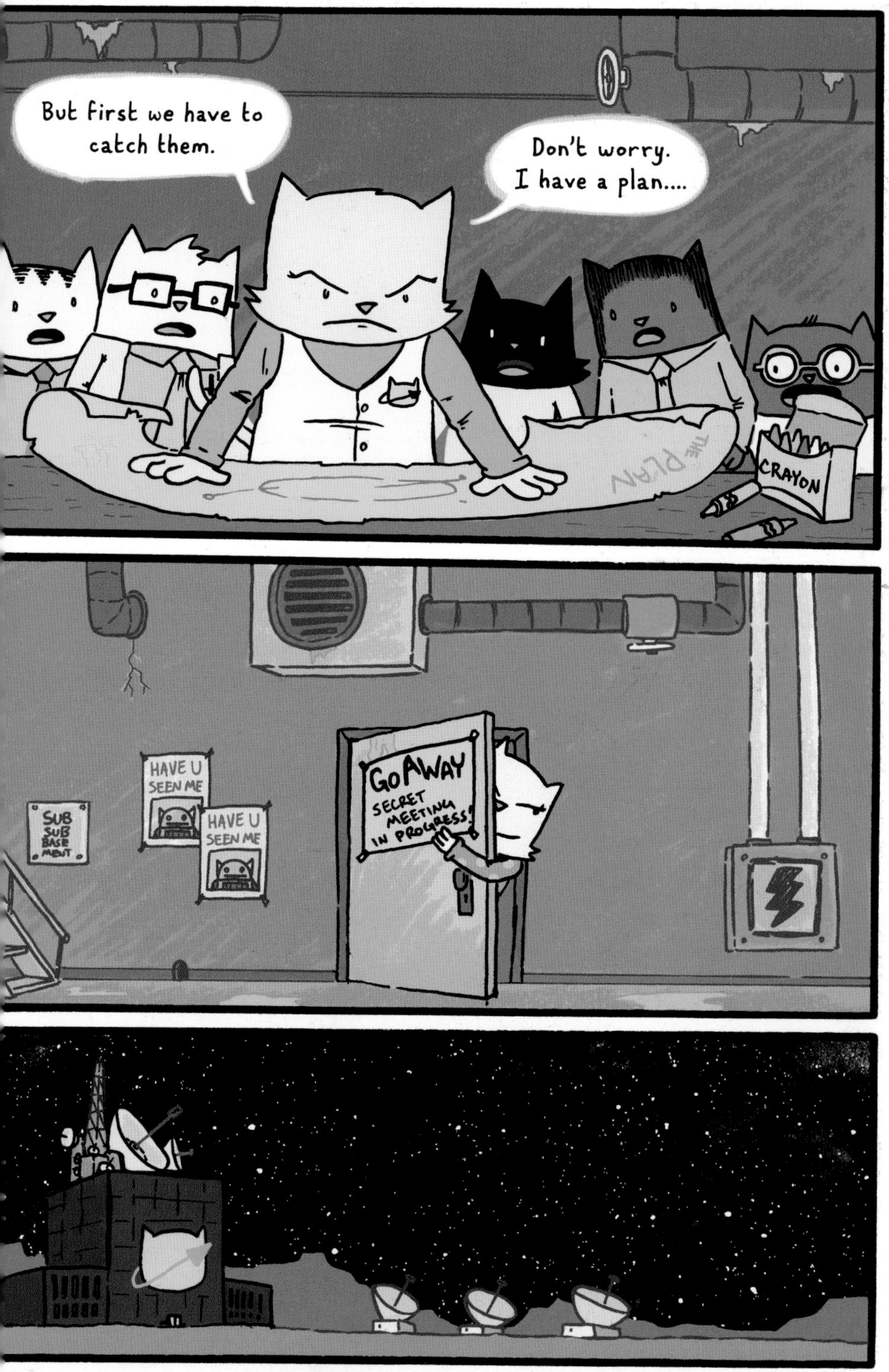
But first we have to catch them.
Don't worry. I have a plan....
THE PLAN
CRAYON
SUB SUB BASE MENT
HAVE U SEEN ME
HAVE U SEEN ME
GO AWAY
SECRET MEETING IN PROGRESS!

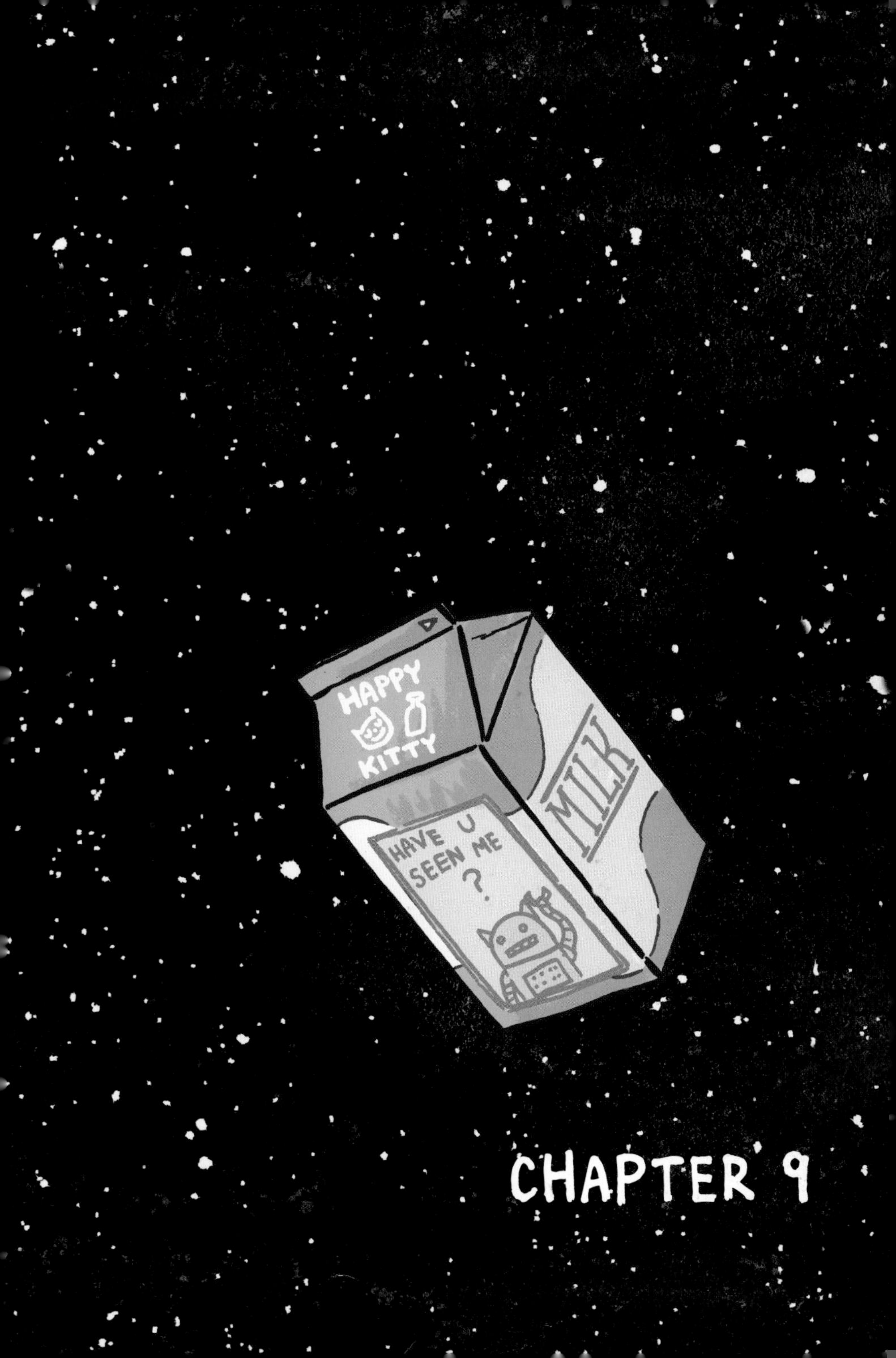
HAPPY
KITTY
MILK
HAVE U SEEN ME
?

CHAPTER 9

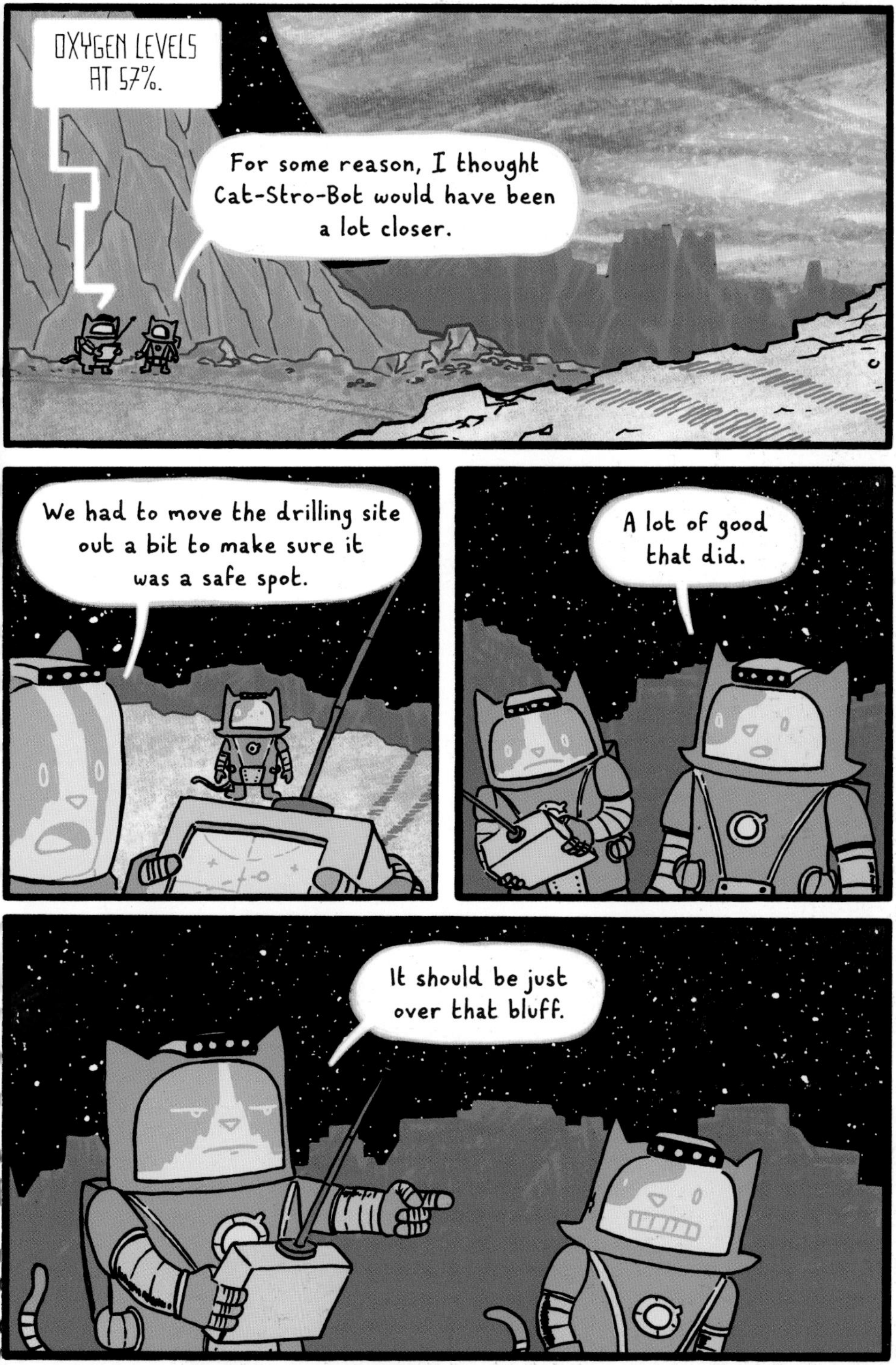
OXYGEN LEVELS AT 57%.
For some reason, I thought Cat-Stro-Bot would have been a lot closer.
We had to move the drilling site out a bit to make sure it was a safe spot.
A lot of good that did.
It should be just over that bluff.

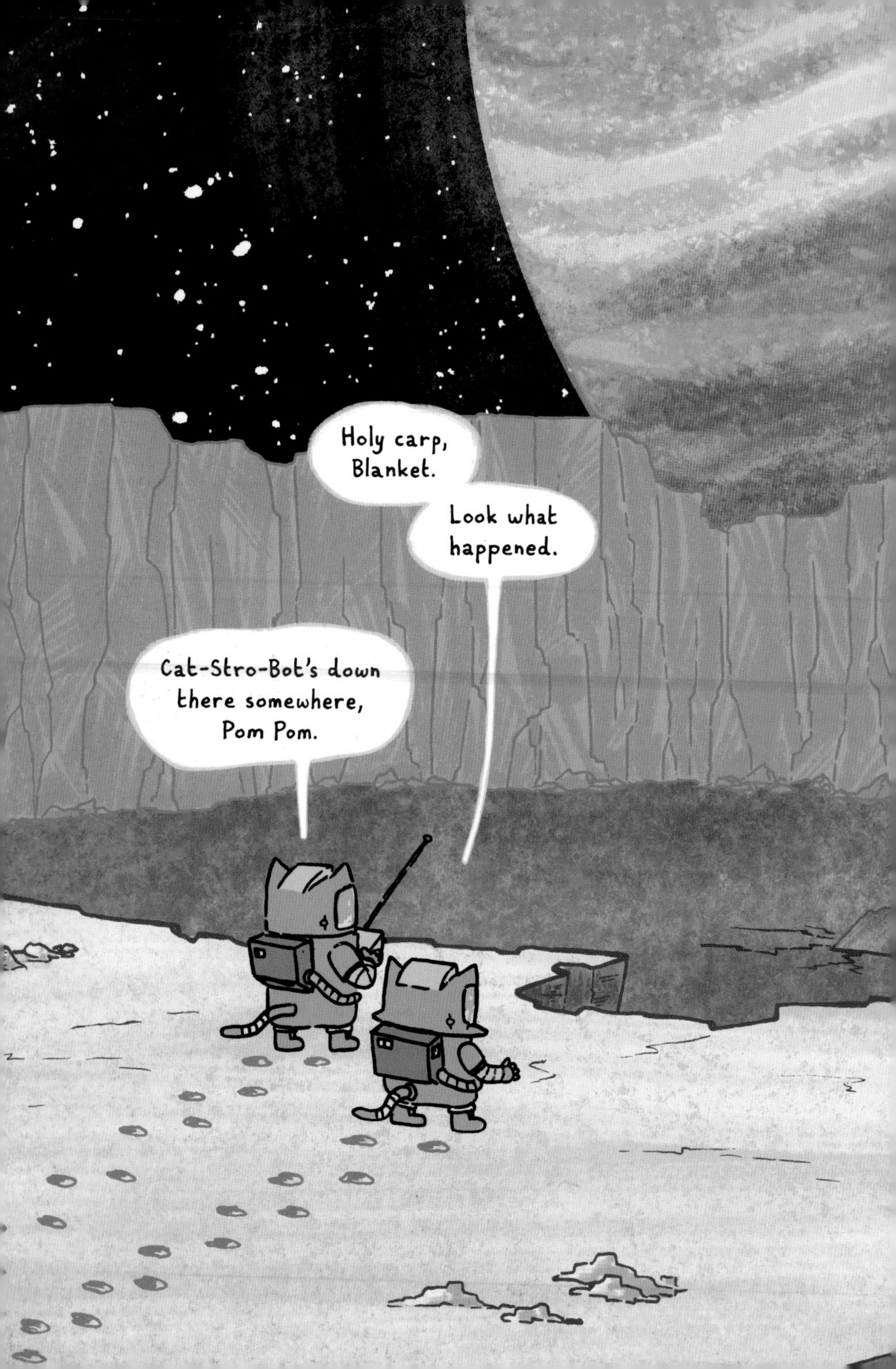
Holy carp, Blanket.
Look what happened.
Cat-Stro-Bot's down there somewhere, Pom Pom.

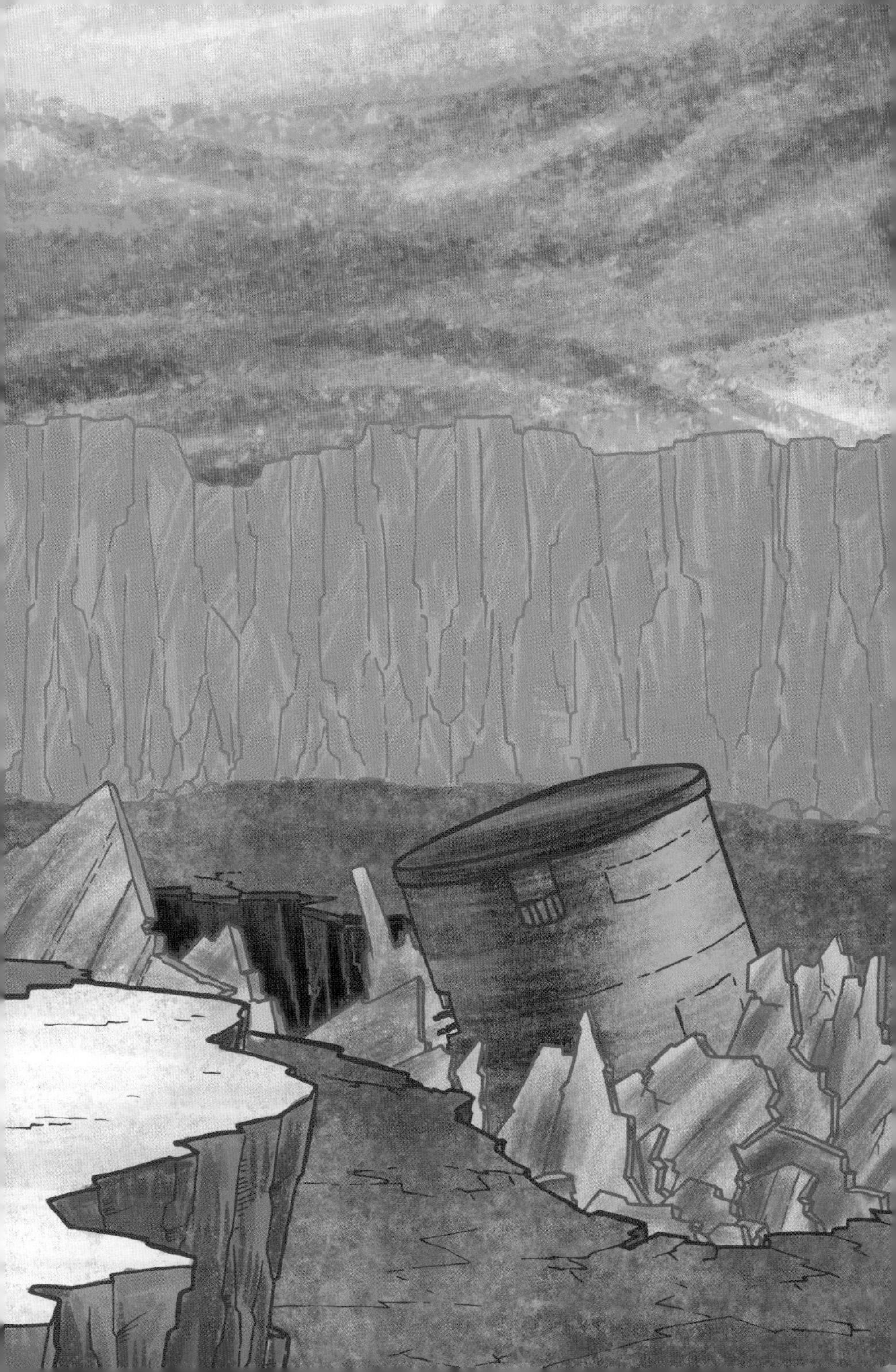

This hole is pretty deep.

I don't think we can climb it.

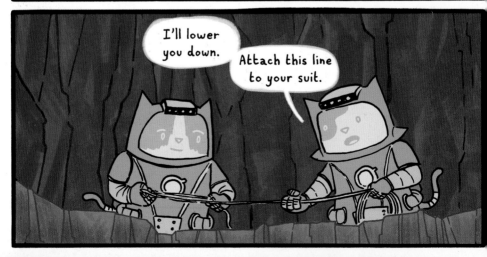

I'll lower you down.

Attach this line to your suit.

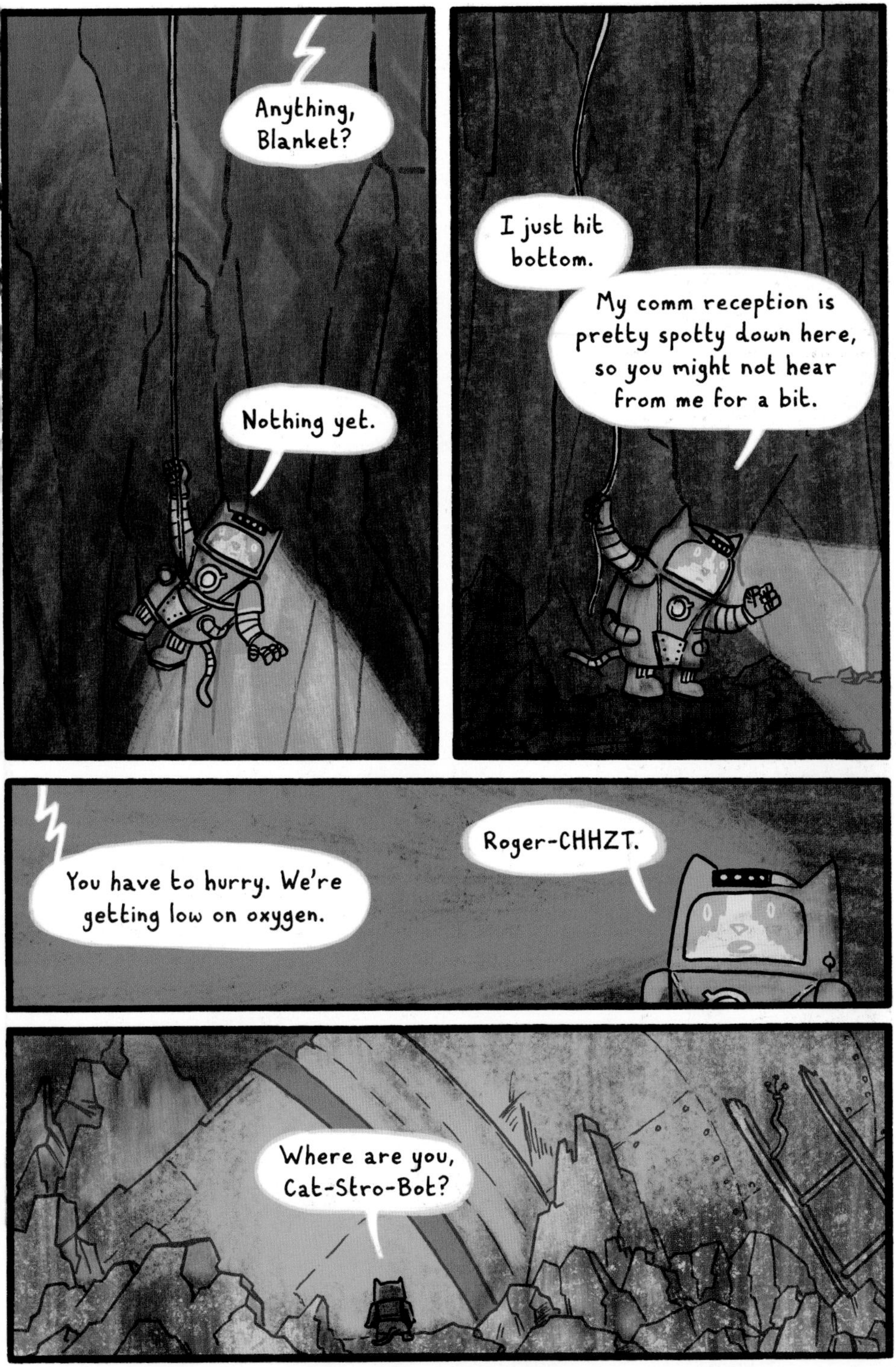
Anything, Blanket?
Nothing yet.
I just hit bottom.
My comm reception is pretty spotty down here, so you might not hear from me for a bit.
You have to hurry. We're getting low on oxygen.
Roger-CHHZT.
Where are you, Cat-Stro-Bot?

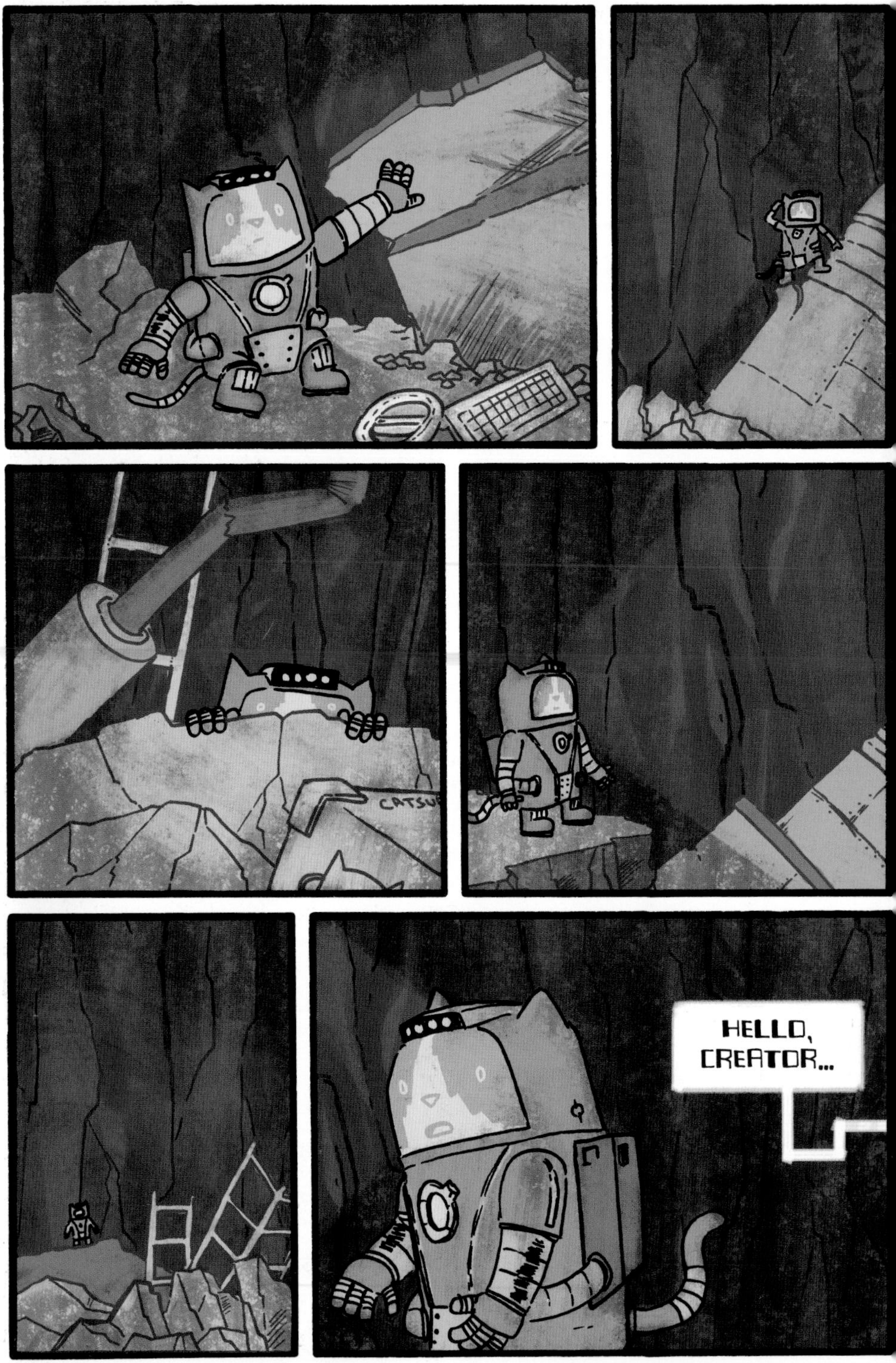
HELLO, CREATOR...

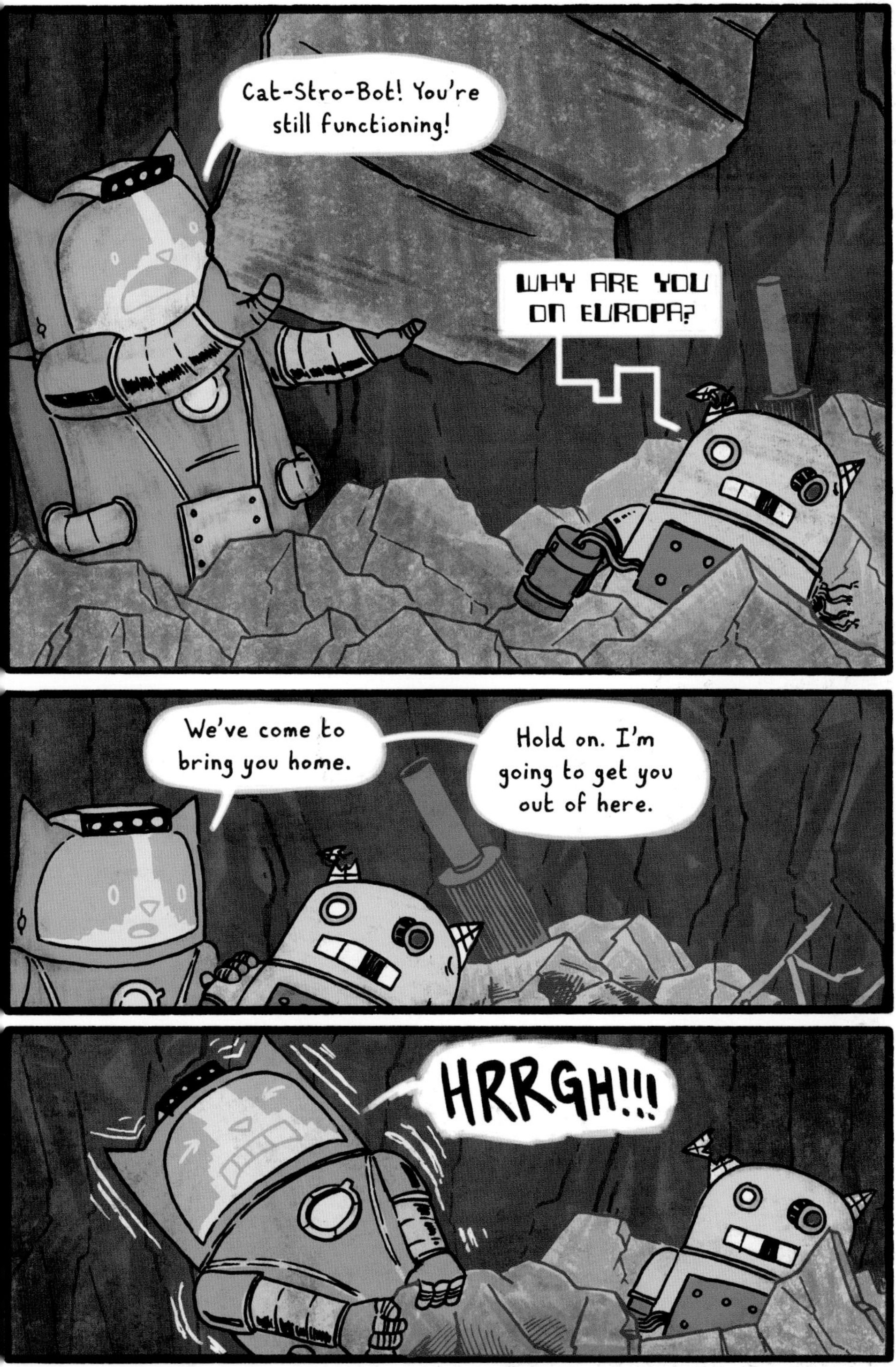
Cat-Stro-Bot! You're still functioning!
WHY ARE YOU ON EUROPA?
We've come to bring you home.
Hold on. I'm going to get you out of here.
HRRGH!!!

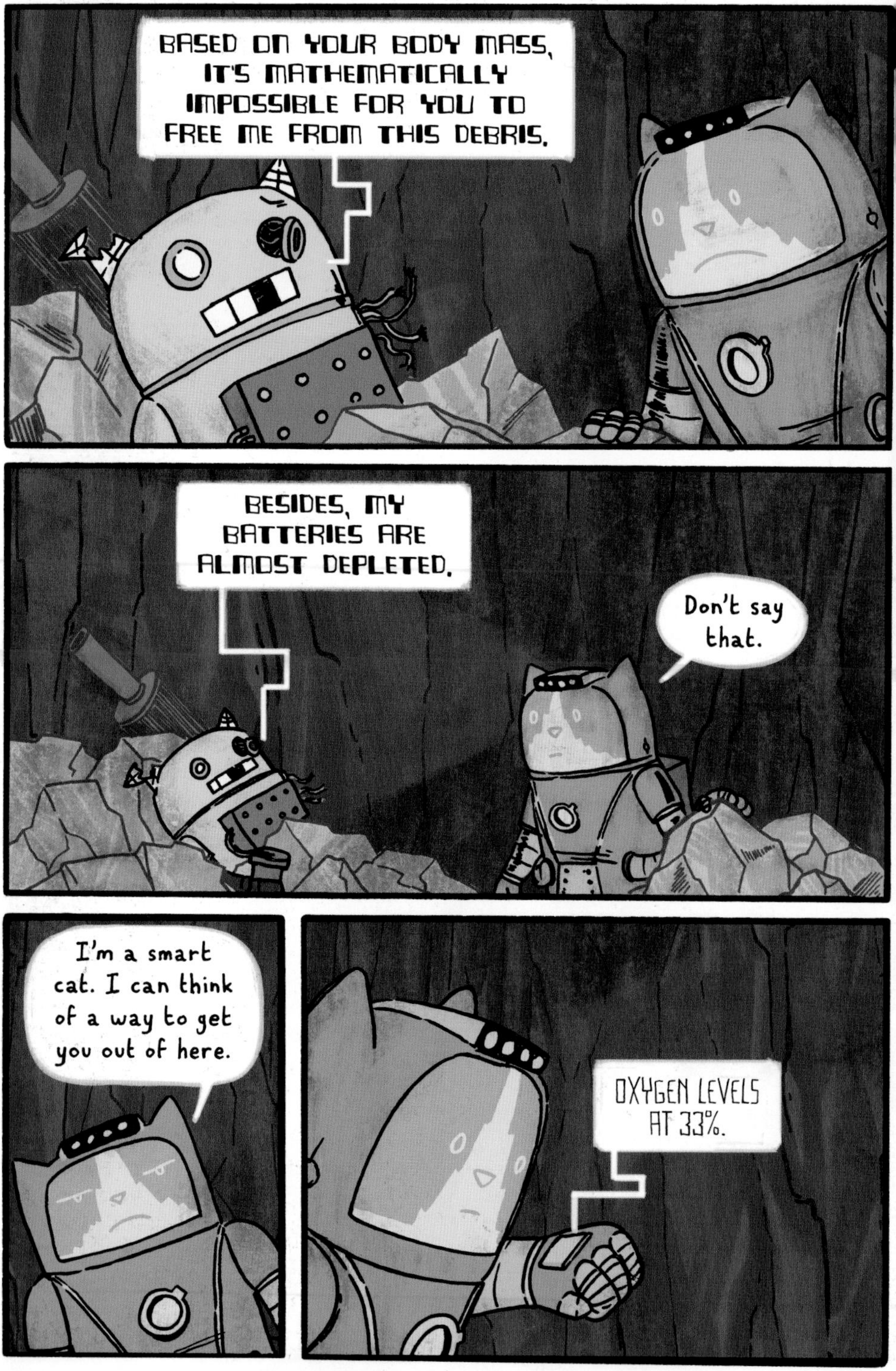
BASED ON YOUR BODY MASS, IT'S MATHEMATICALLY IMPOSSIBLE FOR YOU TO FREE ME FROM THIS DEBRIS.
BESIDES, MY BATTERIES ARE ALMOST DEPLETED.
Don't say that.
I'm a smart cat. I can think of a way to get you out of here.
OXYGEN LEVELS AT 33%.

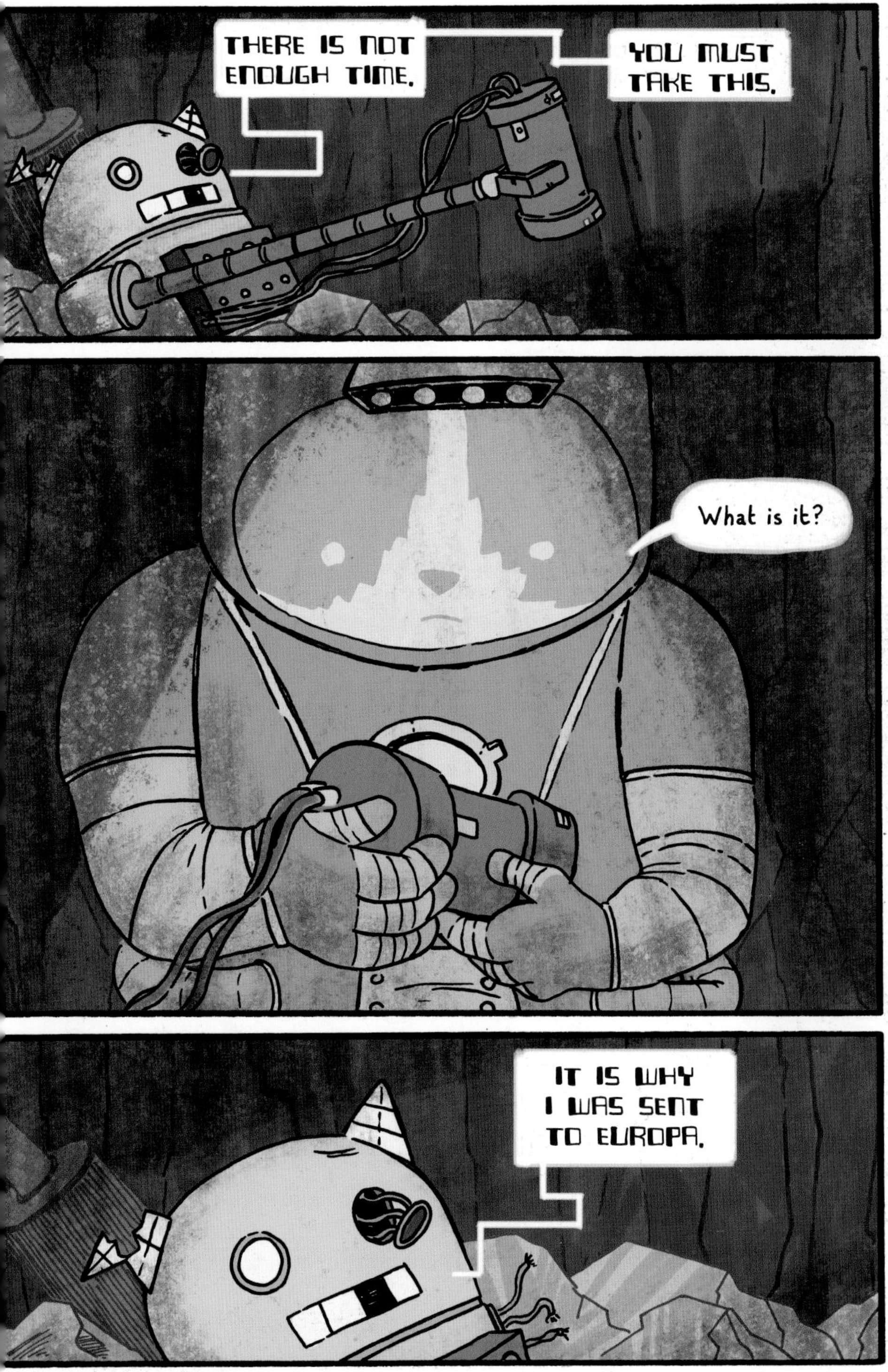
THERE IS NOT ENOUGH TIME.
YOU MUST TAKE THIS.
What is it?
IT IS WHY I WAS SENT TO EUROPA.

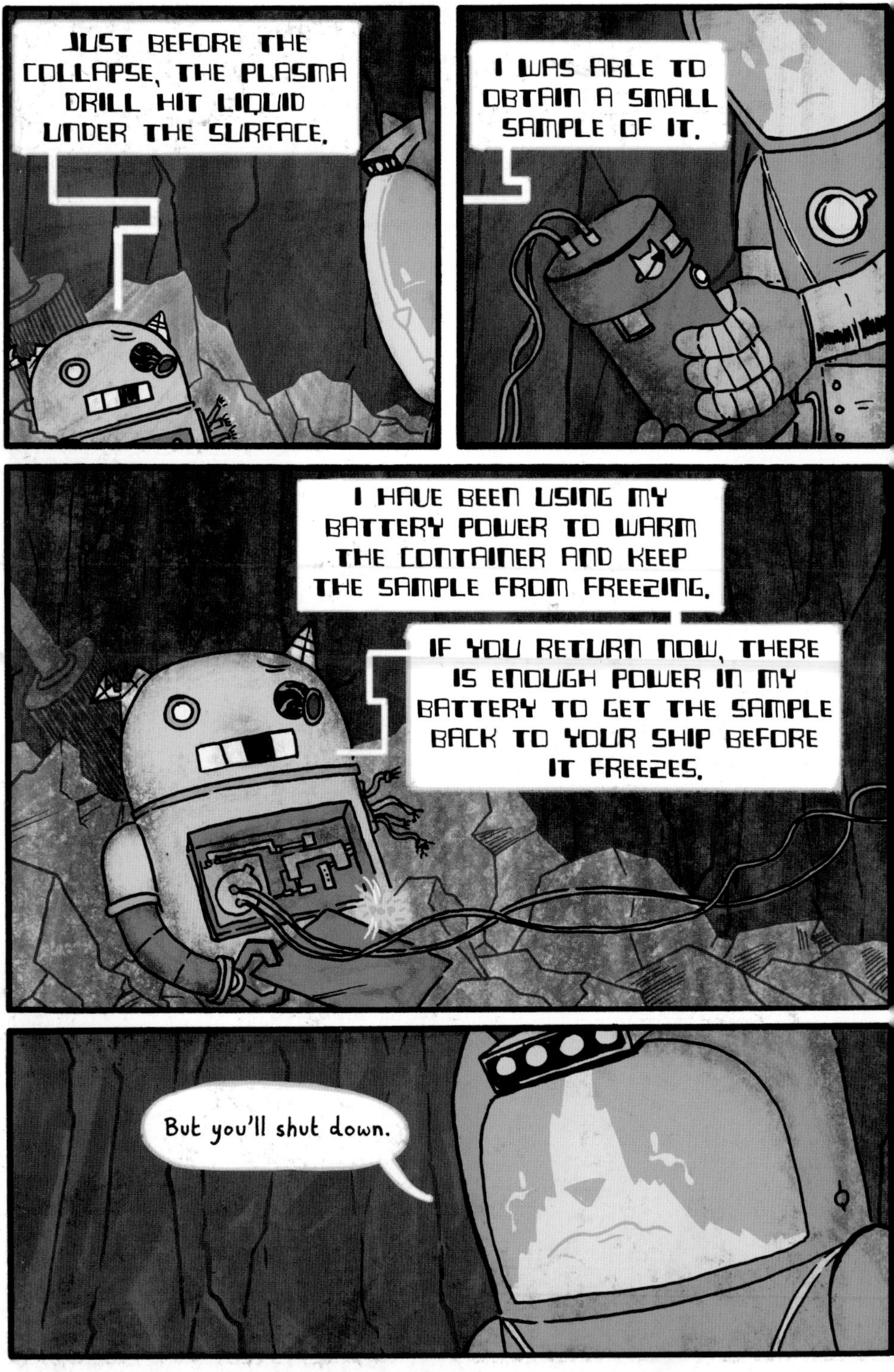
JUST BEFORE THE COLLAPSE, THE PLASMA DRILL HIT LIQUID UNDER THE SURFACE.
I WAS ABLE TO OBTAIN A SMALL SAMPLE OF IT.
I HAVE BEEN USING MY BATTERY POWER TO WARM THE CONTAINER AND KEEP THE SAMPLE FROM FREEZING.
IF YOU RETURN NOW, THERE IS ENOUGH POWER IN MY BATTERY TO GET THE SAMPLE BACK TO YOUR SHIP BEFORE IT FREEZES.
But you'll shut down.

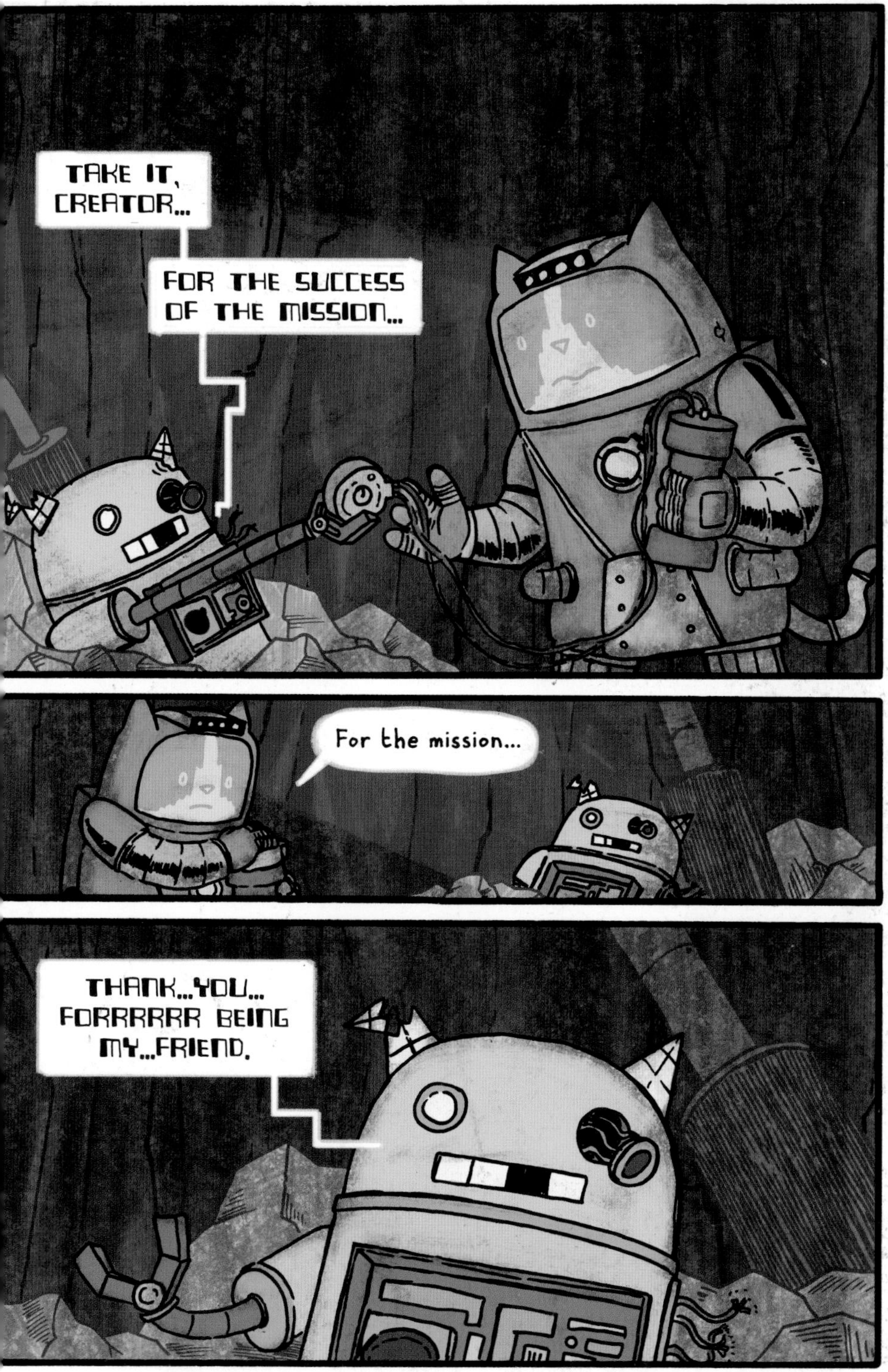
TAKE IT, CREATOR...
FOR THE SUCCESS OF THE MISSION...
For the mission...
THANK...YOU... FORRRRRR BEING MY...FRIEND.

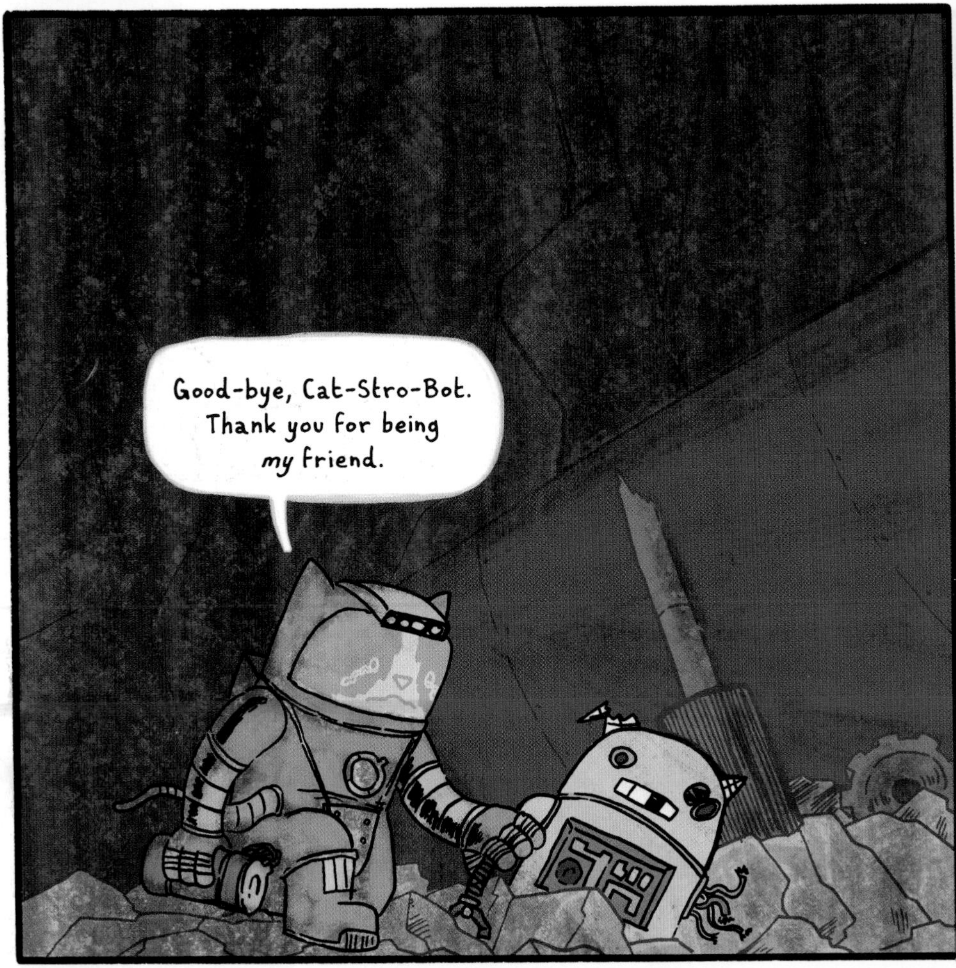
Good-bye, Cat-Stro-Bot. Thank you for being *my* friend.

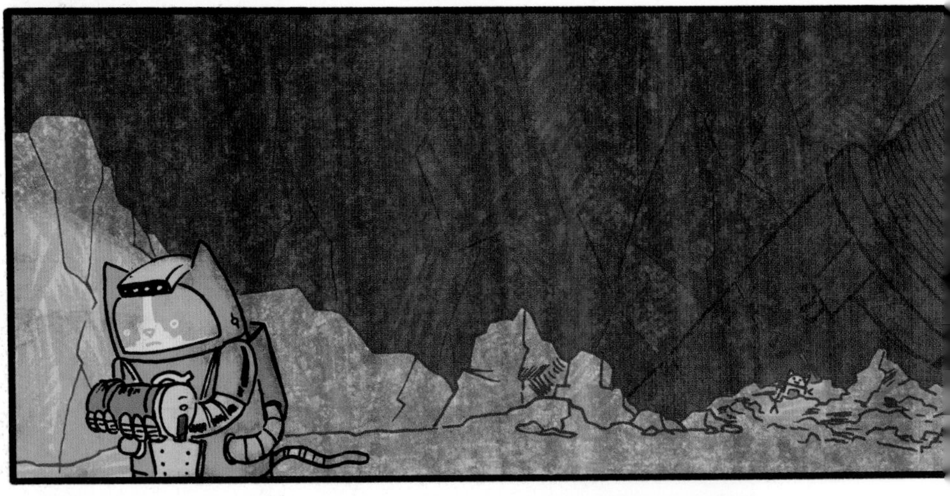

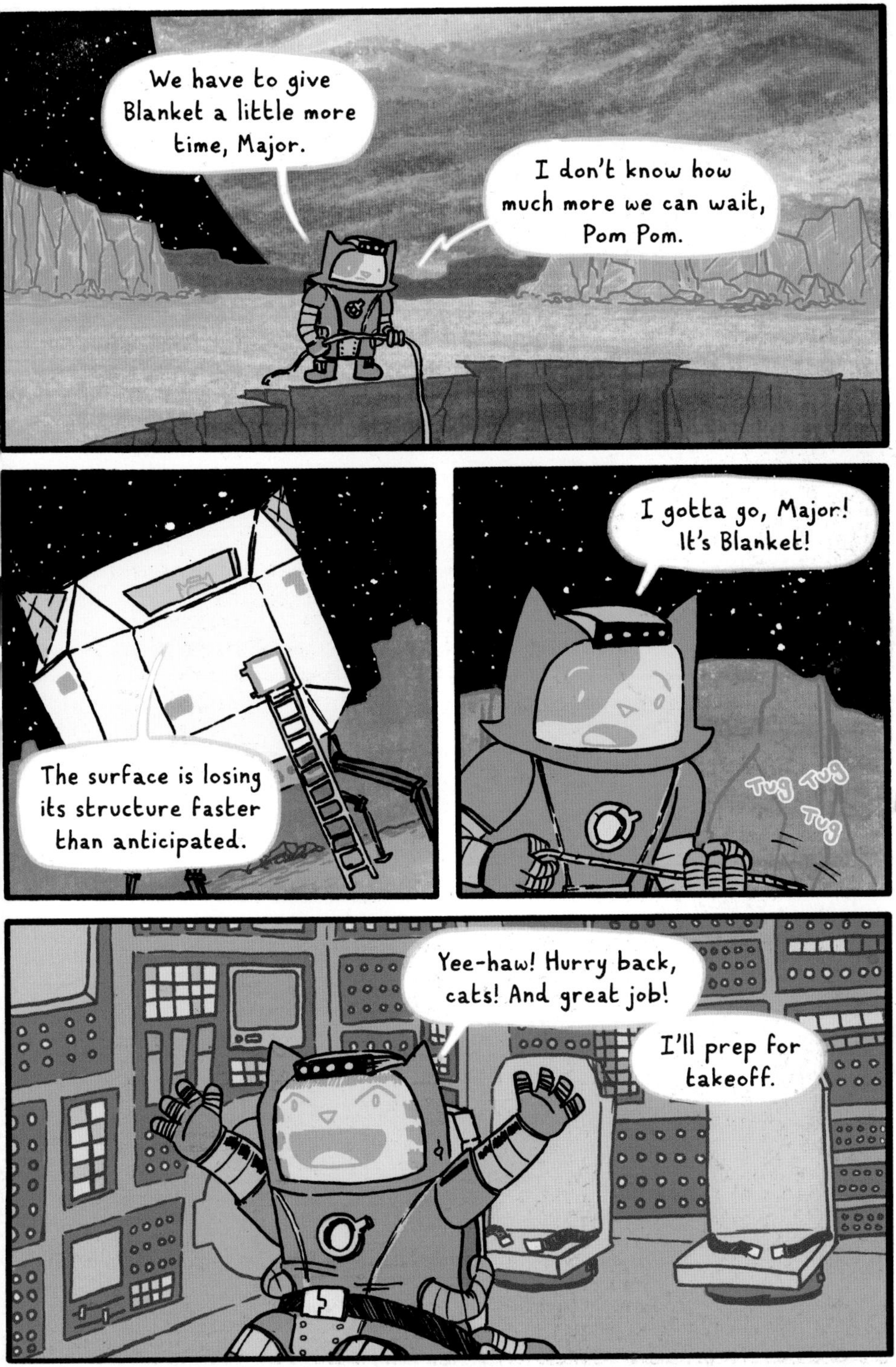
We have to give Blanket a little more time, Major.
I don't know how much more we can wait, Pom Pom.
The surface is losing its structure faster than anticipated.
I gotta go, Major! It's Blanket!
Tug Tug Tug
Yee-haw! Hurry back, cats! And great job!
I'll prep for takeoff.

Blanket! Golly, am I glad to see you.
Here I am.
Did you find Cat-Stro-Bot?
I did.
And?
I couldn't save him.
Oh, Blanket. I'm so sorry.

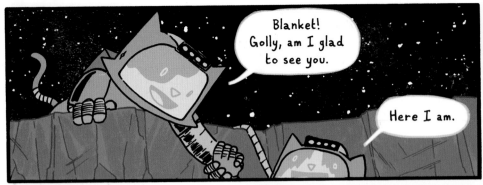

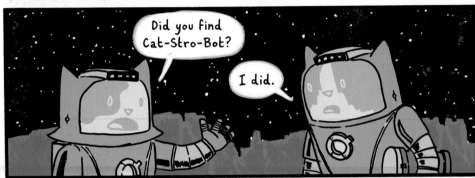

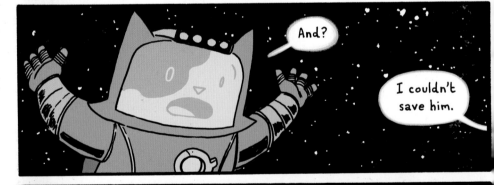

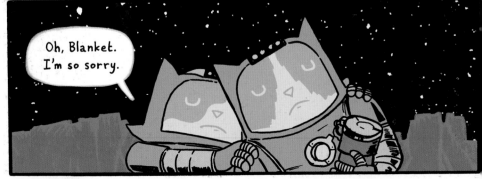

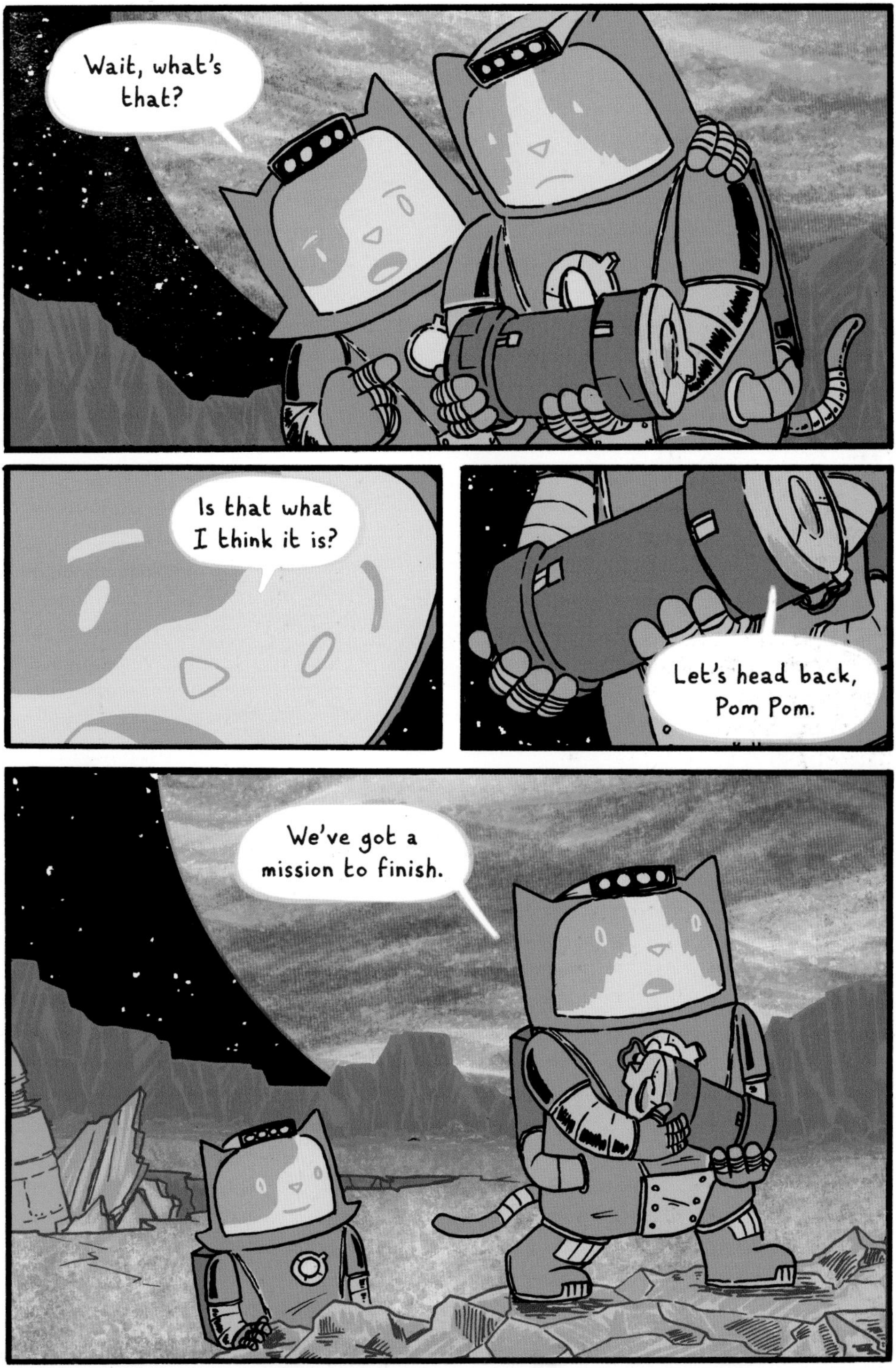
Wait, what's that?
Is that what I think it is?
Let's head back, Pom Pom.
We've got a mission to finish.

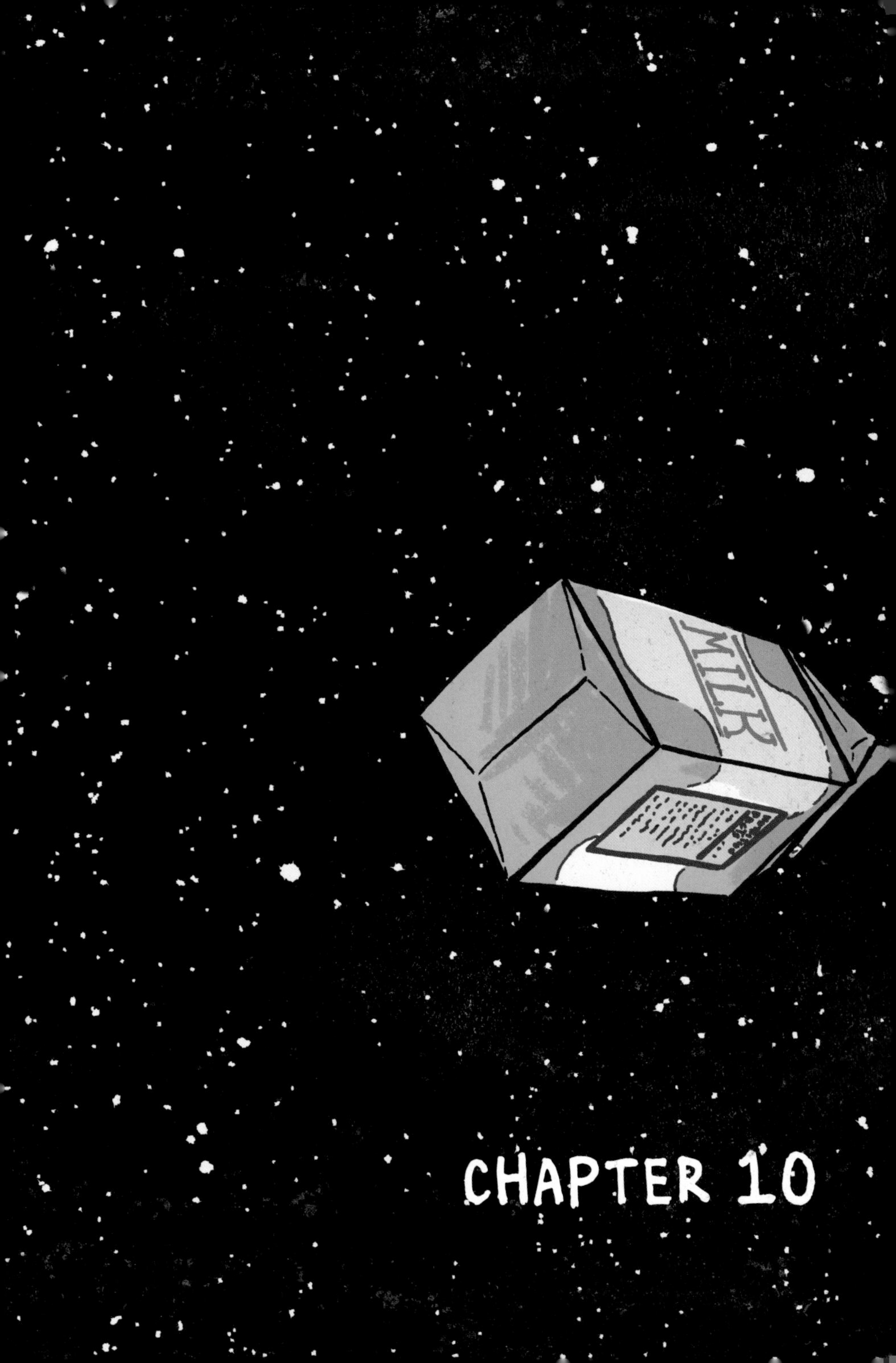
MILK

CHAPTER 10

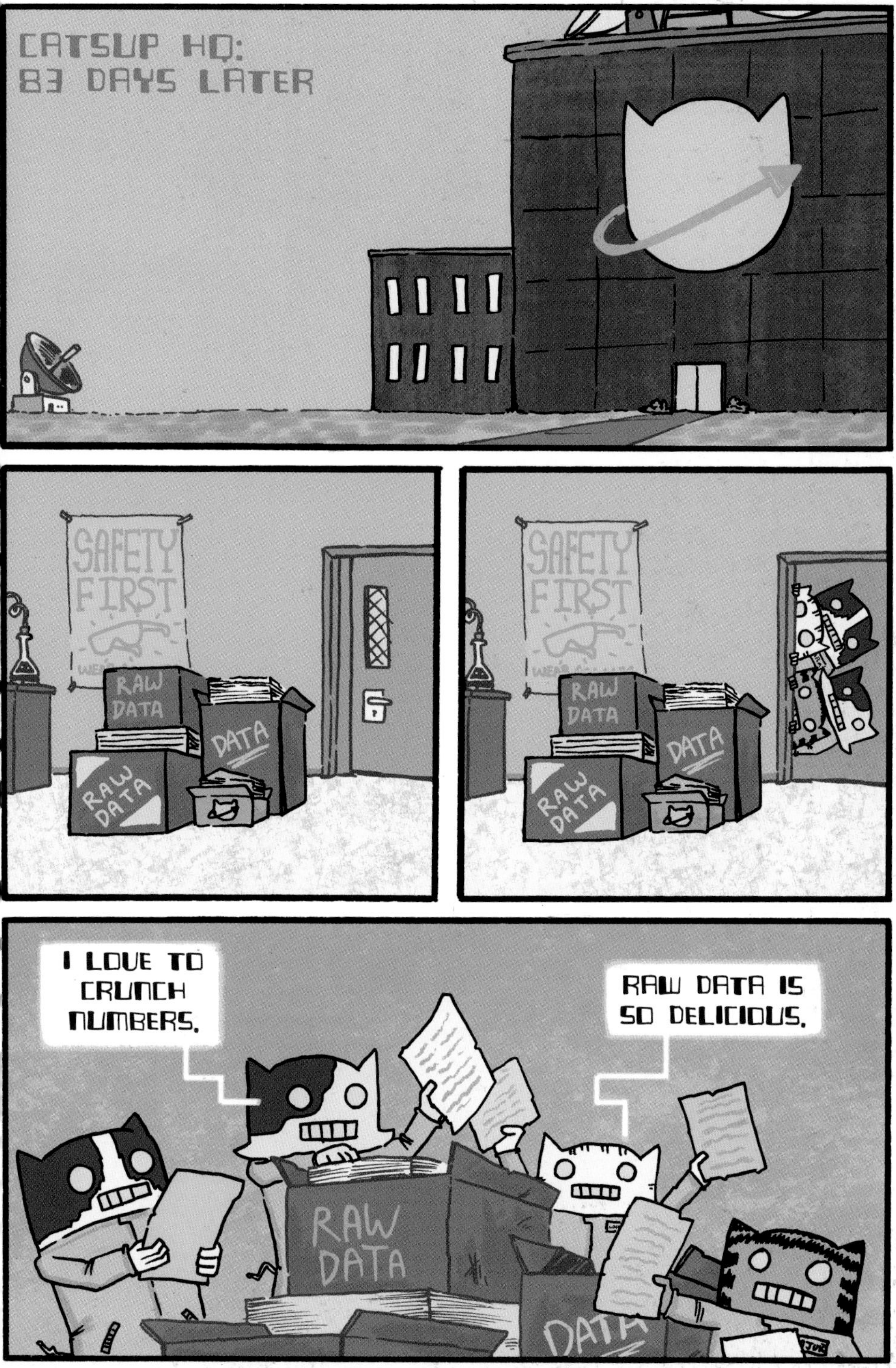
CATSUP HQ:
83 DAYS LATER
SAFETY FIRST
RAW DATA
DATA
RAW DATA
SAFETY FIRST
RAW DATA
DATA
RAW DATA
I LOVE TO CRUNCH NUMBERS.
RAW DATA IS SO DELICIOUS.
RAW DATA
DATA

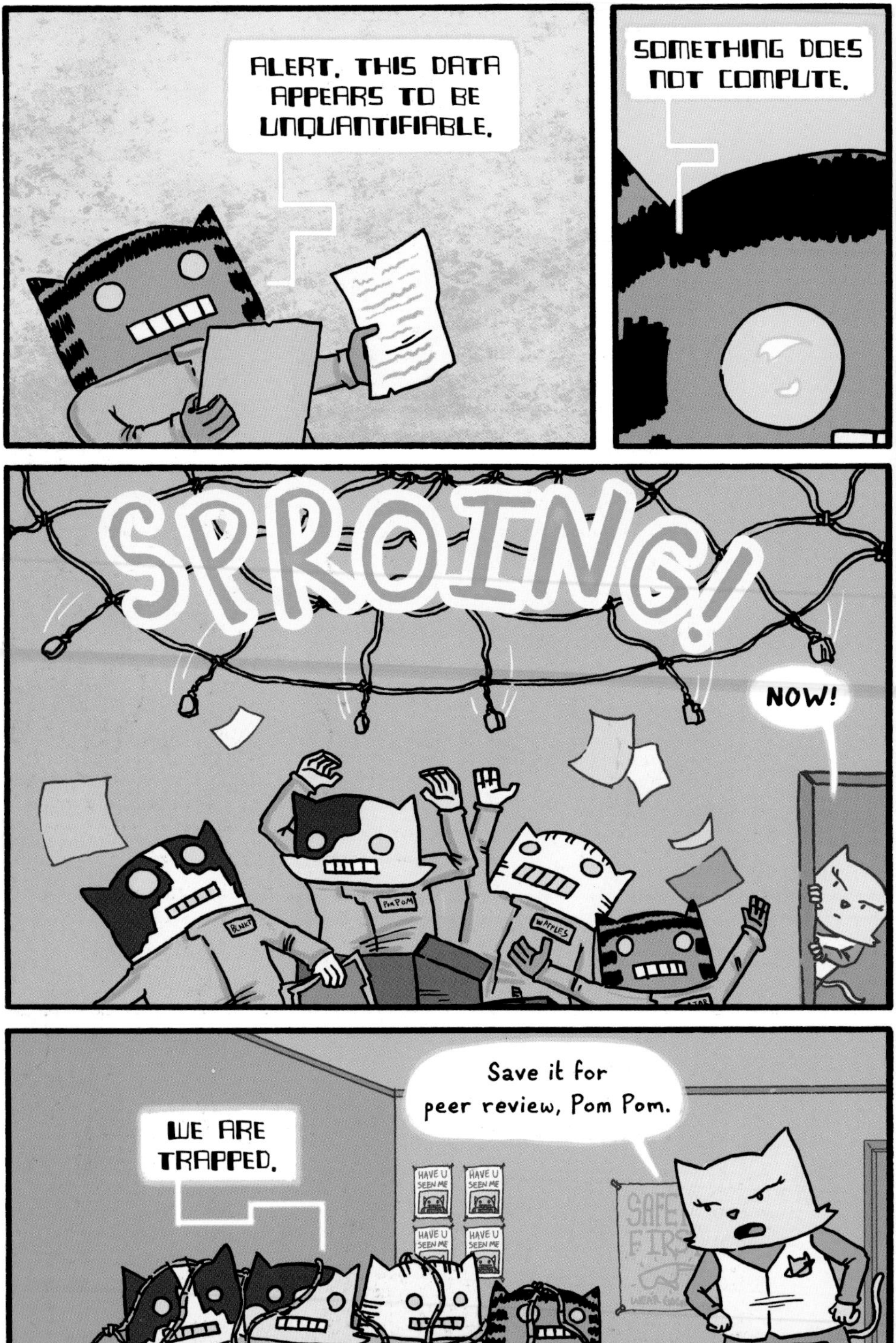

ALERT. THIS DATA APPEARS TO BE UNQUANTIFIABLE.
SOMETHING DOES NOT COMPUTE.
SPROING!
NOW!
WE ARE TRAPPED.
Save it for peer review, Pom Pom.

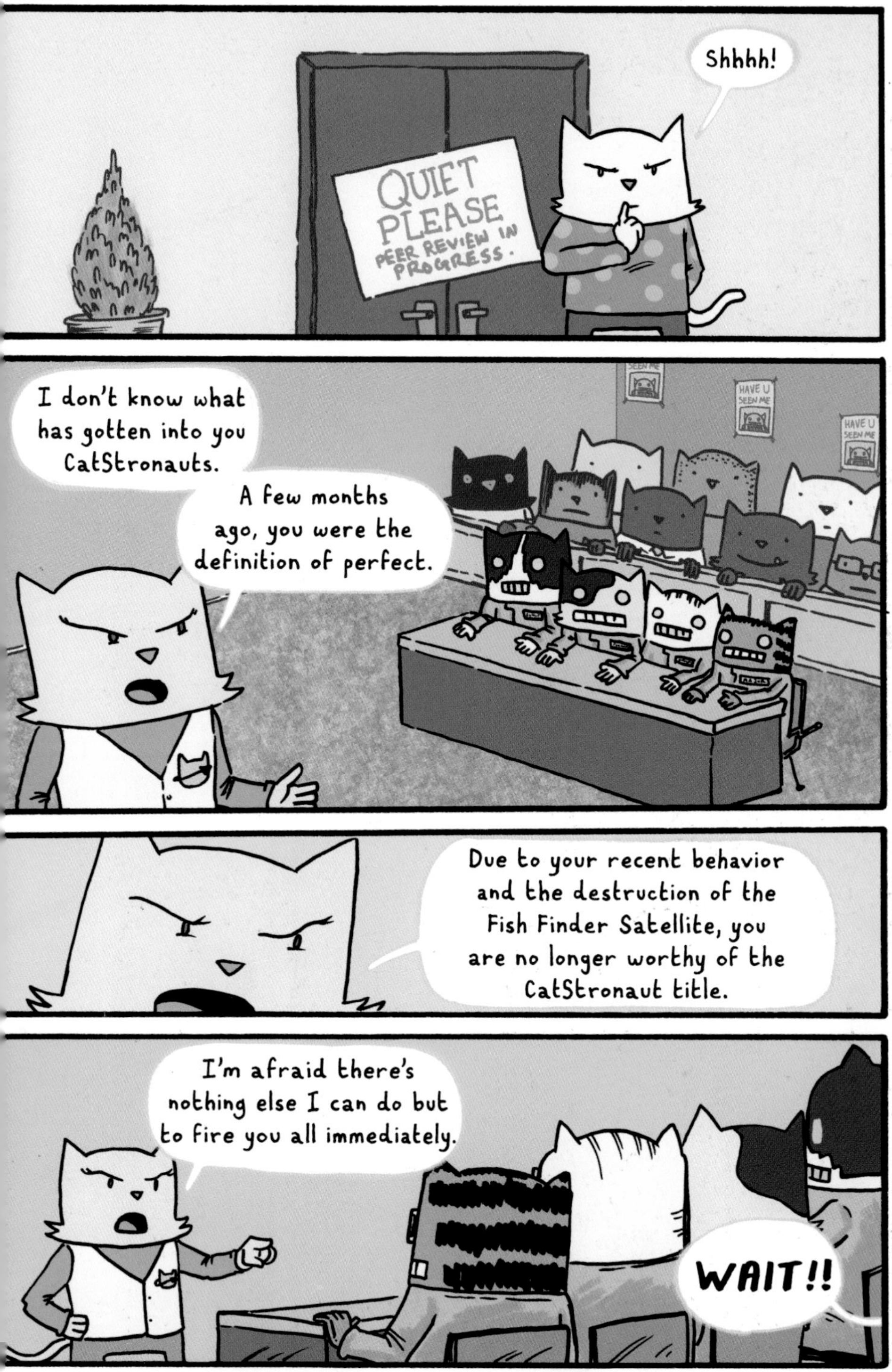

QUIET PLEASE
PEER REVIEW IN PROGRESS.
Shhhh!
SEEN ME
HAVE U SEEN ME
HAVE U SEEN ME
I don't know what has gotten into you CatStronauts.
A few months ago, you were the definition of perfect.
Due to your recent behavior and the destruction of the Fish Finder Satellite, you are no longer worthy of the CatStronaut title.
I'm afraid there's nothing else I can do but to fire you all immediately.
WAIT!!

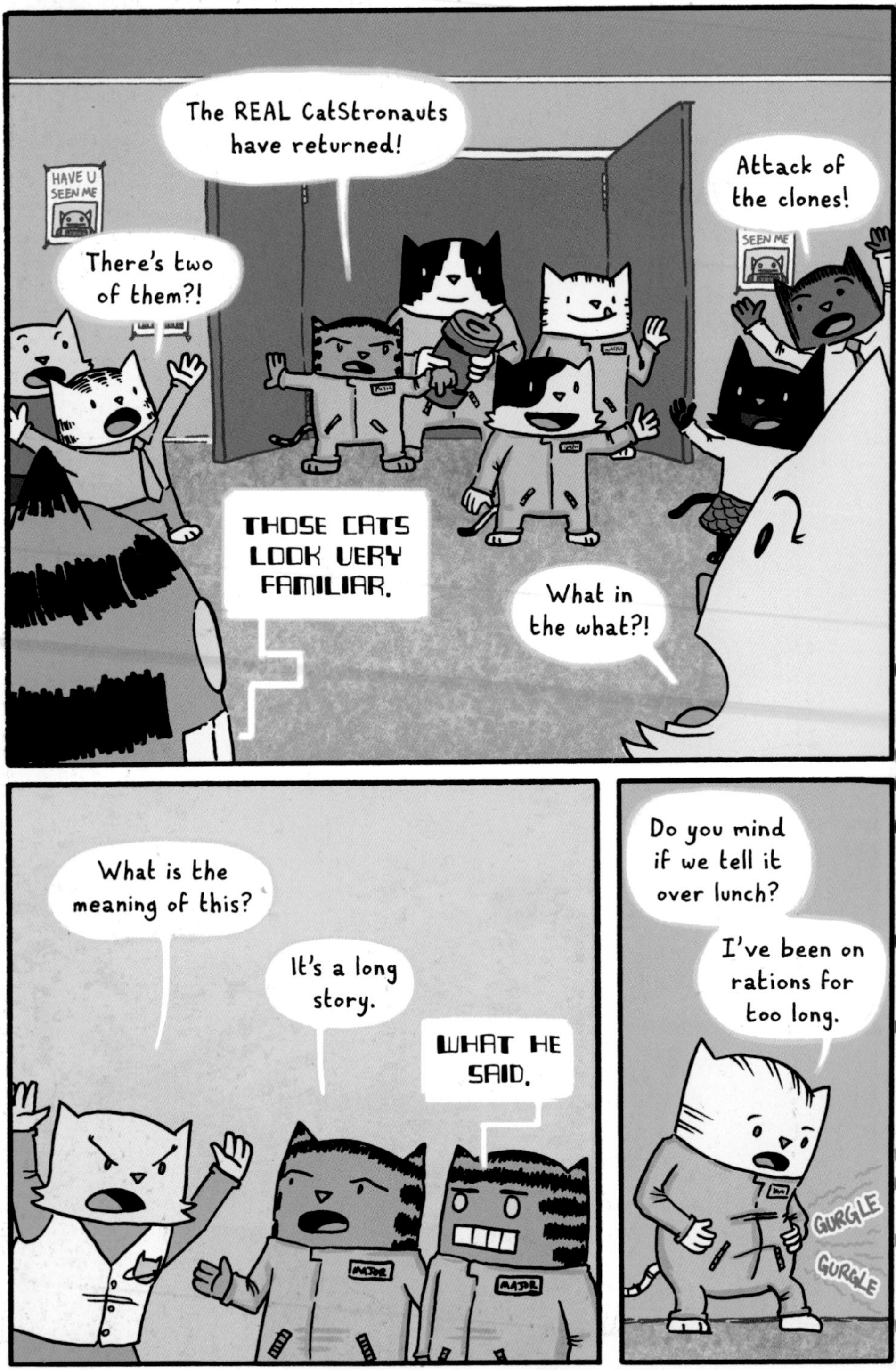
The REAL CatStronauts have returned!
There's two of them?!
Attack of the clones!
THOSE CATS LOOK VERY FAMILIAR.
What in the what?!
HAVE U SEEN ME
SEEN ME
What is the meaning of this?
It's a long story.
WHAT HE SAID.
Do you mind if we tell it over lunch?
I've been on rations for too long.
GURGLE
GURGLE
MAJOR
MAJOR

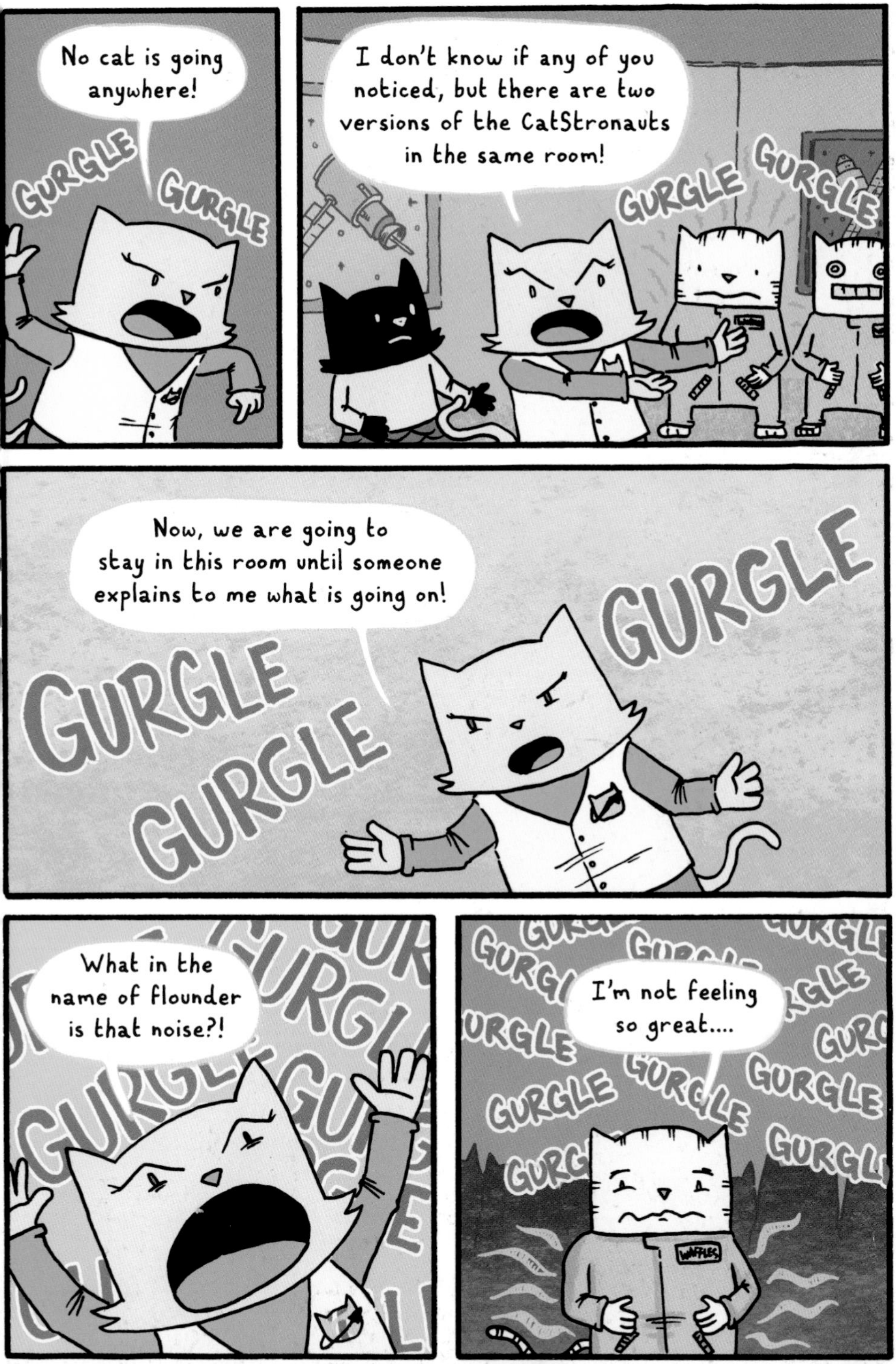
No cat is going anywhere!
GURGLE
GURGLE
I don't know if any of you noticed, but there are two versions of the CatStronauts in the same room!
GURGLE
GURGLE
Now, we are going to stay in this room until someone explains to me what is going on!
GURGLE
GURGLE
GURGLE
What in the name of flounder is that noise?!
I'm not feeling so great....
GURGLE
GURGLE
GURGLE
WAFFLES

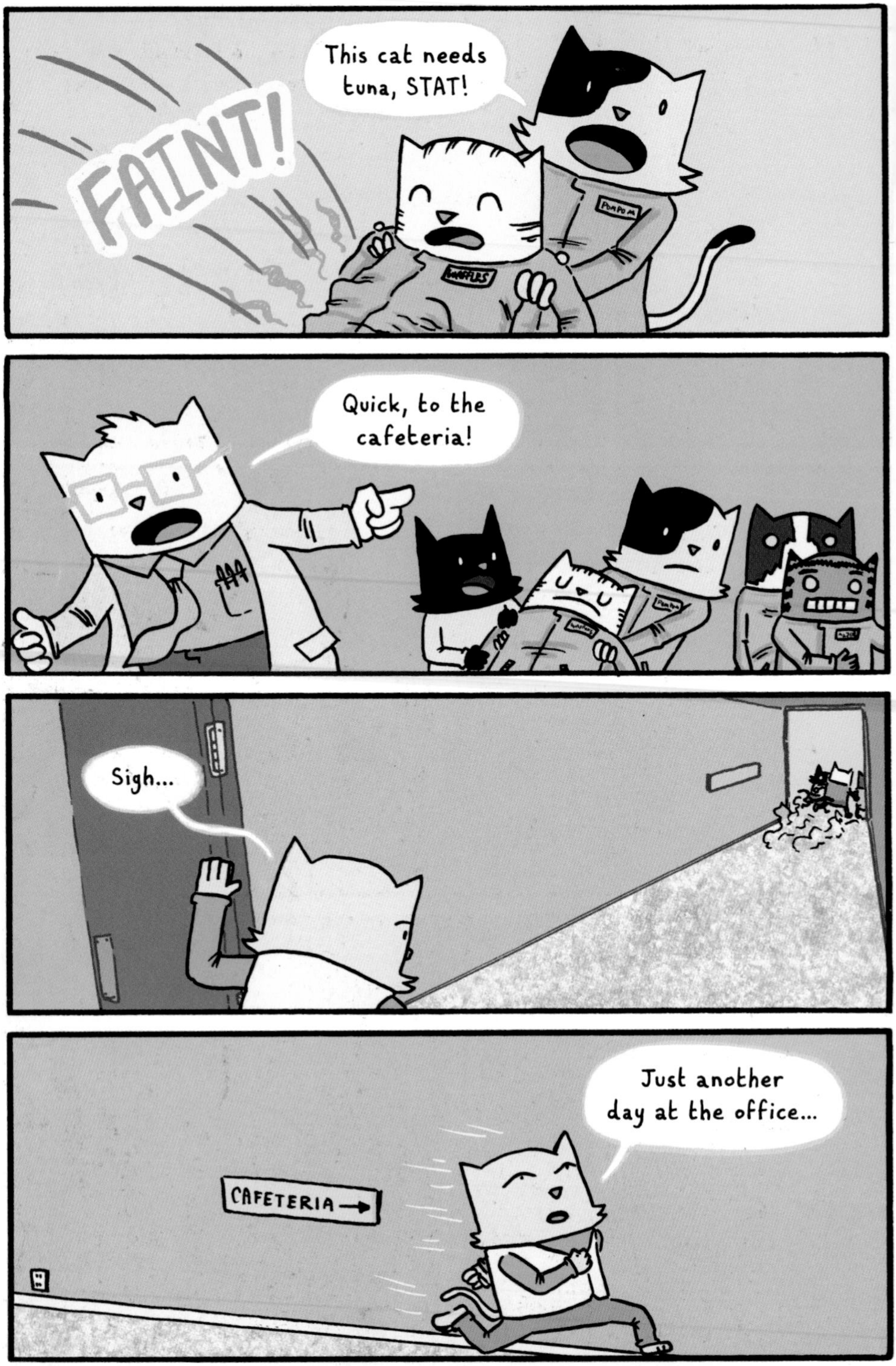
FAINT!
This cat needs tuna, STAT!
Quick, to the cafeteria!
Sigh...
Just another day at the office...
CAFETERIA

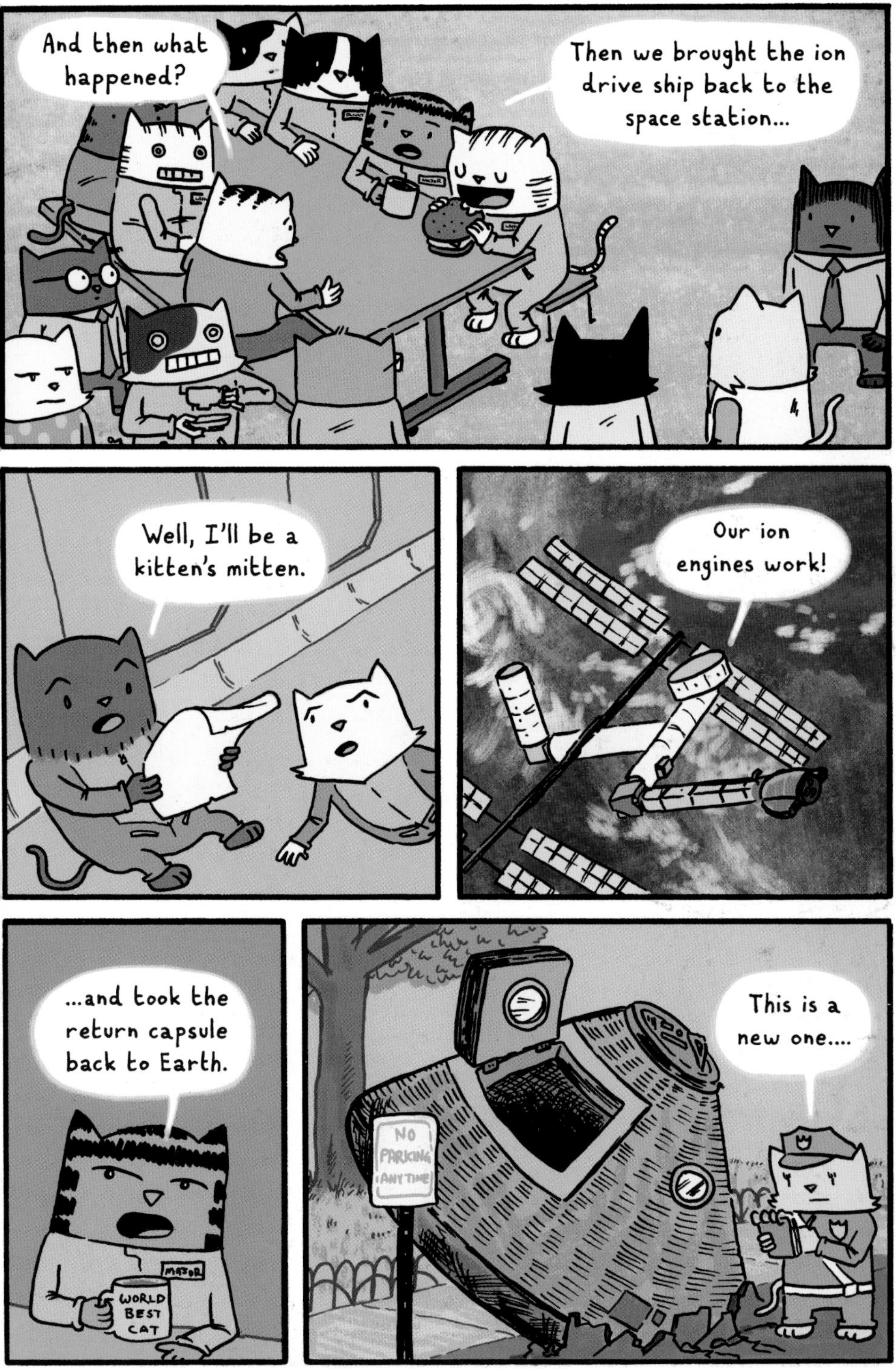
And then what happened?
Then we brought the ion drive ship back to the space station...
MAJOR
Well, I'll be a kitten's mitten.
Our ion engines work!
...and took the return capsule back to Earth.
MAJOR
WORLD BEST CAT
NO PARKING ANY TIME
This is a new one....

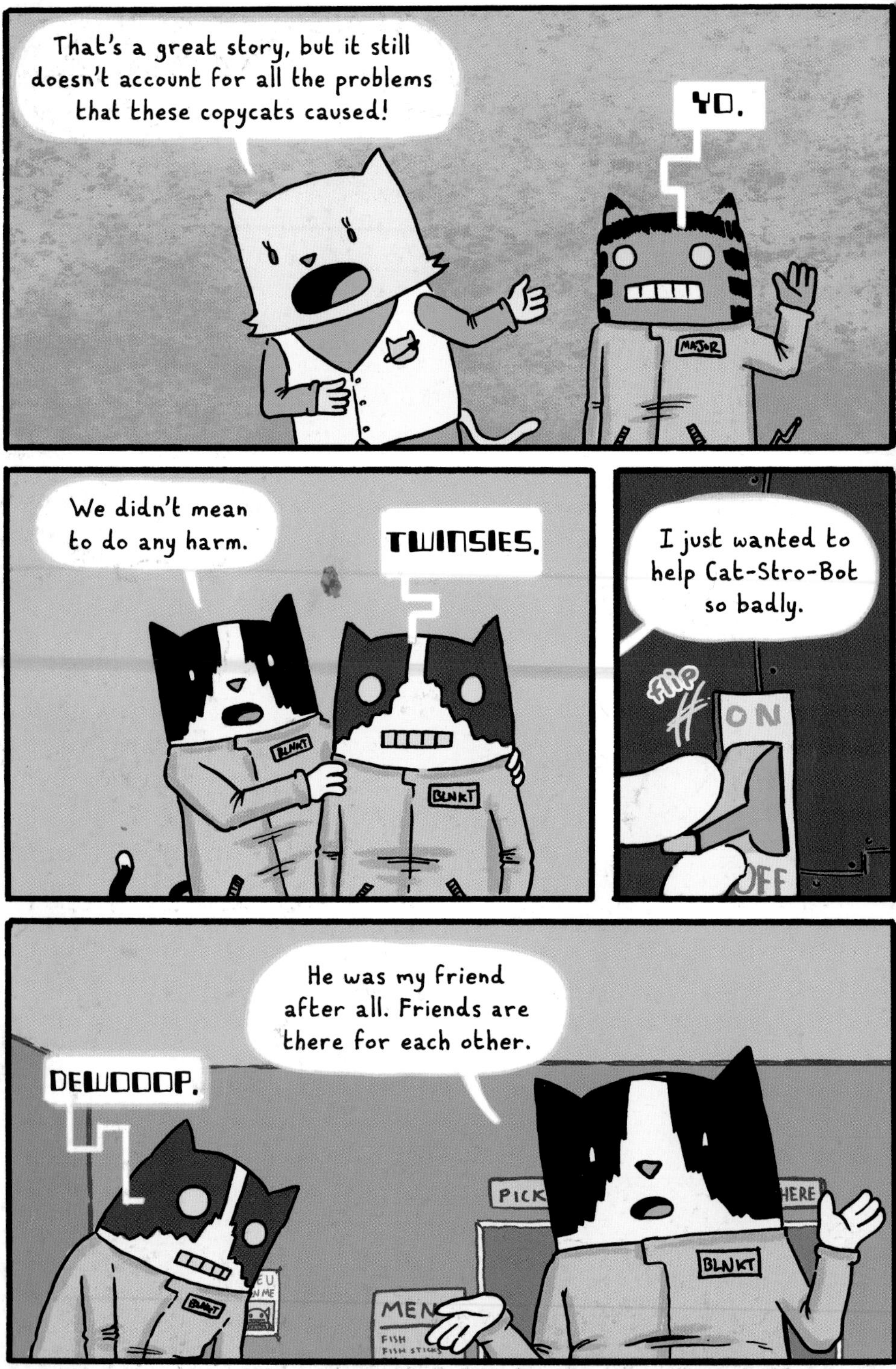
That's a great story, but it still doesn't account for all the problems that these copycats caused!
YO.
MAJOR
We didn't mean to do any harm.
TWINSIES.
BLNKT
BLNKT
I just wanted to help Cat-Stro-Bot so badly.
flip
ON
OFF
He was my friend after all. Friends are there for each other.
DEWOOOP.
PICK
HERE
BLNKT
BLNKT
MEN
FISH
FISH STICKS

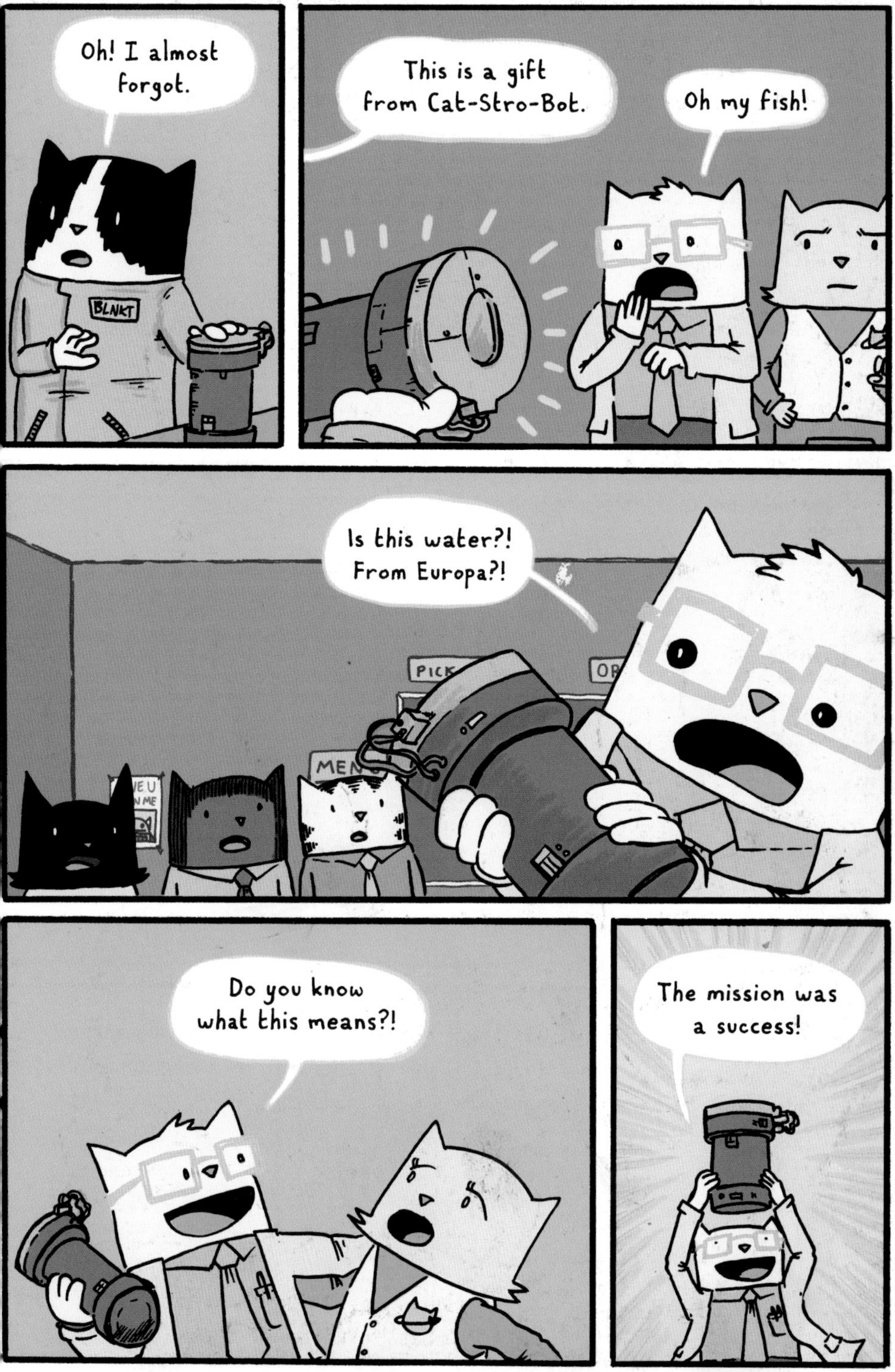
Oh! I almost forgot.
BLNKT
This is a gift from Cat-Stro-Bot.
Oh my fish!
Is this water?! From Europa?!
Do you know what this means?!
The mission was a success!

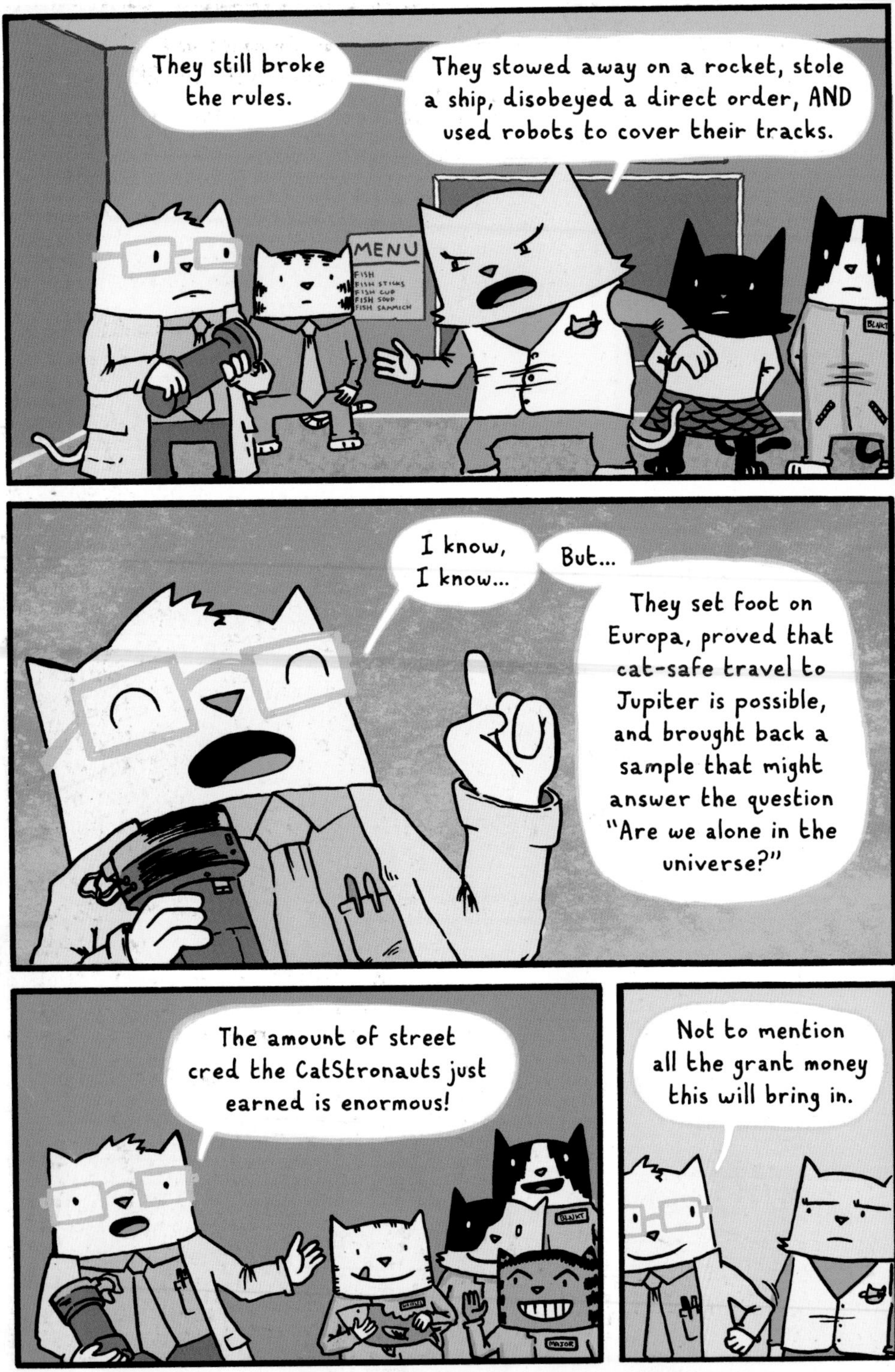
They still broke the rules.
They stowed away on a rocket, stole a ship, disobeyed a direct order, AND used robots to cover their tracks.
MENU
FISH
FISH STICKS
FISH CUP
FISH SOUP
FISH SAMMICH
BLNKT
I know, I know...
But...
They set foot on Europa, proved that cat-safe travel to Jupiter is possible, and brought back a sample that might answer the question "Are we alone in the universe?"
The amount of street cred the CatStronauts just earned is enormous!
BLNKT
MAJOR
Not to mention all the grant money this will bring in.

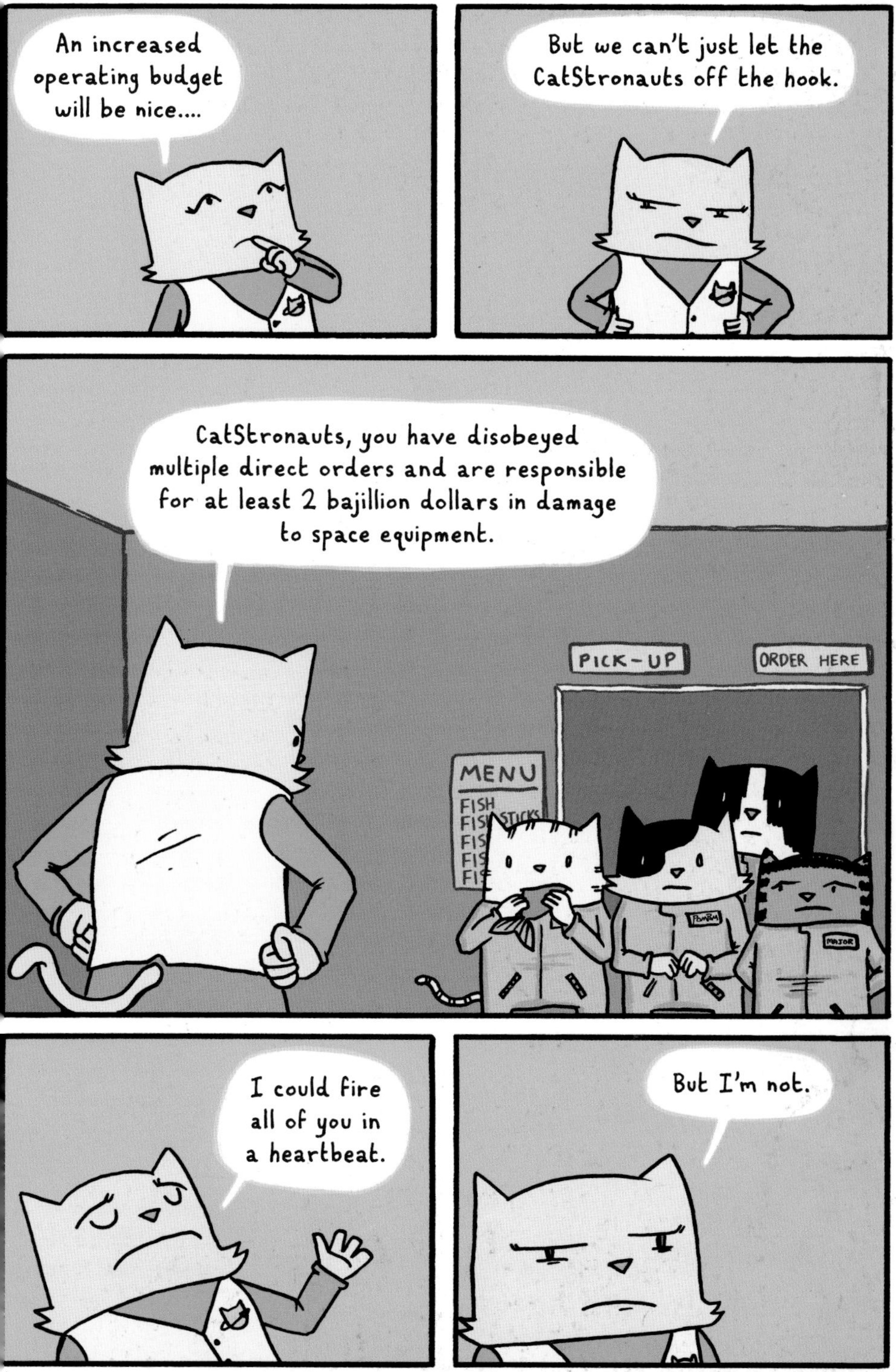
An increased operating budget will be nice....
But we can't just let the CatStronauts off the hook.
CatStronauts, you have disobeyed multiple direct orders and are responsible for at least 2 bajillion dollars in damage to space equipment.
PICK-UP
ORDER HERE
MENU
FISH
MAJOR
I could fire all of you in a heartbeat.
But I'm not.

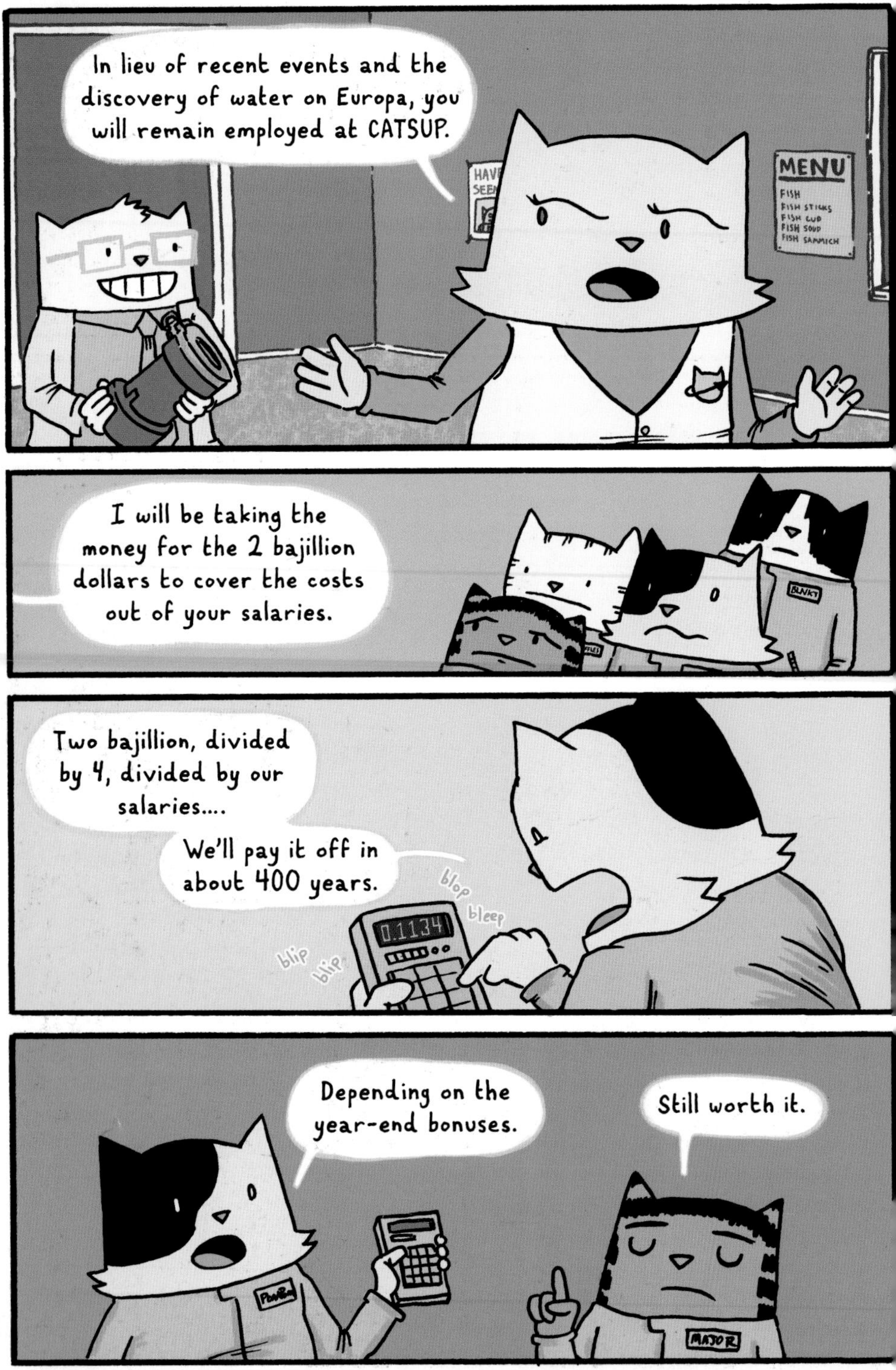
In lieu of recent events and the discovery of water on Europa, you will remain employed at CATSUP.
MENU
FISH
FISH STICKS
FISH CUP
FISH SOUP
FISH SAMMICH
I will be taking the money for the 2 bajillion dollars to cover the costs out of your salaries.
Two bajillion, divided by 4, divided by our salaries....
We'll pay it off in about 400 years.
0.1134
blop
bleep
blip
blip
Depending on the year-end bonuses.
Still worth it.
MAJOR

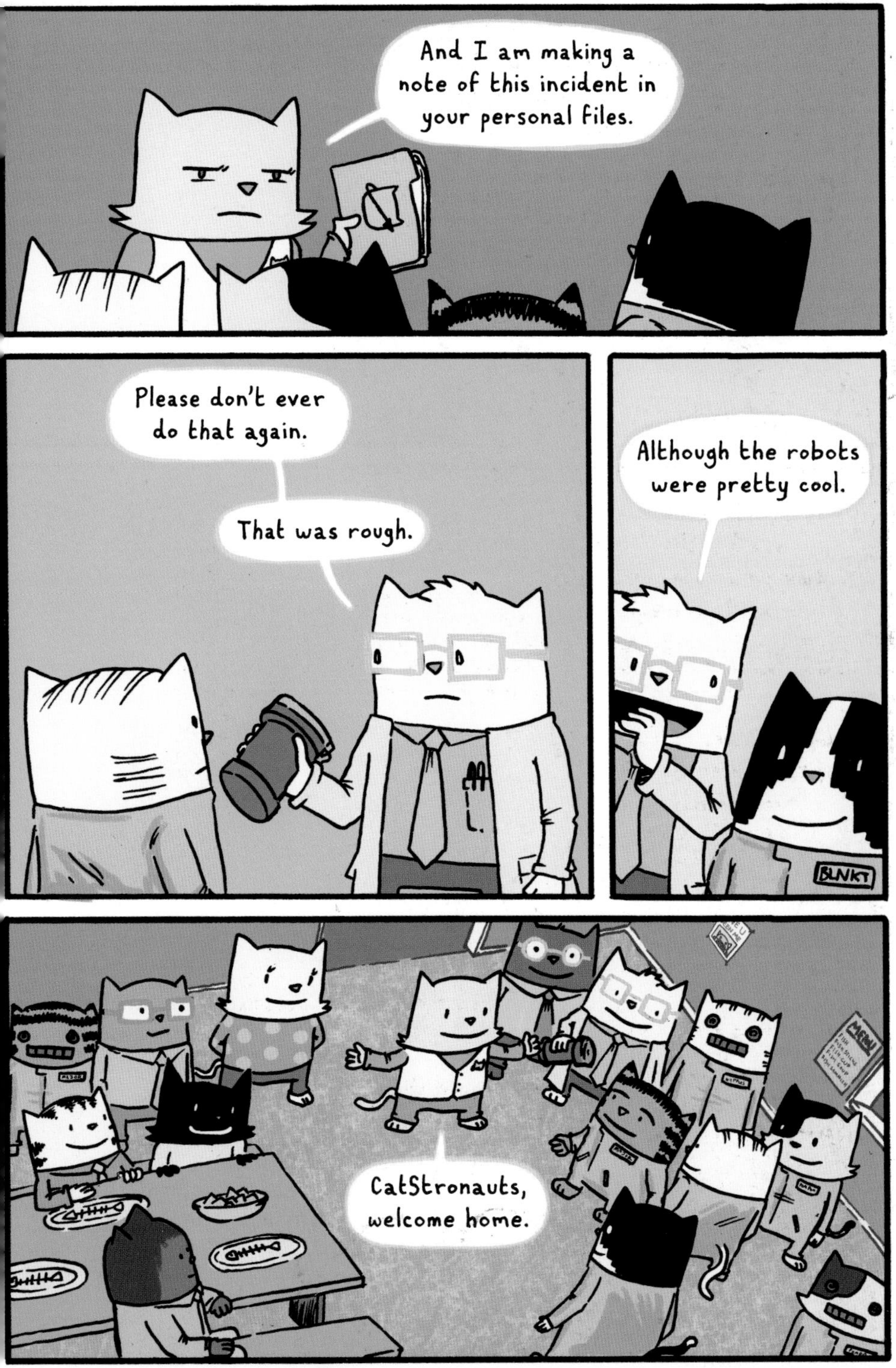
And I am making a note of this incident in your personal files.
Please don't ever do that again.
That was rough.
Although the robots were pretty cool.
BLNKT
CatStronauts, welcome home.

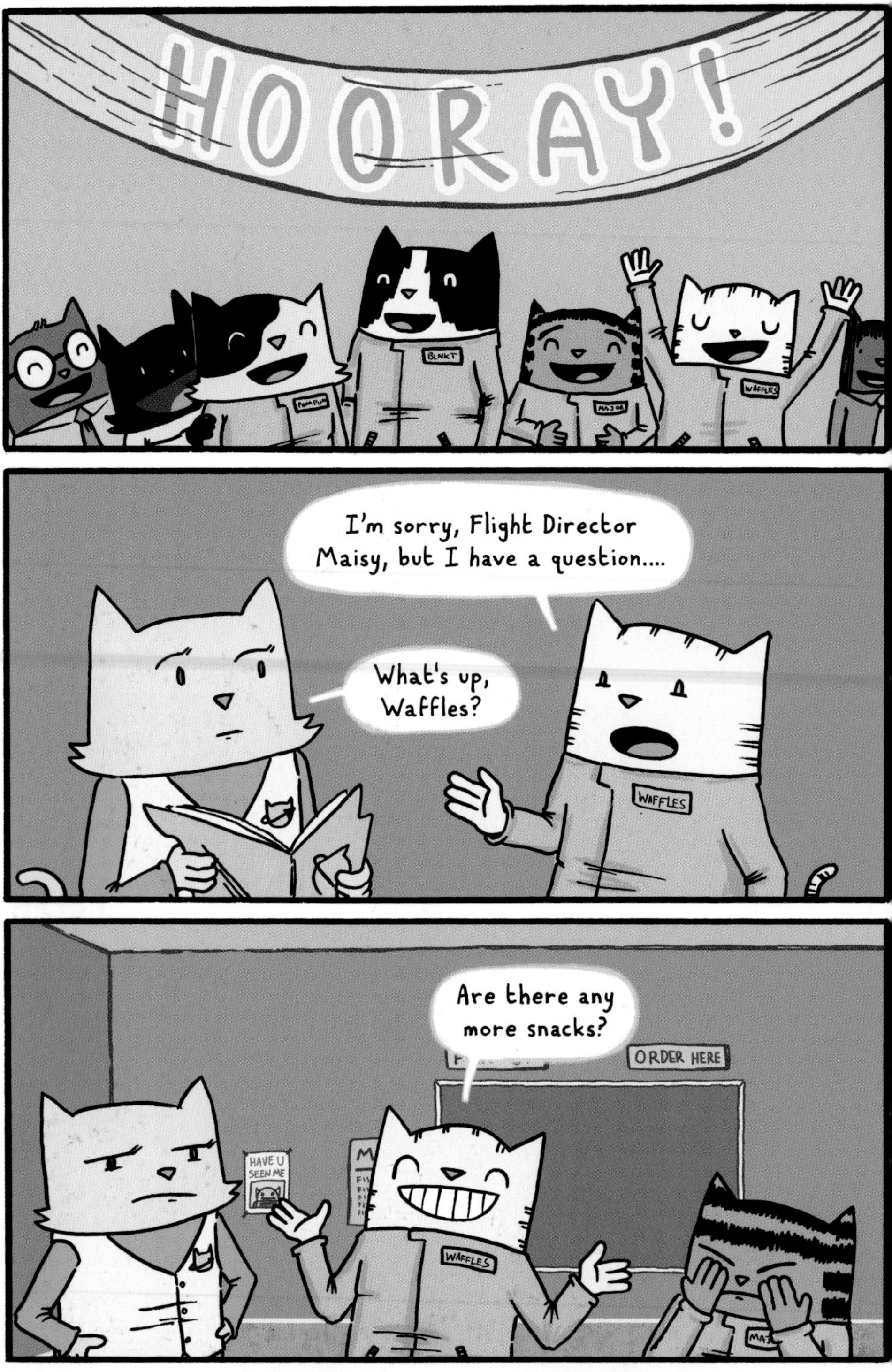
HOORAY!
BLNKT
WAFFLES
I'm sorry, Flight Director Maisy, but I have a question....
What's up, Waffles?
WAFFLES
Are there any more snacks?
ORDER HERE
HAVE U SEEN ME
WAFFLES

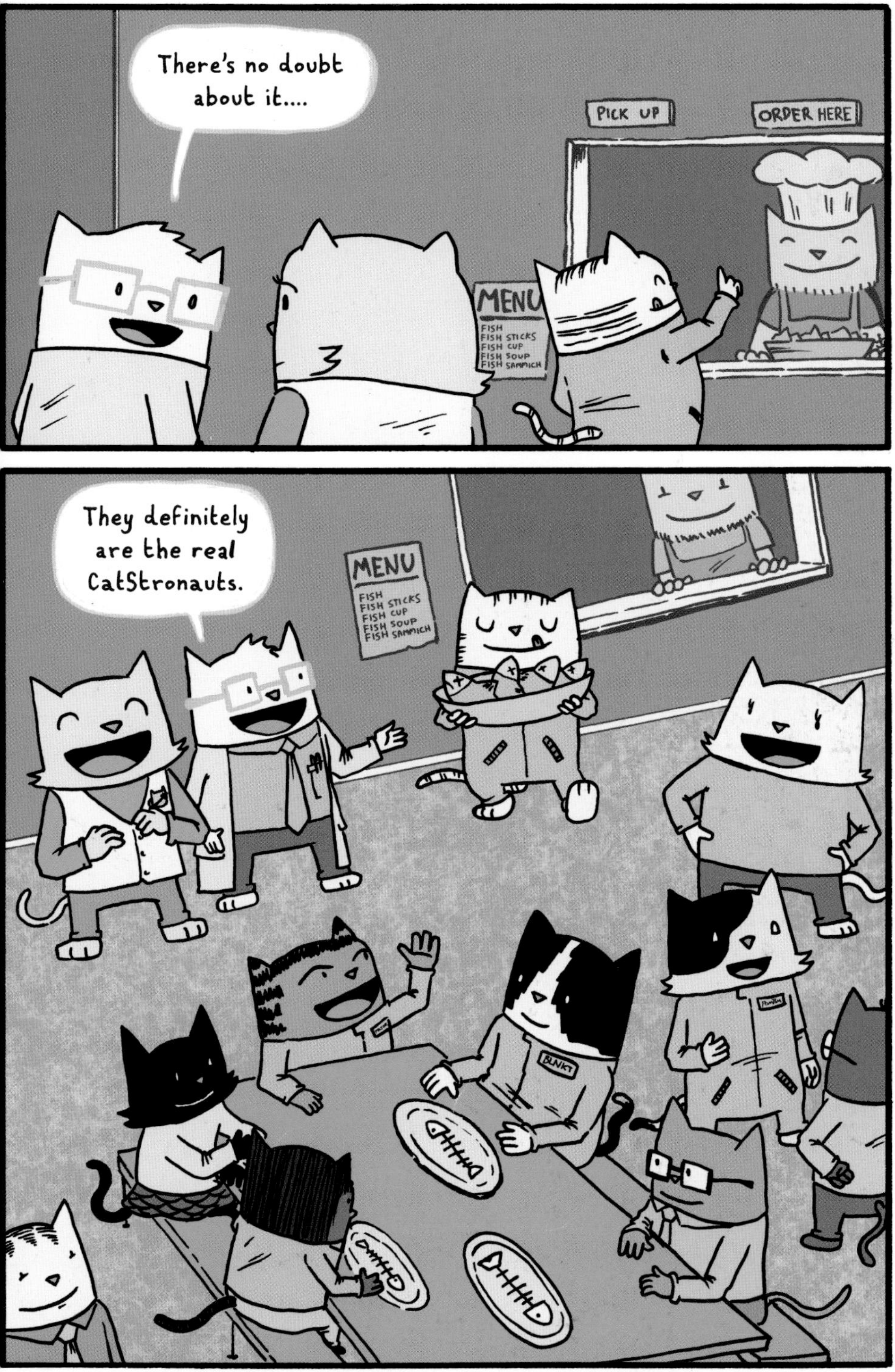
There's no doubt about it....
PICK UP
ORDER HERE
MENU
FISH
FISH STICKS
FISH CUP
FISH SOUP
FISH SAMMICH
They definitely are the real CatStronauts.
MENU
FISH
FISH STICKS
FISH CUP
FISH SOUP
FISH SAMMICH

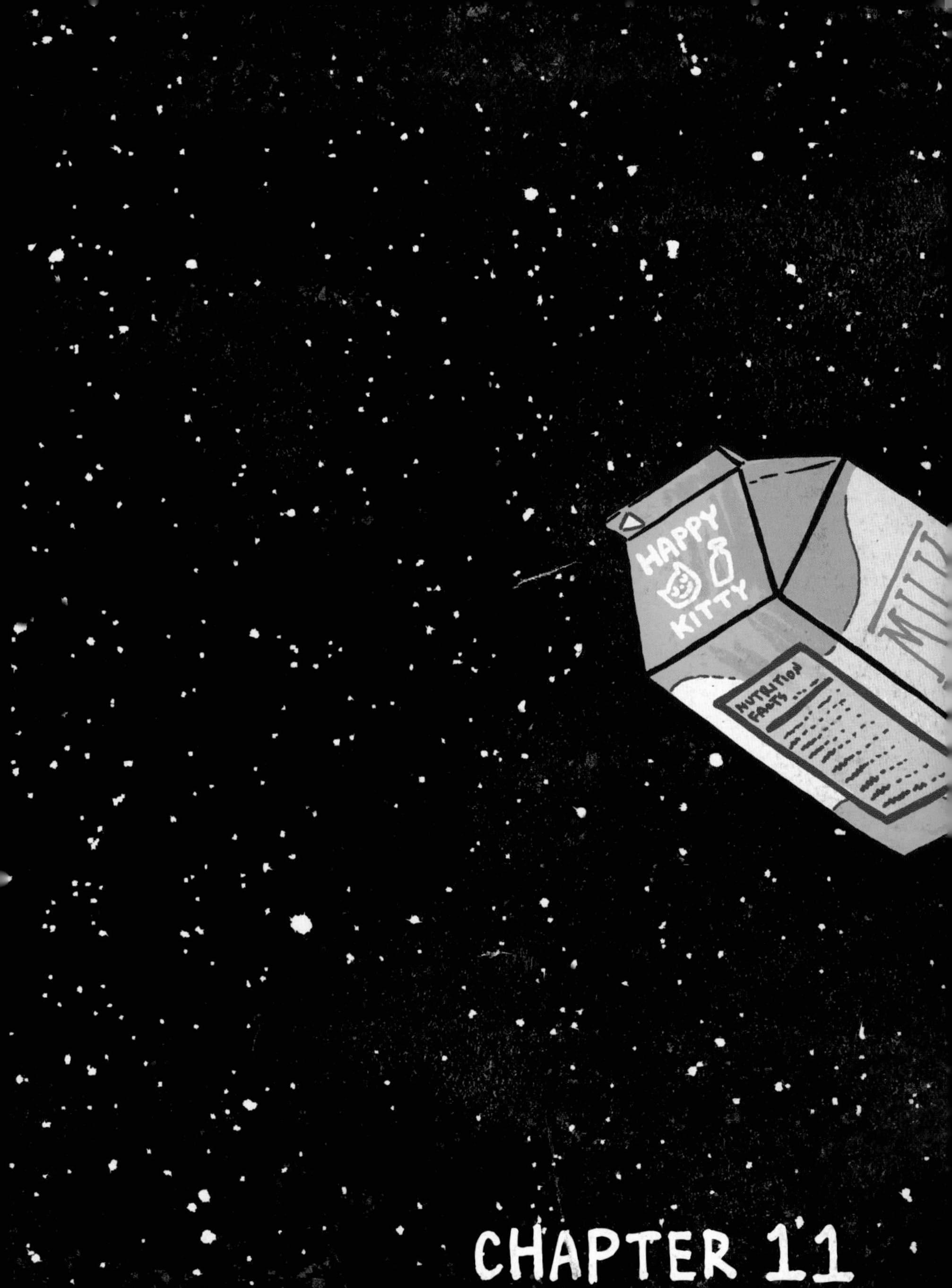
HAPPY
KITTY
NUTRITION FACTS

CHAPTER 11

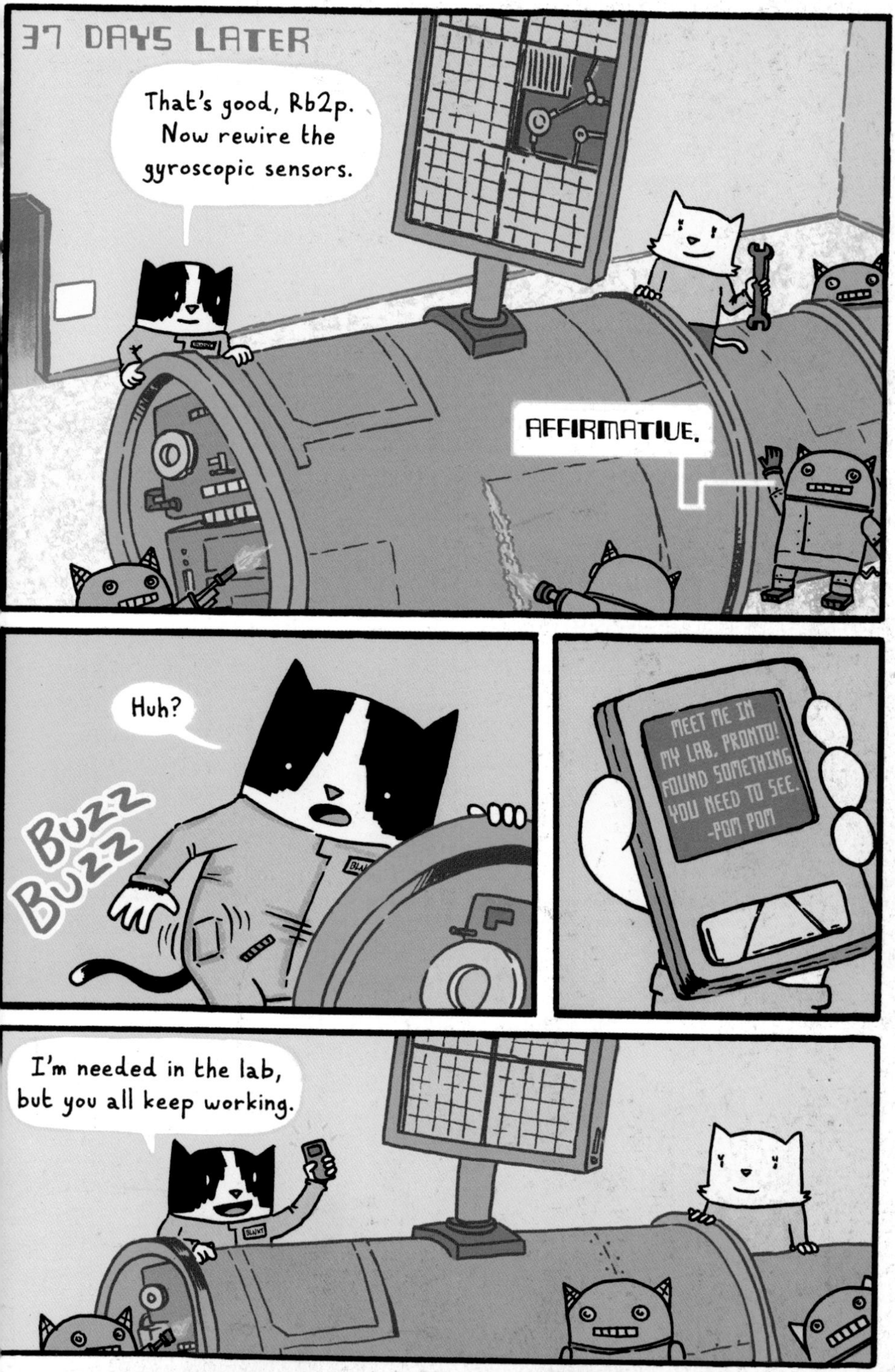
37 DAYS LATER
That's good, Rb2p. Now rewire the gyroscopic sensors.
AFFIRMATIVE.
Huh?
BUZZ BUZZ
MEET ME IN MY LAB, PRONTO! FOUND SOMETHING YOU NEED TO SEE. -POM POM
I'm needed in the lab, but you all keep working.

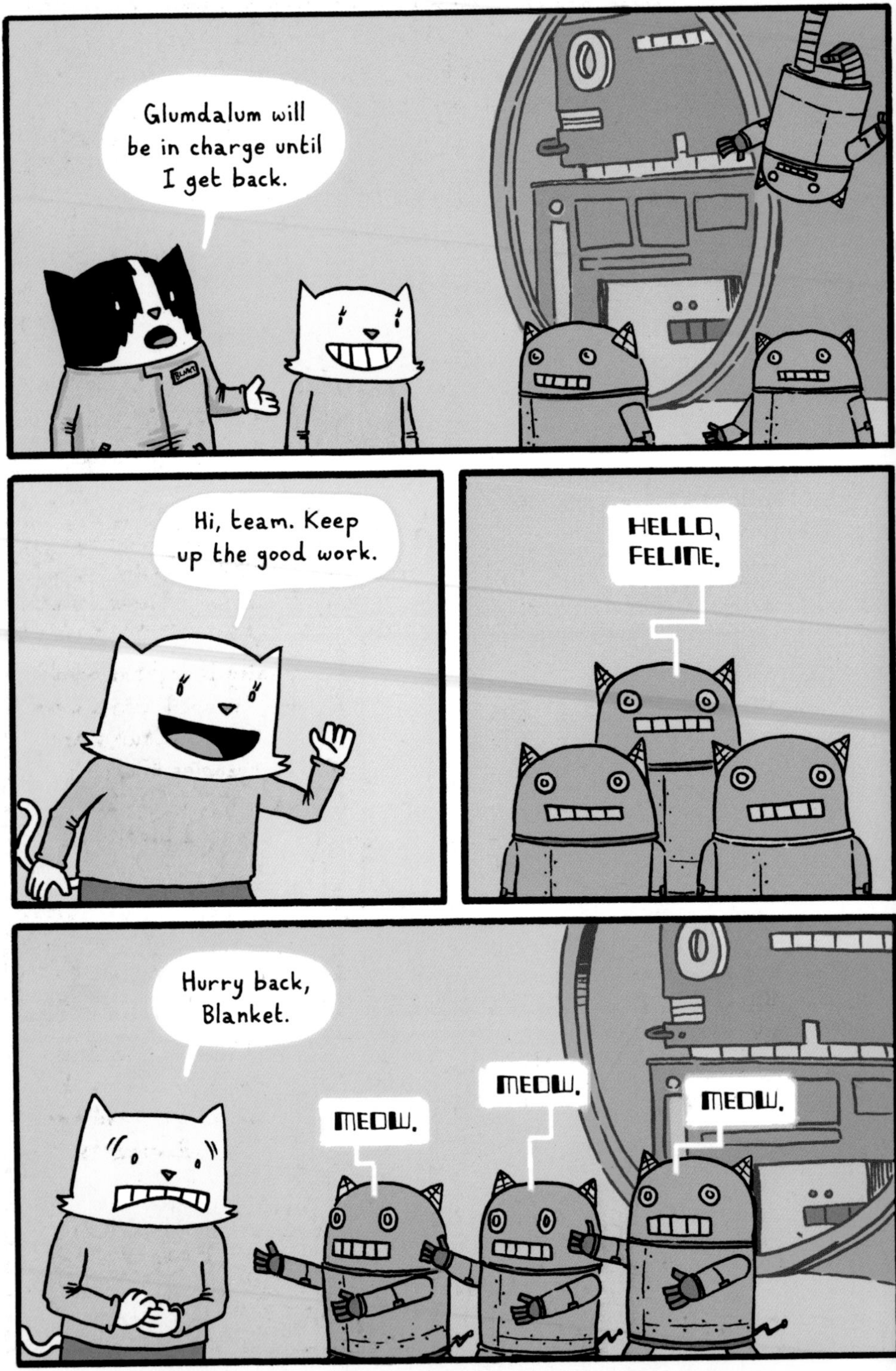
Glumdalum will be in charge until I get back.
Hi, team. Keep up the good work.
HELLO, FELINE.
Hurry back, Blanket.
MEOW.
MEOW.
MEOW.

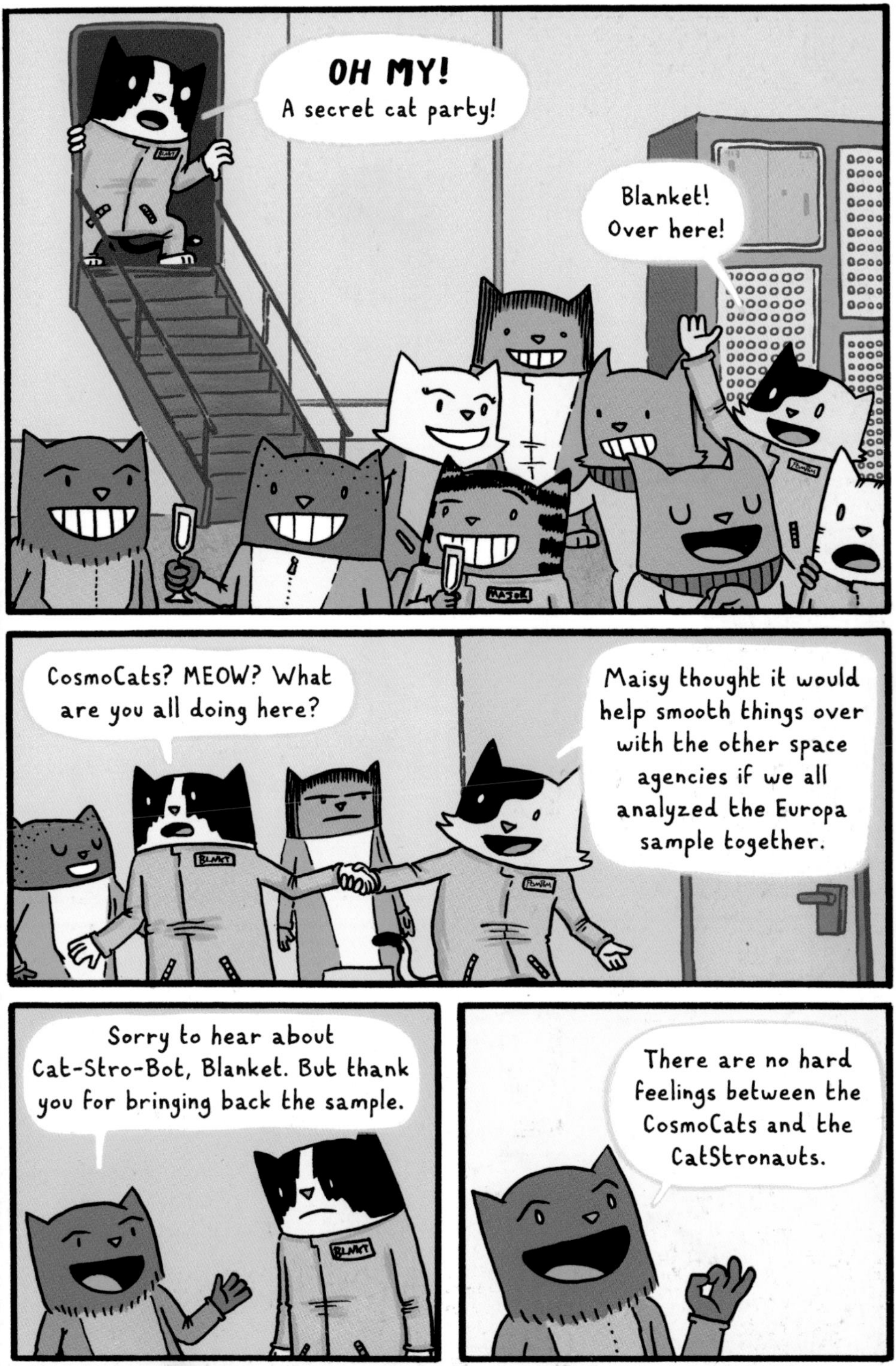
OH MY!
A secret cat party!
Blanket! Over here!
CosmoCats? MEOW? What are you all doing here?
Maisy thought it would help smooth things over with the other space agencies if we all analyzed the Europa sample together.
Sorry to hear about Cat-Stro-Bot, Blanket. But thank you for bringing back the sample.
There are no hard feelings between the CosmoCats and the CatStronauts.

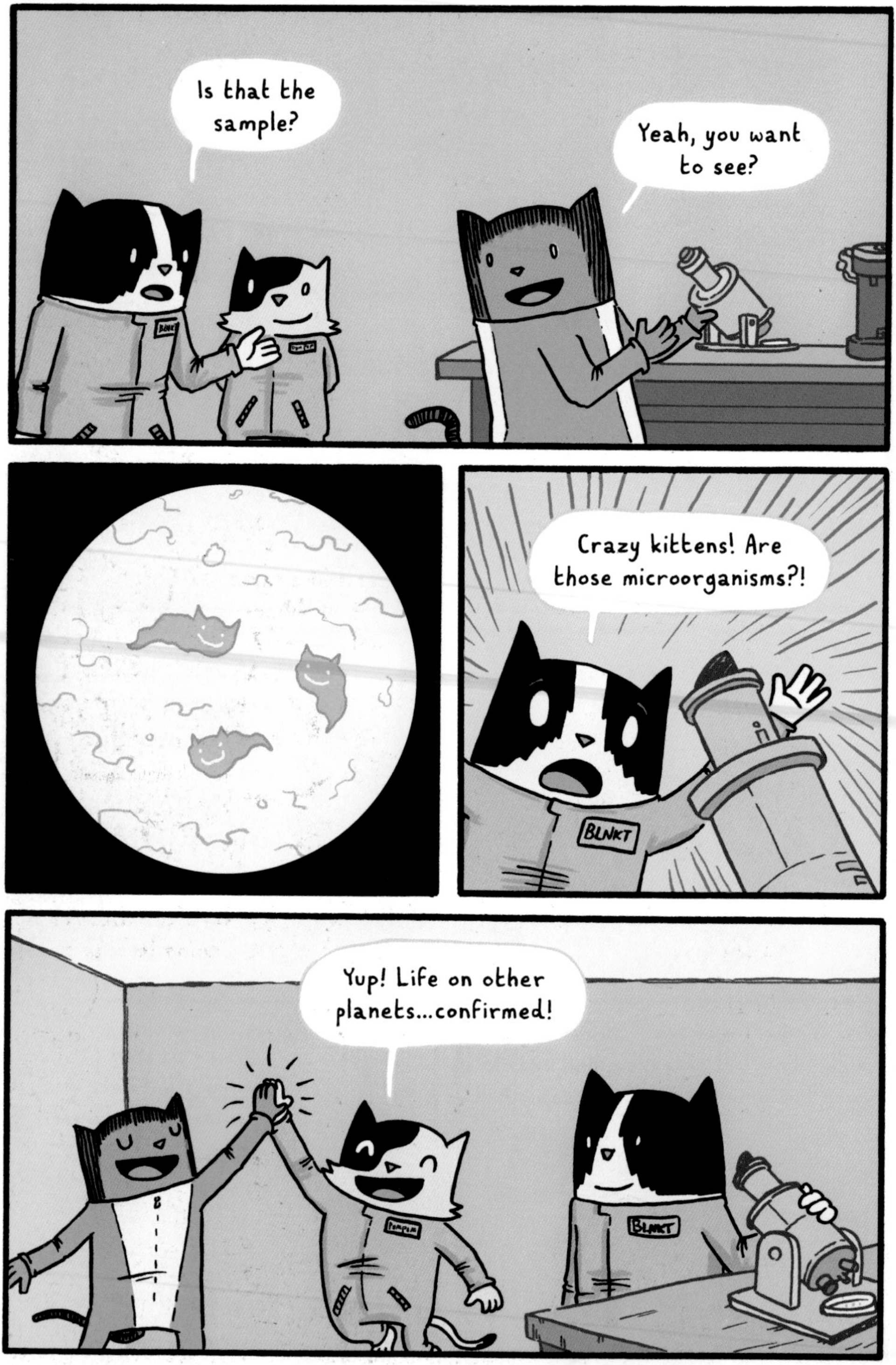
Is that the sample?
Yeah, you want to see?
BLNKT
Crazy kittens! Are those microorganisms?!
BLNKT
Yup! Life on other planets...confirmed!
BLNKT

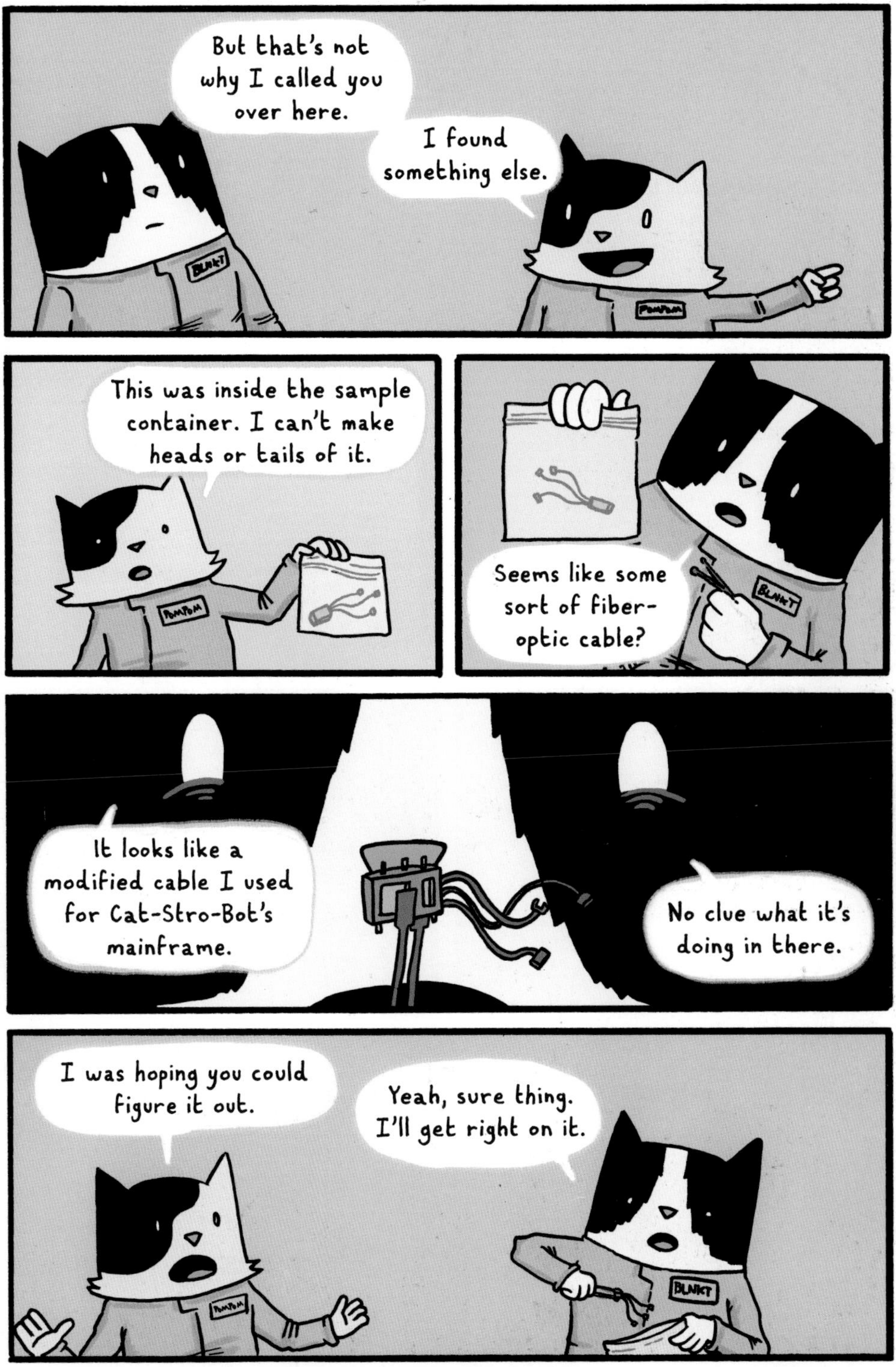
But that's not why I called you over here.
I found something else.
BLNKT
POMPOM
This was inside the sample container. I can't make heads or tails of it.
POMPOM
Seems like some sort of fiber-optic cable?
BLNKT
It looks like a modified cable I used for Cat-Stro-Bot's mainframe.
No clue what it's doing in there.
I was hoping you could figure it out.
Yeah, sure thing. I'll get right on it.
POMPOM
BLNKT

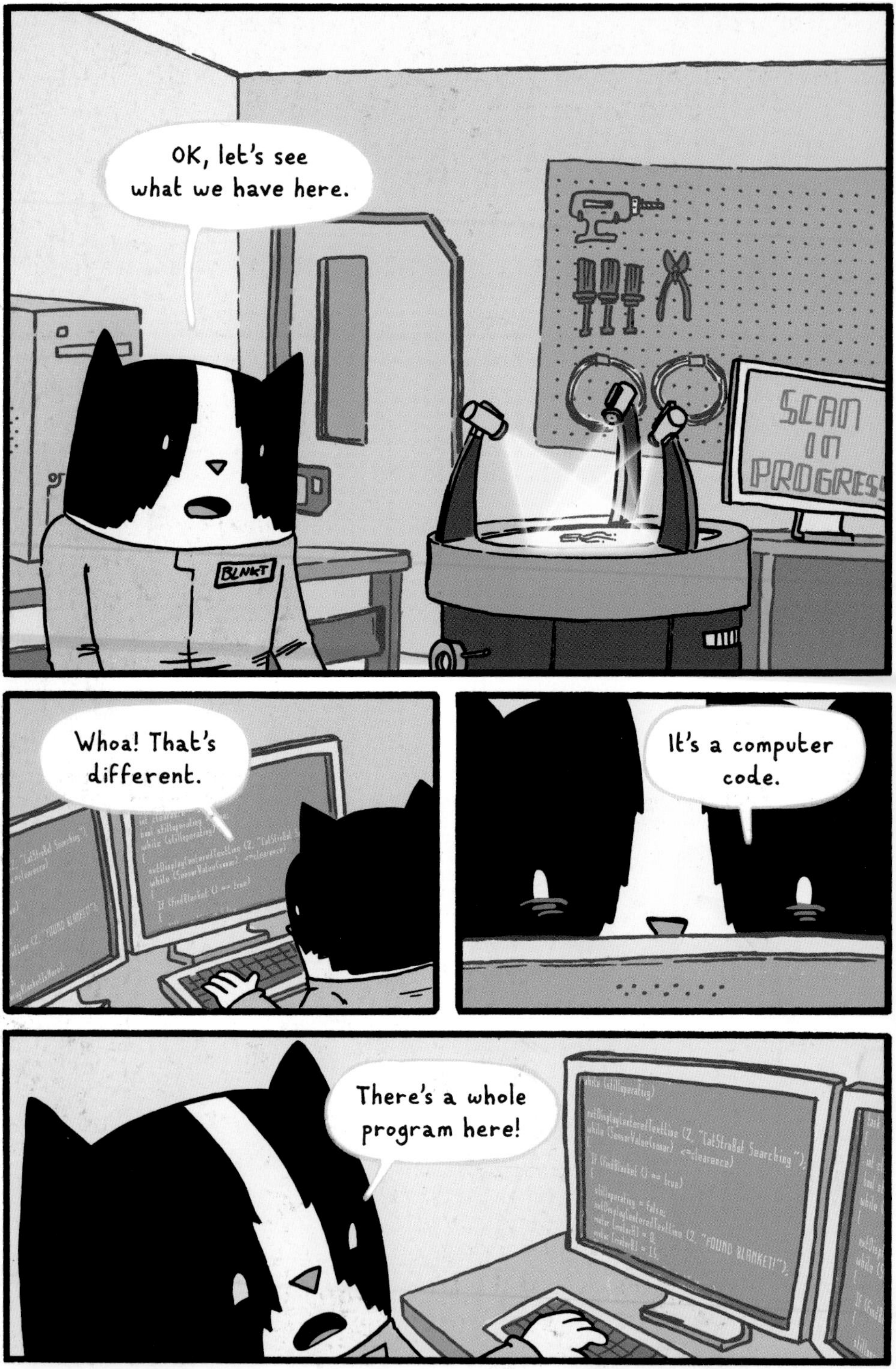
OK, let's see what we have here.
BLNKT
SCAN IN PROGRESS
Whoa! That's different.
It's a computer code.
There's a whole program here!

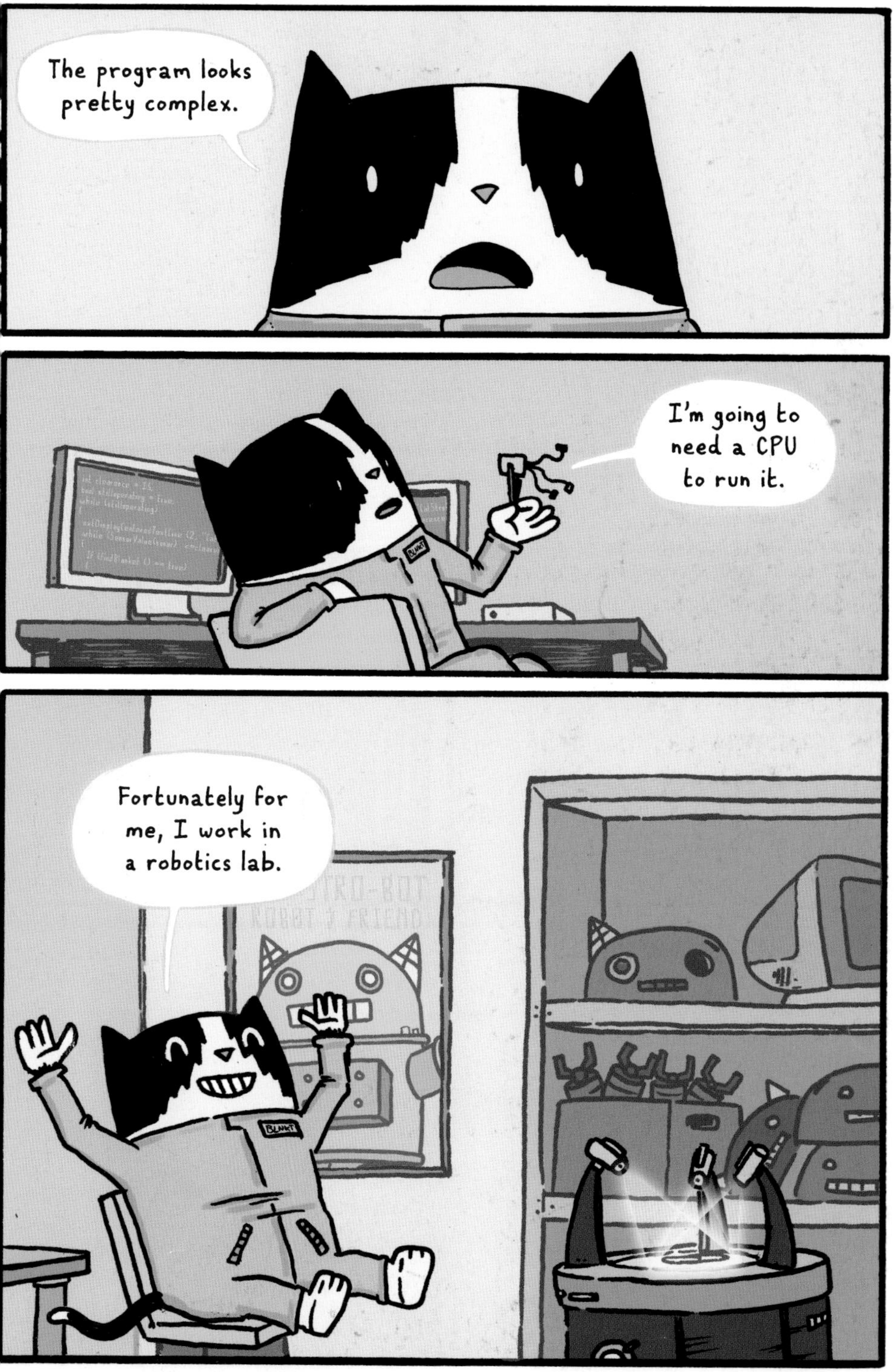
The program looks pretty complex.
I'm going to need a CPU to run it.
Fortunately for me, I work in a robotics lab.

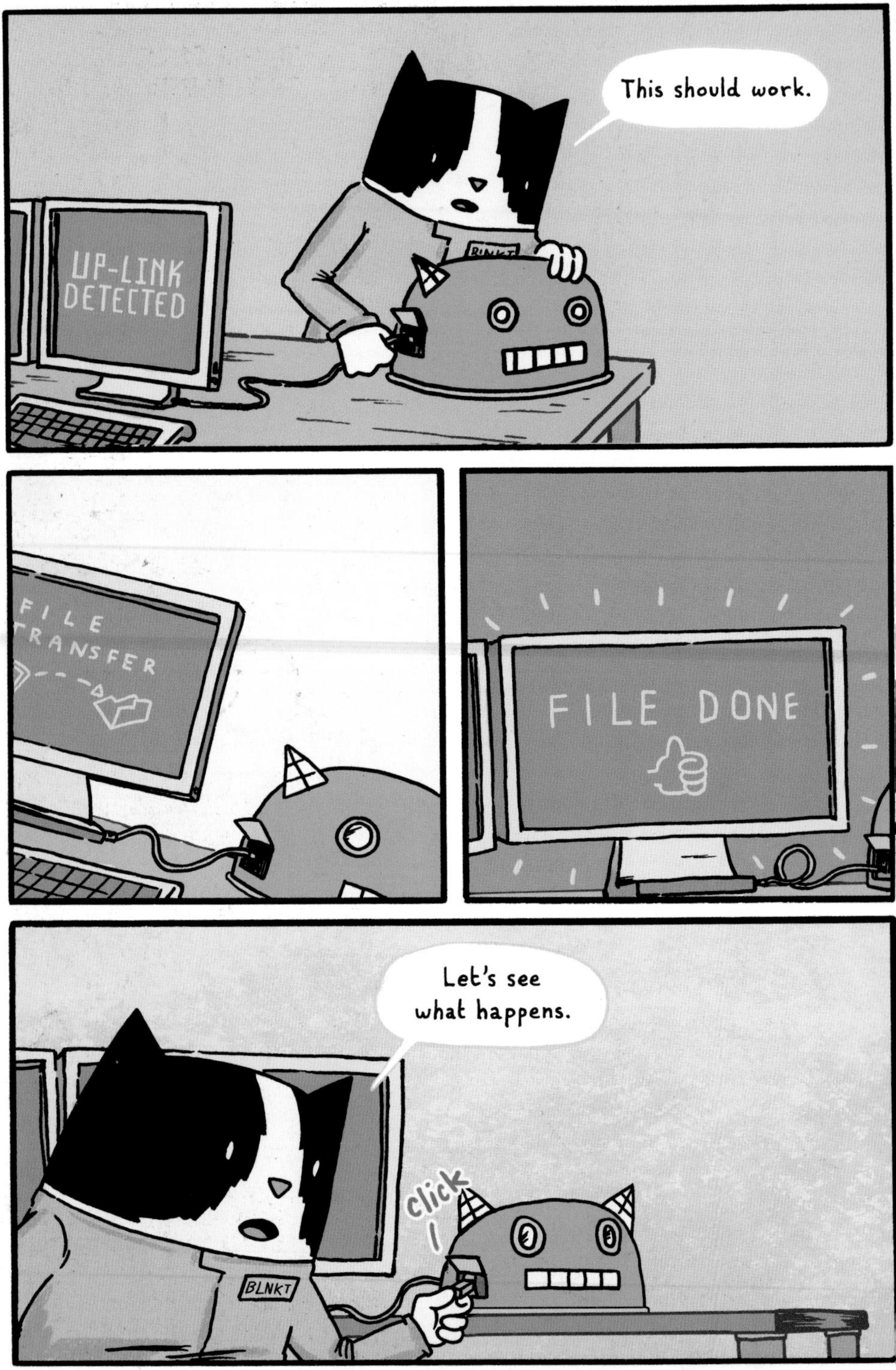
This should work.
UP-LINK DETECTED
BLNKT
FILE TRANSFER
FILE DONE
Let's see what happens.
click
BLNKT

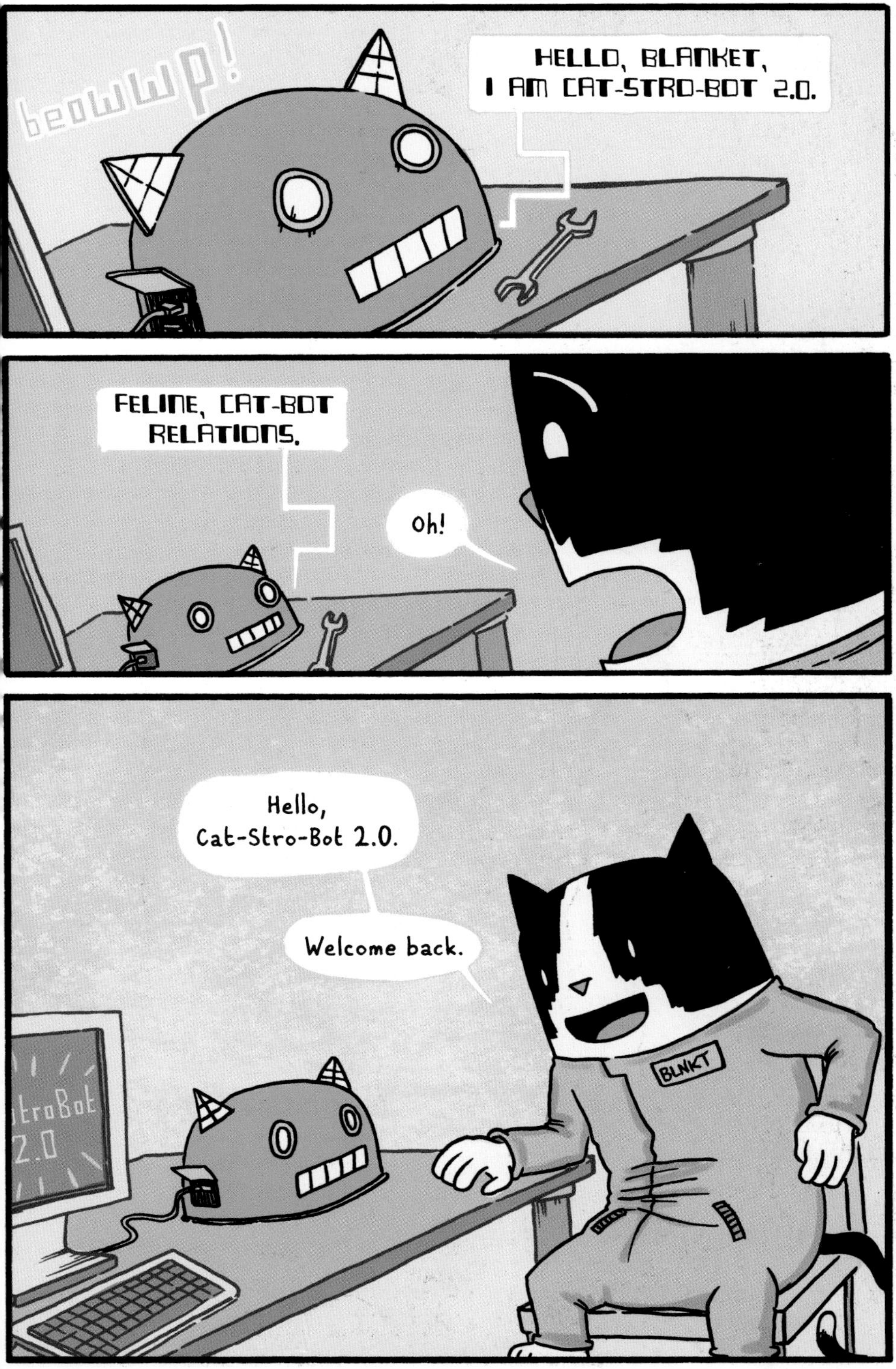
beowwp!
HELLO, BLANKET, I AM CAT-STRO-BOT 2.0.
FELINE, CAT-BOT RELATIONS.
Oh!
Hello, Cat-Stro-Bot 2.0.
Welcome back.
BLNKT

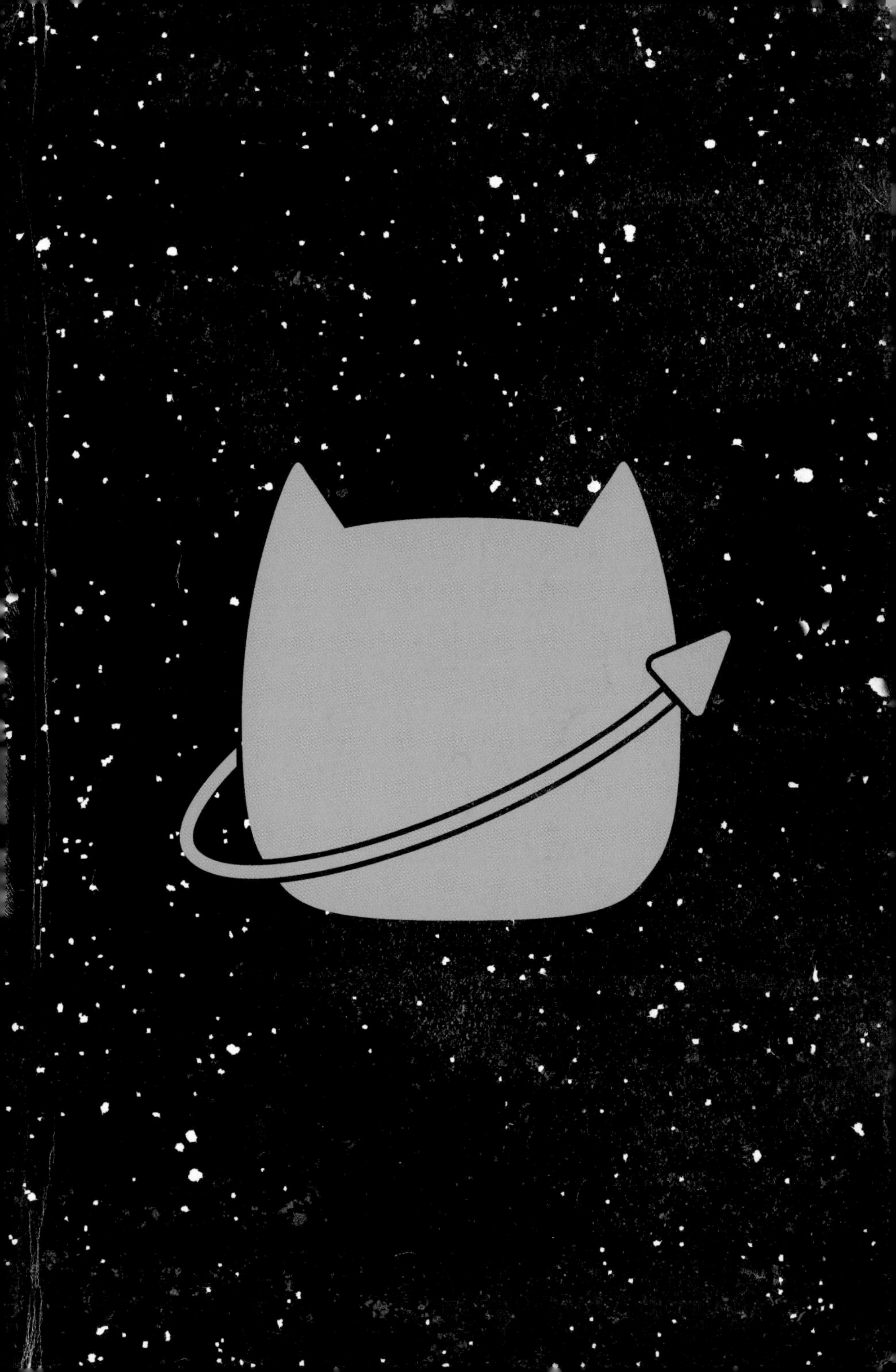

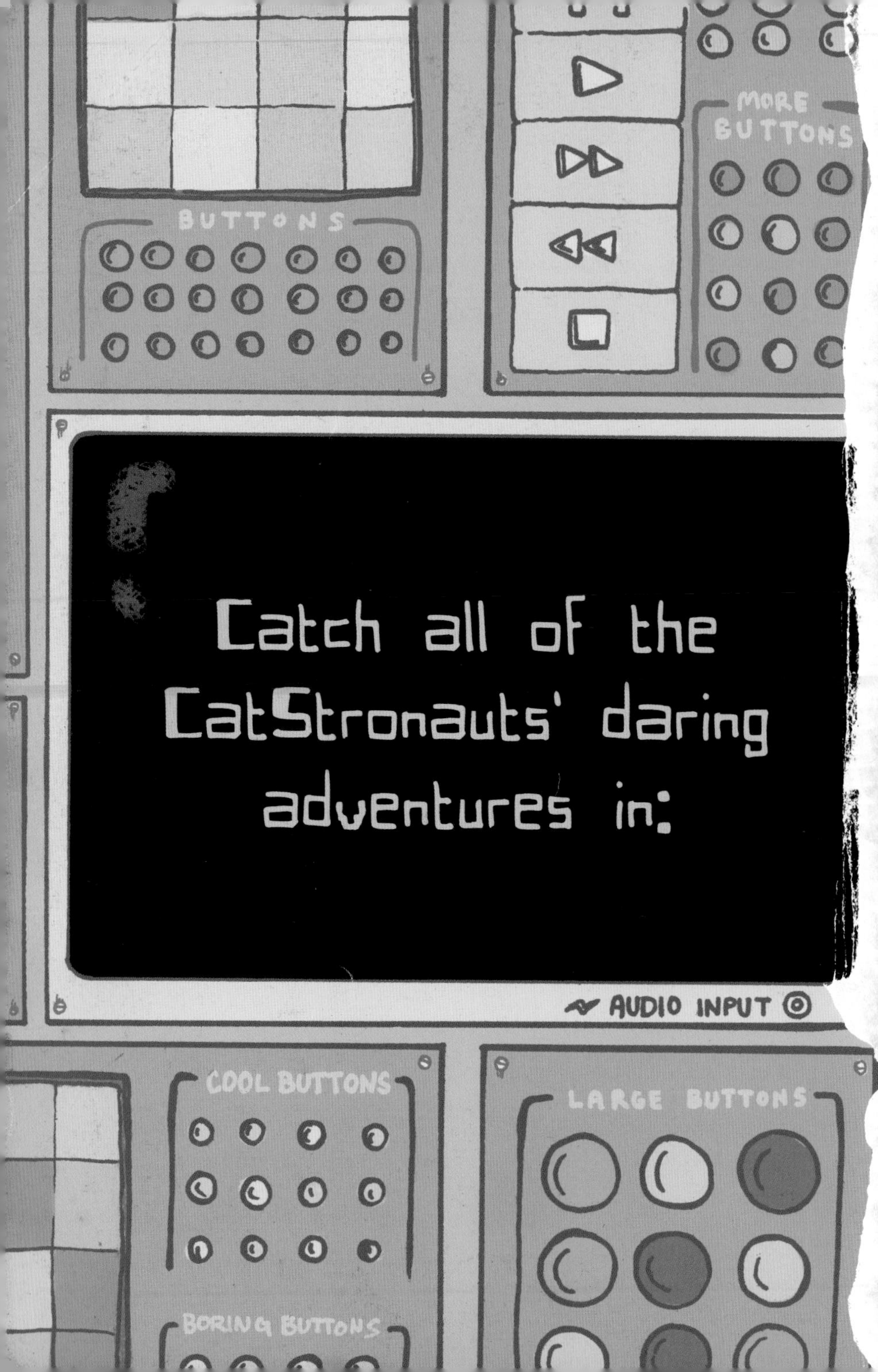
BUTTONS
MORE BUTTONS
Catch all of the CatStronauts' daring adventures in:
AUDIO INPUT
COOL BUTTONS
LARGE BUTTONS
BORING BUTTONS

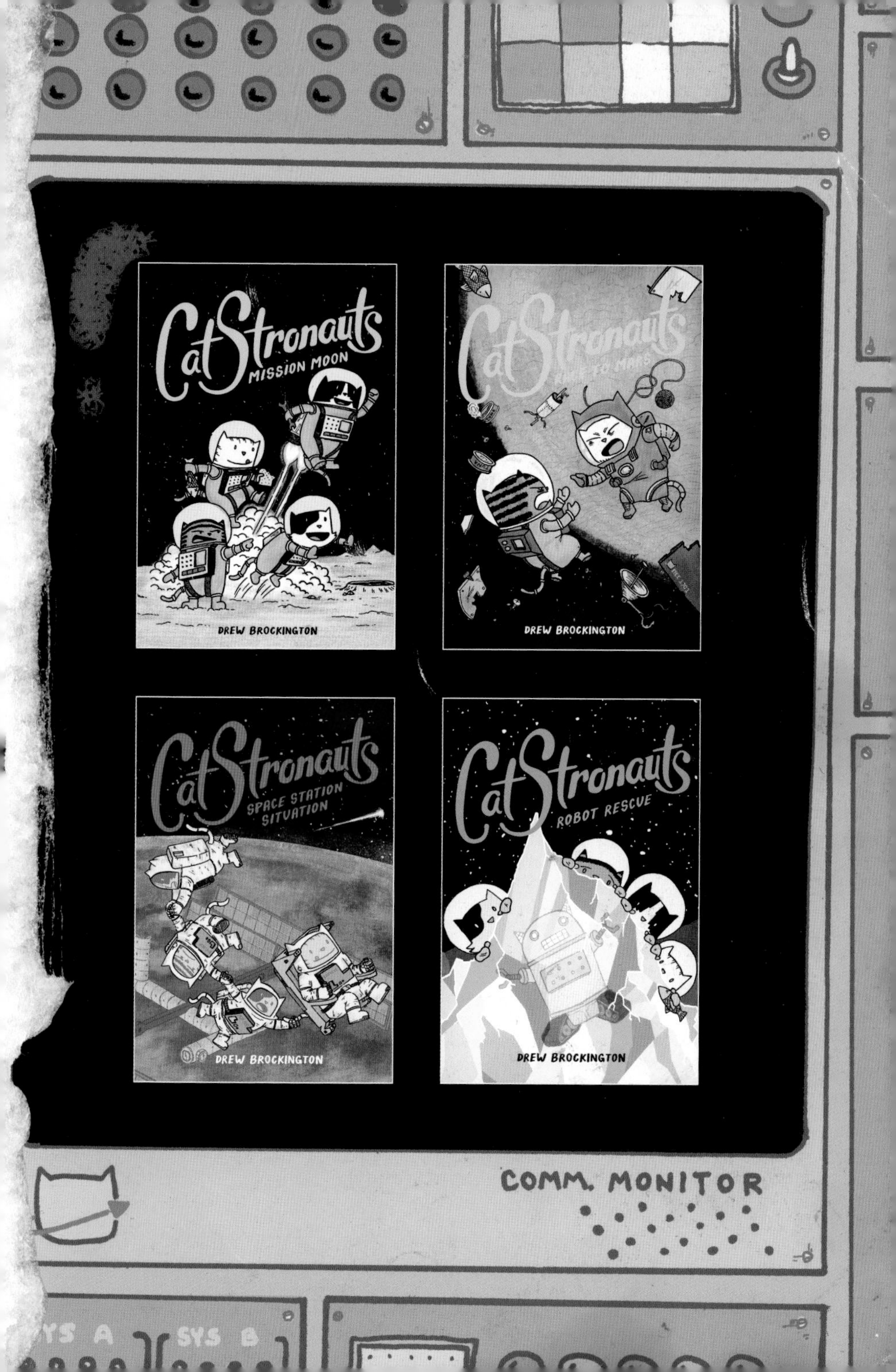
CatStronauts
MISSION MOON
DREW BROCKINGTON
CatStronauts
DREW BROCKINGTON
CatStronauts
SPACE STATION SITUATION
DREW BROCKINGTON
CatStronauts
ROBOT RESCUE
DREW BROCKINGTON
COMM. MONITOR
YS A
SYS B